Lethal Keystrokes

Thanks for reading!

J Drey

LETHAL KEYSTROKES

JOHN D. MAY

GRANVILLE ISLAND
PUBLISHING

ISBN: 978-1-989467-38-1 (paperback)
ISBN: 978-1-989467-39-8 (ebook)

Lethal Keystrokes is a work of fiction. All characters, locales, incidents and technologies portrayed in the novel are products of the author's imagination or have been used fictitiously. Any resemblance to persons, living or dead, is entirely coincidental.

Book editor: Aislinn Cottell
Copy editor: Marianne Ward
Book designer: Omar Gallegos

Granville Island Publishing Ltd.
105 – 1496 Cartwright St.
#14354, Granville Island
Vancouver, BC, Canada, V6H 4J6

604-688-0320 / 1-877-688-0320
info@granvilleislandpublishing.com
www.granvilleislandpublishing.com

Printed in Canada on recycled paper

*None of this would have been possible
without Brenda, who encouraged me
every step of the way and read
countless versions of the manuscript
without complaint.*

CONTENTS

PROLOGUE
SOMALIA 1993

During the heat of day, four-year-old Samir loved to lie in the shade of the Qurac tree. Huge and old, its long branches spread like a giant umbrella over the tin-roofed, crumbling concrete block structure he and his father called home. An old mat woven from long grasses picked in the nearby fields was a cushion against the hard packed dirt, and Samir's back had worn a comfortable resting spot on the tree's furrowed and fissured trunk. The gumminess of the bark had long ago been absorbed by his only T-shirt, much to his father's chagrin.

That afternoon, a light breeze sent dapples of sunlight flitting through the Qurac's feathery leaves and over Samir's eyelids. The shadows mixed with the images of robots and rocket ships that filled his daydreams, until a hailstorm of grit and suffocating dust jolted him into aching awareness.

Replacing his dreams was a nightmare of reality. Shouts, gunshots, the roar of truck engines. Helicopter thunder overhead. Samir scrambled behind a twisted scrap of roof metal he usually used as a fort, and lay frozen as three American soldiers approached on foot, their eyes invisible behind sunglasses, tan camouflage uniforms drawn tight over armored vests and machine guns held in gloved fists. Behind them, kicking up dusty clouds, rumbled a trio of massive fighting trucks, sweeping their cannon-like guns side to side.

His father, also escaping the oppressive heat of the house, was kneeling a few feet away in the street, his forehead resting on his prayer mat. As the soldiers came closer, they yelled and gestured impatiently with their hands to clear the way, pointing at the oncoming trucks. Deep in prayer, with hearing diminished by years of working in the textile factory, Samir's father did not respond.

Red-faced, one soldier jammed the butt of his rifle into the kneeling man's ribs. Samir's father cried out then righted himself. He grimaced at the dusty road and pressed his forehead back to his matt.

Samir's heart beat as ferociously as the helicopter blades above him. Rising to his feet, he sprinted toward the street as a second soldier sent his father sprawling with a hard kick. The third caught sight of Samir and lifted his gun in warning.

Samir's father rolled onto his knees and again began to pray.

The first two soldiers grabbed him by the arms and tried to hoist him to his feet, but he writhed like a snake, kicking and punching. One flailing fist caught the sunglasses of the soldier to his left, knocking them askew. Cursing, the soldier pinned Samir's father to the ground, one forearm across his throat.

The third soldier shrugged and turned his rifle from Samir. He shouted for his comrade to let go. The crack of the gun was loud, even over the din of the helicopters.

The moment the soldiers turned away, Samir ran to his father's side. The old man lay motionless except for his jaw, which opened and closed like a suckling newborn. A bubbling, wheezing sound escaped the gaping wet hole in his tunic.

As the sounds of the soldiers' boots faded, everything turned quiet and still. Samir pressed his face against his father's. He put his mouth to his ear and begged him to live, grabbed his shoulders and shook them gently, then as hard as he could, but there was no response.

Clutching a rock in his hand, Samir stood. The soldiers were nearly at the end of the street. He ran, screaming. A dozen steps away, he hurled the stone with all his might, but it only skidded near their feet. They laughed and kept walking.

Samir spun, looking desperately for help, but the street was empty.

Returning to his father, he lay in the street beside him and wept, breathing in his scent, a mixture of sweet spices and sweat. Eventually there came a great commotion—people shouting, wailing and arguing. Two men, surrounded by an angry, chanting crowd, dragged the body away. Then the roiling, seething mass of humanity departed, leaving Samir forgotten in the dust. He knelt staring at the dirt that had cradled his father. He couldn't bear to touch his crumpled prayer mat, sodden with blood, so prodded it toward the front door with a stick.

Entering his house, he recoiled with shock. Two strangers stood in the single room. A man was sifting through the family's few belongings, while a woman stuffed bags of beans and rice into a cloth sack. They angrily shooed him away. Unsure of what to do, he stood in the street for a while. The sun was low in the sky when he began knocking on his neighbors' doors. No one answered.

He ran to the Qurac tree and slid down the trunk. His father's blood had soaked into the front of his T-shirt, and the wet fabric felt clammy. The gummy remnants of sap now chafed his skin. Shivering, he pulled off his shirt, crumpled it into a ball and threw it as far as he could. He wiped his hands in the dirt then clutched the tatters of his father's mat and hugged his knees tightly against his chest. The squeezing pressure on his stomach, a sharp reminder of his constant hunger, caused him to heave.

Six months ago, Samir's mother had died of starvation, so weak in the last hours before her death that she was unable to hold his sister to her flat breast. The baby, in turn, was too feeble to complain that the breast she suckled was dry. His aunt had taken her away, telling him over and over not to worry, that he would see her again, soon. His father had told him that the American operation, Restore Hope, would ensure the safe passage of relief food trucks, and they would then have enough to eat again.

That, like everything else, had been a lie. He had not seen his sister, his aunt or any other family since. The Americans did not bring peace, or food. They delivered death.

Samir rubbed away the tears that had left wet roads to nowhere under his eyes. He was only a child, but Samir felt a stirring that was more powerful than anything he had experienced before. Something far worse than the pain of hunger in his stomach. This was the day hate entered his life—and consumed it.

DAY ONE

Wednesday
June 27, 2018

CHAPTER 1

Until the late nineties, Tillson, Oregon, had experienced the same fate as many other large American cities. With the slowdown in mining and forestry, unemployment and then crime rates soared. As an antidote, the state's elected officials had done everything in their power to encourage the technology juggernaut Gazzel to locate its headquarters in the once vibrant city tucked into the foothills of the Cascade Mountains. Attracted by the allure of bountiful cheap electricity—generated mostly by the wall of water massed behind the Easton Dam—and reduced taxes, the corporate giant eventually agreed. As predicted, its presence attracted a plethora of tech startups, and in the following years, the metropolis became vibrant once again.

Situated on the edge of the city limits, the verdant lawns of Gazzel's fourteen-acre campus sparkled in the early morning sunlight—thanks to a nightly deluge delivered by the automated sprinkler system. With the workday just getting underway, the large parking lots that dotted the campus were nearly full. Several stragglers hurried along the meandering, tree-lined flagstone walkways toward the immense glass atrium that served as the main entrance to the office towers.

This Wednesday morning, like every weekday, Fatima Khalif was exactly on time as she sat down at her desk. Her nondescript cubicle was one among hundreds of identical workstations in the Foundation Tower, which housed the staff that supported the Dreamers in the Inspiration Tower and the Implementation Team in the Liftoff Tower.

Fatima felt different from the thousands of other employees settling into their work that morning. She was sure that her pulse was beating faster than any of theirs, including those on the company gym treadmills, pounding out their final sprints. For the first time, she was excited to sit in the cramped cubicle of Department 643.

She flinched as a sneeze sounded loudly in her earbuds, followed by several more, each more explosive than the last. Somebody was clearly ill. Either there'd been a break-in at the apartment, or James Wizner had a cold.

Fatima ignored the morning mountain of emails and slew of service requests in the work queue to focus on the live feed. There came a succession of wet snorts, throat clearing and nose blowing. It had to be Wizner; she had established that he lived alone. This was her chance. Hopefully the cold was not so severe that he would be prevented from working at home.

• • •

Across the department floor, Jenny Longstrum leaned back in her chair. It was only approaching first break and her eyes were already aching.

Peering over the corner of her cubicle's bland gray wall, she felt her anger flare. What was Fatima *doing* over there? The woman never took a coffee break, invariably ate her lunch at her desk and always had earbuds in. Most annoying of all, despite her stilted English, she zoomed to the top of the department leaderboard anytime Jenny relaxed for even a moment. All too often, the two of them had to share the weekly productivity bonus. She snorted in disgust. Even now, the other woman's fingers were tapping away energetically on her keyboard.

A year ago, the reclusive ways of the department's newest employee had been a novelty. Jenny and the group would break the monotony of the workday by reporting, via intra-office messaging, the rare sightings of their co-worker away from her cubicle. She did not participate in any office parties or after-work drinks, and never took vacation or sick leave.

Now at lunch, Jenny and her office mates joked about how large Fatima's bladder must be to let her remain glued to her screen through every break. A basketball was the consensus. More seriously, they wondered what secret project Fatima was working on. The entire office was collectively bored out of their minds on the average day; most took any opportunity to leave their desk. Some even pretended to smoke so they could step outside. If Fatima was so enamored with her work, they concluded, she had to be a management spy. Accordingly, they had nicknamed her the SnitchBitch.

Jenny took another peak over her cubicle wall and did a double take. Was that a smile? Fatima's usually humorless face appeared excited. In fact, she seemed barely able to keep still, rocking rhythmically in her chair. Was she watching videos on her work screen? Were these some sort of pathetic dance moves?

Jenny laughed softly and turned back to her work. Oh, she and the girls were going to have fun with this one. She indulged in a brief daydream of sneaking up and catching the SnitchBitch watching farting goat videos.

Nothing would be more pleasing to Jenny than to see Fatima fired. She hated competition for the top spot—and having to share the bonus money that went with it.

• • •

James Wizner had awoken that morning unable to breathe through his nose. Downing several large doses of vitamin C the previous night had done nothing to prevent the tickle in his throat from turning into a full-blown viral attack, and since getting out of bed he hadn't stopped perspiring. Rivulets of sweat still coursed down his back after a second cooling shower. Suddenly freezing, he'd crawled back into bed under three blankets and two duvets, teeth chattering so violently he thought he might chip a tooth.

Driving to work was not going to be an option. As plant manager, he needed to lead by example. Besides, if he passed the virus on now, it would mean putting in endless hours of overtime covering everyone else's sick days.

Regardless of his altruism, he knew the dreaded tsunami of emails would still flood his in-box. He promised himself that later he would log in from his computer and clear out some junk mail, at least. Momentarily he felt better, until another wave of shuddering chills spread across his upper back and down into his belly.

Christ. This wasn't just a cold. He brought his fingers to the end of his nose. Thankfully, his nail beds were not blue. His legs felt heavy, like lead sewer pipes, as he rubbed a foot down each calf checking for the pain and swelling of a blood clot. How he wished his mother lived closer. He could use some reassurance that he wasn't going to die. Better yet, someone to change his sweat-soaked sheets and make chicken soup.

Another round of shakes took hold of his core. He moaned softly and turned over in bed.

• • •

Fatima unlocked her lower desk drawer and made a show of rummaging around. Upon arriving at work each morning, she always removed a USB stick from its hiding spot behind her belt buckle and placed it in her purse. Unauthorized portable memory devices were strictly forbidden, and every employee was subject to a thorough search when entering and leaving the building. In addition, security officers checked the desks inside and out every night.

Covering the encrypted memory stick in a tissue, she snapped her bag shut and blew her nose, letting the USB slide under the cuff of her blouse in a deft, well-practiced motion. Leaning over to close the desk drawer she brushed her pen onto the floor. Her chair swiveled away from the surveillance camera as she extended herself toward it. Shaking her arm, she dropped the memory stick from her sleeve into her palm. Another quick check around, and she inserted the USB into its port in the computer tower under the desk, scooped up the pen and returned her attention to her screen.

A few keystrokes and she was ready. She squirmed with excitement.

Poised to react, she carefully continued her routine work, listening closely to the audio stream. It didn't sound like he was moving around much yet.

She switched her screen to the customer issue docket and smiled. With half the department heading to lunch, she could cherry pick the easily resolvable tickets and regain the top spot on the leaderboard.

• • •

An embarrassing, loud gurgle from her stomach prompted Jenny to tap the ESC button and back out of her workflow until the password screen popped up. She gathered her lunch bag and sweater and stood to stretch. The morning's gym session had rendered her starving. Over the partitioned workspaces she could see Fatima's head: earbuds in, eyed glued to her screen. There was no indication that she would break her habit of eating lunch at her station and then sneaking to the washroom while the majority of the department was in the cafeteria.

Jenny clenched her jaw. Snitch's dedication to work was inhuman. She narrowed her eyes. This lunch hour she wouldn't get to scoop up all the easy calls. Not if Jenny had anything to say about it.

On tiptoes, she approached undetected.

"Coming for lunch?"

Fatima startled. Turning her chair to face Jenny, she fumbled one earbud out. "What? Oh, oh no, not today, thank you very much."

"What are you working on that keeps you so busy?" Jenny edged between the cubicle wall and Fatima's chair, trying to see the icons across the bottom of her desktop. How amazing if there were something out of place—if not unauthorized software, then maybe a thumbnail photo of some guy Fatima was wooing with her good looks and stunning personality. *What a joke, Miss Dowdy would be lucky to marry a relative.*

Darn. All she could see was an array of open quality control worksheets across the top of the screen.

Fatima aborted her program, hitting F1 and blanking the screen.

"Just the usual. But I think I will go to the washroom now. Excuse me."

Jenny stepped aside but lingered for a moment after Fatima walked away. Surveying the workstation, she detected nothing out of the ordinary. In fact, there was not a single personal item on her desktop or any photos pinned to her cubicle walls. *What a loser.* Shaking her head, she heeded the call of her growling stomach and headed to the elevator.

• • •

Fatima almost tripped running down the corridor to the washrooms. Why today, of all days, would Miss Nosy come to bother her? With only a single earbud in and distracted by Jenny's interrogation, it had been difficult to monitor the audio feed. After all this waiting, had she missed the big moment?

At the corner of the hallway, she took a quick peek over her shoulder and saw the flash of Jenny's blond hair as the elevator doors closed. She turned and raced back to her cubicle. She slipped in her earbuds and unwrapped her lunch.

Wizner was inactive. The silence gave her time to think. *Monitoring Wizner while trying to do my best work leaves no time to win prizes for sociability. But I don't always want to stay at my desk for breaks, even if the conversations in the cafeteria are sometimes awkward. I'm never sure if they are laughing with me or at me.*

Then there was Jenny. She frequently went the extra mile to make the workplace uncomfortable. Fatima squeezed her hands into fists and pushed them against her temples. *I must ignore her. I like this job. Here I can prove myself. This is my chance to be independent.*

The tofu and bean wrap tasted like cardboard. Fatima brushed a crumb from her blouse and grimaced. Her clothes were so drab. Besides being blond and beautiful, Jenny had the nicest clothes. And she was popular. *Why does she bother with me, torment me? Just because I sometimes take a share of the bonus money? Clearly, she doesn't need it.* Fatima shook her head. *No, I'm sure that I'm just being paranoid.* After a couple of bites, she rewrapped the rest of her lunch for her afternoon break and started typing.

• • •

The afternoon dragged on, but at long last, the hours of silence in James Wizner's apartment exploded into a burst of heavy snorting and coughing. Fatima felt sorry for the man, but she was glad that something had woken him. She was running out of time. It was almost 3:00 p.m., and in approximately one hour she had to head home. Her co-workers already resented her for her zealous work habits; she didn't want to inflame the situation by appearing to milk the job for overtime.

Her pulse quickened. Footsteps. Wizner was out of bed.

• • •

Convinced that he would never feel warm again, Wizner stood over the bathtub and implored the water to heat faster. Finally the stream running through his fingers began to steam, and he sealed the drain.

While he waited for the tub to fill, he studied his image in the mirror. Never good-looking even at his best, he quickly turned his head at the sight of the drawn, haggard features of a man twice his age.

Wizner soaked until he was prune-like, struggling to stay awake. Finally patting himself dry, he swallowed and coughed, wincing as the whale hook piercing his chest threatened to wrench out his lungs. He wrapped himself in a towel and staggered to the kitchen.

The fridge was bare except for beer and juice. Despite the drops splashing from his brow into his OJ, he preferred the sweat to being cold. Sipping slowly, he grimaced at the tart sting on his the back of his throat. He fingered the tender glands on the side of his neck then checked the skin of his arms. Good, no rash of meningitis.

The microwave display was still blinking from the last power brownout.

"Alexandria, what time is it?"

"It is 3:27 p.m. Pacific Time."

He was reluctant to return to the stuffy confines of his bedroom, which smelled like the consumption ward at a sanatorium. Walking and stretching to relieve the ache crisscrossing his back and shoulders, he entered the living room. Bookshelves overflowed with stacks of comic books, and an enormous flat-screen TV stole the wall. Strewn on the floor around the single big reclining chair was a full armament of gaming consoles.

Winded and dizzy, Wizner stretched out on his chair. His grandfather's tartan wool blanket, used to hide the food and coffee stains on the leather, was rough and scratchy. It made his fever-sensitive skin prickly and uncomfortable, but he needed to rest.

• • •

Fatima listened intently: water flowing, kitchen sounds, a request for the time. Now, footsteps sounded closer. Fatima inhaled sharply. *Please log in.* Surely, a man as important as he was must keep tabs on things during office hours. The footsteps stopped. There was the squished wheeze of cushions deflating and a hacking cough. She checked the time. Ten minutes.

• • •

Wizner sat up. He felt recovered enough to move again.

A small table sat in a corner of the room. It was dwarfed by his prized computer, built with hand-picked components and optimized for high-intensity gaming. Living alone he could play all he wanted. Yes, he knew he was exhibiting signs of addiction—thinking about new strategies to counter the Ajurians during meetings, forgoing his evening walk and invitations to drinks after work to squeeze in another game—but what better way to de-stress than blow up things in Starcraft? He deserved some downtime after all the work he did for this city. Anyway, the machine was a beaut, far better than the clunky laptop provided by his employer. Usually he believed strongly in the separation of work and play and rarely worked from home—but the dreaded emails were no doubt accumulating.

He was cold again. Pulling the blanket with him, he wrapped it around his shoulders and shuffled to the computer, sat down and clicked on the portal to the system server. He entered his password and opened his in-box. The first email entry was an automated request.

"Not another damn meeting."

• • •

Keystrokes! The sound was as beautiful as the first rhapsody she'd heard played by the concert pianist in Davis Theater on her sixteenth birthday. Her foster mother had driven them all the way to San Francisco just for the afternoon performance. She'd been wearing her new birthday dress, and they'd had dinner in a trendy restaurant. She had been so happy then . . . but this was almost as good.

Fatima glanced around quickly to make sure Jenny wasn't slinking up behind her. With several deft commands she opened a work order for Wizner's Alexandria unit, allowing her to save the sample for further analysis. Snipping and pasting the audio segment into the log file, she also placed a copy onto her memory stick.

The instant the ejection light blinked, she discreetly dipped her shoulder and withdrew the device from her computer. Palming it, she drew her hand up onto her lap and slipped it behind her belt buckle.

CHAPTER 2

Samir yawned. Since before dawn he had been BurBur Car's busiest provider, and it already felt like a long day. He checked the time and decided that he could manage one more fare. An empty parking spot on Main Street would be impossible to find at this hour, so he pulled into a loading zone.

As he waited, the usual parade of Western excess passed by: a heavily tattooed, short-skirted woman smoking a cigarette and wearing a huge gold men's watch, tiers of bangles riding up each arm; a parade of massive pickup trucks more luxurious than the homes of most people in the world; groups of teenagers in designer clothes sipping lattes and glued to thousand-dollar smartphones.

Samir detested the immoral and frivolous way of American life—the incessant want-this, want-that attitude. Why was it so important to impress other people with material things and appearances? These same people thought nothing of disgracing themselves by getting drunk and pissing and puking over each other in the back seat of his car.

Unlike many other drivers, Samir didn't mind rising early and fighting the morning rush; it was far more tolerable than the evening and night hours. Even having partaken as a foolish teen, he could never understand why Americans continued to poison themselves with alcohol during adulthood.

No, like his ancestors, Samir knew it was better to live a pure life: to rise with the sun, work hard and sleep with the darkness. It was exactly that attitude that had allowed him to complete his PhD in robotics and artificial intelligence at MIT in just three years—the minimum permitted.

Twenty minutes and no requests. It would soon be time to head home to enjoy his favorite time of day—the hours between the end of his driving shift and sleep—when he did his real work.

He felt most comfortable lost in the labyrinth of complex equations. Solutions others could not see came to him easily; he'd obtained his degree both quickly and with minimal input from his thesis advisor, Dr. William

Novarski. Samir smiled. The man's Eastern European accent had been so heavy it was almost comical. His eyes were oddly fish-like through his pop-bottle eyeglasses, but where the other students mocked him, Samir never could. He liked the man's snide criticism of the 'American Dream', of course, but mostly appreciated that the professor left him alone. It had been extremely gratifying to see Novarski's look of surprise when he presented the final draft of his thesis.

"Samir, so nice to see you. You've been a rare sight in this office."

"I have focused only on this. And I work best in peace and quiet."

"This is truly a remarkable achievement, young man, to tackle such a difficult topic in such a short time."

"Thank you, sir."

"But beyond your work, did you have a pleasant life while you were here? There is more to university than studying." Novarski had laid down the manuscript and smiled. "Social events, discussion groups? Did anything lure you away to enrich the other domains in your life?"

"I have had no time for such distractions."

This had made Novarski frown. "What are you planning next? If I can help with a post-doc position, just let—"

"Thank you. You have been most kind, but I must take a break. I am . . . tired."

"Of course. But don't throw all this away!"

The memory still made Samir laugh. What a silly man.

The car tires squawked and squealed as he drove down into the parking lot beneath the apartment building. He held his breath as he climbed the dank, piss-smelling steps up and out onto the street. *No, Professor Novarski, I am definitely not throwing it all away.*

For the short walk to the newsstand down the street, Samir pulled down his Dodgers baseball cap until the brim touched his sunglasses. At the rack, he selected a Tillson *Herald* and stepped up to the vendor. He held out his money and placed the paper on the counter. Propping open the sections of the paper with an index finger, he pushed until it overhung the far edge. The stooped old man held a tissue under his nose and blew loudly. With a magicians' sleight of hand, he vigorously wiped his bushy moustache and slipped another newspaper from under the counter into the center of the *Herald*.

Every Wednesday afternoon he and Samir performed this choreographed exchange. Alone in the apartment elevator, Samir experienced the usual prickle of anticipation at the sight of the *Al Jazeera*, dated two days ago. He smiled. It was a relief not to feel so alone, drowning in this sanctimonious sea.

The apartment was dark, the curtains pulled tight. The kitchen was spotlessly clean, as always. Monday to Friday, his sister rose hours after he had departed, ate her breakfast and prepared a packed lunch for herself so she would not have to leave her computer at the office, but he never saw evidence of her morning cooking.

Removing his jacket, Samir sat at the flimsy plastic table in the living room and spread out the *Al Jazeera*, flipping to the advertisement section. His finger moved carefully over the job listings, but no keywords revealed themselves.

He was becoming increasingly frustrated by the reliance of his so-called leaders on such antiquated methods of communication. With Americans touting their constant successes against his brothers-in-arms, how was anyone still capable of sending an elaborate secret message? He snorted in disgust.

No matter. Their vision was outdated, and he had his own plans for revenge. A new way. The modern way.

Gathering up the newspapers, Samir opened the apartment door. Checking both ways that the hallway was empty, he walked the twenty paces to the garbage chute and let both papers slide away, the *Al Jazeera* still carefully hidden within the *Herald*. He had no need for further reading.

He checked the time. Soon, the solitude to do anything he wanted would vanish. In his bedroom, Samir flicked on his computer, slipped into his caftan and laid out his prayer mat. By the time he rose from his knees, the screen was lighting up the room. Despite his leaders' inaction, he would continue his own work.

There was no wasted time checking emails; he steadfastly avoided the Internet. The probing eyes of the American government were too ubiquitous on the Web. If he needed to research something not contained in the several reference books stored in his closet, he went to the library. Other than some inane pieces of reading to cover his tracks, he never borrowed a book. He either made shorthand notes or committed the information he needed to memory. Occasionally he took a photo with his phone of more complex diagrams. Later, he always deleted the images.

Pages of algorithms scrolled by on his computer screen until Samir found the lines he wanted to tweak. It was an improvement that had come to him just today, during an idle moment between fares. He smiled. His years of training at MIT had been well spent. There was no way he was going to waste his life driving a truck of explosives into a military checkpoint or popping an assault rifle from under his coat at the mall. He was smarter than that. Believers and infidels alike would be awestruck when they saw the havoc he would wreak; he would be legendary.

After graduation, he had created a list of potential targets in critical industries. The possibilities seemed endless—control of an electrical grid? A bomb to drop on a banking network, a virtual knife to penetrate the soft underbelly of some fat-cat American business? But until he possessed useful intelligence, he could only daydream.

The sound of someone at the door caused him to stand, wary and ready. He checked the time. It was his sister's usual hour of arrival. At the familiar metallic click of the key in the lock, he let down his guard by half, but remained alert until he heard her voice.

"Samir, I am home."

With the clunk of a grocery bag on the counter and the rustle of her coat being placed on the hook in the hallway, he relaxed fully and called out.

"How was your day?"

"Very well, thank you. Did you get lots of fares?"

"The usual. There was a big rush before nine and then it was very slow until lunch. But some of the trips were long ones with big tips."

"That is good. You must be hungry." Her voice was distant, coming from the far end of the kitchen. She knew better than to come into his bedroom. "I have a surprise for you."

A surprise? Samir tidied his workspace and logged off his computer.

She sounded happy, but different from the times she brought home a nice dessert. When he entered the kitchen, she was busy at the counter chopping a large carrot.

"What is it?" He moved to stand beside her, nimbly snatching a piece of cut carrot and placing it in his mouth.

She pretended to chop at his fingers. "Oh, I will tell you at dinner. Now go relax."

"No, you sound excited. What is it?"

"All right, if you can't wait." She walked over to her purse slung over the back of a kitchen chair. When Fatima turned back to him, she wore a smile so huge it made her eyes scrunch shut. In her extended hand was a memory stick. "This man you were most interested in, never used his home computer, except for games. After all these months of waiting, today he was sick and stayed home from work, but he wasn't so ill that he couldn't log on to his computer."

"Interesting, but how do you know he did work?"

"What do you think I have been doing these past months? Counting the money in my mahr so I can pay some man to marry me? I knew you would be angry, so I didn't tell you, but I recorded him one evening."

Samir grabbed her wrist, eyes wide. "That is dangerous."

"I took a necessary risk." Fatima peeled away Samir's fingers. "I barely have time to do my own work during the day." Fatima stepped away. "The games he plays have lots of shooting and yelling. Today was very different. Just typing, and he was angry about having to go to some meeting. I am sure your fancy program can figure it out." She handed him the USB and returned to her food preparations.

Samir felt a tingle run down his spine. Finally, Fatima's job was paying off. Working in the customer support center for Alexandria had allowed her to eavesdrop on prospective prey all day long. They had honed in on several targets, but unfortunately, despite the system's popularity, the vast majority of interactions with Alexandria were at residences, not office buildings. Samir had decided that it was just too risky to record longer evening or weekend sessions; it was far safer to monitor the Alexandria units in real time during office hours.

Besides, the amount of data collected would have been too burdensome. It was better to only record exactly what he needed. This meant, however, that up until now their efforts to get any worthwhile info had been mostly futile. No doubt Fatima's choice had been inadvisable, but admittedly it might have been the only way to get what he wanted.

His appetite for dinner had vanished. Returning to his room he did not bother closing the door. Inserting the USB, labeled 'Vacation Photos', he ran Key Analytics and opened the single file drive.

The harsh staccato of a man sneezing and coughing jarred his ears. Through his studio quality headphones, Samir listened as the person moved closer to the Alexandria unit, then away again. Finally, came a scuffing sound and the creak of a chair.

The keystrokes that followed were clear and not too fast, two-finger plunking speed. Excellent for analysis.

Samir rubbed his palms together. There would be no dinner or sleep tonight.

CHAPTER 3

In the dusty cement stairwell of her apartment building, Jenny pushed herself through the searing pain in her thighs to mount the last few steps. The sight of the large number twenty-three stenciled on the gray fire door prompted a deep intake of air and a sigh of relief.

The ritual of climbing the twenty plus flights two at a time at the end of her workday was retribution for sitting on her ass for eight hours in front of a computer screen. She was determined not to become one of those lard-assed women who bought larger and larger clothes until the supersize counter at Walmart was their only option.

She acknowledged that she was sensitive about her figure. In high school, she had been slim enough but too tall to be a cheerleader. Despite this horrific physical limitation, her enthusiasm and all-American good looks had landed her a spot on the high school team and then as a substitute on the varsity cheerleading squad at Texas U. When she was nineteen, however, she noticed that from the waist down, she just, well, sort of, became thicker. Not fat—she was too fit for that—but heavier, somehow. As a result, whenever she filled in for an ill or injured teammate, she invariably ended up on the lower supporting line with the guys, while the petite little things above soaked up all the glory and admiring looks.

But there was a silver lining. At a third-year mixer event with the football team, she met smart, strong, sweet Mike Longstrum, and he had swept her off her feet—literally. Although he'd made varsity football, he also had his gripes. Big and strong, but not fast enough to be a starter at outside linebacker, he rode the bench year after year. Away from the crowd gathered around the BBQ, they had commiserated over a beer.

Mike must have heard the dejection in her voice as she explained why she was never at the top of the pyramid. He'd put down his beer, reached out and gracefully lifted her over his head like she was the lead ballerina in *Swan Lake*.

When he landed her delicately on her feet facing him, hands still on her hips, she'd leaned in and planted a soft kiss on his cheek.

He'd smiled shyly, looking deep into her eyes. "Perfect."

"I'm not really." She batted her eyelashes.

"That's something I've always dreamed of doing."

"Well, you must have practiced. You're pretty slick."

"Before I had my growth spurt, instead of football as a high school freshman, I tried out for the cheerleading team." He grinned sheepishly. "I thought it would be a great way to meet girls."

"And cop a feel."

Mike laughed. "Well, that too. But what I really wanted to do, instead of tossing Judy Smith—who I had a serious crush on—into the air for a double flip, was to let her slide down into my arms and kiss her."

She'd had no reason for jealousy, but the story definitely diminished the glow that had been warming the moment. "Well, glad that I was able to fulfill—"

Pressing a finger to her lips, he shushed her. "Reality is what counts, and this feels way better than anything I ever imagined."

She felt the same, and the year after graduation, they married.

Her legs felt like lead. Still panting, she reached the door of their apartment and paused. The delicious aroma wafting under the door and into the hallway made her want to recheck the unit number. Mike must have come home early from work and was clearly cooking up a storm.

Normally, she didn't see him until after 8:00 p.m. His work with the FBI necessitated long and unusual hours. Years of experience taught her that his arrival home in time to cook, especially on a Wednesday, was a harbinger of bad news. He would be slated to work the weekend.

The sounds of a roaring exhaust fan and sizzling chicken breasts greeted her as she pushed open the door. Mike didn't hear her enter, and she cast an admiring eye over his wide shoulders and the firm buns peeking through the apron tied around his waist. *I'm a lucky girl.*

She knew better than to startle a Bureau boy. To avoid a kitchen spatula to the heart she cleared her throat as she approached. Still stirring, he turned and smiled. My, she loved those eyes. They had been married for almost ten years, but their greeting hugs and kisses were still long and romantic. Mike embraced her, carefully keeping the greasy spatula from touching the back of her dress. Their lips were still touching when he separated slightly to reach back and stir his concoction of onions, tomato, garlic and chicken.

With a final peck on her lips, he turned his attention back to cooking. "See anyone suspicious today?" He grinned.

Over the years, they had come to adopt light-hearted banter instead of the standard, *how was work, dear?* Mike always said his job of sifting through the masses of Internet surveillance data was too boring to talk about. More to the point, he was forbidden as an FBI agent to discuss his work and well practiced at deflecting questions. After years of quizzing, Jenny had gleaned only that one of his principal tasks was identifying unusual financial patterns that could indicate the funding of terrorist plots.

She shrugged and returned his smile. "Oh, you know, just the usual suspect, that weird woman in the office. Other than that, the same security guard, delivery boy and meter maid."

Mike laughed as he opened the lid on a pot of boiling water, exposing the white bobbing heads of peeled potatoes. "Same old for me, too. But no breaking down doors or shoot-outs at the train station."

After all these years, she knew his humorous remarks shouldn't bother her, but fear squeezed her chest with a tight band. Yes, he was part of the nerd squad usually tasked to sift through the nearly impenetrable depths of the Internet jungle, but when all hands were called upon, Mike geared up with Kevlar and an automatic just like the rest of the team. What really irked her was that he clearly loved it—the thrill of danger, the uncertainty of conflict, the rush of adrenaline, the close camaraderie after the takedown and then relaxing with the team over a beer. *All fine, if you were lucky enough to survive.*

The chicken was tasty, but the veggies were murder victims. She blamed Mike's poor culinary upbringing. His parents had raised him on a bland diet of boiled potatoes and soggy vegetables, and his tastes had never changed. Jenny doused her broccoli with pepper and salt, wishing for a creamy cheese sauce to perk up the wilted spear drooping from the end of her fork.

"This is delicious, darling, but all jokes aside I do wonder about Fatima and what she's up to. She is always so secretive and intense. Whenever I go near her desk she gets all jittery and hides her screen as fast as she can."

Like Mr. Krupp, her stuffy old grade-six schoolteacher, Mike cleared his throat.

"Try not to make judgments. You're only on her case because she keeps to herself," he took a mouthful of water, "and wears a headscarf. At the Bureau, we can't profile someone just because of their religion."

"Really, is that your 'official' answer?"

"OK, mostly never."

"It's not like I can get access to the office security camera, so could I put one of your little high-tech surveillance gizmos in her cubicle?"

Jenny let her comment hang in the air and raised her eyebrows. Mike laughed. His fork was midway to his mouth when he stopped.

"You're not really asking me are you?"

"Just for a day."

"You've got to be kidding. I can't take anything out of the office without permission, and even if they gave it to me, I couldn't loan it to you." Returning his attention to his plate, he filled his mouth and chewed vigorously.

Trying to diffuse the tension, she chuckled. "How about this? Since the government is so broke these days, why don't I offer to rent the equipment?"

She beamed a smile and nodded enthusiastic agreement to her own idea, but her humor seemed to have the opposite effect. Mike pursed his lips and stared at her hard before managing a smile. "Nice try."

"OK, fine, I'll just have to figure something out."

"Honey, leave this stuff up to *highly trained* professionals, please."

Jenny laughed, until it was her turn to realize Mike was being serious. "Oh, come on."

"No, just think. If she really was some sort of terrorist or spy, you'd be putting yourself in terrible danger. Please don't get involved with her."

Jenny pushed food around her plate with a pout. "I'm just trying to help. Come on, you're always trying to find a way to get noticed so you don't have to sit at a computer all day. I know you don't have the time to be looking under every rock for a juicy clue, but this could be the big one."

Mike put down his utensils and pushed back his chair. "But getting caught doing illegal shit would end my career."

"You've got to take a chance now and then. Come on, one little peek. You can explain it away." She stood, wrapped her arms around his shoulders from behind and planted a soft kiss on his cheek. "You've trusted my instincts before. You know, like the time I told you to not to believe that bank dweeb in Turks and Caicos."

She felt him tense, then melt beneath her hands. "All right, fine. If it will make you happy, give me her information and I'll run her through the database."

• • •

Chuck Schelmer parked his pickup truck under the light post closest to the entrance of the Streamline factory. The surrounding acres of asphalt parking were sparsely covered. There had been a dramatic drop in demand for luxury trailers recently, and the warehouse ran a skeletal night shift.

To counter the dust swirling in the gusty wind, he tucked his lunch bucket under his arm, dropped his head and shielded his eyes with the other hand. Beside him another truck door slammed.

"Hey, Schelmer, taking another zombie shift? Whadda' ya need the money so bad for?"

"I could ask you the same, Spitwell. You just work a double?"

"Ya, 'nother fucking donation to our pinko government." Spitwell pulled down his US Veteran's cap to block another gust.

"At least I got a wife and kids. What's your excuse, did the bar call in your tab?"

"Ha ha. Seriously, Schelmer, I know the sitch with your daughter. I's not just your foreman, I got connections. Could see you make a lot more money. Legit."

"How's that?"

"You're a farmer, registered, right?"

"So?" Chuck started to walk away. He knew the company Spitwell kept.

Spitwell grabbed his arm, but let go quickly. "You get me some supplies and I'll make it worth your while."

"What?"

"I's thinking of starting up a little grow-op, and I need some fertilizer, the high nitrogen stuff."

"Goodnight, Spitwell. I gotta do my physio-rehab paperwork before I start." As Chuck departed, he heard Spitwell's raspy exhalation and grimaced as a cloud of unfiltered cigarette smoke enveloped him. He walked faster.

Behind him the other man's voice was low, phlegmy and too close. "Y'all think about it."

There was a loud hork, followed by a splatter of spittle that landed beside Chuck's foot. "Think very serious-like, Schelmer, cuz we ain't finished discussin' this matter. See ya tomorrow."

● ● ●

The floodlights of Rosepark Field were dark. On the moonlit artificial turf of the ten-thousand-seat stadium, Hamid Hassan planted his left foot and executed a lightning fast dodge to his right, then streaked down the flank toward the goal. He executed another feint left and right before he cut sharply away from the sideline, the ball following him as if attracted to magnets in the toes of his shoes. With a final burst of speed, he closed on the net, its white ropes barely visible in the watery moonlight. Running flat out, he drew his left foot across the ball for a powerful curving shot.

He pulled up to watch, squinting. The ball appeared to be heading past the far corner of the net, but over the final yards of its trajectory, its arc narrowed and tucked inside the post. Drenched in sweat, Hamid stood alone on the pitch, his arms raised in triumph.

At an early age, coaches and fellow players had recognized his talents, but Hamid's dreams of playing English Premier League soccer remained buried in the rubble of war. Of course, born in a conflict-ridden country like Somalia, he was always a long shot anyway. The colonial wounds left by Italy and Britain had festered into a devastating civil war for his homeland, but Hamid knew the final blow to his dream had been the American betrayal.

Muscles aching, he walked slowly to his gym bag where it rested on the home bench. His towel was musty but served its purpose of sopping up the salty sweat dripping into his eyes. Removing his cleats, he pulled on his sweat suit and laced up his running shoes. The soccer ball fit neatly inside his bag.

With the final reconnaissance of the stadium complete, his decision was made. Gear slung over one shoulder, he passed under the stadium seating and through the maintenance area to the door of the storage vault. Checking that he was unobserved, he pulled out the keypad and tools from the bottom of his bag. The job was not complex and he was finished in a matter of minutes. Everything was ready for the show Saturday night.

At the employee entrance, he slid in his magnetic strip card and entered the code required to operate the gate. He kept to the shadows of the fence until he was well down the block before crossing the street.

The first message would go out tonight. He checked his watch. Everything should be done before midnight, allowing him time to watch the rebroadcast of this evening's soccer match between Barcelona and his favorite team, Real Madrid.

• • •

Downtown, Abarque Abouani slid his wide janitor's broom along the terrazzo floor of the long main corridor of Rackford Technology College. The three-story brick building took up an entire city block on Third Street, next to Tillson's old city hall. At ten thirty, night classes were winding down and soon the aging building would be all his.

Finishing up his cursory tour to make sure the school was empty, he locked the front doors. He exchanged his broom for a mop and filled a wheeled metal bucket with hot water and lots of soap. With the handle of the mop, he propelled the cart along the hallway. In front of the women's washroom he stopped and propped the handle against the wall.

That distasteful job could wait. It didn't matter the nationality, after a day's use all washrooms were disgusting affairs. Every night he dealt with a soggy carpet of toilet paper and hand towels, miss-aimed evacuations and sticky soap blobs sprayed helter-skelter on mirrors and countertops.

Taking a hand-duster with him, he unlocked the door of room 102 and entered, sliding the door latch closed behind him. He tossed the polyester feather duster on the instructor's desk and crossed to the server, tucked in an alcove on the far side of the computer lab.

The computers at each workstation were switched off at night to conserve energy, but the more powerful server powering the class intranet remained on. Abarque considered modern technology nothing but a vehicle for Western decadence, but for what he needed to do, a computer was necessary. He had previously tried using one at the public library, but its functions were restricted. Then one evening, while moving all the lab desks and equipment out to clean and wax the floor, he had discovered a treasure.

Straining to move the monstrously heavy instructor's desk at the front of the class he had inadvertently pushed one corner over the edge of the raised lecture platform. The desk had lurched at a precarious angle, and only the drawer slider-stops prevented their contents from spilling onto the floor. The exception was the thin, top middle drawer. Everything, white board-markers, paper clips and assorted pencils flew across the floor, revealing a long white paper taped to the bottom. The string of alphanumeric figures appeared to be a password, and indeed it was—for the server in the side room.

Abarque retrieved a USB key from his pocket and pulled up a chair. Amazingly, the computer's password was still the same. With the USB key inserted, he clicked on Settings and opened the innocuously named 'icon maker' tab to unleash the software that masked his online identity.

At his last prayer session before he left Somalia for America, his Al-Shabaab trainer had slipped the tiny memory stick into his hand and uttered only one sentence of explanation. *Waterproof this and hide it inside a toothpaste tube, install it on a computer and never use the Web without it.*

From his training, Abarque knew what to look for on the Internet, where to find it and why. The webpage flashed brightly and he blinked. A white background with the black outline and numbers of a sudoku puzzle cast an eerie glow over the alcove. The ratings amused him—easy, medium, hard, evil and diabolical—but the coded message he sought was not there. Everything was normal, to the letter, to the number.

No call to arms tonight; America was safe for another day. Now it was time for him to clean up its shit and piss.

CHAPTER 4

Billy Shanopski's basement apartment was in his parents' house, a postwar bungalow on Cherry Street. A passerby looking at the permanently curtained windows would find it difficult to believe anyone actually lived in the lower level; Billy's bedroom was eternally dark except for the glow of his computer screen. He slept all day and used his lights at night infrequently, only flicking a switch in the bathroom or when he mounted the back stairway to raid his parents' kitchen fridge. Living underground like a troll, he also behaved like one, by the Internet's definition. He liked the parallel.

Most of Billy's life consisted of honing his World of Starcraft skills, with the goal of becoming a world champion in the blossoming 'sport' of competitive electronic gaming. Due to time-zone considerations, he kept unusual hours so he could do battle against the best players scattered around the globe, especially those in South Korea. His 'sports uniform' consisted of sweatpants and an Oakland A's T-shirt. This ensemble also served as his pyjamas. For comfort's sake he removed his baseball cap to sleep. The colors were still pristine, having never seen the light of day.

Billy Shanopski was also an American patriot and a good-guy hacker. He was a proud deputy of the AIPL, the American Internet Protection League, a loose network of Internet savvy persons whose mandate was to monitor the net for terrorism threats and other illegal activities.

Founded by the Protector of The Realm, known solely as JonSno, the league prided itself on uncovering information that the understaffed police agencies of the USA government couldn't. Over time, they had proven that their information was credible, but their methods were so secretive that the AIPL was under surveillance itself by the very government organizations it pledged to assist. Billy loved the irony.

Whenever he wasn't gaming, he passed through the portal to the dark web, whose deep virtual shadows hid all sorts of menace: illegal trade in guns, drugs, child sex slaves, snuff porn and stolen information. Anything craved by the evil side of human nature existed there. Encryption was often employed, but surprisingly the most dangerous messages were often sent by the least sophisticated.

In cyberspace, Billy was known solely as TyrBus84, the hacker tag paying homage to his favorite football player, LA Rams wide receiver Tyrone Busapor. Billy's talents lay nowhere near the playing field, however, nor even the light of day; the online community knew TyrBus84 as a genius in encryption busting.

His main claim to fame had been bringing down a pedophile ring based in Hungary six months ago. Using a myriad of encrypted, password-protected sites, the perverts had escaped detection for years, until one night Billy followed a cryptocurrency trail to an IP address that had popped up on his watch list.

Although he was lucky enough to intercept one of their encryption codes, it was not complete, and it had taken hours of work to open one of the files. What he saw revolted him: a young girl, her naked image captured in full light while a black hood masked her tormentor's face. Only the man's eyes, boiling with savage pleasure, were visible. The blank, emotionless expression in the little girl's eyes still haunted Billy.

Squinting, his eyes tired, Billy refocused his gaze to take in his own faint reflection on the computer screen. "Unfortunate looking," is how he'd overheard his mother describe him to one of her tea-party friends. The large, humped nose protruding between an unevenly sized pair of dark, beady eyes somewhat drew attention away from the port-stain discoloration that blazed across his forehead above the smaller eye. A straggly beard covered a small, recessed chin, and a moustache hid his harelip, which was surgically repaired when he was a child. His speech was perfect even if his appearance never would be.

What he saw was someone who needed sleep. The dark circles under his eyes were in stark contrast to the pasty pallor of his skin. Maybe he should grab some leftovers from the fridge and sleep for a few hours before going on patrol. Then again—he squinted at the screen, his Spidey senses tingling.

Several months ago, an innocuous chat group had caught his eye. He'd come to learn that the blander the messages, the more suspicious. Nobody planned garden parties on the dark net. Intrigued, he had reviewed past posts, trying to parse their ambiguous wording. No, he had decided, the site wasn't for child porn—this conversation could be another other kind of evil.

He had put the blog on his watch list, but it had remained dormant for months. Now, he stared at the red notification bubble. With a flurry of keystrokes, he brought up the page.

One new post was pinned to the top of the blog, containing one lone word. *Saturday.*

DAY TWO

Thursday
June 28, 2018

CHAPTER 5

By 8:00 a.m., the heat was already radiating off of the stone steps leading up to the office tower. Fatima fidgeted with her belt as she pushed through the revolving door. The three USB keys taped to the back of her belt buckle were chaffing against her skin. She wished there'd been more room in the leather handle of her purse where she'd cut a slit for the fourth device behind the thin metal of the designer's emblem.

Beyond the physical discomfort, she was scared. She hated the pressure that Samir put on her. She could lose her job, or worse. She loved her brother and wanted to help, but his search for revenge was starting to feel unhinged. What would she do if he were arrested? If they both were?

Fatima dry swallowed in a vain effort to sooth her parched throat. Walking through the cavernous lobby toward the security station, she tasted a mouthful of queasy anxiety but was reassured by the familiar, bored-looking guards at the checkpoint. She stepped into the line of employees waiting to be processed.

The primary function of security screening was to prevent firearms from entering the workplace. There had never been an incident at Gazzel, but two years previously, the estranged partner of a woman had shot and killed her and three co-workers in a nearby industrial area.

The second function was to permit the random search of purses, backpacks and pockets for hard drives that could be used to download corporate secrets.

The security guard staffing the counter by the metal detector was as efficient and unfriendly as usual. Well versed in the routine, Fatima placed her lunch bag and open purse in a plastic tray without being asked.

Blindly rummaging through her purse, the guard swept his hand toward the next station, muttering a perfunctory, "Thanks, ma'am."

She pushed her tray into the scanner and proceeded through the arch of the metal detector. The other guard frowned at the buzz of the alarm and directed her hand scanner around Fatima. It spat out a rapid sequence of beeps.

"Please undo your belt."

Placated that there was nothing behind the buckle, the guard waved her on. Fatima collected her things and walked quickly toward the bank of elevators.

Last evening, her beloved brother had been ecstatic with the information she had obtained from Wizner, but this morning he was despondent. He had wakened her early.

"Fatima, you brought good information. Now, we don't have to monitor the other targets. Concentrate on this man. I need more sonic data so I can map his keyboard. Get as much as you can." He'd laid the extra USB keys on the end of her bed and left for work.

Fatima felt a wave of relief. While Samir had sleuthed for the 'right' people who were also in the Alexandria customer database, his moods had ranged from despondent to table-pounding bursts of rage. She could only hope that besides his improved disposition, her role in whatever this was would be finished soon.

Always secretive, Samir had never revealed his plan to her, but she wondered if he had known in advance about the upgrade to Alexandria that they were exploiting. One day each year, Gazzel invited everyone in customer support to the corporate amphitheater for an advance product release presentation. At the last conference it had been announced that Gazzel was adding multiple microphones to Alexandria. The upgrade would enable the device to triangulate the position of a sound's location and tailor its assistance according to where a person was situated in their house—reminding them when they entered the kitchen to check the milk supply, or at the front door to take an umbrella because rain was in the forecast. It was part of the company's big push into domestic robots.

Fatima didn't really understand the technology but surmised that it was sort of like the sonar dolphins used. Samir, on the other hand, was an expert in such things. His PhD research had made him a world leader in audio location software to increase the precision targeting of drones.

When she'd finished recounting the information from the presentation, all Samir had said was, "Praise Allah."

It was ironic that their victim had paid hundreds of dollars for something that could spy on him so easily. Yet, despite the sophisticated equipment, their success depended completely on the man staying home sick for another day.

At her cubicle, Fatima powered up her computer and slipped her handbag and lunch sack into the large bottom drawer of her desk. Before closing the drawer, she spread open the slit in the strap of her purse and teased out the USB stick. When she was sure no one was watching, she loosened her belt and sat down. Leaning forward and pretending to look for a pencil in the container beside her screen, she slipped the memory keys into her palm. Checking again that she was unobserved, she placed the keys in the sliding plastic tray in her center top drawer and hid them underneath her large collection of markers and sticky-note pads.

Reflexively, she used her left hand to block the view of her keystrokes while she entered her password. A quick look at her in-box revealed nothing urgent, so she clicked the WORP icon on her desktop.

The Work Order Request Program was the bane of the existence of everyone in the department, but it was the reason they got paid. Every customer query, complaint, suggestion or possible hardware malfunction was routed through the program. The task of the twenty persons in the department was to vet each item. If it was obviously hardware related, they notified the customer that their concern was being passed on to the engineering department. Everything else, Fatima and the other customer assistants were expected to deal with. Most additions to the list came from emails and were queued up and assigned to a staff member as they became available. Phone calls also appeared at the top of the list, highlighted in blue, and were doled out to the team in rotation. After each customer engagement, they had to fill in an encounter form that became part of their WORP resolution report.

The truly evil thing was that WORP ranked everyone's clearance rate and posted it in a floating box on the desktop that could not be closed or minimized and was updated every ten minutes. The idea was to encourage the speedy resolution of problems. Their department manager, Mrs. Perks, monitored this competition and used it as the basis for incentives that were awarded 'live' during the day and at the end of each month.

The power of the WORP score didn't stop there. A quarterly summary report went into each customer assistant's human resources file as the crucial measure of job performance. It was the most annoying idea ever dreamt up by an efficiency expert, and the staff jokingly, referred to the process as 'Survivor, the Office Edition'.

Fatima clicked on the fake report that she had created for Wizner's Alexandria. Every time she opened and closed the WORP file she flagged it as under review by engineering, so that none of her co-workers could see it. The best thing was that whenever she pretended to refer the file onward, the program rewarded her with a point for a resolved problem.

• • •

In her cubicle, Jenny stared at the WORP assignment screen. Their F9 key was a toggle to the daily resolution summary, or DRS, and upon tapping it she smiled. With yesterday's results, her streak of seven first place finishes was intact.

Jenny prided herself on being a consistent top performer. Lucy was strong competition when she wasn't bummed about some friend's comment on her daily Facebook post. The middle rankings were inhabited by minimalists. She had to give credit to Sarah and Philomena for consistency, but management would throw a party if they ever broke a sweat. Then came the truly untalented led by Leo, the solitary male in the department. The only way he broke into the upper echelon was during summer vacation, when most of the competition was out of the office.

But there was something more pressing on her mind than her winnings today. Fatima. *What was going on with her?* The woman was consistently near the top of the pack, but yesterday her result had been dismal, placing her ahead of only Janice, who was on vacation. Had she become bogged down in a difficult telephone interaction? Typically, her resolution of problems by email was above average, but her over-accommodating style and misunderstanding of American slang increased the time she spent on live calls. Jenny was sure that the customers believed they were dealing with an offshore call center when they dealt with her.

A blue highlighted customer phone call popped onto the top of the list, interrupting Jenny's train of thought. Her competitive juices flowing, Jenny instantly scooped the call with a double click. Adjusting her headset, she stood, pretending to stretch, and cast an eye across the office to Fatima's corner. *Why wasn't she pulling her weight?*

CHAPTER 6

Heidi Schelmer slipped the last of the breakfast bowls into the dishwasher as her husband pushed through the front door into the mudroom, toeing off his work boots with two heavy thumps.

"How was work, hon?"

"You know it would be cheaper to wash the dishes by hand. How much do those damn soap pucks cost, anyway?"

Heidi slammed the door shut and pressed the wash cycle button. "I know you're taking extra shifts, Chuck, but please, give me a break. You want me taking care of three kids, getting us through calving season by myself, *and* cooking, housecleaning, doing laundry —and now washing and drying dishes?" Her eyebrows arched toward the ceiling.

Chuck put up his hand. "Sorry, sorry. I'm just feeling a little stressed. Becky's last hospital stay used up the last of her forty days for the year. If she gets sick again—"

"I know, I really do. We'll just have to keep her well." Heidi sat down across from her husband and took his hand. "So. How was your night?"

"I ran into Spitwell. What a piece of work. He wanted to know if we'd sell him some nitrogen fertilizer."

"What in the world for?"

"It doesn't matter."

"Why?"

"The guy's a dangerous fuck." Chuck reached for his coffee mug.

"How much is he offering?"

Chuck sputtered through a mouthful of coffee. "You can't be serious."

"No, no. Sorry. I just don't like seeing you working yourself to the bone." Heidi squeezed Chuck's hand. "We're a team. We'll get through this."

"Yeah, you're right." Chuck slipped his hand out of Heidi's grip and rubbed it across the stubble on his chin. "Everything will be fine."

Hamid didn't relish waiting outside Mr. Ashton's office. The cheap plastic chair was sticking to his sweat-damp pants and scraped on the uncarpeted concrete floor as he alternated lifting each buttock for relief. He wondered why the owner of ACE Security would want to see him before the day's shift even started. Was he in trouble? He couldn't afford to lose this job. The security credentials that gave access to the stadium were key to his plans for Saturday night.

Hamid's strategy was basic and therefore more likely to succeed than Samir's grand schemes. It could happen now, with certain results. He was sick of waiting for his friend to give the go-ahead for his own 'big thing'. Why not keep it simple? Pick a crowded target and execute an attack. As de facto leader, wasn't he, Hamid, the one who should choose what the group did?

Still, he had respect for Samir, even if they didn't always agree. They had come a long way together from the dusty grime of Somalia and the refugee camp in Kenya.

At first, Hamid had not known what to make of Samir, but he'd been intrigued by the boy who slept in the closet of the school each night—introverted, thin as a stalk of grass, a supersmart kid who preferred to sit in the shade and read books rather than join the soccer games with the other boys.

He remembered the day religious extremists had torched the school for allowing girls to enter. The pile of burning textbooks in the courtyard had attracted a swarm of boys singing and dancing in celebration of their freedom. A sworn enemy to academics, Hamid had watched in amazement as Samir pulled one after another burning book out of the flames, wrapping each in old cloth like it was a jewel. While everyone else had been filled with joy to escape the confines of the hot, stuffy classroom, Samir curled up under a tree to learn math from the texts he had rescued. Taking pity on the now shelterless younger boy, Hamid had brought him under his wing.

In the following insufferable years spent as orphans, the unlikely pair became a formidable alliance. Samir, the intellectual and visionary; Hamid, the hard-working foot soldier.

In fact, each owed the other his life. In Somalia, a fight with a pair of teenagers over a tin of beans had led to a knife being held at Samir's throat. Without thinking, Hamid charged at Samir's assailant, knocking the pair to the ground and loosening the boy's grip on the knife. But instantly, the other teen jumped him and while they fought Samir won the race to the knife and slashed it across his captor's arm. The pair fled, leaving him and Samir trembling like leaves in a windstorm. Battle tested and now armed with a knife, they repelled a few more would-be robbers until their reputation as untouchables became legend.

Finally, the misery of the refugee camps in Kenya had forged both teens' naive desires for jihad into steel; the most important link between them was their shared hatred of America and fervor for a violent reckoning.

Eventually they were separated when an American family adopted Samir and his sister. Not as fortunate, Hamid was an adult by the time his claim for asylum was finally accepted by Germany. Despite time and distance, however, their bond had remained strong.

It had been a long, arduous journey to join his friend, including time spent in England and Canada. Amidst this, unknown to anyone including Samir, he had slipped out of Germany and fought briefly for ISIS in Syria. While the training he received was invaluable, Hamid quickly tired of running from one pile of rubble to the next. He decided that he wanted to have a bigger impact and jumped at the opportunity to participate in the next direct attack on America. Was that chance not priceless?

But recently, Samir kept making excuses to postpone any action. *Did he still have the same passion?* Hamid chastised himself. Who was he to doubt his friend's resolve? Samir's reasons for revenge were deeply rooted, and Hamid believed in him. But he moved too slowly.

Finally, Mr. Ashton's booming voice sounded through the closed door.

"Hamid, come in."

"Yes, boss, what's up?"

"Sorry to make you wait. I was just signing up an important new customer." The man removed his glasses and rubbed the bridge of his nose. "Hamid, I have already warned you once about this. You mustn't use the company vehicle for personal use. We can't have the van with our Logo on it parked . . ." Ashton cleared his throat and lowered his voice, avoiding eye contact, ". . . parked in front of a goddamn mosque."

Hamid clenched his fists tightly but kept his face impassive. He forced his voice to sound respectful. "Sorry, sir. It won't happen again. I will pay for the mileage."

"That's not the point." Ashton opened his palms in conciliation. "Look, Hamid, you know that it would be the same for a strip club. You're my best employee, that's why I let you keep the truck. I appreciate that you like to work, shall we say, flexible hours, and as long as the work gets done I'm happy. But no more parking at the mosque."

Hamid swallowed hard. He did not want to risk a dispute that could lead to losing use of the van entirely. His only alternate means of transportation was a bicycle.

"Understood, Mr. Ashton. It will not happen again." Not ever.

"One more thing. I thought I told you to shave off that scraggly beard."

"Yes sir, soon." He rose stiffly. "Is that all, sir?"

"For now."

"Thank you." Hamid whipped the office door closed behind him but regained his composure in time to catch it before it slammed. "Fat bigot," he muttered under his breath.

On the way to the truck, he thought of his plan. It must happen, and the sooner the better. Stabbing the key into the ignition, he could think of nothing more satisfying than lining up assholes like Ashton in his gun sights. It was time to buy the man a ticket for the Crazy Girls.

CHAPTER 7

Just like his wife in her cubicle across town, Mike sat staring at a computer screen in frustration. It was a relief when the ringing of his desk phone interrupted his dull perusal of the Bureau's database.

The call was a reminder from the department secretary, Tula Jones, about his ten o'clock meeting. He felt a prickle of panic. His early departure from work the previous night had left him with a shitload of paperwork to prepare for this morning's case review session.

He pursed his lips, annoyed with himself. He had spent so much time on Jenny's little witch-hunt, but Fatima Khalif was either just a nobody, or very good at concealing any terrorist leanings. Her name wasn't on any surveillance lists and her immigration paperwork was as boring as a beach in the desert. He wasn't even sure he was looking at the right person. The database search had uncovered several women of a similar age with the same name in this city alone.

Sorting his case notes into some semblance of order, he rushed off to his meeting. It was a miracle he managed to keep his job.

• • •

An hour later when Fatima's clearance rate remained in last place, curiosity overcame Jenny. Well ahead atop the leaderboard, she was in a sound position to take a coffee break.

She logged off, slung her purse over her shoulder and grabbed the apple on her desk. Heading toward the lunchroom, she abruptly veered past Fatima's workstation and stood behind her.

Caught off guard, it took the other woman a few seconds to blank her screen. The instant was long enough for Jenny to catch a glimpse of a rarely used application—the trouble-shooting page that allowed Gazzel to monitor an Alexandria unit's recordings. Its purpose was to analyze any errors made by the home assistant in the execution of user requests. The customer name had flashed away too quickly for Jenny to catch anything but part of the last name, Wiz.

Jenny inhaled sharply. It was frowned upon for a customer representative such as Fatima to use the analytic module. Protection of consumer privacy was a big deal in the press right now, and the wrath of public advocacy groups could be very damaging to business.

When Fatima turned around, her posture was tense. Wide-eyed, she blinked twice rapidly, then her gaze slid away.

Jenny stepped closer. Was Fatima involved in something unethical—or worse, criminal?

"Time for a break? I think Len is coming." Jenny tried to sound friendly.

Fatima returned her attention to her keyboard, avoiding eye contact. "No, thank you very much. As you can see, I must do my work."

"Oh, come on, Fatima. What could be so important?"

"Jenny, you are very excellent at your work. I am falling behind. Maybe another time when I can keep up to everyone else."

"OK, I understand." Taken aback by the flattery, Jenny struggled to find some encouraging words. "I'm sure you'll be up there with the rest of us soon."

Jenny gagged at her own cheerleader sweetness. Ugh. Turning on her heels toward the elevators, she shot one last look over the department. The fresh line of sight showed her something else unusual. At the base of Fatima's computer, a USB key protruded from one of the two ports near the floor.

Now, that was a definite breach of security. Invigorated, Jenny strode back to her cubicle. There was no time for a break now. She was on a mission.

● ● ●

Fatima exhaled slowly. She hoped that her self-deprecating tone was enough to appease her Barbie-doll, all-American nemesis's unnatural interest in her.

It had been a close call. The monitoring module open on her screen had originally been used for testing during the development stage of Alexandria. Customer support personnel rarely used it now. Only with guidance from her brother on what to look for in the long lists of technical support programs had she uncovered it. In fact, she was sure that some newer department workers would not even be aware of its existence. Unfortunately, one person who would know was Jenny—she had served as a tester on the beta launch.

Anxiety was making Fatima's stomach uneasy. Maybe a glass of water would help. Ejecting the USB key, she tucked it under the pens in her desk tray and closed the drawer. Even though she wouldn't be away for long, she was certainly not leaving with a non-official piece of hardware sticking out of her computer.

● ● ●

Lying in wait, Jenny clutched a file folder to her chest and pretended to be busy at the copy machine. A large euonymus plant positioned along the wall partially concealed her presence in the tiny glass-walled room at the end of the department floor. She watched as Fatima turned down the opposite hall toward the washrooms. If she upheld her usual pattern, Jenny had less than ten minutes.

She rushed forward, her ankles slightly wobbly over her high heels as she rounded the corner into the main office space. She fought against breaking into a run, and like a NFL wide receiver breaking for an out pattern, she made a sharp cut toward Fatima's cubicle. Stooping behind the chest-high office partitions, she covered the last few paces and plunked down in Fatima's swiveling chair.

A tap on the space bar brought up the sign-in screen. A good corporate girl, Fatima was logged off. Damn, there was nothing incriminating on the desktop and—she checked—the USB key was gone.

Casting a darting look behind her to make sure Fatima was not on her way back, Jenny silently slid open the desk drawers. They were empty except for the usual forms and manuals. The floor of the shallow center drawer was bare except for bloc notes and a small stapler. The usual paperclips and markers filled the sliding plastic tray.

Adrenaline coursing through her system, she shut the drawer with too much force and it popped back out, spilling several markers onto the floor. She bent forward, scooping up the pens and stuffing them back into the tray slot. As she did so, her fingers hit something smaller, stubby and rectangular. A USB key. Sorting through the contents of the tray, she discovered three more unmarked keys.

Jenny wasn't sure how much time had elapsed, but she couldn't tolerate the anxiety any longer. Halfway back to her cubby she spotted Fatima returning out of the corner of her eye. She held her breath as she watched the woman's dark eyes studying her work area, but there was no reaction. Jenny slumped down out of sight in her chair and logged on. Time to get back to number one on the board while she contemplated what to do next.

• • •

Fatima relaxed. Nothing seemed out of place after her excursion to the washroom. She was impatient to resume her monitoring. She had continued to hear distant coughs and sneezes in her ear well past Wizner's usual time to go to work this morning. Encouraging signs, but now she wished that he would hurry up and get out of bed.

Pushing her earbuds into position, Fatima pulled up the command-monitoring program, already open to Wizner's incident report page. She pulled out the center desk drawer to grab the USB key she had been using.

It wasn't there. Feverishly pushing the pens aside, she let out a quick sigh of relief. There. It must have shifted position with the drawer movement. Shaking her head, she placed the key on her lap under a fold of her dress.

CHAPTER 8

Wizner awoke with a start, drenched in sweat. Spasms of chills were running up and down his torso. Just how sick was he? Should he go to the hospital? The company's Health Maintence Organization?

The HMO doctor provided by the company health plan was a knob; Wizner was reluctant to subject himself to his care. At his last mandatory annual examination, the guy had spent the entire time pestering him about his weight and blood pressure rather than answering Wizner's questions about how to avoid toxins in the food chain. Wizner was sure his 'care' had more to do with reducing long-term expenses for the HMO than addressing his own medical concerns.

Coming to full alertness, he opened his eyes and blinked. He decided he felt too sick to go to work but not sick enough to spend the money on an ambulance ride to the hospital.

He must have slept twelve hours. Squinting at the sunlight slicing into the room between the slats of the window blind, he brought one arm out from under the covers and drew his hand across the dark duvet. It radiated heat. No wonder he was broiling. He was covered not only by his mother's old quilt, but an additional two blankets he must've grabbed at some point in the night. Maybe he didn't have a fever. He ran a hand over his face. His brow was warm and moist but not burning. He would live.

Despite a very wobbly gait, he made his way to the kitchen and plugged in the electric kettle, a relic also inherited from his mother. When she'd moved into a retirement home at eighty-one, he had been the beneficiary of most of her physical belongings. Up to that point, his apartment had been rather bare. His sister in Wyoming took cash in lieu, which suited him well. He was the acknowledged family moron with money, and not a lot of decorating taste.

With only a little fever and his cough abating, he should be fit to return to work Monday. Meanwhile, in between naps he could catch up and prepare for the endless monotony of meetings that started every workweek.

The trip across the living room provoked a round of dry hacking that stopped him in his tracks. The only good news was that the discomfort in his chest had eased. During the night it had felt like the linings of his lungs were being ripped to shreds with each cough.

Supporting himself on the back of a chair, he paused to recover and check his breathing. Good, it wasn't short. He'd read in a health blog that, besides dehydration, a lack of wind power was an ominous development in the flu. He placed a finger on his carotid artery, checking for any irregular beats indicating heart inflammation, then quickly removed it. Another site he used had warned that you could provoke a stroke if the pressure of your finger dislodged a cholesterol plaque.

He plopped down on the couch, shielding his eyes. The sun was already striking the wall to his left. "Alexandria, what time is it?"

"It is three twenty-seven Pacific Time," came the synthetic, clipped, yet somehow still alluring voice from across the room. Sitting next to his gaming rig on a short stone pedestal recycled from his mother's garden sat his Alexandria—blessed with programmed intelligence and the voice of an angel.

Snatching a tissue from the box on the side table next to the couch, he blew his nose clear—well, at least one side—and flipped on the TV to the 24-hour news channel. He had a long-standing compulsion to watch several minutes of the day's news events to make sure the world still existed every morning. Satisfied that the west coast had not fallen into the ocean, he finally sat in front of his computer and tapped in his password for the work portal.

"Oh, shit, look at all this crap."

His in-box showed another seventy-five messages since yesterday, the majority of them worthy of nothing more than a cursory read.

"What do these people do all day?"

He deleted the thirty or so postings from the in-house buy-and-sell forum en masse. Among the rest, he prioritized a few to look at later when he felt stronger, then emailed his secretary saying he expected to be at work on Monday.

He clicked on the system icon and logged in. After ten years in the job, harvesting the numbers he needed for his weekly Monday morning presentation to the corporate brass was as easy and familiar as popping gophers with his dad's twenty-two back in North Dakota.

• • •

Finally passing level thirty-four of Zombie Androids Attack, Billy was crowned a Rank II Master at approximately 3:45 a.m. After forty-seven days of trying and this final, epic, ten-hour battle, he was exhausted and fell backward out of his chair onto his bed.

He was awoken at 1:30 p.m. by his stomach growling like an overfilled coffee grinder and his large, noise-canceling earphones digging into his skull. He rolled over and moaned. To avoid their reprimands, he planned his foraging trips up the back stairs around his parents' schedule, and his mother was always home Thursday afternoons. He still carried vivid memories of their last encounter: his mother's pained expression, the pleading tone in her voice. "You should be out looking for a girlfriend," and with a deeply furrowed brow, his father, "And a job."

He did agree that some sort of life above ground would probably be a good idea. When exactly had he evolved into this sunlight-adverse creature who avoided clean clothing and human contact? When did he begin thinking that people using pseudonyms online were genuine companionship? *Maybe not soon enough*, he thought, recalling the high school taunts over his unusual appearance when he tried to make 'real' friends.

Pushing his greasy, tussled hair out of his eyes, Billy tapped the space bar to awaken his computer. Nothing interesting had happened since he slept except that, thanks to his South Korean friends, he had fallen to number three on the leader list of ZAA. He couldn't fix that now, however—it was time for a sortie into the dark web.

Beyond his usual crusade against the pedophiles, he planned to spend a couple of hours scrutinizing the shifting sands of supposedly anonymous IP addresses, looking for patterns of strange activity that could link some ambiguous message back to ISIS or any other terrorist organization.

In particular, he kept an eye out for unusual traffic spikes on any dark site before or after a terrorist attack. News clipping apps kept him up to date on extremist activity, both homegrown and foreign. Unfortunately he was constantly adding sites to his watch list. But the longer he was in 'the game', the better his predictive ability was becoming. He hoped one day he could prevent one of the horrendous massacres that constantly peppered his feed.

Shit. That damn blog had no new posts. Something was going down two days from now, he was sure of it. But that wasn't enough to be useful. He needed the 'what' and the 'where'. Without a playbook, he was still in his three-point stance waiting for the ball to be snapped.

He yanked off his headset, crept up the stairs and pressed his ear to the door leading into the kitchen. It was imperative to fuel up for some practice rounds of Starcraft before the next big match against WizKid88.

CHAPTER 9

Fatima was on a tear, dispatching a slew of user inquires when Wizner coughed. She immediately pressed alt F7 to record.

This time the sound coming through was closer to the intelligent speaker. Her brother had said that any data from the room with the computer would be helpful. This was perfect. She recorded more coughing, throat clearing and nose blowing followed by a snippet of news broadcast, footsteps, chair squeaks, a computer mouse scraping on a hard surface. Clicks, and then the gold, a brief burst of keystrokes—likely a password.

The light on the USB blinked rapidly to indicate that the computer was spooling the recording directly to the memory stick, then returned to a steady glow.

Samir wanted a high-resolution file that would chew up available memory space like a hungry goat. She was glad. It would be a relief when all four memory sticks were full and she could concentrate on her work; when her clearance rate fell it attracted too much attention from Jenny.

• • •

Jenny terminated the call on her headset and entered her summary of the encounter. Pleased with herself for maintaining her professional decorum with a very irate customer, she clicked the checkbox indicating 'fully resolved to client's satisfaction'. With that her name bumped up to number one, finally ahead of Lucy Langmore.

Once again Fatima's name was anchoring the list. What was going on? Now agitated, Jenny couldn't focus on her work. Mike's job made her acutely aware that the possibility of danger lurking where you least expected it. When she couldn't sleep, the stories Mike loved recounting ran like a horror movie in her head: the doting grandfather who decided to protest one last time against the IRS with a Winnebago full of explosives, or the worst sleep-killer, a nice Irish nanny who was actually a serial baby-killer.

Should she take her concerns to Mrs. Perks? It should be easy to get Fatima fired. But one rule of detective work Mike always espoused was the need to observe the suspect for as long as possible without endangering the public. It was about building a solid case and gaining a glimpse at the bigger picture, if there was one. With Fatima gone, the trail might go cold.

Jenny could not find any active files starting with the fragment of the last name she had seen on Fatima's screen. If a customer had no active issues, why would Fatima have pulled up the file? 'Wiz' couldn't be a common start to a surname. She put the letters into the system-wide customer database, but to her surprise was rewarded with too many possibilities.

But why waste more time guessing? To hell with what Mike said: sometimes the man was too cautious. Privately, she suspected it was why he hadn't been promoted yet. It was time for some up-close and personal snooping. With determined strides she marched across the department.

Preoccupied with formulating the right questions, Jenny banged her elbow on the edge of the partition as she rounded the corner into Fatima's aisle. Crap. She could hear a desk drawer sliding shut. When she arrived Fatima was already half-turned in her chair facing her.

"Oh, hi, Jenny. Thank you, but I think I will take my break here, as usual." Fatima's smile was pinched.

"I'm not here for that. I want to know why this morning you had the instruction monitoring screen open for a client who isn't in the outstanding encounter queue."

She couldn't keep the anger out of her voice. Standing with her arms crossed over her chest, her grip was so tight that her fingernails were burrowing into her sides.

Fatima's face turned crimson. Suddenly she stood and took a step toward Jenny, her hand digging in her dress pocket. Jenny stumbled backward, the heel of her pump catching on the carpet. Was Fatima going to pull out a pair of scissors? Right here?

She grabbed Fatima's wrist and twisted hard. "Don't even think about it."

Fatima lurched into her grip.

"Ouch, you are hurting me!"

Jenny wrenched Fatima's hand from her pocket. A tissue floated to the ground.

"Oh my God. I'm sorry, I thought . . ."

She dropped the offending wrist and took another step backwards.

"Thought what?" Fatima scooped up the tissue.

Jenny shook her head. *The best defense is offence.* "I want to know what you're doing."

"Please don't tell anyone, please. I. . . I. . . I am so embarrassed." Fatima dabbed at her eyes. "I am using Perfect Match dating site and I have first date with an American man. But I am so scared I won't know what to talk with him about. I know it is very incorrect but I was checking what music he likes, what his interests are so I can make the good conversations."

"Oh my God, that is so wrong."

Jenny was dumbfounded. She was still thinking about what to do when Fatima approached, her arms extended.

"I know it is, but I am so scared. I am so lonely."

She wrapped herself around Jenny, sobbing.

Held tightly in Fatima's embrace, her own arms trapped, Jenny could not move. Enduring the awkward situation in silence, she finally spoke over the top of the shorter woman's head.

"OK, but it has to stop right now or—"

"Oh, thank you, thank you." Fatima squeezed tighter and sobbed even more vigorously.

With difficulty, Jenny disengaged herself and placed her hands on Fatima's shoulders, forcing a sympathetic smile.

"Just go, relax and be yourself. You'll be fine. He's an American male, so ask about his favorite baseball or football team."

Fatima nodded. "Yes, that is good. Thank you so much."

Free of Fatima's grip, Jenny stepped sideways to gain a view of Fatima's workstation. In her rush to stand, Fatima had ripped her earbuds out of place. The white chord dangled over the edge of her desk.

Taking coffee breaks at their cubbies, many of her fellow employees listened to music on an MP3 player or their smartphone. Previously, Jenny had never paid attention to where Fatima's buds terminated their journey.

But now she saw they were plugged into an auxiliary output of the telephone/computer analog-to-dbx digital audio converter situated under the phone set. Normally, the cable from the second jack on the front left went directly into the computer. This permitted analog phone conversations with customers to be digitally recorded in the interaction file. In case of a dispute, management could review what transpired during a call.

Not only were Fatima's earbuds inserted into the system, there was an additional cable from the computer attached to the second input on the rear of the dbx system. Fatima was listening to live audio from the computer and sending a digital copy back to her computer.

"You're not only eavesdropping on your new boyfriend, Fatima, but you're recording it." Jenny put every ounce of steel into her voice that she could command.

Fatima stepped back toward her desk, half blocking the view to her computer.

"Oh, no, no, I wouldn't do that." Her voice was tight with nervousness.

Jenny stepped closer, craning her neck to see around the woman, but Fatima slid sideways. Crossing her arms, Jenny cast an eye over the rest of the desktop but saw nothing amiss.

"Why would you have the computer output routed to the dbx system, except to record it, bypassing the incident reporting program?"

Fatima flinched but remained silent. Sensing an opening, Jenny pounced. "This morning I saw an unauthorized USB key in your computer, now this. Whatever you are doing is distracting you from your job. Your clearance rate is lousy. Obviously you're not doing company work."

Jenny grabbed Fatima's elbow. "I think it's time we went to see Mrs. Perks. And you better bring your purse 'cause you ain't coming back to your desk, honey."

Fatima pulled away from Jenny's grasp.

"No! Please." Her accent seemed to get thicker as words poured out. "My English is not good as everyone and it makes me a bad performer and I want very much to be better. Sometimes I listen to the records of my telephone talking with customers so I can be improved."

Jenny slid her hands down her cheeks and over her chin. She supposed it was plausible.

Fatima bent her head in shame. "Please, I need this job. I found a way to record again my part of the conversation so if quality assurance makes a checkup it will sound the best. Especially if customer is not as happy as they should be. Please, nothing bad. I am still trying to learn American and do a good job."

For a second time, Fatima burst into sobs. An unexpected swell of compassion washed over Jenny. She inhaled deeply, shook her head in confusion and then in disgust. She couldn't go to the manager's office without a good case. If Mrs. Perks fell for Fatima's sob story, Jenny might even be the one who got fired.

"I'm sure Mrs. Perks would be supportive of your attempts to improve your language skills, but I think it would be a better idea for you to join us girls for lunch and coffee breaks. That would give you a chance to practice your English instead of spending all your time in your cubicle. It's certainly a safer option than cheating and monkeying around with the equipment."

"Monkey-ing around?"

"See! Exactly the kind of thing you would learn by hanging out with us more. It means doing stuff you aren't supposed to." Jenny felt the anger coming back into her tone. Crinkling her face into a super smile, she continued. "So . . . break?"

"Oh, yes, thank you very much. Please let me put my desk proper and I will meet you in the lunchroom. You are a very kind person."

Jenny said nothing, striding briskly toward her workstation. This time when she swiveled her head to look back, Fatima was still in her chair facing her. When their eyes met Fatima's blank expression instantly morphed into a watery smile.

Rounding the corner of the aisle, Jenny shook her head, stomped her foot and snorted in frustration. She didn't know if she believed a single word the woman had spoken.

CHAPTER 10

Hamid drove past Rosepark Field slowly. Ace Security didn't have many big corporate contracts; the mainstays of the business were worried home or shop owners. The new subcontract for security and surveillance improvements to the staff entrance and maintenance area of the stadium, home of the local major league soccer team, was one of the larger jobs he'd been involved in.

Having unfettered access to such a large public venue was an opportunity too good to pass up. The huge billboard above the entrance announced that the Crazy Girls concert on Saturday evening was sold out. With this gift from Allah, his new plan would be much easier than the airport attack.

It had been too risky to check his work last night. The sound of the large metal door opening would be better concealed by daytime traffic noise. He stopped the van and aimed the remote control out his window at the storage vault. The door immediately began rising, revealing dozens of stacks of folding chairs.

He clicked the door shut again. By Saturday afternoon, with the chairs on the stadium floor for the concert, the room would be empty. He and his team would arrive several hours before showtime. Within seconds, the van would be through the outer gate and parked inside.

When the audience was fully seated, the stadium lights would be turned off except for the exit signs. In the darkness, he and his team, armed with assault rifles and hand grenades, would move into position. Then he would detonate a grenade—more for the noise than the destruction. In the ensuing pandemonium, the panicked crowd would stampede down the narrow staircases. Easy pickings. The off-duty cops policing the event would be challenged to find his team in the chaos, let alone stop them. The carnage would be colossal.

He'd debated when to tell Samir. His friend liked to keep electronic communications to a minimum, and Hamid didn't want to risk a face-to-face meeting so close to the assault. Since they agreed on the importance of compartmentalization, perhaps his friend would have to hear about his magnificent sacrifice just like everyone else, on CNN.

There was no doubt Samir's plan was larger in scope, but in defiance of good military planning, it relied too much on Samir himself. Personally, Hamid could not wait any longer for fancy schemes that had a high risk of failure. Access to something like Saturday night's concert would not materialize again anytime soon—the stadium was closing after the last home game in August to allow for a year-long refurbishment.

Everything was a go. He must post a call to arms tonight. It was time to have a cake of revenge—and eat it too.

CHAPTER 11

Preoccupied with SnitchBitch's behavior, Jenny squirmed in her chair, arms wrapped around her chest, her Diet Coke untouched. After her invitation, Fatima joined the group in the cafeteria for all ten minutes of afternoon break. Clearly preoccupied, the woman had nodded her agreement to everything and contributed nothing before rushing back to her cubicle as if she were missing the last train to Clarksville.

Fatima's presence at break did not lessen Jenny's suspicions, just the opposite. She was sure the 'socializing' was just another ploy to distract from all the unusual goings-on of the past two days.

Ugh. She couldn't concentrate. Blanking her screen, Jenny pulled out her phone.

"FBI, Mike Longstrum speaking. Special Services Deptartment."

She didn't bother with any lovey-dovey platitudes. "Did you find out about Fatima?"

"Why, what's up?"

"I think she's eavesdropping on someone and recording it." Breathless with excitement, she could barely complete the sentence.

"Whoa, honey, slow down. Who, why?"

"She was looking at a customer file in the auditory monitoring module, and there was a USB key in her computer."

"Translation, please."

"We're not supposed to use that program. It allows her to listen to the audio from an Alexandria home system in real time. She was bypassing the system to make a recording of someone whose name starts with the letters W-I-Z and putting it on a memory stick."

"So did you go to your boss?"

It was a reasonable question, dammit, but—"What is that useless tit of a woman going to do?"

"Did you ask Fatima what she was doing?"

"When I confronted her she said she was checking out her new boyfriend so she could have a 'more American conversation' when they met. Like she wants to know who his favorite country music artist is. Ha!"

"OK, it's not cool that she is being a high-tech stalker."

"Mike, this could be a lot bigger than some workplace thing!"

"Why do you think this is a matter of national security, Jenny?"

"You know where she's from."

"Oh, wow, that is racist."

"Your point?"

"I can't have this discussion, especially at work. Look, honey, we can talk about this when I get home. I've got a ton of stuff to do or I'll be here all night."

"Did you check her out on the database?"

"You know that I can't do random searches without a reason on file, or the privacy monitor will have my ass."

"Please, Mike."

"OK, I did take a peek, but there are several people with similar names. Without something like an address or date of birth, I can't be sure who I'm looking for."

"I can't get into the human resources files." Jenny knew her voice was trending toward shrill.

"You could just ask her."

"That's too obvious. She'll freak for sure!"

"Look, honey, I gotta go, love you. I'm sure you'll figure it out. Bye."

· · ·

Mike hung up without waiting for her reply and rubbed his ear. When Jenny was excited her voice was loud, even when she tried to whisper.

When she latched on to one of her crazy ideas, she was obsessed as a cat with a mouse. He shook his head. Honestly, sometimes he thought his job was harder on her than on him. When they'd started dating she wasn't a paranoid person, but now she seemed to perceive danger everywhere. Then again, the world was a different place than even a few years ago.

Regardless, supper conversation tonight promised to be interesting.

· · ·

At three fifteen with all four memory sticks full, Fatima did something unusual. Shutting down her workstation, she walked over to the manager's office. She peaked around the corner into the room and cleared her throat. Mrs. Lauren Perks looked up and slid her reading glasses down her nose.

"Yes, Fatima?"

"Very sorry to disturb you, Mrs. Perks, but I do not feel well. I do not wish to make anyone else sick, so I would like to go home please."

"Oh, OK, that is very considerate of you." Perks pushed her glasses back up her nose and started typing again. "Please let me know ASAP whether you are coming into work tomorrow."

"Yes, yes I will. Thank you, Mrs. Perks."

Fatima lifted her head only after she was out of Mrs. Perks's sight.

• • •

While Jenny chewed on her anger, she declined another customer call. To hell with her clearance score. Mike, her normally supportive husband, had dismissed her concerns out of hand. She was staring past her computer screen at the blank wall over the storage cabinets, swinging her chair in a gentle arc back and forth, when someone passed through her field of vision in a blur.

Oh my God. It was Fatima, heading to the elevators. Jenny bounced a finger on the space bar to reveal the hour. It wasn't even close to clock out time.

Barely aware of her own actions, she bolted from her chair and marched to Lauren's office. *Damn.* The door was closed and Perks was on the telephone with her back to the glass wall—the boss's shorthand for *do not disturb.*

Jenny swallowed hard and frowned. Well, that's just how it was going to be today, no help from anyone. Time to cash in her good employee chips. She could claim illness or maybe a family emergency. Even if she just crashed a date with the American sweetheart, it would let Fatima know that she was on to her.

In the lobby, the security check seemed to take forever. When she finally pushed through the revolving atrium doors, Fatima was boarding the number fifteen bus. It wouldn't be smart to board the same one. The quickest solution was a taxi—but the stand was empty. She guessed cabbies didn't make a habit of sitting curbside until the end of the workday. *Surveillance is a lot harder than they make it look on TV.*

Slipping off her heels, Jenny sprinted across the street to the staff parking lot. There was still hope. One advantage of arriving early was a choice spot in the shade near the exit. Also, she knew the bus followed a very direct route on its way downtown. All she had to do was to catch up before Fatima got off.

CHAPTER 12

Heading to work for his evening shift at the tech college, Abarque stopped at the Acme Hardware store nearest the school. In the gardening section, he selected two small bags of SuperGrow high calcium nitrogen plant fertilizer, 15-0-0, and walked to the checkout counter.

"Good afternoon. On the school account, please."

Al Smith smiled. "The plants must be hungry again."

"Oh, yes, very. I wish the school board wouldn't buy so many for me to care for. I have enough to do already."

"I'm surprised you don't burn the roots with that stuff."

"Oh, I am very familiar. The soil in Somali is very poor."

"A little gardening must be a nice break though, to get outside, away from mopping floors."

"In that you are very right."

"You know, it's a better deal to buy a bigger bag. I could order some."

"Oh, thank you, but my budget for these things is very small." He signed his name. "Thank you. Have a nice day, Al."

"Same to you."

Outside the school, Abarque looked over the sad display of petunias and ornamental shrubs that wrapped around the building. What a waste of good soil. There was enough space in the flowerbeds to grow sufficient food to feed two families. He shook his head and headed downstairs to the basement.

With his eyes closed, he counted the number of paces from the last step until he reached the custodial storage locker next to the utility room. Unlocking the door, he entered. There was no need to use the light—every nook and cranny of the room was emblazoned into his memory.

Running one hand along the wall, he felt the hard plastic of the first container of soap on the second shelf from the bottom of the rack and picked it up. Counting along to the fourth bucket, he popped the lid and emptied the soap into his mop bucket. He refilled the empty container with the two bags of fertilizer, slid it back into place and stuffed the spent bags into the bottom of the partially filled black garbage bag wedged underneath the rack. Pushing the mop bucket back into the hallway, he locked the door behind him.

In the utility room, he slipped a mop off the wall rack and filled the bucket with hot water. He tipped half of the suds down the drain and refilled it. The remaining water frothed with bubbles. It was amazing how clean you could make floors using hard work and soap. Lots and lots of soap.

• • •

Fatima settled into the hard plastic seat and swallowed, suppressing a surge of burning bile. Closing her eyes as the bus lurched forward, she inhaled and exhaled slowly until calm replaced fear. Even if Jenny went to Mrs. Perks, what was the worst that could happen? Certainly, she could be fired for breaching customer data, but nothing would link it to Samir and his plan. Besides, they would never let her go for something so small. She ticked too many boxes on the affirmative action hiring checklist.

To clear her mind, she focused on the people and places passing by. Fatima loved the bus ride home. Everything in Tillson was so green, so different from Somalia. And unlike the claustrophobia of Africa, the buses here were rarely full. Luxuries aside, the acceptance of and safety for a single woman traveling alone were bigger joys. This was the freest part of her day.

The winding route provided a scenic tour along the Hanson River before the bus headed uphill to the downtown area. It was beautiful. The original settlers had been smart to build on the high ground of the large plateau that extended down from Balderston Mountain. From the river, the views up to the city were spectacular, especially when the maple and ash trees turned color in the fall.

She watched through the window as the bus passed the gaggles of joggers and bicyclists crowding the trail alongside Masta Creek. A large tributary of the Hanson, its crystal clear waters flowed through the center of the enormous park on the northeast corner of the city center before being diverted underground and joining the main watercourse.

Not everything here, however, was picturesque or comforting. As the bus bumped along, Fatima frowned as the scenery on both banks of the river became ugly. The rapid expansion of the past century had forced subsequent commercial and residential construction to occupy the flood-prone low ground closer to the water. Fortunately, the Easton Dam controlled the runoff in the spring to prevent large-scale destruction. The gigantic lake formed by the dam filled each spring with snowmelt and rain and provided Tillson with abundant drinking water. Yet it also scared her. Even when she escaped the arid dust bowl of Somalia, she'd ended up living in rain-starved California. It made her uncomfortable to be close to such a massive amount of water.

But she wouldn't trade living here for a few less raindrops. This was where she found her first job, and with that the sweet taste of possibility. Here she could become independent and make her own decisions. Not just to ride the bus alone, but the power to say no to men, men like Samir whose violent solutions to the injustices in the world threatened the hopes and dreams that America was beginning to foster in her. This new country of hers was far from perfect when it came to race, religion and social inequalities, but at least here there was a dialogue, a recognition that suppressing people and ideas was wrong.

Yes, America the country had done her country ill. Yes, she still believed in the teachings of the Quran—but maybe no longer the jihadist interpretation that her brother did. But Samir was family, and respect of family was fundamental.

She took another look, first at the men and women enjoying the lush green landscape, then the harsh, drab industrial sprawl of factories and aging warehouses, and nodded to herself. Yes, she thought, the contrast summed up her feelings perfectly.

• • •

Jenny ignored the blaring horns as she ran a red light. Mike would kill her for such dangerous behavior, but when she pulled around the corner at Thirty-Fourth and Third she was rewarded. At the far end of the block, a woman about Fatima's size and shape and wearing the same dull brown hijab was hurrying along the street away from the bus stop. With her head down, she turned and entered a small grocery store.

Jenny parked across the street and waited. Ten minutes later the woman exited carrying a white plastic bag. Now, Jenny could clearly distinguish Fatima's features. Leaving the car and following on foot a safe distance behind, Jenny kept pace until her quarry disappeared into a tall, sixties-style apartment building at 620 Sixth Avenue.

Her mission accomplished, there was nothing more she could do. The next obstacle to overcome was her darling husband's reluctance to use work resources for unauthorized purposes.

Fortunately, she knew exactly how to get what she wanted. Food always worked—and a few other things too. On the way home, she'd go to the grocery store and pick up a few trusted favorites. Perhaps she wouldn't even have to make dinner if she served him a glass of wine in her naughty little black nightie.

• • •

Fatima slammed the apartment door behind her and let the grocery bag drop to the floor. She had never felt so glad to be at home. Weak in the knees, she pressed her back against the wall. It wasn't just Jenny; she was sure that people in stores and on the street were looking at her differently. Blowing out a breath, she shook her head. She was becoming paranoid.

After a few more deep breaths, she slipped off her light jacket and hung it on the hallway hook. At the kitchen table, she undid her belt and ejected the USB keys onto the tabletop with a clatter. From the strap of her purse she extracted the fourth. Relieved, she crossed the kitchen and placed the kettle on the stove.

Just as she reached for a tea bag, the hall door opened. The sound made her jump, and the sight of her brother did little to comfort her. His eyebrows rose, then furrowed as he saw her.

"Why are you here?"

"It is my home too, brother." She forced a smile.

"Yes, yes I mean you are home very early. Why are you not at work?"

She bit her lip. She had to say something.

"I couldn't take it anymore. Sneaking around doing your dirty business, so you can do what, blackmail this man," she dipped the tea bag into her cup, fingers shaking, "and turn off the lights?"

"This behavior will raise suspicions."

"Of what?"

"You don't need to know."

"No?" She yanked the hot tea bag out and threw it at him, but Samir caught it deftly and tossed it on the kitchen table. "You're so caught up in 'the cause', you refuse to acknowledge the danger you put me in!"

Her hands were shaking so much she almost dropped the sugar bowl.

"I have the right to know more. I almost got caught listening to Wizner today—I had to say I needed to know about him because we were going on a date. I'm risking everything for you. So tell me."

"No, it is better that you don't know."

"Why are you still so angry? Don't we have a good life here?"

"What? A good life? We're not here for a good life. Don't you want to avenge our father's death?"

"I never knew the man." Fatima turned and poured her tea into the sink, her mouth sour.

"I think you are beginning to like this superficial, pizza-gobbling country too much. Think what those Americans did to our homeland."

"That was the government, not everyone."

"Oh, come on." Samir slapped his palm on the fridge door with a pop that made Fatima jump. "What about the Smiths?"

Fatima put her hands on her hips. "You mean our wonderful adoptive parents who saved us from the refugee camps in Kenya?"

"Yeah, the ones who pushed 'America is great' at us 24-7."

"They were only doing what they thought was right."

"Really? Did they really think that ice cream cones at Baskin and Robbins and trips to the mall could make us forget our pain?"

"Living in California and eating ice cream wasn't all bad." Fatima tried to smile.

"Be serious. They just didn't get it. Remember when 'Dad' took me to an American football game so that we could 'bond'? How was a boy from Somalia who played soccer with a tin can and dried goat turds as goalposts supposed to learn football, or even care?"

Samir turned away from her sharply, looking like he wanted to flip a chair. His gaze fell on the memory sticks scattered across the table. Abruptly, his features brightened. "I see that you had success."

"Yes. Take them far away from me, please. I am never taking them to work again."

"We'll see about that." His face suddenly transformed into a placating smile. "You shouldn't worry so much. They will never figure out why you are making the recordings. No one in the world has the software to decipher—anyway."

He scooped up the handful of devices like a gold speculator snatching a fistful of nuggets, and left.

Fatima balled her fists. Holding back tears, she jerkily made a fresh cup of tea. She cradled the warm cup in her hands and went and sat in the living room. Samir was right; they had changed.

As teens, they had been intent on seeking revenge for America's transgressions against their faith. But Samir was always more extreme, and when he went off to college his ideals had hardened into fanaticism. But now she had doubts. Shouldn't the damage be directed against powerful people in Washington, the ones who waged the wars?

She flicked on the TV. Perhaps some distraction would dampen the storm of conflict in her roiling thoughts. All she found were reruns of *The Office* and *Three's Company*. Humor she didn't understand. She turned it off. Perhaps a nap was in order; she was exhausted. She had come home sick, hadn't she?

• • •

Samir couldn't wait to get started but found himself staring out the window of his room watching the pigeons nesting in the gutters of the building across the street. He was worried about Fatima. Her help was essential, but she was right, he was putting her at risk. This final stage of the battle was his alone. He wanted her to live. Twenty-five and beautiful, she would make a good wife. But would she make it without him? As her older brother, had he been too protective, too strict? He stroked his beard. Knowing her stubbornness, she'd survive despite him. In fact, maybe she'd be better off when he was gone.

This was not, however, the time for further contemplation. Time was running short. He drummed his fingernails on the desktop. Soon he would no longer be able to prevent Hamid from proceeding with his unimaginative airport plan.

He stretched, loaded the first USB device and hit return.

The sound analytics program performed a scan but came up empty. The second stick yielded a beep. He hit the space bar, rewound and listened. A person moving about and then sitting followed by clicks—typing. Annoyingly, there was a low rumbling sound interfering with the sound quality and obscuring the keystrokes.

He rewound and adjusted the filtering parameters. A low husky male voice came through, thick with mucous, whispering a few letters and numbers.

Could it be? Making further adjustments, he replayed the segment, perspiration beading on his brow. After a pause there were more keystrokes. He would analyze those later. Then a loud voice almost deafened him.

"Oh shit, look at all this crap. What do these people do all day?"

Samir couldn't believe it. Rewinding, he highlighted the signal pattern where the password had been entered.

Letting his computer do its work, he leaned back in his chair.

The algorithm was simple. With the data from Alexandria's multiple directional microphones, distances could be calculated with a resolution within an inch. This was accurate enough that he could map small groups of keys on a standard keyboard by their relation to the most frequently used ones: the space bar, return and delete.

Passwords were usually a random chain six to eight characters long, containing upper and lowercase letters, numbers and special characters. Additional information such as the cadence, key strike strength and keystroke combinations used for common words—such as *the*, *and*, and *it*—helped refine the analysis.

The program returned only a few keystrokes with high probable identity. Samir increased the volume of the audio and laughed out loud as the rough voice came through again, the speaker clearly mouthing several characters aloud as he entered them. This was a sign from Allah.

Not all the audio was interpretable, but in conjunction with the keystroke analysis he would soon have a list of possible solutions for the password. Hopefully there would not be too many. Most security software allowed less than five incorrect logins before freezing the account.

Samir ran his hand through his hair then placed it on his gurgling belly. It would take time for the computer to spit out the possibilities. He had a few minutes to eat.

Fatima was not in the kitchen and her bedroom door was closed. He shrugged. Sometimes he did not understand his sister, but her well-being was not his concern at this moment. Of course she was nervous, but she had also changed. Western life had softened her. In the past they had spoken about serious issues, but now their mealtime discussions were guarded, and they argued over the most trivial of matters. His sister kept the house clean and prepared a good meal, to be sure, but he did not need to hear silly stories about her work. They had more important things to focus on. It was a shame he could not tell her what he planned to do. Maybe if she knew the powerful message of his deed and the glory it would bring to them, she would be stronger.

He rifled through the refrigerator, scattering several clumps of beans and rice as he dumped a plastic container of leftovers onto a plate and shoved it in the microwave. Suddenly beyond famished, he stood over the counter and stared at the spinning meal, desperate to shovel overladen spoonfuls into his mouth as fast as possible.

Glancing down at the food he'd spilled, he reprimanded himself. Desperation was a hard behavior to break, after living the early years of his life unsure when or if the next meal would arrive. But it was a long time ago that he was a lonely boy sobbing in the street. Now he was a man, hardened by years of adversity. One ready to avenge the murder of his father by arrogant America, convinced they were the greatest, the strongest and always the victor.

If he succeeded tonight, he could finally fulfill his destiny. Hamid would understand the full potential of his plan, and together they would bring darkness to these twisted people. After that, he had no idea what would happen. Hopefully something better would arise from the ashes, but he would not be alive to find out. That would be for Fatima to build.

He used a damp cloth to wipe his mess into the garbage. Suddenly overcome with nervous excitement, he grabbed the edge of the counter to control the shaking of his hands. If he were to succeed, he must remain calm and focused. He tossed the dishrag into the sink. Fatima could clean up the rest when she made dinner.

His physical hunger satiated, he returned to his computer. On Lakeridge's corporate website he brought up the log-in page for the employee portal that allowed people to work from home.

While he waited for his program to generate a list of possible passwords, perspiration beaded on his forehead. The tension was what he imagined a chain-smoking, gin-addicted gambler, glued to a Vegas slot machine, waiting for the next banana to fall into place must feel.

Eventually, nine combinations appeared. Too many, but with the benefit of Mr. Wizner's partial vocalization, he reduced the possibilities to just seven. There was a 71 percent chance of success before being blocked.

Holding a lungful of air, his pulse pounding in his temples, he tried the first, second and third. Rejected.

On the fourth he expelled his breath. He was in.

CHAPTER 13

When Chuck pulled into his usual parking spot at the Streamline factory, Spitwell was sitting on the concrete base of the lamppost waiting for him. The glow of the man's cigarette flared in the semi-darkness. Standing, he flicked the still-lit butt toward Chuck's truck.

Before Chuck could collect his dinner pail, Spitwell was tapping on the driver's window. "Roll it down."

Chuck growled, then lowered the window. "Yeah, what's the hurry?"

"Just trying to save you the trouble. I gave the night shift to someone else."

"What? Come on. You know how much I need the money."

Spitwell only shrugged.

"You could have at least saved me the drive."

Spitwell crossed his forearms and rested them on the truck door. "Suppose I could've, but this is just a little taste of what's comin' if you don't play ball." Spitwell leaned in close enough that the scent of stale beer wafted in with him. He slipped a piece of paper into Chuck's top pocket. "I'm working a seven to three this Saturday. You know my truck. Have the shit in the back by end of shift." He broke off his piercing stare to cough and spit.

Chuck unfolded the note. "This stuff doesn't grow on trees. You gotta order ahead, fill out special forms."

"Exactly." Spitwell pushed back from Chuck's truck. "Enjoy your sleep."

• • •

Rows of cryptically named icons popped up across the top of Samir's screen. The stamped envelope was obviously the email server. Clicking in and scrolling down the correspondence in Wizner's in-box, it seemed most of the contents pertained to mundane office affairs.

Samir launched a search for subject lines with the word 'meeting', and a long list filled the page. Skimming through revealed a frequent topic—operational security.

Popping to another tab, he opened his own email and sent a request to James Wizner for an interview, briefly outlining his research in the areas of infrastructure security and cyber threats. Thanks to some sloppy IT maintenance on the part of MIT, Samir still had a valid account despite his departure eighteen months earlier. He signed the message Professor S. Khalif of the Department of Computer Science and Robotics.

Returning to Wizner's in-box, Samir marked the received email as read and composed a reply in which Wizner agreed to a meeting at ten o'clock the following Tuesday morning.

It would seem natural for a manager such as Wizner to host frequent visits from outside consultants. Scanning for the words 'security' and 'guest' yielded the details of a visit from a regional director. Downloading the file template he found attached in the correspondence, he inserted his own name and sent the form to the head of security from Wizner's email account, requesting a guest security pass be created.

Closing the email program, he scrutinized the remaining icons. He clicked the tiny representation of Zeus with a lightening bolt and entered Wizner's password. Immediately a pop-up box appeared:

Access Denied.
Please enter your employee number
and today's password.

Just another obstacle to overcome. It was a relief to know there was no fingerprint or iris scan, but there still could be other requirements.

He returned to the main page again and clicked on the tiny spreadsheet icon. Another pop-up appeared spewing an incomprehensible stream of what appeared to be real-time stats. Selecting another, rather boring, icon depicting smokestacks resulted in the message "Restricted Access. Contact Your Network Supervisor."

He exited the program.

Despite the limited access, Samir was exhilarated. He had a foot in the door. His mind whirled. First, he must alert Hamid before his friend went ahead with his mundane idea.

He did not pass judgment on believers willing to serve Allah with the ultimate sacrifice, but he could not understand their impatience to be martyred for a jab when they could deliver a knockout punch.

Of course, in preparation, Hamid already knew much of Samir's plan, but not this final stroke of genius. It had been difficult to convince his friend to wait, when he himself had been unsure exactly what was possible. Now, with the missing piece, they could strike a much stronger blow. Now he could make his friend understand the immense glory his addition offered. Now he was certain that Hamid could be persuaded to abandon his unimaginative airport idea. It was flashy, but low-impact. With Samir's computer expertise, their efforts would be more sophisticated, on a larger scale, and would deliver a long-lasting legacy. He, Samir Khalif, represented the next generation of warrior—one that used technology to turn the infidels' own 'advancements' against them.

On the NowCar app he quickly composed a post stating that he was driving to Naskas Falls, California, tomorrow afternoon. 'Anyone interested? Share the gas costs only.'

While he waited for a response, he opened his closet and lifted his dark blue suit off the rod. Not too wrinkled or stained, it was presentable, even if the style and the accompanying tie were several decades out of date. That was a good thing. What else would a privileged white man expect from a third world immigrant professor?

Pushing the rest of his meager clothing collection aside, he dragged the two boxes sitting at the back of closet forward and felt along the baseboard trim behind them. He was proud of his ingenuity. The tightly mitered seam was barely detectable to the naked eye. Only by finding the slightly raised edge with his fingertips could he even tell it was there.

With one fingernail, he pried away the piece of wood held in place with Sticky Tack. Near the floor, the drywall was broken, as if it had been damaged during installation. He slid his hand under the rough edge and groped until he felt the crinkle of a plastic bag.

The solid metal of the Colt .45 against his hand was reassuring. From a separate bag, he removed his cache of bullets and loaded the chambers. Returning the gun to its hiding spot, he replaced the trim and stood, closing the closet doors with a quiet click.

• • •

"Mike?" Jenny shook her husband's shoulder, but he was sound asleep. The hearty dinner of shrimps, steak and a nice bottle of wine had been a romantic success, though the actual lovemaking had been a bit of a disaster. Tired and a bit drunk, they were both left wishing for more but unable to go the extra distance.

Worst of all, the major mission of the evening was a failure—Mike was still reluctant to help her find out more about Fatima. All he'd done was mumble that he didn't have the time before drifting off to sleep.

She drew back the covers and slipped on her housecoat. It was the one that Mike always made fun of as being homely—"Come on, Granny, let's get your walker and go for a stroll to the nursing home canteen for a cup of tea."

So what? The pink velour wasn't stylish or sexy, but it was super warm, as were her furry slippers. The polar opposite, Mike loved to be in bare feet and sometimes even wore his flip-flops in the snow.

They were different people, for sure, but usually on the same page for important things—except where Fatima was concerned, apparently. Jenny growled quietly to herself.

Mike's work laptop was on the hall table. In the dark, she sat down on the couch and lifted the lid, blinking at the sudden brightness of the screen.

She wiped her sweaty hands on her pajama legs and stretched her neck, the vertebrae cracking, before she placed her fingers on the keyboard. She hesitated. Hadn't she promised herself never to be this person? But this was important, damn it!

Long ago, she had figured out Mike's method for remembering his password. Well actually, he had explained it to her, exasperated by how frequently she forgot hers.

Each month he was required to create a new one for work, and there was a security check to ensure that it was sufficiently dissimilar from the previous version. Mike started with a base word, Lizbeth, Jenny's archaic-sounding third name that she detested. To that he added two digits, such as 1 or 2, and a special character like a parenthesis. The first day of the new month he moved inward on the upper keyboard row of special characters and changed the last pair of numbers in sequence, so 3, 4, for example.

Several weeks ago, while bringing him his morning coffee, she'd seen where he was in the progression. The end of the month was twenty-eight days ago. She was able to log on with her first attempt.

First she searched his email in-box for any correspondence from Tula Jones, the young, far-too-pretty department secretary who made her attraction to law enforcement officers obvious. Jenny was sure that handcuffs and bedposts figured prominently in Tula's bored work daydreams.

Relieved to find nothing incriminating, Jenny clicked on the general database and entered what she knew: Fatima Khalif, 620 Sixth Avenue, Tillson. The screen blanked except for an hourglass draining sand, flipping over and over. Man, the Bureau could use some increased computer power. Five seconds. A long header snaked across the width of the screen: a name and address box, then a string of column titles containing the usual FBI gibberish of abbreviations. Ten seconds. There. Apartment 1210, DOB 8/3/1993, born Tabda, Somalia, followed by a row of mostly empty boxes. Another few seconds, and the screen lit up with an additional hit, a brother—Samir Khalif, age twenty-nine. Actually, it was Dr. Khalif, PhD. Both siblings had emigrated from Somalia nearly thirteen years before and obtained US citizenship, Samir in 2010 and Fatima in 2013.

Once after one too many pre-dinner drinks, Mike had let slip that files in the database were marked with a yellow, red or orange flag based on level of concern for terrorism. There were none beside either name.

Jenny logged out. Without further passwords, she could only access information from the basic database, but she had her own arsenal of weapons as well. At work, she could run advanced in-house Gazzel informatics on the professor. Hopefully, the search would reveal more interesting and useful details than Fatima's dreary existence had. Also, she needed to figure out a way to narrow the Wiz list of Fatima's supposed 'boyfriends'. If she could provide enough suspicious evidence, Mike would have to agree to investigate the siblings.

• • •

Energized by the excellent response to his blog post, Hamid had stayed up late into the evening planning. Although he knew none of the nine fighters personally, they were all sworn to sacrifice themselves, body and soul. He trusted in their ability to fire a machine gun, anyway, and that was the important part.

He still felt jittery with unused adrenaline. Pulling up the Premier League stats, he watched until he fell asleep, hunched over his laptop.

The opening notes of "Stairway to Heaven" roused him. He winced at the stiffness in his neck. As he stretched over the edge of his futon, the hard corner of a book dug into his ribs. Grunting in discomfort, he shoved it away, irritated by the clutter.

Restricted to the smallest room in the boarding house, his belongings always stayed spread out over his futon. But it was all he needed, except the landlady had strict rules against cooking in the room; the only appliance she allowed was an electric kettle to make tea. Overall, however, she was perfect. There was no smoking or alcohol permitted, she provided clean sheets every week and best of all, she asked no questions.

Hamid's phone's screen glowed with an alert from NowCar. Yes, one thirty tomorrow at Naskas Falls would work. That left more than enough time to get back for the concert. He typed out a reply, agreeing to share the gas cost and meet at the mall.

He smiled. Samir had likely decided on the small town because it was an unlikely destination, and they were both amused by the similarity to the Somali word for 'breast'—*naaska*.

• • •

Billy yelled, slamming his hand on his desk.

"There's no way you could have seen my stockpile on Tertain without a hack, you cheating bastard."

It was almost 4:00 a.m. and after three solid hours of combat, his status emblem was still shining bronze. Not fair.

He exited the game. Was it a Japanese dude that had died from metabolic breakdown after gaming non-stop for three days? He shook his head and sent a mental probe around his body. *No way am I that bad.*

It was late and everything in off-line America was quiet. Time to posse up and check out the sites he had under surveillance. You never knew when the bad guys might stir.

First on his hit list was the 'Saturday' site. He furrowed his brow. There was a new post. "Bday this Saturday night at Romy's apartment on Standford, beer and wings followed by eating cake at eight." Was it normal for a host to specify when the cake would be served? *Too weird.* It was time to delve deeper into the blog's past posts.

One message struck him. "Time to secure our existence"—*that's definitely a white supremacist dogwhistle.* Pulling up his notes, he began cross-referencing the site entries with dates of terrorist events, homegrown and foreign. *Ha.* Almost exactly one year ago, there was a slew of posts to the site just hours after a brutal massacre at a mosque in Arles, Texas. Bursting into a prayer group, five neo-Nazis with assault rifles had slaughtered eighteen innocent people before fleeing.

Billy thought for a moment. Only four months ago, the Bureau had thwarted a terrorist attack in Times Square attributed to ISIS. He tapped in the dates; another spike of odd remarks. Flurries of messages occurred even around less publicly known terrorist events.

Overall, the pattern pointed toward attacks on Muslims, and the highest correlation was with attacks on mosques. Were the postings congratulations or commiserations? Who was going to kill whom?

Although previous messages were reactionary, these appeared to be more about planning. This Saturday? If so, what was the target? A prayer session? A special event? The image of blazing candles on a cake came to mind. Were they going to torch a mosque? And if so, which one?

He reread the party post. General Standford was an iconic name in the region, particularly Tillford, due to a large battle led by Standford against Native Americans in the late 1700s. The uniqueness of the name was powerful evidence that this was something local, maybe even planned by known homegrown white supremacist, Max Spitwell.

Billy's only contact at the FBI was the local agent heading up the Online Sexual Crimes unit, but maybe she would listen to his theory and pass it along. It would be almost impossible to track this site back to its source, but Uncle Sam was becoming more resourceful every day. Who knew what could come of it. All Billy could do was point them in the right direction.

DAY THREE

Friday
June 29, 2018

CHAPTER 14

Heidi Schelmer groaned and rolled over in bed. *What time was it?*

Her eyes barely open, vision blurry, all she could make out was five somethin' on the green-lit digital clock. Next to her ear, the baby monitor wailed. She smacked it off. Fortunately, her own children were old enough to no longer warrant such surveillance.

Beside the bed, her overalls and a baggy shirt lay waiting. The floor was freezing, and she hopped from foot to foot as she quickly dressed. At the back door she slipped on her muckers—sturdy, knee-high rubber boots with a good tread. Shivering in the chill air, she reached back to grab a tattered jacket.

The previous evening, she had left the barn lights on in happy expectation of a new calf, but now the plaintive lowing of the mother-to-be was heart-wrenching. She was in trouble.

A few minutes later, arm sheathed in a plastic glove up to the shoulder, Heidi determined the calf was sitting breach. Pushing with all her strength against its haunches made no difference. Damn, this was a job for her strapping husband. But Chuck was acting weird. When she got up to pee in the middle of the night, he'd been watching TV in the living room. It had still been dark when he woke her up to tell her he was going over to Mission Hill Farm Co-Op store near Winona before his seven o'clock shift.

Chuck wouldn't be home until after eleven tonight—his last shift had been unexpectedly cancelled, he said, so he'd taken a double. It was going to be another long day doing everything alone, but hopefully the extra cash would pay today's vet bill.

As she walked back to the house to put on a pot of coffee, she made the call to Dr. Jack. Hopefully, Becky, Tim and Peter were still asleep. Someone in this household had to get some shut-eye.

• • •

When Samir woke, he acknowledged the acceptance from Hamid. To maintain his routine, he would drive his usual clients to work before heading to the pickup location, an obscure area of the parking lot at the super-sized shopping mall on Highway 56.

As Samir slipped on a loose T-shirt and jeans, his thoughts turned to the plan. What else could they learn about this man, Wizner? What would make him more vulnerable to manipulation? After the joy of initial success, Samir had been confronted with the reality that he still lacked the vital information he needed. It was going to take more than deciphering a few keystrokes to unlock the treasure he sought. Could his dear sister unearth something that they could use for blackmail?

He couldn't wait. Treading heavily down the hallway, he knocked on Fatima's door. A sleepy mumble was her only response. He opened the door and stepped into her room.

"Fa, I left the USB keys on the table. Collect more data, anything that might be useful. Personal stuff like what he searches for online."

Fatima rolled over, rubbing the sleep from her eyes. "No, brother! I told you. I am tired of you and your schemes."

"Trust me, Fatima, this is the last time. Please do this for me."

He backed out of the room before she could reply. His sister was clearly having one of her 'female days', but there was no doubt in his mind that she would do as he bid. She always did.

• • •

Fatima waited until she heard Samir leave the apartment before she rose and entered the kitchen to make breakfast. At the doorway to the living room she stopped short. The cursed USB sticks lay on the table like poison candy. Slamming her bowl on the counter, she turned and ran back to bed, drawing the sheets up to her chin.

The ticking of the wall clock still echoed in her ears, even with the pillow over her head. She dreaded getting up, going to work, but lying here also felt unnatural and was certainly doing nothing to calm her nerves. Samir was right. She prided herself on never missing work; it would be more suspicious to stay at home.

Fatima contemplated her options. She could leave the USB keys behind. No—when Samir came home and found them, he would be unbearably angry. He had never hit her, but something in his eyes when he was in a rage told her that he was capable. Could she make them disappear somehow, perhaps say the security guards confiscated them? She could practically hear his voice accusing her of being sloppy. Sometimes, she almost wished he would just kick her out, but she knew he would never willingly let her out of his control. She groaned. She had no other choice.

The morning had been a busy one, but senior agent Wendy Adams finally took a minute to catch her breath. Last month she had received a promotion into first-level management as the lead officer in charge of investigating online sex crimes. She was excited about the job but less so about the myriad of time-consuming videoconference meetings that were an apparent requirement with her new responsibilities.

Admittedly, the external high-level discussions were often a welcome distraction from mundane intra-department chores, but there was one routine task she looked forward to: the Friday debriefing. The weekly review of her department's work served as a chance to touch base in person with all her staff. During work hours, the social life of her team was as lively as the cryogenically preserved crew of a deep-space probe. Hunched over their computers wearing bulky ultra-high-definition headphones, they rarely spoke as they concentrated on detecting the slightest nuance in video or audio that might provide a vital clue to a new bust.

Fortunately the weekly debrief was filled with dark humor. Usually, other than stuff involving children, it was a hilarious and sometimes even titillating journey through Internet perversion—though occasionally it drifted away into a bitch session. Like last Friday. That shit show had been just another reminder that as team leader she spent too much time putting out fires.

The one sanity-saving perk she enjoyed as manager was the separate office space. Sliding over the padded armrest of her faux-leather, high-backed chair, she settled in to begin the daily tedium of email maintenance. Hopeful for an exciting new lead, she started with the encrypted in-box for her anonymous informants.

There was no way in the vast Internet world that the FBI, with its limited resources, could monitor everything. Just like out on the streets, they paid for tips or used incriminating evidence to turn suspects into informants, but generally speaking, without face-to-face 'persuasion' the Internet was a tougher beat to patrol. Luckily, sometimes, the good guys just appeared out of the ether—like TyrBus84.

On several occasions in the past year, the young hacker's information had proved essential in the arrests of some truly sick people. Best of all, bless his soul, he never asked for money. To allow himself to be vetted, they had met once, briefly, and only after she promised never to reveal her source. Since then, he had completely transformed his online identity from Gunner#%21 to TyrBus84, and his communication included an imbedded code for validation that only she knew.

Securely opening the large attachment in his most recent message, she could see that this was not the usual material. A birthday party? Was TyrBus84 off his rocker?

Apparently not yet—reading through to the conclusion, she admitted the guy made a convincing argument. But her expertise was child pornography, not terrorism. That would be the domain of Dan Smithers and his team. Until vetted by the IT boys and girls, security policy did not allow external email attachments to be uploaded, but they could be spooled to a secure printer.

The print copy of the file was bulky. To comfortably walk it across the office, she stuffed the block of paper into the plastic shopping bag she kept under her desk for her spare shoes.

It was just a quick trip down the hallway into task force delta's room. Dan's office was empty, but across the expanse of open-concept space, she could see Mike Longstrum, one of his senior analysts. He was immersed in his work, typing with one hand and gulping down a supersized takeout coffee from the other. He was the guy Dan would delegate this to anyway.

"Morning Mike—or is it afternoon already? Got something for you."

"What's that? Donuts, or the original manuscript for *War and Peace*?"

Wendy appreciated that Mike could make her laugh. It was a quality sorely missing among most of the weirdos in her department. "I've got this cyber hacker vigilante dude who sends me pretty good tips, but this one is not in my wheelhouse."

She plopped the bag onto his desk just as the plastic handle stretched and gave way. "He's trying to convince me that a white supremacy group is going to attack a mosque in this area on Saturday night."

"Thanks. Just what I wanted, more work." Mike sighed, flipping the edges of the formidable stack. "Do you want your bag back?"

Wendy laughed. "No, save it for when you bring me donuts."

"For what?"

With her index finger, she tapped the top of the pile. "This intel, because with it you're going to thwart a mega mosque massacre and earn a promotion."

• • •

Mike watched her leave. Despite the non-regulation high-heeled shoes, she moved gracefully with strong strides. Did she notice that every guy raised his head to admire her as she passed by? Probably. That woman didn't miss much.

He always welcomed a visit from the easy-going manager, not only because she was stunning, but because the tenacity and dedication she brought to bear on her work was inspiring. Recently, she had single-handedly taken down some truly revolting perverts. The stuff she was forced to look at on a daily basis was disgusting—he wasn't sure if he could handle it.

He fingered the ream of paper; it was daunting. But if Wendy deemed this tip worthy of the walk over here, then he should take the time for a quick perusal. Besides, his other task at hand was inducing severe brain numbness.

The war on terrorism was never glamorous. Immersed for countless hours tracking the transfer of illegal funds and looking for the tiniest mistake was not only tedious but also frustrating, as the jurisdictions involved were usually reluctant to cooperate.

He skipped to the cyber-nerd's conclusion. The document intrigued him. This guy had meticulously documented traffic peaks on certain sites in relation to well-published acts of racist or terrorist violence. It surprised him to see mention of some events that never hit the press—in particular, two recent missions in which the department took down the bad guys before they acted. The FBI, to protect sources and the Bureau's methodology, had suppressed all information. Somehow this guy was accessing confidential material.

Obviously, a leak in the department was a concern, but if this tipster was correct there was an imminent threat. His priority was to report this to Dan Smithers, his immediate boss and station head. He fought a grin. It was serious business, but this could be an opportunity to personally head up a task force—a chance to get out on the street and fight the bad guys face-to-face.

In preparation for a punchy presentation, he rapidly scanned the most pertinent sections of the document, highlighting as he went. Scooping up the documents, he jogged through the maze of desks in the department.

At Smithers's ajar office door, he straightened his tie and knocked.

"Enter."

"Morning, Sir." Mike took a seat across from Dan Smithers. "Wendy received this last night, and I think there's something to it. If we don't react and something happens, people are going to get hurt, and we'll be the bad guys once again." He leaned forward and handed over the papers.

Rapidly turning the pages, Smithers read the portions Mike had marked. "This is pretty vague stuff. We can't even be sure of the target location."

"I know, but Wendy trusts this guy. I think we should act on it."

"I'll have to shoot this upstairs."

"Sir, that will take time. Perhaps we could get started right away?"

Smithers removed his glasses and pinched the bridge of his nose while he thought. "OK, Mike, I suppose it won't cost us anything to send out a warning to the Islamic leaders to be vigilant. They can decide whether or not to cancel their services.

"That's it?"

Smithers shrugged. "There are insufficient resources to do anything other than appear to be doing something."

Mike leaned forward, his expression intense as he tried to keep the frustration out of his voice. "Can we at least broadcast that we are increasing our presence in light of worrisome intelligence information?"

"OK, that much I can approve. Maybe we can get the bad guys to abort. That might help validate Wendy's source."

"All right. I'd still like to spin the most likely perps. The Lone Star Men are the most violent—"

"No, Mike. I love the idea, but the budget is too tight. We can't afford the manpower, especially without approval from above. Keep this local. If they do abort, we know with more certainty that something was planned in our area."

Trying not to frown, Mike rose to his feet. "OK, boss. I guess if a bunch of people die that would be also be a good test of this guy's theory."

Without waiting for a reply, he left, not bothering to close the door. He flinched as the thump of a fist on a desk rang out from Smithers's office. The accompanying voice was muted but discernible.

"Fuck, Mike, what do you want me to do?"

• • •

Chuck sat in the front seat of his truck, his lunch pail open between his legs. Normally, he ate with the guys at the picnic tables at the back of the plant. His co-workers were a decent bunch despite the cigarette smoke and disgusting jokes. But Spitwell was shift foreman today, and if he joined the lunch crowd, he knew things would go sideways fast. Spitwell and his buddy Kevin Lowry always cracked racist jokes; the cruder the humor, the more they laughed. Chuck preferred to avoid them, and he especially didn't want to risk seeing Spitwell now. Besides, eating alone would give him time to think.

Spitwell's list was becoming smudged with the nervous sweat between his fingers. The memory of the fistful of lies he'd spun at the Co-Op this morning made him grimace; he'd nearly caved and confessed at the clerk's single raised eyebrow.

He pounded a fist on the dashboard.

"I can't do this!"

There was still time to take the stuff home and put it in the fertilizer tank. But they needed the money. Was it worth it?

His appetite vaporized, Chuck popped the glove compartment and rummaged around for the cigarette lighter he kept for emergencies. The piece of paper in his hand caught fire easily. He held on until the flames threatened his fingertips then threw the remnants out the window.

• • •

Hamid stood in the designated location at the back of the mall. Parking the company van in the shipping and receiving lane behind the storefronts would not arouse suspicion; Ace Security had several clients here.

His stomach growled loudly. Pressed for time, he had worked through his breaks. Hopefully there would be leftovers from the enormous lunch Fatima always packed for Samir.

Right on time, his friend's car approached. The vehicle barely stopped moving before Hamid had slipped into the passenger seat and closed the door. As they headed toward the expressway, they exchanged nothing more than "Allah Akbar."

Merging into the flow of traffic, Samir spoke as he checked his mirrors. "I have good news. Finally, last night our wait was rewarded. The path to victory has been illuminated. I have broken into some of the network I've been researching."

"That is good news. But what does it mean, 'some of it'?"

"Do not ask, you know better. I just need a bit more time to gain control. Then we can proceed as planned."

"I am sorry, my friend, but I couldn't wait any longer. I have already given the go-ahead for a plan of my own, tomorrow evening."

"The airport? No, you must wait!"

"No, something better."

"What? But I should know—"

"Compartmentalization, operational secrecy." Hamid grinned briefly, then shrugged and turned to stare out the side window. "Besides, things are well underway."

"I plead with you to postpone. If you bring attention to us now, everything I have worked toward will be lost. Together, Hamid, we can be the masterminds of the greatest attack on American soil since 9/11. Not just shooting up a few infidels, but really making them suffer."

"You always want bigger and better. It is time for action, not words."

Samir slapped the steering wheel. "Remember what we talked about?"

"But you never said when or where."

"Yes, that is true. I couldn't be certain, not until now. But before this, did you not trust me enough to gather the materials and find the special weapon I requested?"

"Yes, but I grow impatient waiting for this grand vision of yours. We have no time for dreams. The longer we wait, the more we risk detection."

"Hamid, it is no longer a dream. We can do this, and soon. Are we not a team? We survived the same camps, the same injustice. We must fight together."

Hamid closed his eyes and massaged his temples with his fingertips.

"How much longer do you need?"

"I am very close, only days."

"This better be good."

"Oh, it will be worth it. I promise."

Hamid stared out the window in silence for several minutes. "Do you still think of Somalia?"

"Yes, my friend, I remember the pain of our homeland always."

"We have come a long way from sharing a blanket in that abandoned house."

"Indeed. I was always afraid that roof would collapse the rest of the way."

Hamid laughed. "Me too. I remember you screaming that night when the wind blew away another piece of the tin. But at least we could see the sky. I loved laying there under the stars while you told me stories about traveling in the clouds to other worlds. Especially the ones about making robots."

"They were the dreams of a little boy wanting to control something in his life."

"Remember how we planned the most wonderful meals to eat if we ever got out of that hellhole?"

"We were so hungry. But we survived—because we made an excellent team. You could steal food from under the nose of a king."

"And you could make a smartphone out of scrap metal."

"Hamid, we are still a good team, only our mission has changed. We need to trust each other just like we did then. My plan is the right one."

"As long as these people pay."

"Yes, my friend, Somalia has endured imperialism for too long—from the British and the Italians."

"And especially what the Americans did," sneered Hamid.

"Praise Allah, we will make them suffer dearly for every transgression." Samir turned off the highway and retraced their path back to the mall, stopping in a distant corner of the parking lot.

"Together we will strike a blow so hard that these infidels must accept that it is our turn to rule."

"Very well. I will postpone. But I warn you, if you don't succeed I will proceed with something else very soon."

Hamid leaned in as he closed the door. "Let me know ASAP. I need time to organize. Parts of your plan require different equipment and expertise than mine."

"Sunday at prayers we can talk."

CHAPTER 15

Jenny stretched and rubbed her aching wrists. It was exhausting being both a cyber sleuth and keeping up with her work. She had already put in a full day's effort and it was just coming up to afternoon coffee break.

Before the rest of the department trickled in, Jenny had spent an hour searching the Web for information on Dr. Samir Khalif. So far, pretty much all she had determined was that the man had graduated from MIT with a PhD in computer engineering in 2016. It seemed suspicious that there was nothing regarding a current occupation. Weren't tech students usually hired before they even finished their degree? It couldn't be coincidence that he and his sister lived in the city containing the headquarters of Gazzel, a technological powerhouse. Had he ever applied to work at the company? If so, human resources should have had his résumé on file.

She also learned that several of his research papers had been published in highbrow scientific journals, but not much more than that. She tried reading the abstract of one article but struggled to understand the technical terms. The gist seemed to be that by mimicking how owls located their prey, he had figured out a way robots could accurately locate the source of a sound.

Jenny half stood to take a peek at Fatima. Despite arriving late and looking tired and pale, she had maintained a torrid clearance rate, second only to Jenny herself. For the first time, Jenny felt guilty. Perhaps the poor woman really had been sick yesterday. Was it possible that her suspicions about the SnitchBitch were misplaced?

With her docket clear for the moment, Jenny exited her workflow and took a look around before accessing the outside Internet again. Entering her password, she acknowledged that her activities were being monitored in the interest of the company's privacy act.

Over lunch, she'd thought of a few additional search ideas, but not one yielded a result. Samir Khalif was an Internet anomaly. He had no presence on Twitter, Instagram or Facebook.

Finally, she found one item from a tourist blog thanking a BurBur Car driver named Samir for recommending a Somali restaurant in Tillson. She hadn't known there was one. How many Somali men in town had the name Samir? It had to be him.

• • •

Hamid mulled over what Samir had said. His friend was right. It would be wise to choose the option that delivered the biggest bang for the buck, as the Americans liked to say. But it meant canceling the attack on the Crazy Girls concert —it would be impossible to do both. No matter which plan they executed, the city would be shut down tighter than the skin on a drum for a long time afterwards. Hamid felt a little disappointed that it would not be his idea. He only hoped that Samir's was truly superior, so he could be proud of his part.

Tonight after work he would send out a message to cancel the assault on the stadium, then he would wait until the Sunday meeting with Samir. If they decided to proceed, he must allow enough time for his two most trusted fighters, Farzaad and Mouri, to arrive. They were not just martyrs, they were well trained in military tactics, explosives and most important of all, they were fearless.

There was one more person he must include, a man he had recruited over a year ago, with another use that precluded wasting his life on the Crazy Girls attack. But now he would be needed. The man loathed technology, however; Hamid would have to make contact physically.

He looked at his watch. There was still time to attend the prayer session at the little pop-up mosque downtown before getting started.

• • •

On her way to the office that morning, Fatima had resisted the urge to toss the USB keys into a public garbage bin. She'd spent half an hour more in bed agonizing over them and had to claim bad traffic to excuse her tardiness once she arrived at the office.

Hampered by her late start, she had forgone lunch to clear the overnight backlog of customer queries. So far there had been no activity picked up by Wizner's Alexandria unit. Soon it would be break time. Her nerves were on edge. Would nosy Jenny arrive, pretending to be friendly when all she really wanted to do was to pry? As a precaution, Fatima disconnected the extra cables to the dbx box.

A quick check of the time showed that she had a few minutes before afternoon break to accomplish the first task her brother had given her. Since she was already in the customer database updating her stats, it would only take a second to download all the Gazzel analytics about Wizner onto the smallest of the memory keys.

Finished, she logged off, slung her purse over her shoulder and stood. She peered over the office dividers. Jenny was hunkered down over her keyboard, typing away intensely. It was time to shake things up.

Moving as quietly as she could, she crept up behind her co-worker.

"Jenny, are you ready to go on break?"

The other woman turned her head so quickly Fatima thought she might snap her neck. "What—Oh, hi, Fatima. Yes, of course, give me a second."

Before Jenny could blank her screen, Fatima saw something that sent a chill through her core. Jenny had a search window open, and her brother's name was in the query box.

• • •

Mike tapped his pencil on the cover of the procedures manual, faster and faster and with increasing vigor, eliciting annoyed 'ahems' from the surrounding agents, until Ken Jenkins's voice silenced him.

"Hey, Pitbull, cut it out. You trying to be Keith Moon?"

It wasn't just Smithers, thought Mike, reining in his drumming. With the explosion of threats to the USA, both external and from within, the excuse that 'they couldn't spare the manpower' was becoming altogether too frequent throughout the entire Bureau.

This month marked his nine-year anniversary of being on the force, and the flat line trajectory of his career was beginning to wear on him. How he had ended up on the geek squad, he had no idea. His place was out in the field leading a team.

Actually, he knew why. Graduating from university with a double major in business and computer science, he'd figured that the Bureau's anti-terrorist squad would be a perfect fit for his skills. During his time as a novice agent, he also thought he'd proven to his superiors that he possessed the mental toughness and physical attributes to make a great field agent. Instead, citing his educational background, he was named subsection lead in the cyber intelligence group. The promotion was nice, but he didn't fit in with his nerdy co-workers, who had apparently missed the disbursement day for personality. He grimaced. Wendy had just handed him a fantastic opportunity to demonstrate his initiative and on-the-ground operational smarts, and it had all fallen flat.

Get a grip! You earned the nickname Pitbull for a reason. Aggressive tenacity. Perhaps tonight, he could spend a few hours of his own time surveilling Max Spitwell, known leader of the Lone Stars. They were the most likely group to be planning an attack of this scale. The home front was covered as he had already told Jenny that he would have to work this weekend. Putting in the extra time could pay off with a big bust.

It would be nice to have a search warrant or a court order for a cellphone tap, but that took time and authorization. What he did have was full access to the file on Spitwell detailing his home address, vehicle and plate number, as well as his favorite hangouts. The guy would be easy to recognize from his crystal clear black-and-whites, taken at a white supremacist rally the previous October.

Unpaid overtime was the norm in the office—in fact, an expectation. At least this shift would be one of his own choosing. It meant, however, trading Friday night mojitos with Jenny and the gang for a bout of illegal surveillance. He grimaced. Jenny. Now he'd be a jerk to deny her less-than-legal requests. Yes, it was a double standard, but he had justification. He was in procession of hard intel, just not the required paperwork. Jenny was going on mere intuition, which could prove brilliantly right or catastrophically wrong.

He preferred slow and steady, by the rules. Mostly.

$$\bullet \ \bullet \ \bullet$$

Exhausted, Heidi sat down with her third cup of coffee—or was it the fourth? She had lost track. It was well past lunchtime, and her stomach was growling. The vet had been successful in manipulating the unborn calf for a safe delivery, but the procedure ate up most of the morning. Though she dreaded Dr. Jack's bill, she couldn't help but be pleased at the birth.

In the midst of the hubbub, she had still managed to organize the boys for the last day of school. Once they were on the bus, she'd begun Becky's treatment. This morning, with the arrival of the warm, moist summer air, her daughter's lungs were heavy with mucous.

The poor girl's daily routine was worthy of an Olympic athlete. Every morning she arose sopping wet and chilled to the bone from sleeping in a salt-water mist tent. Born with Cystic Fibrosis, the underactive cilia in her airways could not budge the abnormally thick secretions produced by her lungs.

The artificial sea breeze helped loosen the congestion overnight, but still she had to receive postural drainage two or three times a day. In preparation for this treatment, she inhaled twenty minutes of a nebulized mist delivered by an air compressor. Then for forty-five minutes she lay in nine different positions on an incline board while Heidi or Chuck delivered gentle percussion with cupped hands over specific zones of her lungs. After each position, Becky attempted to dislodge the mucous by forcing herself to cough.

Heidi used to joke that she would never have the droopy arms of an old lady thanks to the daily toning they received—until rotator cuff tendonitis forced her to resort to a mechanical device with a padded 'thumper'.

After the treatment, Becky spent another fifteen minutes deeply inhaling an aerosolized antibiotic with her hopefully more 'open' lungs. Because the thick secretions also prevented digestive enzymes from exiting her pancreas, Becky had to swallow a small bowlful of replacements with every meal. Despite eating like a child in a candy shop, the girl could never fill out her clothes.

Eight-year-old Becky was determined that her health would not deny her a single thing. With a contagious enthusiasm, the red-headed fireball took part in a surprising number of school activities. Sports like volleyball required less lung capacity, and her light weight allowed her to jump high enough to be better than the weak members of her public school team. Heidi always wondered where her daughter found the wind to make her voice soar like a songbird's in choir.

Outwardly optimistic, Chuck and Heidi knew full well that Becky walked through life balanced on a knife-edge. Lurking everywhere, the common bacteria that healthy lungs subdued with ease could overwhelm Becky. A severe chest infection could take her at any time.

They also knew that all too often, the never-ending stress of supporting a chronically ill child proved too much for a marriage. The couple considered themselves lucky that the battle for Becky's life had drawn them closer, not split them apart.

By contrast, Becky's two brothers were as healthy as well-fed mules. Little Peter, or "The Accident" as Chuck called him, constantly griped about the inconveniences Becky's health caused him, but Tim took his job as protective older brother very seriously. Mature beyond his years, he was always willing to pitch in with house and farm chores when his parents were busy with Becky's needs. Only occasionally did he show signs of jealousy at the amount of attention his sister received, but he responded well to extra doses of TLC.

Heidi poured the last of the stale coffee into her mug and refilled the carafe. There were still chores to be done.

• • •

Wizner stood at his kitchen counter, holding his sides as he coughed. Yes, it still hurt, but without the fever, he felt improved enough to prepare properly for work on Monday.

Crossing the living room with a cup of tea, he fired up his computer. Fed up with the endless, useless emails, he ignored them all except for the encrypted message containing his daily password to facility operations. Fortunately, the code to unlock the password was simple to memorize and never changed.

Not sure how long he would have before the next bout of fever, Wizner set about gathering the data required for his weekly system status report.

• • •

Fatima's whole body felt numb, as her mind filled with a dull buzzing. *Why was Jenny checking on Samir?*

"I said yes. Did you hear me?" Jenny was staring at her, hard. "Are you coming to break or not?"

"Ah, that would be all right. I will see you there."

Fatima could barely contain the urge to run to the exit. Perhaps she should have a relapse of her illness and go home and never come back—but she was so close to completing her mission. She felt a sudden swell of resentment push aside her fear. Who was Miss Cheerleader to stop her? Doubling back to her cubicle, she waited until Jenny disappeared down the hall to the elevators.

Fatima's pulse quickened. She fumbled with the first USB and dropped it. A quick look over the partitions. All clear. Down on all fours she recovered the device and inserted it. Initiating the data collection, she continued until all the memory sticks were full. The recording was music to her ears, a concerto of clicking keys. Samir would be delighted.

• • •

The tiny makeshift mosque near First and Devine was nothing more than a double garage, converted by a true believer. After 9/11, however, larger well-known mosques had suffered serious hate crimes. Remaining low profile seemed prudent.

Abarque slipped off his shoes and took a prayer rug from the rack at the entrance. There were already several people on the floor. Fortunately, his favorite spot was still available. Slightly apart from the others, he orientated his mat and knelt.

Several minutes later, the sound of a rug slapping down beside his disturbed his concentration. He opened his eyes and peeked sideways. It was a man with a storm cloud of a face: an immense bushy black beard, tight lines on his cheekbones and a forehead that puckered the skin between his eyebrows into a knot.

Abarque had not seen Hamid in over a year, but it was hard to forget the intensity of his dark piercing eyes. One day after prayers, the man had invited him for an espresso, claiming friendship because they were both from Somalia.

But the conversation had been one-sided. Abarque only listened intently as Hamid listed compelling arguments for why they should attack America in the name of Allah. Besides jihad being a religious duty, did he not hate the Americans' broken promises of peace and their self-righteous arrogance? Not only in Somalia but also throughout the Muslim world. Had he forgotten the death of his uncles in Mogadishu?

Caught up in the moment, Abarque had agreed. The task the man asked him to do seemed safe enough—buy plant fertilizer, lots of it. Several months later, however, Hamid returned, his demeanor darker, less friendly, and his request was much different. *Are you prepared to die in the name of Allah?*

Even Abarque knew that only one answer was ever allowed to that question.

Returning to his recitation, Abarque closed his eyes but was soon bothered again by the edge of his mat being lifted. Blinking, he caught sight of Hamid's hand returning to position. The piece of paper he'd tucked under the edge of Abarque's rug was partially visible. Puzzled, he shot the man a questioning look.

Keeping his hands and forehead pressed to his mat, Hamid whispered out of the corner of his mouth.

"Be ready, my friend. The time has come."

Abarque flinched as a wave of dread rolled through him. Light-headed, he closed his eyes tightly and dropped his forehead onto his mat.

The cadence of his prayer increased. Using the words as a mantra, he tried to meditate away his anxiety. When he opened his eyes, Hamid was gone.

After the session was over, he remained kneeling for several minutes. Finally, he slid his hand under his mat and over the note, concealing it as he lifted the mat and stood. Not everyone in the mosque shared the same ideas.

On a busy street corner several blocks away, he opened the note while waiting for the light to change. It contained a website and password. Before he'd reached the other side of the street, he had the information memorized. Shredding the paper with trembling fingers, he dropped a few pieces into a garbage can then distributed the rest in two others on the way to work.

Abarque walked more slowly to work than usual, taking the time to enjoy the warmth of the sun on his face. *How strange that when you face death, you are instantly glad to be alive. Everything becomes sharp and clear and beautiful, no matter how ugly it really is.* He realized that he was already mourning his own death. Shouldn't he be content that his soul was about to transcend this planet, leaving behind all its injustice and pain? Did he doubt?

The Friday exodus out of the city was already in full swing, the Americans setting out for the weekend to rediscover nature with motorbikes, ATVs and boats. At the McDonald's across the street, the drive-through queue circled the building and trailed out of the parking lot, blocking the curb lane. At the touch screen, a man leaned out his window, repetitively stabbing at the quarter pounder meal deal button while three youngsters watched TV in the back seat. In the parking lot, a woman screaming into her phone toted an enormous paper bag and a tray of super-sized drinks back to her truck. All for just three people.

Abarque shook his head and picked up his pace. The school would be deserted now, all the better for him. He could check the computer in room 102 and go home early to enjoy what may be his last days of this life.

At work, he parked his mop bucket outside the computer lab and unlocked the door. Halfway across the room, he doubled back to the hallway to verify he was alone. It was a totally unnecessary precaution. He was more alone than a night watchman at the morgue.

From memory he located the new website and entered the passcode. He let out the breath he was holding at the empty screen. Yet Hamid's words echoed in his head. "The time has come."

He would have to check every day for the call.

CHAPTER 16

Mike sat in his car, warming his hands on the cardboard cup of his takeout coffee. Max Spitwell was an easy man to locate. His file had listed the isolated strip bar off Route 4 as his preferred Friday evening hangout. The seedy dive was an anonymous location where hard-working guys from the Streamline factory could unwind after a long week of welding mobile home chassis.

In the still darkness, Mike was nearly falling asleep from the boredom. All he'd had to watch was the unsteady comings and goings of the bar's intoxicated clientele. Finally, the front door of the bar swung open and several figures made a staggering exit. One man, his hat pulled down low over his face, walked toward the truck that Mike had pegged as Spitwell's.

Following the Ford 350 as it wove along the back roads, Mike contemplated pulling the guy over for impaired driving. He wasn't a highway cop, however, and had no roadside breathalyzer.

It was obvious that Spitwell was heading home, but merely following him there was of little use. *Without official sanction, what could I possibly do to prevent an attack? Illegally park at the end of Spitwell's driveway to block him in?*

Mike jabbed a finger in the air. "That's it!" What if he could spook Spitwell into canceling the attack? That would provide circumstantial evidence to his complicity. Not ideal, but something, and if it saved lives it would be worth it.

He began to break all the rules of surveillance. At the stop sign, he didn't wait for Spitwell's pickup to dip over the first hill before turning to follow. At the gate to the Cedar Springs mobile home park, he paused just momentarily before following and parking a short distance away. From the shadows, he could see Spitwell cast a double look over his shoulder as he entered his trailer.

Under the light of the waning moon Mike studied the park. It had been mostly clear-cut, and the lots were generous, fairly isolated and demarcated by lines of tall pines. The extra space around each trailer was filled with homemade sheds and second and third vehicles. There appeared to be no amenities other than a rectangular wooden gazebo near the road sheltering a row of large gray garbage bins.

Over the next two hours, there were no visitors or detectable activity. At approximately eleven thirty the solitary light at the back of the trailer was extinguished. Was the early bedtime tonight in anticipation of a big day tomorrow? Mike decided to wait to ensure that turning out all the lights wasn't a ruse for Spitwell to sneak out.

Everything remained quiet. It was nearly midnight; Mike couldn't stay awake any longer. He reached for the keys in the ignition. The thought of curling up beside Jenny was far more appealing than one more minute freezing his ass off in this car.

A sharp crack exploded behind his left ear. Reflexively he dove for cover across the front seats, drawing his service revolver and twisting to confront the source of the noise.

Steadying his shaking grip with his other hand, he swung the barrel left and right. He could see nothing but darkness. Behind his head, a loud thump shook the vehicle. Awkwardly, he wrenched around, but saw nothing. Scrambling his hand across the seat under him, he squirmed to retrieve his phone.

Another loud smack against the driver's window sent another shock of adrenaline through his veins. Bringing his leg up, he pushed himself further across the seat so he was half sitting, propped up against the passenger door, his revolver in a two-fisted grip.

"Open the door." A gruff voice barked.

Mike still couldn't see a thing. "Make yourself visible. Who are you?"

"I'm asking the same thing about you."

Spitwell appeared in the window, a lopsided grin on his face.

"Put both hands were I can see them." Mike gestured with his gun.

"You talk like a cop. What ya doin' snooping around here."

"Routine patrol."

"Bullshit." Spitwell raised a shotgun into sight. "This is private property, so you see, I got a right to defend myself." He patted the gunstock. "I suggest you move along unless you got a warrant for something."

With that Spitwell turned and walked nonchalantly back toward his trailer.

Mike holstered his weapon. Not a pleasant end to the evening, but his mission was definitely accomplished. Spitwell knew they were on to him.

• • •

His hands still smelling of floor soap, Abarque sat cross-legged under the harsh light of the bare bulb that hung from the ceiling of his tiny bachelor apartment. The room was sparse; he had known this day would come, and soon after Hamid's visit, he had purged most of his already meager belongings. Why bother wasting money on anything of value? A mattress on the floor, a cushion to sit on and minimal basic kitchen supplies were the only worldly things that he now owned. His home was devoid of electronics—which he knew, even before his recruitment, only delivered sin—and literature, except the only book worth reading, the Quran. Even if he had wanted to spend more, every month the majority of his paycheck immediately disappeared on rent, food and the money he sent to his widowed sister, Jamilla, leaving him with just enough for necessities.

Apart from his fear of death, Jamilla's situation was what truly troubled him about his recruitment. Still living in Somalia under unthinkable conditions, her only hope for a better future was up to him, her sponsor. Unless he was still working in America, there would be no money for the greedy immigration lawyers.

As the memory of Jamilla's hopeful brown eyes rose in his mind's eye, he realized that he had made a decision, even through his fear. Now was not the time to become a martyr. After he gave those zealots what they wanted, he would refuse to join them. Certainly these men would understand his commitment to a single mother of two children. The holy Quran was clear about the duty to family. It was not a perfect solution; he might be branded as a coward and executed by his compatriots. He would have to prepare for the worst eventuality and tell Jamilla what she needed to do.

His monthly pay from the college would be deposited in his bank account sometime tomorrow. He would send the immigration lawyer every penny. Hopefully, it would be enough to finish the process. Writing and placing the check in an envelope, he put it aside and began a letter to his sister. He did not want to scare her by talking about the life insurance policy from work, so he chose to be vague. Unfortunately, his life wasn't worth much.

• • •

There had been no time for a training session at the soccer pitch this evening. As soon as he got home, Hamid had sat on the end of his bed, his computer across his knees, and accessed the blog site that he curated. For years he had meticulously followed world events and posted in response—mostly celebratory messages following mosque attacks, however much it sickened him. His followers in turn peppered their comments with slogans that he had provided.

The original soldiers who had answered the call for the birthday party on Saturday would be disappointed that their sacrifice was not needed, but they should understand. Sudden changes were a common occurrence in this business, and if Samir's plan were a go, he would need believers with different skills.

Until this moment, Hamid's focus had been on the final preparations for Saturday night's battle. Now, waiting for Samir allowed him time to be pensive. As he waited for responses to his new post, he lay back on his bed and contemplated how he had come to this point in his life.

His revelation of the injustice in the world began early. His parents died of AIDS, and when food, water and freedom were also removed, his simmering rage began to boil. Still a young child, he'd had no outlet for his feelings except to kick around a half-inflated soccer ball, until target practice by American soldiers on patrol entirely deflated his dream of becoming the Somali Pelé.

He had no time for the luxury of school. Living on the street was a full-time job. One morning, while he was hunched over a garbage can licking the remains of chicken suqaar from a discarded paper plate, Diric, the school-teacher, had placed a gentle hand on his back. "Come."

He didn't know it at the time, but that was the first moment that changed his life. School is where he encountered his polar opposite, Samir.

Later, he and Samir were herded across the border into one of the many sprawling refugee camps in Kenya. Orphans there were sometimes 'adopted' by caring aid workers or members of the Kenyan army who oversaw the camp. Samir, the intellectual, was taken under the wing of a Canadian doctor working with Doctors without Borders. The woman had earned a PhD in physics before entering medical school and loved that Samir was interested in learning everything she could teach him.

A soccer-possessed army officer became Hamid's guardian angel. At first the man would spend his work breaks watching Hamid and the other boys kicking around a tin can. One morning he moved closer, his hands clasped out of sight, and beckoned the boys over. He asked if he could join in their game. When the boys agreed, he revealed, to their screams of delight, the shiny new soccer ball hidden behind his back.

In the following weeks, the man helped the boys hammer scrap wood into goal posts and supplied some tattered cloth for 'netting'. A talented player himself, the army officer recognized Hamid's gift for soccer and offered coaching tips after the matches.

Evenings lying side by side on their pieces of cardboard, Hamid and Samir shared different stories from their early childhood days. In a very strange sense, even surrounded by barbwire fences, they felt freer than they ever had.

But soon afterwards life became dismal again. The soccer soldier and Samir's doctor's rotations ended, and the government of Kenya grew weary of the cost associated with the camps. They began cutting back on food and water, and hope grew hard to find.

Then the course of his life changed again. Ismid. He remembered his and Samir's awe when they saw the man for the first time. Different from anyone in the camp, he did not sulk around or act defeated. On his daily walk through the tent city, he carried himself tall, almost proud, as if he was just passing through for a few days. One evening he stopped to talk to them in his deep, commanding voice.

"Boys, let me warn you about the future. There are organizations coming to offer you a better life in America." He pointed a finger at each of them. "But do not be tricked by their lies. They may take you to Disneyland and feed you rich foods, but you will always be second-class in America."

They listened raptly, nodding their heads even though they didn't understand everything.

Ismid's visits became regular and so began their education on the ways of Al-Shabaab and its aspirations to grow from its roots of local clan and gang warfare onto the global stage.

According to Ismid, all the evil in the world originated in the desire by infidels to crush Muslims. Night after night, under a tent lit by a dim lantern, the man only dared to whisper his teachings. Yet his speeches were still fiery, filled with passion as he explained how this injustice had started with the Crusades over a thousand years ago and was still happening today.

Hamid still felt the same surge of fear and inspiration when he recalled their final meeting. Ismid had glared at them and pounded violently on the dusty crate that was their table, nearly upsetting their one flickering candle.

"Who is the biggest perpetrator of this war on Islam?"

"America!"

Ismid delivered another closed fist slap to the table. "America must pay! Will you answer Allah's call?"

The intensity in Samir's eyes had been almost terrifying. They'd held hands and nodded vigorously.

"Yes, Commander, we will go to the United States."

Ismid nodded. "Remember, this is not for a trip to Disneyland. You go with a mission. A deadly one."

When Samir nodded, Ismid turned to Hamid. "And you?"

"Yes, I understand."

Ismid had wet his thumb and finger to extinguish the candle and left. Huddled together in the darkness, neither of them was able to sleep. Hamid remembered whispering that he really did want to see Disneyland and the painful jab in the ribs from Samir.

Shortly afterwards, the adoption agencies arrived. At thirteen he and Samir were not as easy to place as younger children, but when Samir stated he had a younger sister, his value went up. Within two months the authorities had located Fatima. The siblings were reunited and shortly afterward flown to California to be adopted by a young couple.

Hamid was devastated. He swore that no matter the cost, he would be with Samir again.

He endured several more years in camps before he was shepherded by the Al-Shabaab into a training camp in Somalia. The group was dedicated to freeing Somalia from foreign influence, but in 2012 stronger links with al-Qaeda were being formed. The new al-Qaeda branch in Syria, al-Nusra, needed trained soldiers, so in 2013 Hamid was sent to Syria. A self-taught electronics specialist, he'd proven his genius by salvaging battle-damaged Russian and American advanced weapons for the jihadists. Leadership soon recognized his potential for greater things and repurposed him.

He made his way to Germany and finally arrived in North America as part of the Canadian government's asylum program in 2015. On a starless night in the deadly cold of winter, his trek through the Quebec forest into Vermont was far more difficult than Samir and Fatima's plane trip to California. Unlike them, when Hamid arrived in the United States there was no one there to welcome him except a rip-off taxi driver.

• • •

At one o'clock in the morning, nothing was worse than cold, plain perogies. He didn't even have any sour cream or bacon. *I really need a microwave down here.*

Putting aside his dinner plate, Billy turned back to his computer. Time to pull on his vigilante hat and go for a ride around the Wild West of the dark web.

Dammit. The pedophiles were at it again.

He quickly lassoed the emails, site links and Bitcoin addresses and transaction IDs into a file and uploaded it to his friendly contact at the FBI. He wouldn't bother deciphering any of the crap. That's what the feds got paid big bucks for.

Not that they seemed very good at it. It had been eight months since he identified this phony office supply site as a concern. How many more victims had been claimed in that span of time? Of course, the feds had to work through all the stuff he didn't have the patience to do: infiltrating and case building before bringing the creeps down.

The 'Saturday' site showed a few replies: 'thumbs up' and 'beer and chips?' If his decryption of the messages was correct, the white supremacist 'birthday party' on Saturday appeared to be abandoned. 'B-day canceled, sorry, see you next year!" *Hopefully not.*

He fired off a quick message to his contact about the cancellation, but hopefully they were already monitoring it. He wanted to rush upstairs to tell his parents: he, personally, was responsible for preventing a massacre. The hours spent on his computer in their basement were not wasted—he was a contributing member of society. And finally, they should get off his fucking back about getting a job.

But he remained in his chair. Really, would his parents care? Their life consisted of *Jeopardy* and buying state lottery tickets. It was probably best not to wake them up. If he made them angry, they might start charging rent and demanding a financial contribution for groceries.

His good deed done, Billy was impatient to enter the gaming arena and pit his stealth tactics against the South Koreans. While he was busy saving the world, those bastards had probably never left their consoles.

DAY FOUR

Saturday
June 30, 2018

CHAPTER 17

"Where were you last night?" Jenny rammed two more slices of bread into the toaster.

"Sitting outside the School House Strip Bar off Route 4," replied Mike casually, keeping his eyes on his toast as he meticulously spread peanut butter over every square millimeter.

"Outside?"

It would not be wise to stoke his wife's mistrust any further. "Yes, outside. I was conducting surveillance on a bad guy."

Jenny sat down across from with him, her arms crossed over her chest. "Anything good?"

"Nah, the guy went to bed earlier than me."

"Are you going into the office today?"

"Sure." Her pout disappeared. She grabbed her purse, pulled out a paper and laid it in front of him. "While you're there, can you run this name and address?"

He sighed. "Oh, honey, what now?"

"It's Fatima's brother. Isn't it suspicious that a guy with a PhD in computers is unemployed in this town?"

"And if he were a white guy, it wouldn't be out of place?"

"That has nothing to do with it. The guy is an expert on high-tech listening devices for robots."

"That makes him excellent husband material."

"Come on, Mike, be serious. I told you his sister is doing some weird stuff at work. Maybe it all fits together."

Mike realized that there was no winning this argument. He needed to concentrate on taking down homegrown murderers—it would be expeditious to just appease his wife.

"OK, fine. I'll try and find some time this morning to check him out."

Jenny stood and wrapped her arms around Mike's shoulders. "Thank you."

"And honey, I have to go out again tonight, same deal. Also, I got made last night, so can I borrow your car?"

• • •

Samir drove for BurBur Car on weekdays and sometimes Saturday afternoons, if there was a sporting event or a music concert. Extra money to support the cause was always welcome.

Despite the Crazy Girls concert at the soccer stadium this Saturday night, he would stay home. He needed to find out everything he could about James Wizner. Digesting the vast amount of Gazzel analytics data Fatima had downloaded was going to take hours. Last night, progress had been excellent until his heavy eyelids exerted their will and forced him to grab a few hours sleep. Today, he felt refreshed and ready to get back to work.

Wizner's passwords for Facebook and Instagram were identical and short. KeyAnalytics had provided an almost perfect match, requiring merely a bit of trial and error to get the last number. Apart from learning details about his family and social life, Samir could see from the man's search history that he was an active gamer, liked country and western music and was a huge fan of the local major baseball team, the Angels.

Each work morning Wizner's digital assistant ordered the same coffee from Starbucks for pickup, and every night at approximately seven it ordered exactly the same takeout—either Chinese or pizza. His most frequently performed Internet searches were the next day's weather, traffic reports for his route to work, dictionary definitions, baseball trivia and organic vitamins and supplements.

Several hours into his investigation, Samir remembered Fatima's cover story and reopened Facebook. He needed to protect his little sister. It took only a few minutes to create an account for Fatima using a photo of her uploaded from his phone. It was fun to set up an exchange of messages between her and Wizner, and to arrange a date for the following week. He chuckled at his last entries.

'What color is your hair?'

'That is only for a husband to know.'

Returning to the trash bin of Wizner's work emails, he determined that the security code for the operation side of the plant changed every morning. An encrypted email was sent out to the select few who needed to know just before 7:00 a.m. Unfortunately, it was going to take a concentrated effort to decode. He needed a cup of tea first.

Slightly perturbed, he paced the kitchen floor waiting for the water to boil. Further analysis of the power plant informatics had revealed an even more daunting obstacle to his success: access to the sensitive portions of the console operations required additional security.

Overcoming this challenge was crucial. It had been a calculated gamble, asking Hamid to wait while he attempted to gain full access to the plant operations. If he failed, Hamid's wrath would be unbearable. He couldn't lose the trust of his friend. He must succeed by tomorrow.

Samir stretched out on his bed, tea in one hand. In the living room, the television was blaring some American garbage. Why Fatima wasted her time with such nonsense he would never understand, but at least she did useful things like sew clothes while she watched.

Rejuvenated by the caffeine, he set to work. He'd come so far; he could finish this.

In keeping with his desire for anonymity, he rarely attended the mosque, but the obscurity of a large crowd was another safe way for him and Hamid to meet. While the worshippers at the mosque mingled, they could sneak off to the library corner. Really though, there was not that much to talk about. Their objectives had been clear for a long time. Hamid only needed to be filled in on the details of this latest addition.

• • •

When Mike rounded the corner, Wendy Adams was walking away from his workstation. She looked better wearing no makeup, dressed in Yoga pants and an FBI T-shirt than most women did all dolled-up for a Saturday night out. On top of that, she possessed more brains and common sense than most veteran agents. He wished he were half as confident.

"Morning, Wendy. Glad to see that I'm not the only one crazy enough to work Saturdays. What's up, you have something for me?"

Smiling, she turned back to his desk and flicked the corner of a sheet of paper on his blotter.

"I didn't pick up this email until this morning because, unlike the nerd who sends me the stuff, I sleep at night. Anyway, it looks like the planned attack for tonight was canceled late last evening."

"Really, when?"

"Eleven-ish last night according to this guy. I don't know what you did to warn them off, but it worked."

Mike nodded. The timing fit. Either his purposefully bumbled surveillance or the disinformation the FBI disseminated late in the afternoon yesterday did the job. Either way, Max Spitwell must have canceled his plans.

"Yeah, I—" He cut himself off. *The fewer people that know about my unauthorized surveillance, the better.* "I owe you. Thanks. Looks like your hacker friend has earned some cred. I'll let Dan know."

"No problem." Wendy sat down on the corner of his desk looking concerned. "By the way, Mike, is everything OK at home with Jenny?"

"Sure, why do you ask?"

"My boyfriend is Tillson PD. He saw you lurking outside a strip joint last night. He ran the plates, but when he saw your name, he didn't bother you."

Mike laughed. "I was just following up on a lead."

"Sure." Wendy gave him an exaggerated wink and turned to leave.

"It's just—"

Wendy stopped. "What?"

"Jenny is driving me a bit crazy. She is constantly asking me to investigate people she thinks are terrorists."

"Ah, she's a wannabe. It's normal among spouses. The underemployed partner has career envy but probably doesn't even know it. She is a bright woman. Maybe she's bored, or feels left out and is missing you. Perhaps her intuition has picked up on signals that you don't even know you're sending. Or she's just trying to help you get ahead. It is normal, trust me."

"But—"

Wendy shook her head and stood to leave. "You should spend more time with your wife."

She is probably right, thought Mike. He should count himself lucky. Jenny knew the nature of his work and his tenacity when confronted with something he thought was important. He chuckled. If he were ever going to court mischief, he would court Wendy, not a stripper.

Performance review season was coming soon. He had to admit the tedium of following the latest torturous money trail back to ISIS made him feel like he was trapped in a dark, sealed box sucking on a collapsing paper straw for air. With this gift from Wendy, there couldn't be a better chance than now to show some initiative.

Let's go, Pitbull! Mike grabbed the printed email and headed down the hall. There was someone else in the office that always worked weekends. Divorced for years, Dan Smithers had never remarried. A workaholic, he joked that when he had to choose between his job and marriage, he got it right the second time.

Mike knocked lightly on the door and stuck his head through the gap. "Hi, boss, you got a sec?"

"My my, aren't we dedicated? What's up?"

"I need a search warrant for the home of Max Spitwell."

Smithers took off his glasses and chewed the end of the earpiece, his eyebrow furrowed. "For what reason?"

"We need to look at his computer."

"What do you expect to find?"

"Wendy heard from her hacker again last night. Our ploy to dissuade the attack on the mosque worked. A message to cancel was posted on the blog last night. If we can link Spitwell to the website . . ."

"Look, you know better than that. There is no legal case here yet."

"Yeah, but I thought I'd ask anyway."

"Mike, I'm sorry but that's it. It's done. From the get-go, the bosses upstairs were reluctant, and with the attack aborted, they won't have any interest now."

"I've got a gut feeling about this."

"Look, you're telling me that with the help of Wendy and her hacker you can keep tabs on Spitwell's plans. Intervening now won't make an easy case—too circumstantial. So wait. If we catch them in the process of implementing another attack it would be an open and shut case."

"That could be extremely dangerous."

"Granted, but it seems like you have a credible source. The next time there's a threat I want you to go full out." Smithers leaned forward with his elbows on his desk. "Mike, you did good work."

"Thanks. Hey, if we get another chance could Wendy be on my team?"

Dan leaned back in his chair and chuckled. "It seems everyone wants Wendy helping on their assignments these days. Dream on. She's in a different department. Now, get out of here."

• • •

Fatima switched off the TV. It was already the middle of the afternoon and there had been no sign of Samir, but what he did behind his bedroom door she did not care to know.

Did she dare go alone on their weekly trip to the halal grocery store? Normally, she avoided shopping at a regular supermarket during the week unless it was absolutely necessary to pick up something quick on the way home from work. For the big shop, Samir liked to supervise. She was sure he used that super-intelligent brain of his to calculate the cost per ounce to three decimal places. But frugality was not likely his real motive. It was to keep an eye on her. What a paradox. It was OK for her to go to work because it suited his purpose but not to shop alone?

She padded down the hall and stood outside Samir's room. "Brother, it is getting very late. We need groceries."

His voice was a strange, husky bark. "I'm too busy. You go."

She tingled with anticipation—an outing alone, away from her brother's puritanical oversight. Along Eighth Avenue she could peruse the fine boutiques that showed all the latest fashions, clothes Samir would forbid her to even look at. More importantly, she could peruse the young, handsome man who stocked the shelves at the market.

Today she would be free to linger in the aisle and perhaps summon the courage to start a conversation. Maybe she could ask him a question about one of the products that only a manager might know. It would be very nice to find out he was not just a stock boy. Samir would never allow her to marry someone who did not have a strong future.

She blushed at the thought. Was he single? Would she have the nerve to ask? What if he said yes? Her mind zoomed ahead. She imagined the nikah ceremony, the young man proposing in front of Samir. She tingled at the thought of saying qabul three times. Sometimes her brother was harsh, but she had no doubt that he would be the proudest uncle on the planet.

• • •

Mike was eager to get home. If he was going to spend another night conducting surveillance on Spitwell, he'd better spend some time with Jenny first. But he couldn't return empty-handed. Tapping into the active case databank, he ran a search on Samir Khalif.

Nothing. Oh well, at least he could say he tried. He could still pick up something nice for an early dinner on the way home.

• • •

Restless after morning prayers, Abarque had spent the better part of the day walking. He loved the broad sidewalks lined with tall shade trees. Even though he had no interest in the shops and their trinkets, or the gaudy sidewalk cafés, it was nice to see people smiling, not fearful and flinching at the sound of every dropped box or revving truck engine.

It was now evening, and he needed to rest his bruised feet. At the park near his apartment there was a small pond with a waterfall, often visited by ducks and geese. He loved watching the birds swim around the dark pool of water. Whenever he wanted to push away his worries, he bought a small bag of popcorn and tossed handfuls over the surface. The ensuing ruckus of flapping wings and squawks never failed to make him smile. It reminded him of the bedlam around the relief caravans during food dispersals.

On the far shore a little boy was making putt-putt engine sounds and guiding a bright yellow plastic boat through the water with a broken branch. His mother, bouncing on her toes to sooth the baby snuggled against her chest, supervised his every move—joys he would never know, should he fail to escape his comrades.

Abarque hated to leave, but soon it would be time to go to the college to check again for a message. Tossing the last of the popcorn over the water, he brushed off his pants and resumed his walk.

The school was dark except for the exterior lighting and a bare bulb outside the main office. The back of the school was completely shadowed; the exterior lights there were on a timer. He didn't know how to adjust the controls, so just before he left at the end of last night's shift he had removed the bulb over the rear door.

With practiced precision he paced out the distance to the stairwell. At exactly eight strides his toe struck the kick of the bottom step. In a similar fashion, he made his way through the building to room 102 and the computer terminal.

The glare of the screen forced him to cover his eyes for a moment. Squinting at the bright display, he logged in . . . and clasped his hands together while looking skyward. "Praise Allah." No new posts. It didn't mean he would sleep well tonight, but he was thankful for another day of life.

He still, however, had the second half of his task to accomplish. Abarque double-checked the hallway and headed to the industrial chemistry science lab. On the far wall of the room was a double locked storage locker. His master key opened one deadbolt lock, but the other required a non-copyable key that hung on a nail in the side panel of the top drawer of the school secretary's desk. It had to be signed out by an instructor, and the cupboard's inventory was verified regularly.

Abarque scooped a tablespoon of aluminum powder into a glass container he'd plucked from the recycling bin, and one of potassium chlorate into another. On the way back to the janitor's room, he detoured to the school office and quickly returned the key to Mrs. Harrison's hiding place.

• • •

Samir rubbed his eyes, then his grumbling stomach. He needed to eat.

Things were progressing very slowly. So far, he was only confident in the last four keystrokes—0810—of the code to decrypt the daily password. He groaned and stood up. In the kitchen, Fatima was standing at the stove stirring a pot.

"Fa, I'm starving."

"Eggplant, zucchini and tomato over farro."

"You went shopping without me?"

"I could not wait."

Samir cast an eye at the time on the stove, "Oh," then he sat down heavily at the kitchen table and rubbed his eyes vigorously.

"I have not seen you all day." Fatima dished out a generous portion, carefully wiping the drops from the edge of the plate. "Are you OK?"

"Oh, yes, just working hard."

"I hope the information I brought home was useful. People tell so much about themselves on social media. Are they not afraid of hackers?" She placed a steaming bowl on the table in front of him.

"Yes, thank you, I . . ." Samir paused. "*Of course.*"

He picked up his bowl and grabbed a spoon from the drawer before Fatima could set the table. "I must continue my work. Sorry, sister."

His stomach forgotten, he returned to his room and immediately opened a data dump of Wizner's Facebook account. And there it was: the names and birthdates of the man's sister and mother, one born in August, the other October—08, 10. Was the remainder of the key some combination of parts of their names, perhaps?

In the KeyAnalytics program, he refined the search with the additional information and sat back. He took a spoonful of his lunch, but too excited to eat he soon pushed the bowl aside. It was going to happen. Soon.

• • •

Mike rubbed at the depressions on the bridge of his nose. The standard issue binoculars were powerful, but heavy.

This time he had parked across the road from Spitwell's abode, in the entrance of an abandoned quarry. The overgrown shrubs were perfect for concealing his presence.

The lights were on in Spitwell's trailer. His truck was parked beside it, but only the nose was visible. The ramshackle structure attached to the side of the trailer hid the contents of the pickup bed.

At the third trailer in, about ten people were gathered around a fire circle with cases of beer parked at their feet. One man teetered away from the group, weaving around tree stumps then along the narrow gravel road between lots to deposit a box of cans and bottles in the trash with a reverberating crash and clatter.

None of the participants appeared to be Spitwell. It was already 6:45 p.m. If something was going to go down tonight, there should be activity soon.

As if he'd ordained it, a Ford 150 rounded the bend in the road and came to a gravel-crunching, dust-spewing stop in front of Spitwell's. From Mike's notes, this would be his second in command, Kevin Lowry. Spitwell must have been waiting because he was out the trailer door and into the passenger seat in less than ten seconds.

The truck did a fast 180 and headed out on the highway toward Tillson. Mike put away the binoculars, waited ten seconds, and followed.

DAY FIVE

Sunday
July 1, 2018

CHAPTER 18

Jenny, her head propped on one elbow, watched Mike's relaxed face as he slept. He was still handsome and desirable, even with early etchings of worry lines around his eyes. He was a keeper. Her keeper. She smiled.

A few minutes earlier she had awakened from a dream that one of their Sunday morning lovemakings had created a baby. The dream had carried on as they moved into a new house with a gorgeous kitchen, a huge craft room for her hobbies and a yard big enough to grow flowers for arrangements and lettuce and tomatoes for BLT sandwiches. The lingering aroma of fresh homemade bread left her feeling happy and hopeful, even after she was wide awake.

She kissed him softly. "Good morning, sleepyhead. It's after ten."

He blinked and murmured, "Hmm, nice."

Man, he was cute, but she felt restless. "Come on, the day's a wastin'."

"Just a few more minutes, hon. It was a long night."

"I know, it was after three when you got home. Sorry I couldn't stay awake last night. I really did myself in at the gym while you were at work. Did you catch the bad guys?"

"Nope, I just followed this guy to every bar in town until I was sure that nothing was going down."

"That's it. An epic bar hop."

Mike raised himself on one elbow and poked her on the arm. "Hey, I got a list of the license plate numbers of all the guy's buddies. I can run them through the computer tomorrow. Besides, I had to make sure that it wasn't a trick."

Jenny jabbed Mike playfully on the chest with the tip of a finger. "What kind of trick?"

"Can't say." Then he plopped back down onto his pillow. "I'm beat."

"I'll go make us some coffee." Jenny sat up beside him and ran her fingers through his hair. "I've been thinking about Fatima and Samir and . . ."

Stretching his arms above his head, Mike groaned softly. "Slow down. Give me a chance to wake up."

"Fair enough." She kissed his forehead, then stood and slipped on her dressing gown.

Minutes later, Jenny returned with two steaming mugs. Snuggling back in beside her husband, she ran a finger down the length of his nose. "As I was saying, I've been thinking."

"Them . . . still?" Mike shook his head and took a sip of his coffee. "Sorry, hon, I think they're pretty naturalized. They've been in the country more than half their lives, and there's nothing suspicious on file."

"OK." Jenny nodded absent-mindedly, lost in her thoughts. "Wiz."

"Wiz what?"

"Sorry, just talking to myself. The guy Fatima is listening to. I wonder what about him is of interest to her?"

"His rugged good looks? She said he was her new boyfriend." Mike reached up and brought Jenny closer for a kiss.

Oh, you devil. You sure know how to distract me. Jenny melted into his arms.

· · ·

Chuck Schelmer ran his hand across the bedsheets, searching for Heidi. As he slowly regained consciousness, he could hear the kids in the kitchen ordering up the number of pancakes they could eat, in multiples of ten.

Reaching for the glass of water on the bedside table, the pain in his shoulder made him wince. The extra shifts were taking a toll on his body. When the company HMO put him on modified duties last year he had lied his way back to full-time, but now he was paying the price.

He took a sip of water and lay back again, staring at the ceiling. Normally, the stress of their financial problems made his sleep restless, but worrying about what he had done for Spitwell had turned restless sleep into full-blown insomnia. He'd probably only caught three hours, max.

Through the curtains the weather looked clear and sunny, good for the corn crop. It also meant a few guys would call in sick and he could pick up an afternoon shift. Getting a little more sleep would be nice before the supervisor called. He rolled onto his other side and caught sight of his cellphone. The display was blinking: one missed call, unidentified caller. He pulled the pillow over his head and moaned. It was probably the cops, or worse, the FBI. *How am I going to get out of this mess?*

· · ·

Fatima liked Sundays. Samir was not as grouchy as he was on workdays when he arose before dawn, and often he would sleep in and she could experience a morning of forbidden joy watching the Shopping Channel. Cries for help from Samir's bedroom occasionally interrupted her entertainment, but she knew better than to try to awaken or comfort him. His room was like sacred ground that only he could walk upon.

She turned up the volume. It was always the same. He'd never spoken to her of the details, but witnessing the death of their father must have been a horrible thing. A baby at the time, Fatima was spared his anguish, but she knew that it was the foundation of his hatred for everything American.

Separated from Samir at such a young age, she'd grown up knowing little of her brother other than his name. From the first moment that they were reunited in Kenya, she'd sensed the differences between them.

Time and distance were not the only divide. Samir's soul inhabited a dark place, forged not only by death, but also by his life as an orphan forced to find shelter in rubble. He'd learned to trust no one and grew up loving nobody, except maybe that delinquent, Hamid. She'd never trusted that beady-eyed boy—he'd take food from your bowl without blinking.

In contrast to Samir's suffering, Fatima's life had been much easier. Her aunt had fed her bottles of goat's milk and bowls of mushy rice while her brother ate other people's garbage.

But she was old enough to remember the chaos after the Americans left Somalia and the day that the United Nations declared her country a failed state. When various Islamic militias failed to make things better, the Americans had come back. Under the guise of providing humanitarian aid, they'd waged their destructive war—she later learned that it had more to do with countering the Russians' growing influence in the Horn of Africa than any peacekeeping. Eventually, after the night her aunt mysteriously disappeared, she too was shipped away to a refugee camp.

Although they shared the same resentment about America, Samir was such a bitter person it was difficult to be around him. During their time in the refugee camp, she had avoided him and Hamid as much as possible. They were only forced back together as brother and sister by the adoption agency.

Trying to distract herself from the painful memories, Fatima turned up the volume even more. Her love of the Shopping Channel was an addiction acquired during their life in California with their adoptive parents, Marjorie and Jack Smith. She and 'Mom' had spent hours ogling the cheap jewelry and clothes, though they rarely bought anything. She missed Marj. Since moving to Tillson, Samir had forbidden any contact.

The aging parquet floor squeaked behind her.

"What are you doing?" Samir's voice was hard. "Turn that materialistic propaganda off."

"There is nothing wrong with looking."

"You have become too obsessed with the worldly life. The Smiths corrupted you. You took their bribes."

"Oh, come on, Samir, you also took everything they offered. Do you really think that ridiculing them behind their backs rights the wrong?" She started to wave her finger but stopped. This was dangerous ground with Samir.

"It is important to respect the teachings. All things are owned by Allah."

"Your morals weren't high enough to prevent you from helping your fellow students cheat by doing homework for them, for a price."

"All my money is for Allah's use."

"You hypocrite. You ruined high school for me! You controlled me like a father. It was fine for you. While you made me wear a hijab and clothes so baggy they could be mistaken for tents, you wore blue jeans and went to parties."

"It was right to keep you away from that clique of scantily clad girls. Besides, your social failings had more to do with your shyness and bad English than fashion." Samir clicked off the TV. "Anyway, remember, we had some good times."

"Maybe, but you never helped me with my English or my schoolwork. You always spoke Somali to me. Oh, that's right. Samir, so brilliant, science and math teachers falling at your feet and scholarships thrown at you. You forbade me to socialize, bossed me around then you went off to MIT and left me holed up in my room with no friends."

"Yes, but it was me that took you away from that and brought you here. It was me that helped you get a job."

"I had a good job helping the new refugees from the homeland."

"All that did was give you scabies and ruin your English. I taught you about computers."

"To serve your own purposes."

"Allah's purpose."

Fatima groaned. The argument was ending the same way it always did.

Samir knelt beside her chair. "Are you not still a believer? Am I not still your flesh and blood?"

"Of course."

"Then you must continue to help me."

"But I'm scared."

Samir stroked her hand as he spoke.

"Don't worry, my dear sister. It will be over soon." Slipping an arm around her, he hugged her briefly. "I love you. I must go and pray now."

After he left, Fatima went to the kitchen to make tea. The conversation had upset her, but she very much loved her older brother. It wasn't just for the teachings in the Quran that he would defend her to the death. She had no doubt that he loved her back. And he hadn't always been so grumpy. When he wanted to be, he was funny, hilarious even. Many times, back in high school, she almost peed her pants when he imitated the dull drawl of teachers and idiotic antics of their fellow students. But she couldn't remember the last time he'd told a joke.

She had missed his company while he was away at MIT. Zealous about his work, Samir had rarely made contact and did not return to the Smiths' until he graduated. And when he did, it was life changing.

He'd only been home a day when he burst into her bedroom.

"Gazzel is hiring. In Tillson, Oregon. They provide on-the-job education and training. It would be a fantastic opportunity. We could go together."

She'd agreed—her life certainly wasn't going anywhere living at home. But the transition had not been easy. The hiring window at Gazzel was temporarily closed when they arrived, so Samir drove a BurBur Car to support them. Money was tight, but living with her domineering older brother was easier than she thought it would be at first. His attitude toward a woman's place in society appeared to be shifting forward by a century. Although he was more than content that she stay at home to perform all the menial tasks, every evening after supper he taught her about technology.

It was fifteen months ago when Gazzel introduced their new product, the digital home assistant Alexandria, that she began to suspect that Samir's eagerness to advance her education was solely because it was to his advantage to do so.

When the hiring notices for the device's support team appeared, Samir meticulously prepped her for the interviews. He even allowed her to buy some new, more modern clothes, though he insisted on the same drab colors and a headscarf.

It was ironic that Samir's dedication to his purpose also served to weaken his grip on her. Winning the job at Gazzel had filled her with pride and self-confidence. She'd embraced the opportunity and worked hard to prove her worth to the company. It was also her first glimpse of a different life for herself. A more liberated life, filled with the promise of becoming the person she'd hoped to be but had never dreamed was possible. That promise was spoiled shortly after she started the job, when Samir asked her to spy.

She had reached a compromise with herself. When she finished this last thing Samir had asked, she would go no further and would spy no more. She would build a new life for herself here in America, a life of honesty and dedication—not to revenge, but to healing.

Hearing the apartment door close behind her brother, Fatima clicked on the TV to savor the images of jewelry, shoes and dresses in peace.

• • •

The large Isgani mosque on the edge of town was bursting with the faithful this morning. Despite being surrounded by fellow believers, Hamid and

Samir could not risk conversing as they knelt on their mats. There could be informants, even here, so only after prayers did they separate themselves from the rest of the congregation and move toward the small resource center on the edge of the room.

"Do we proceed?" Hamid whispered as he thumbed the pages of a book.

Samir nodded and selected a thick picture book of historic religious sites. "Yes, are you ready for your part?"

"I have been for a long time."

"True, and I am thankful you canceled your plan, my friend, because for mine I need you alive, in position and ready on my command Tuesday night."

"Of course."

"The rest of the new men understand the importance of their roles?"

"Most definitely and they are eager." Hamid could not keep the irritation out of his voice.

"Good, now we must pray to Allah that all goes well."

"Yes of course, brother. But what is the new part of the plan?"

Hamid's eyes opened wide as Samir explained.

"This is good," he said.

After Samir clarified the final details, he embraced Hamid. "Already we are blessed with the weather we prayed for, heavy rain for two days and then clear with a good wind from the north on Wednesday."

"Praise Allah."

"The next time you hear from me will be the command to execute."

"Understood, my friend," replied Hamid, closing the book before melting into the crowd by the exit.

CHAPTER 19

Heidi cast an eye across the hazy sky. It was only late morning and already the air was sticky and wet, the thermometer pushing 84 degrees. This kind of weather worried her. The humid air trapped pollution and pollen, and the heat irritated airways, making them spasm. All this would make it harder for Becky to breathe—plus, the body used more oxygen working to stay cool. When she was fighting a lung infection, cool, dry air was a necessity. Unfortunately, their home air conditioning system had a small leak and was losing pressure in the coolant loop. A new compressor filled with modern, environmentally friendly refrigerant was nothing they could afford right now.

Yesterday afternoon, after several weeks of being housebound for calving season, she and Chuck had promised the kids a fun outing to celebrate the last birth and the end of school. But Becky needed air conditioning, not a water park.

She looked at Tim and Pete, already dressed in their bathing suits, and sighed. At the last minute Chuck had taken a double shift at the plant, so once again she would have to be the one to disappointment them.

She racked her brain for an alternative to the wave and slide park, and finally decided on the West Creekside shopping mall. It wasn't far and it was air-conditioned.

"Hey guys. How about mini-putt at the mall and then super-duper ice cream cones?"

Pete sprouted an enormous pout and plopped down on the floor, pulling his towel over his head. On the verge of tears, Tim's voice quivered.

"But you said we were going to the water park."

He clearly knew the change of plans was because of his sister's condition. Speaking to the floor, his voice was barely audible. "I wish she was dead already."

"You do not and you know it! Any more nonsense like that and we aren't going anywhere. Now get changed."

Tim stood his ground. "I want to go swimming."

"I know, honey, but it's too hot and muggy today for Becky. Besides, I think it would be more fun at the mall." She lowered herself to look into his eyes, gently cupping his cheeks with her hands to make him hold still.

Tim pulled away, refusing to look at her. "Why can't Dad take me and Pete?"

"He has to work."

"That's all he ever does!"

Becky stifled a cough and leaned against the kitchen wall. She knew better than to intervene. There was nothing she could say that would take away Tim's resentment of her.

"Sounds great, Mom." Her voice was squeaky with phlegm.

Seeking some small victory, Tim asked, "Can we at least see the new Star Wars movie afterwards?"

"We'll see. Becky may need an extra lung treatment later this afternoon."

Tim's expression firmed into fury, and he stomped away into his room.

• • •

Hamid wasted no time riding his bicycle directly from the prayer session to the Safe Place storage facility. Heeding Mr. Ashton's warning, he couldn't risk the company van being seen out on a Sunday, let alone at the mosque. The last thing he needed now was for the boss to make him hand over the keys.

There was no security guard at Safe Place, just a keyless lock and video cameras. Careful to shield his face from view, he entered the code, then locked his bike to the chain-link fence and walked to the back of the lot.

Everything in dingy, eight-by-eight-foot unit 56 was as he had left it a year ago, albeit dustier. The open boxes still overflowed with the household junk that he had bought at garage sales. Old pots and pans, TV sets, lamps with dented shades, cassette tapes—it didn't matter, it was all crap. He didn't care if any of it worked or not; it just had to look like the stuff people normally put in storage. Behind the front row of boxes and under a stack of folding chairs were two trunks, the only valuable objects in the collection.

It took him several minutes to clear enough space to drag the larger one forward. Transported halfway around the world, the case was battered, the padlock fussy and the key bent. The combination of frustration and nerves made him break into a sweat as he coaxed the lock and key to cooperate.

Finally, the lid popped open, revealing a top tray filled with musty newspapers and photographs of some unknown family. They looked Russian, or maybe from one of its previous republics like Kazakhstan. He didn't care. The larger, bottom portion of the trunk appeared to be filled with blankets and sheets, but under a false door was the weapon that had nearly cost him his life and all his money.

Reassured, Hamid closed the case. Its assembly would have to wait until he had his tools. Now he turned his attention to the smaller container, which held an impressive cache of arms. From his pocket he removed a cloth and a can of gun oil to start the cleaning ritual that all warriors performed before battle. It had disappointed him not to have done this yesterday morning in preparation for the stadium attack that *he* had planned, but Samir had been right. What they were about to do now would be so much better.

There were fewer guns to prepare now that there would be just four fighters, so he took his time, relishing the aroma of the oil and the feel of the cold steel in his hand. In one packsack he placed assorted supplies and in another a cache of grenades.

When he got home, he would alert his warriors that a different kind of party was a go.

• • •

Side by side on the couch, Mike and Jenny lounged, each hidden behind a section of the *New York Times*. A leisurely perusal of the enormous Sunday addition was a ritual they relished as a respite from the hectic pace of the workweek.

"Look, Mike, here's a three-bedroom on two acres in Stone Ridge with a granny suite."

"Which granny?"

"For the last time, my mom is all alone and would be great with kids. Your mother still thinks I'm the bimbo cheerleader who'll never be good enough for her only son."

Mike's work phone hummed, vibrating across the coffee table.

"Saved by the bell."

He picked up. "Longstrum."

Jenny tossed down her newspaper with a derisive snort and went to the kitchen to search for brunch items. She sometimes worried she would never get entirely used to the constant interruption in their lives. She knew that Mike would be a great father, but he would have to learn to make the time.

The phone conversation was brief. She heard the paper rustle as he stood up from the couch and left the living room. When she peeked around the corner, Mike was in the bedroom throwing on clothes like a firefighter about to miss the ladder truck.

"What's up?"

"The case I'm working." He strapped on his holster. "There's been an anonymous tip."

CHAPTER 20

Mike hesitated before knocking on Dan Smithers's office door. It was partially open and the man's voice was booming out over the empty department.

"Yes today. Yes now!"

The phone slammed down.

"Boss?"

"Get your ass in here."

"What is it?"

"Well, we might have caught the break we need. A call from a pay-as-you-go cellphone saying Spitwell bought materials for a bomb."

"Well, not last night he didn't, and this morning he'd be too hungover to make much more than a Bloody Mary."

Smithers gave him a quizzical look.

"I mean . . . we know the attack was called off, so he could be biding his time."

"So you're fairly certain he'll be at home and alone." Dan smirked.

Mike looked away. "Yes."

"Regardless, it's time we bring him in. I just got off the phone for a search warrant. By the time the Tac team is ready, it should be here."

"Not taking any chances."

"It could be a trap. You know how these guys like using government agents for target practice. Don't worry, Mike, this is still your baby."

Less than an hour later, Mike was peering once again at Spitwell's ramshackle trailer, the grime coating its yellowed siding much more apparent in daylight. From his vantage point in the bushes, everything appeared quiet. The blinds were down. The man was likely watching a ballgame and nursing his hangover.

Around him, the tactical team was deploying. Their leader, Julie Peters, rarely said much; she didn't have to. Mike admired her professionalism as she positioned her personnel with hand signals and terse one-or-two-word commands issued through her headset.

Four squad members on the far side of the trailer were in containment positions. At the rear, two men were crawling forward, slithering around piles of junk and stumps of felled pine trees.

At the same time, the three-person main approach team led by Peters edged forward to their launch point. Unfortunately, the terrain and the position of other trailers dictated that the final charge would be risky—across a fifty-yard stretch with absolutely no cover.

When Peters raised a clenched fist, Mike inhaled and held his breath. They waited. Nothing would happen until the main team lobbed a stun grenade through the trailer's rear window.

Beside him, Dan Smithers drew his gun. "You ready?"

Mike followed suit and nodded.

"This is what it's all about."

The crack of a rifle and following crash of breaking glass shattered the quiet. The front window of the trailer exploded, sending brilliant shards flying outward. Spitwell had fired the first shot.

A terrible moaning sound came from the primary assault team. One agent was down. Stretched flat on her stomach, Peters crawled toward the downed officer while triggering her comm headset.

"Medic up. Upper chest wound. Conscious." Peters's staccato voice blared in all their earpieces.

The instant the medic arrived to apply a compress, Peters logrolled behind a large boulder at the corner of the overgrown rock garden out front of the trailer next to Spitwell's. Calmly, she rested the barrel of her rifle on the railroad-tie retaining wall and sighted through the scope. Her weapon recoiled twice. The return fire was immediate and sent a shower of stone chips rattling off her eye shield, forcing her to take cover.

More automatic weapon fire rang out from the trailer. The tree branches over the head of the medic dragging his teammate to safety exploded, showering them with splinters of wood and bark.

"They need help. Let's go."

Smithers sprinted across the gravel road and took cover behind the trunk of an immense pine tree. Mike followed in a zigzag pattern and squatted beside Smithers.

Smithers was panting. "Whew, haven't done that in a while. Mike, you spend more time on the range. Can you get a shot?"

"Not from here." Mike scampered forward toward the garbage station. He hurled himself to the ground behind the concrete base supporting the large metal bins, steadied his revolver and aimed into the middle of the unbroken section of the trailer's front window.

Before he could fire, a loud pop erupted from the trailer and the remaining windows shattered. He recoiled as the stun grenade propelled jets of smoke and debris horizontally through every opening. On the far side of the trailer there came a crash followed by the crunch and screech of tearing metal as the Tac team breached the side door.

Mike dashed the final distance forward. Still cautious, he crouched below the trailer's front windows, but there were no more shots. He slipped around the corner to the trailer's threshold; he couldn't see through the fog of dust and smoke, but sounds of a vicious struggle could be heard from deeper inside.

"Keep him alive!"

The rear ends of two Tac team members knocked Mike backward as they dragged Spitwell's limp form down the single step to the ground before dropping him with a dull thud. Blood oozed from the man's ears and nose, and a lengthy laceration spread down from his lower lip to his chin.

Mike kneeled and checked Spitwell's carotid artery to reassure himself that the man was still alive. Eager to secure the evidence of bomb components, he edged along the side of the truck into the attached shed.

"Stop!" Dan grabbed Mike's arm. "It could be booby-trapped. Let the bomb squad handle this."

CHAPTER 21

To help clear his head, Mike took the stairs from the interrogation room to the office level. After pleading with the doctors to secure Spitwell's release from medical care and enduring hours of the man's contempt during interrogation, he felt drained. At Smithers's door, he didn't bother knocking. Dan looked up from his work, coffee cup pressed to his lips.

"You've been going for hours. Is he talking?"

Mike slumped in the padded chair across from his boss. "Not yet."

"Well, he's not going anywhere. The associate DA has already filed the charges, attempted murder of a federal agent."

"But not the bomb? Come on, the dogs went crazy. The empty nitromethane containers, plus the amount of nitrogen the informant said he bought—he has all the makings of a good-sized bang."

"It's just the informant's word. Without proof of purchase, there's nowhere to start looking." Dan pulled a small stack of paper from the laser printer behind him and started initialing and signing them. "The trouble is, without the nitrogen and a detonator, it isn't a bomb yet. Does anything check out?"

"He claims the fertilizer is for growing some pot and the nitromethane is for the drag racer he's part owner of. He says the nitrogen is stored at his grow-op, which is hidden in the woods, but he isn't going to tell us where."

"He's got all the answers, doesn't he? So basically, we're screwed."

"Not yet. We'll have the results from explosives' swabs in the morning."

"Yeah." Smithers gave a forced smile. "OK, Mike, take another go at him then let's call it a night. Nice work identifying the newest members of the Lone Stars. They talking?"

"Nope. How are the guys from the Tac team doing?"

"One's home from hospital with bruises and a broken tooth. The other came out of surgery an hour ago and is doing fine."

Mike downed his coffee and took a quick look at his watch. "I need to wrap this up. Jenny will be having a bird."

Mike took his seat at the table in the interrogation room. Despite the cuts and bruises covering most of his face, Spitwell smirked defiantly at him. Mike made a show of arranging his papers and switching on the tape recorder. He kept his voice calm and reasonable.

"Again, tell me why a man who calls himself the leader of the Lone Stars, a known white supremacist organization, and has the makings for a bomb in the back of his shed, isn't at all suspicious."

Squinting his swollen eyes into narrow slits, Spitwell curled his upper lip and looked up at the ceiling. "Where's my lawyer?"

"It's Sunday. I'm sure he is on his way, but you're not walking."

"It don't matter." Spitwell tried to raise a fist, but the cuffs chained to the table brought him up short with a jerk. He locked eyes with Mike, his voice calmer. "My boys are quite capable of carrying on the good work all on their own. You can't stop us now."

Got you. Mike raised an eyebrow. "Stop what, exactly?"

"Lots of shit," Spitwell smiled slyly, "to express our God-given freedom." He winked slowly. "You know, by growin' a little weed."

"Well, your boys have all been brought in for questioning." Mike paused. Spitwell's left eye twitched. "That's right. Even the newbies. Randy Newell, Tyler Smith."

Spitwell snorted. "They won't talk."

"Hmm, the kid who can barely grow a moustache? Adam? He seems ready. So why don't you take control of your own destiny here?"

"I ain't going to say another word."

• • •

Under the cover of darkness, Abarque entered the back of the college. Unable to sleep the night before, he had spent the day dozing and reading from the Quran, but he still felt strangely groggy. Slowly, he counted the last steps along the unlit school corridor to room 102 and slid his hand downwards. Feeling for and then finding the lock, he inserted the key.

Skirting the desks, he once again entered the side room. The computer sat on its desk like a tombstone. A deep sense of foreboding came over him as he sat down, his heartbeat a fast warning. He wanted to run, to take care of Jamilla, but the commandments of Allah swam in his mind. He tensed his hands into claws and dragged his nails deeply up his thighs, inhaling slowly through clenched teeth. He reached for the keyboard.

The brightness of the screen made him blink, but the message was clear, black letters stark on white neon. The party was Tuesday night.

DAY SIX

Monday
July 2, 2018

CHAPTER 22

When he pulled off his headset, the silence was a panacea to Billy's overloaded ears, long past fatigued from the frenzied soundtrack of explosions and missile fire. He loved the stillness of this time of night. There were just a few hours left before dawn, and a fridge raid before bedtime seemed wise.

Returning to his room with a banana and a chocolate yogurt, he sat down at his computer and switched to the dark net.

"Oh, shit."

He wiped the brown spittle of yogurt off the keyboard with his sleeve.

It hadn't taken long for the bad guys to regroup. He shook his head, reading aloud.

"Stag night. Tuesday. Usual bar on General Standford. 8:00 p.m. start."

Again, there was the reference to Standford. This was unquestionably local shit. The target had to be the Tillson mosque, the giant one on the edge of town.

Hopefully, Billy had earned the trust of his contact at the FBI. A quick email to alert them that something was going down tomorrow night would have to suffice. First thing tomorrow he would send all the collaborating data, but right now, he needed to sleep.

• • •

It was before dawn in Hastings, Idaho. At the Padari Cabral Bakery, Farzaad Nuur inhaled deeply, savoring the aromas wafting from the oven. Never would he grow tired of this smell.

In Kabul, he and his family had been fortunate; their small bakery had occupied a prime location on a bustling street. At first, Farzaad had hated the hours—the demanding early morning business meant rising in the middle of the night to fire the ovens—but with time he learned to relish the quiet solitude of working when most people were asleep. His father had slowly taught him their trade, one that had been passed down from generation to generation.

That seemed a long time ago now. After his parents died, life was tough, but despite his youth, he had learned to run the shop by himself. His work ethic allowed him to survive and support his younger brother, Mouri.

By the grace of the United Nations education initiative, Mouri had been able to complete the first two years of an engineering technician diploma under the tutelage of a German-trained chemical engineer. Farzaad always knew that his brother was intelligent, but it surprised him that despite spending most of his time in cafés instead of going to class, Mouri received very high grades.

Then two bombs changed their lives forever.

The first destroyed Mouri's school located near the diplomatic zone in Kabul. Luckily, Mouri had been sipping coffee at his favorite haunt at the time. The school never resumed operation.

The second explosion occurred shortly after. One afternoon, a wired car directed at a diplomatic convoy detonated near the bakery. During the resulting street battle, American heavy arms fire destroyed the shop completely.

Farzaad had distributed the baking supplies to the needy and left Kabul, taking Mouri with him. Like most Afghans, he had no love for the Taliban, but growing up in the nightmare that was his country, he despised the foreign invaders more. Especially the Americans. The loss of the bakery had been the last straw in a long line of grievances, and he knew it was time to fight back.

It hadn't taken much to convince his impressionable younger brother to join the fight in the name of Islam, though Mouri remained irreverent. Farzaad could never be sure whether his little brother had agreed because he truly believed in the cause, or merely out of his desire for adventure.

In the years prior to their arrival in America, they had traveled with jihadists across Iraq and Syria, but with the constant defeats of ISIS by American-assisted troops, the dream of an Islamic State was in jeopardy. Rather than die fighting in a pile of rubble, Farzaad decided it would be more impactful to attack the enemy directly. Tired of living in hardship, his brother had readily agreed.

When the brothers approached the elders with their request to leave the caliphate, they were not looked upon favorably. Farzaad had employed all the skills of persuasion he'd honed from years of up-selling bread to his customers. When he emphasized the brothers' powerful passion to become martyrs and their willingness to take the war to American soil, the leaders had finally accepted their idea and offered assistance.

Although eager to leave Syria, they couldn't risk fleeing as illegal refugees. It would be senseless to pledge their lives, only to wash up on the shores of Italy, drowned after capsizing on the Mediterranean.

Entry to America through legitimate channels would require undergoing intense scrutiny. Fortuitously, due to chaotic government situations in Iraq and Syria, the database used by the UN to perform the initial vetting of asylum seekers in the refugee camps was incomplete. Assuming a Syrian identity was relatively simple, but single male refugees would still raise suspicion. Fortunately, there were plenty of widows with children willing to escape by marrying a fellow emigrant. He and his brother quickly found suitable families.

When Portuguese baker Mr. Cabral, approaching retirement in Hastings, had begun searching for help in his store, he'd discovered that few young people in America were willing to work such exacting hours. Desperate to preserve his shop, he'd approached a local Baptist church that was sponsoring Syrian refugees. Farzaad's application fit Mr. Cabral's needs, so the church group sponsored him and Mouri, and their 'families'.

Mr. Cabral could not afford to hire them both. In gratitude for the community's support, Mouri volunteered as a caretaker for the church.

Arriving with nothing but a few suitcases, the brothers, their wives and their children settled into a furnished property provided by the parishioners. The two women and five children lived in the house while Farzaad and his brother slept in a makeshift room in the garage. The money from Farzaad's job at the bakery barely supported both families, but the community readily accepted them, and they often found food or boxes of used clothing left on their porch.

Shortly after their arrival, a man named Hamid made contact. Together the three men met several times to discuss various plans of revenge. Their last meeting had been more than a year earlier, but although the first flush of exhilaration had long faded, Farzaad had kept his faith in Allah, knowing that their time would come.

Thus, before leaving for work at 3:00 a.m. each day, Farzaad faithfully checked his onion. This was his little joke. He had always detested the smell and taste of the vegetable, but to enter the dark web it was necessary to use a search engine bearing its name. Yet, each day, nothing.

Patience was difficult for Farzaad, but keeping Mouri occupied was even harder. Trained in the streets of Kabul, his brother's chief talent was sneaking in the back doors of shops and picking locks. But thievery was not a skill valued in America, and Mouri showed only passing interest in baking, and certainly no aptitude.

But this morning, the scent emanating from the oven smelled particularly sweet to Farzaad, because finally the call to action had come. The night before, the long-awaited invitation to the party had been posted on the correct site, verified by embedded code words. Assured that retribution was finally going to take place, Farzaad felt very calm inside. He trusted that Hamid and his compatriot from Somalia, Samir, would not be wasting his and his brother's talents on something less than impactful. Now, he and Mouri could make their sacrifice, for everyone who had died before them. This was their fate.

The timing was perfect. Traveling tomorrow and missing work on Tuesday night would raise no suspicions as Wednesday was the Fourth of July holiday.

As far as he knew, there was no watch-list for car rentals. They could easily drive the six hundred miles on Tuesday afternoon after work.

Farzaad slid the long tray of golden-brown buns out of the oven. They looked and smelled like perfection. Thanks be to Allah, he was good at whatever he chose to do, because tomorrow night he would need to be flawless.

He had no doubts about himself, but he couldn't help wondering if his brother would be up to the task. Most days, Mouri still acted like a teenager: out late, sleeping in and as conversational as a firebrick in the bread oven. He preferred the company of his cellphone.

Outside the window, the rays of sunlight starting to dapple the street prompted him to glance at his watch. Five thirty. Once again, his brother was late. Frustrated, Farzaad wiped the sweat from his brow with his apron and slid the next tray of buns onto the cooling rack.

"Greetings, brother."

The unexpected interruption made Farzaad jump.

"You are late."

Mouri appeared fully awake, which made him suspicious. What had he been up to all night?

"Where were you?"

"Bible studies."

"Your sinful ways will be the end of us." Farzaad tossed the hot metal tray in his hands onto the counter with a rattling clatter. "It is insane what you are doing. If the preacher catches you with his daughter, all of us will be run out of town."

"In the name of Allah, all of my sins will be forgiven in one glorious act. So I best collect as many possible." Mouri's face bore a roguish grin.

"That is a very wicked interpretation of the teachings. Well, it doesn't matter anymore. Very soon you will have your chance to redeem yourself."

Mouri blanched. "What do you mean?"

CHAPTER 23

It was barely light outside when Wendy unlocked the door to her office. She made a habit of getting to the office before six on Monday mornings, as she detested starting the workweek snowed under with paperwork.

Early hours were no hardship to her. Since the age of fourteen, she had risen early to run ten miles before most people were sipping their first coffee. Her dedication had made her a high school track star and garnered her a lucrative scholarship from the University of Iowa.

In the four years of her degree, Wendy failed to medal in any individual event on the track. As a member of the four-by-eight-hundred-meter foursome, however, she had captured gold at the national championships in her final year.

This Monday it was more important than usual to be ahead of things, as Wednesday was a statutory holiday. After a quick shower and breakfast, she had slow-jogged the short distance to the office. Exchanging her running shoes for heels with one hand, she tapped the keyboard of her computer with the other.

A red-flagged email sat at the top of her queue. TyrBus84 was concerned. Last night there had been a substantial up-tick in traffic on the same presumed white supremacy site as a few days ago. He'd concluded that there existed a high probability of an attack on a local mosque tomorrow night and promised to send more information soon.

Wendy paused. Her plate was full, but it was never too early to call an ambitious agent like Mike Longstrum.

• • •

Mike grabbed for his phone and silenced the ring as fast as possible to avoid waking Jenny.

"Longstrum."

The fog of sleep lifted quickly as he listened.

"Thanks, I'm on it." Rolling over in bed, he kissed Jenny. "Gotta go."

"But it's still dark."

"The bad guys might be on the move."

"What? You're strapping on the flak?"

"Yeah, explain later. I gotta get to the office and pick a team so I can be ready to roll if this lead pans out."

"Be safe." She reached for his wrist to pull him back to bed. "Will you have time to check out Samir and Fatima?"

Mike groaned. "Honey, I've got bigger fish to fry."

"You're exhausted. You're not going anywhere just yet."

"But—"

"It'll be worth your while."

Mike groaned, one leg already in his underwear as he hopped to the closet. "Sorry, babe. Next time."

• • •

Chuck held out a cup of steaming coffee for Heidi.

"Here you go, sleepyhead. Would you like bacon and eggs? I already made the kids some egg Mcmuffins."

Stifling a yawn, Heidi accepted the coffee.

"Not just yet. What's with the super dad and husband routine? You get fired?"

"Na, I just thought I'd get some things done around here. Besides, my shoulder's been bugging me."

"Sure, but as soon as Spitwell rings you'll be double-shifting again."

"He won't be calling for a while. At least I hope not."

"Why's that?"

"I heard he got into some trouble away from work." Chuck burped, a mouthful of acid reflux making him grimace. "Sorry, my stomach is a little upset."

"See, I told you that you need to relax." Heidi waved a finger at her husband and took a sip of coffee. "If it's true, good riddance. The man's a pig."

She slid out of bed and gave Chuck a hug.

"I sure can use the help. Becky needs extra chest treatments."

"I'll get the boys to help with chores."

"Good. How about two eggs over easy, no bacon?"

"Coming right up."

• • •

Fatima, feeling light, unburdened without the USB sticks, took the time to read the social events blog before she started on her customer files. A best ball golf tournament or a Trivial Pursuit pub night seemed too ambitious, but maybe she could try the monthly lunchtime BBQ next Friday. They must serve veggie burgers. She looked around. There was no soothing place for her eyes to rest on the beige fabric of her cubicle. Perhaps it was time to bring in some pictures.

It would be easy to fulfill the one small request Samir had asked of her this morning. During dinner last night her brother had been delightful, expressing his appreciation of everything that she had done for him. He was like the brother she dreamed of, full of jokes, eager to praise her. Perhaps they could turn a new page, once this plan of his was over.

Submerged in clearing the long list of customer problems that had accumulated over the weekend, Fatima was surprised when the morning break arrived. Today, without needing to constantly monitor Wizner, she could spend time actually being social. Gathering her snack bag and purse, she walked to Jenny's cubicle, only to see that she was not in today. Just as well, the woman made her nervous.

It was too early yet to answer the one question that Samir asked. There would be plenty of time when she returned to her computer to find out if Wizner had been well enough to return to work today.

• • •

Frustrated by Mike's dismissive attitude and resistance to amorous bribery, Jenny had lingered over her first coffee, contemplating what action she could take on her own. Deep in thought, she'd neglected to check the clock until it was already well past eight. *Dammit.* She was never late.

Despite her impatience to do something—anything—Jenny couldn't come up with any ideas. She might as well go to the office. Even though Mondays were always incredibly busy, with the computer power at her disposal perhaps she could figure out who Wiz was and why he was important. Plus, she could keep an eye on Fatima.

She arrived just at the end of first coffee break, in time to see Fatima and two other girls reentering the department together. Charlene and Debbie appeared to be listening intently as Fatima spoke. Then all three broke into giggles and shared a friendly laugh.

Charlene placed a hand on Fatima's arm as they parted ways. "Don't worry, girl, your English is just fine."

What was going on? Suddenly Fatima was Miss Socialite?

Jenny logged onto the status board. The team was on fire cleaning up the weekend backlog, but her smile soured when she saw that Fatima ranked first again. *Enough of that shit.* Jenny quickly selected the next incident report in the sequence and opened the file. She had to free up some time to work on her own project.

Her stomach was growling; she'd skipped breakfast to save time. She reached inside her bag for an apple. How ironic that she was the one eating in her cubicle now.

• • •

Fatima checked the time. Almost lunch; it seemed like a good time to check up on Wizner. Verifying she was unobserved, she opened his account, switched over to the diagnostics module and selected his Alexandria unit.

She chuckled. The log contained several real error codes. She opened an audio file that had been triggered on Saturday by a misunderstood command. No wonder, with the amount of nasal congestion in Wizner's voice. She could hear him on the phone telling someone, maybe his mother or girlfriend, that he felt weak, his cough was ripping out his lungs and he was worried he was dying. The only reason he wasn't nauseated and having diarrhea anymore was that he had stopped taking anything by mouth except copious amounts of water. Now, he was peeing up a storm. Yes, he knew that his father suffered from diabetes and yes, he was aware that it ran in the family. But wasn't he a bit young for that? The conversation ended with his promise to go to the emergency room if he felt worse.

Sunday evening he was definitely up and about; there was a lengthy error entry caused by his sneezing and coughing. This morning he had inquired about the local weather, the traffic and ordered his coffee. After seven thirty, no further recordings had been activated. He must have gone to work. Opening her desk drawer, Fatima reached into her purse and turned on her cellphone.

Company rules demanded that all personal devices be turned off during office hours. To make her call she needed some privacy, just for a few seconds. She removed her purse and lunch bag from her desk drawer. It would not seem unusual to leave for break a few minutes early to avoid the pre-meal rush at the washroom. A quick stall check verified that the room was empty.

Samir answered after one ring. "Yes?"

"Hello, brother. Dinner is in the fridge. Just reheat it in the microwave on full power."

"Thank you."

• • •

Before making his way to his own cubicle, Mike made up for his late arrival at work by heading directly to Wendy's office for a briefing.

The senior agent appeared snowed under behind the stacks of files on her desk. She handed him a printout without looking away from her computer screen. "I took a quick look at the material my guy sent. He compiled several years of communications on the site and matched it against known incidents. I agree with him that the tone of the latest messages suggests imminent activity. Likely tomorrow night, but I'll leave the final call up to you."

Mike nodded his thanks. Scanning the document as he walked, he made a quick stop at his computer and pulled up the upcoming events page on the Isgani mosque website. Downing his remaining coffee in two big gulps, he headed to Dan Smithers's office.

"Hey, boss, got a minute?"

"Sure." Smithers waved a sheet of paper then slid it across the desk toward Mike. "I just got a prelim on local nitrogen sales. Nothing from J&J Farm, but Mission Hill reports a large one to a local farmer."

"It's a bit late in the season isn't it? The crops are in the ground. We better check this guy out."

Smithers nodded and indicated the chair. "What you got?"

"I think the Lone Stars are planning an attack on the Isgani mosque just outside of town in Wasin County."

"How's that?"

"Wendy received another alert about the white supremacist website. It appears to be a call to action tomorrow night at the same hour the mosque is hosting a guest speaker. The timing is right. It must have been posted by Spitwell's lieutenant, Kevin Lowry, right after we released the gang yesterday."

"IT hasn't broken into Spitwell's computer yet, so we haven't directly linked him and his followers to that website." Smithers leaned back in his chair and crossed his arms across his chest. "How are you so sure that it's local?"

"The message refers to a local bar on General Standford Street. There aren't too many of those around."

Dan nodded agreement. "OK, who's the speaker?"

"Some bigwig imam from New York."

"I guess it all fits." Smithers rubbed his hand along his chin as he thought. "Yeah, and these guys may think this is a great way to start off the Fourth of July celebrations."

"Wouldn't they just." Mike could feel his pulse beginning to bound. "We could bring the Lone Stars back in for another round of questioning."

Smithers shook his head. "We have nothing on 'em. And the problem is, that after the false alarm Saturday and now two casualties, I'm not sure the regional brass will go for anything without something more substantial."

Mike's anger surged. "Saturday wasn't a false alarm, I—we prevented a—"

"That's not the way they see it." Smithers shrugged, pushed up the glasses on his nose and resumed working.

Mike stood. He hesitated for a moment, then placed his hands on Smithers's desk and leaned forward. "OK, so we keep it quiet, in-house. Since we have the drop on the bad guys, we can keep this small, just our team, no Tac squad."

"What are you thinking?" Smithers looked up, slipping off his readers.

"Surveillance ASAP and a stakeout team, just for Tuesday evening."

Smithers chewed vigorously on the arm of his glasses for a moment. He closed his eyes, leaned back in his chair and stretched his arms over his head. When he rocked forward, he landed his forearms on his desk with a thud. "OK, go with it, catch them in the act. You gotta play outside the sandbox now and then. But for Christ's sake, keep it clean, no collaterals."

"Yes, sir, but I'll need some help."

"Yeah, sure, I'll free up a few warm bodies for you, but it's going take me a bit to organize."

On his way back to his workstation, Mike grabbed a coffee from the machine in the hall. Reentering the main office, Tula called him over, holding out a pink message slip.

Mike reached for it absentmindedly, immersed in thought. "Thanks."

Tula smiled and maintained her grip on the paper. "Anytime."

Mike nodded at Tula's playful smile while reading the note pinched between her long, red fingernails. "Excellent!"

Tula lifted her eyebrows in surprise and beamed.

"Tell lockup I'm coming down."

"Anything else?" Tula stood and pulled the hem of her sweater down firmly.

"Tell Dan I'm going to put the heat on Spitwell."

Mike strode away without noticing the warm flush enveloping Tula.

CHAPTER 24

Wizner opened his office door one-handed, juggling a large coffee as he struggled to prevent his packsack from slipping off his arm. It irritated him to be late for work. The doctor's appointment this morning had proved a complete waste of time. He'd fully believed he was going to die Saturday afternoon and made an online booking through the HMO. But by Sunday he felt mostly recovered but kept the appointment—it could be the start of something serious, after all.

The doctor, in his usual condescending manner, dismissed his concerns about diabetes with a protracted sigh. "You had the flu. Seems like you're on the road to recovery. There is no sugar showing on the urine dipstick test, so you don't have diabetes. Do you need a note for work?"

"No need, I'm management now," he'd retorted tersely, irritated at the dismissal. "What about all the peeing? Maybe I have Conn's syndrome, you know, brought on by the virus."

"OK!" The doctor threw up his arms. "As far as I know, there's no such thing as virally induced Conn's, but just to ease your mind—"

He typed something quickly and ripped a lab requisition off the printer, almost throwing it at Wizner. "This is for a hemoglobin A1c test for diabetes and a set of electrolytes. You can head to the lab on your way out. You don't need to be fasting."

Already way behind schedule, Wizner grabbed the prescription but hadn't bothered with the blood test.

While he waited for his computer to fire up, he fished out the second of the three lanyards he was required to wear in addition to his security pass, a double-sided plastic card that covered the key points of the plant's safety and emergency action plan. Wearing two was burden enough, so he normally left the third in his desk drawer. Besides, now that he was management, he rarely used the red dongle.

The company logo finally disappeared from his computer screen and the bane of all management staff popped up: the list of the day's meetings. Kicking off the festivities was a system review in ten minutes. Tomorrow was just as crazy—performance evaluations, monthly budget assessments and in the middle of it all, a visitor appointment at ten. Who was Dr. Samir Khalif? He didn't recall having OK'd the meeting, but apparently he had. The software had automatically inserted the meeting date and time into his calendar from an email he'd sent last Thursday. In his in-box was a notice that security had approved a visitor pass for Dr. Khalif. He shook his head. He must have done it while he was delirious with fever.

• • •

Without moving a muscle, Mike stared at Spitwell across the table. He counted slowly to sixty and then switched on the tape recorder. "Ten thirty, July second, 2018. Agent Mike Longstrum interview with Maxwell Spitwell."

"It's just getting worse for you, Max, so how about you make it easy on yourself and tell us about the bomb. I'm sure the DA would take your cooperation into account."

"What fucking bomb?"

Mike placed the sheet of chemical analysis in front of Spitwell. "We found dynamite residue in your shed."

Ignoring the paper, Spitwell snorted derisively. "Yeah, yeah. My son lifted four sticks from the ski patrol's avalanche control stash, up at Big Valley Resort. Hid it in my shed. When I found out, I told him to get rid of it."

"What'd he want it for?"

Spitwell leaned back in his chair, shaking his head in disbelief. "Whatdaya think?" He chuckled. "To blow up shit."

"What exactly?"

"He and his buds make YouTube vids. Hear ya can make a good buck. Crazy fucking world."

"We know you're planning something tomorrow night. We've got eyes on your dark web blog."

"The darkie web. They taken that over too?" Spitwell's laugh turned into a chesty cough. "Can't you see I need a smoke, man?"

Mike crossed his arms across his chest and shook his head. "Cut the shit. You know what I'm talking about."

"Hey, Mr. Federal Agent, don't get all uppity with me. I pay my taxes. It's my hard-earned money that pays the likes of you. For what? So you can protect everybody else but the men and women who built this country?"

"I'm here to protect what is American: freedom, liberty—"

"Spare me." Spitwell held up a hand. "Speaking of freedom, I haven't seen my lawyer yet."

"He's on the docket to see you at ten."

Spitwell suppressed another coughing fit then swallowed several times. When he spoke, tears welled in his eyes and his voice was a gravelly rumble. "Can a guy at least get a drink of water?"

"In a minute. We know you're going to attack the Isgani mosque."

Spitwell cleared his throat loudly, then cast an eye about for a place to spit, but seeing none, he turned back to face Mike. With a taunting smirk, he opened his mouth slightly with a glob of yellow phlegm on the tip of his tongue and made a spitting motion.

"Nice." Mike kept his face calm. "Family trait?"

After a moment of tense silence, Spitwell swallowed exaggeratedly, then laughed. "A visit to the mosque, sounds good, real good. A few rounds from a AR-15 will teach those fuckers they can't take over the world."

"Strong words. Why don't you tell me everything right now, otherwise we'll deal with your brothers on Tuesday night, and it won't be pretty."

"You ain't got shit, so go fuck yourself." Another round of coughing bent the man in half.

Mike shoved a bottle of water across the table. "No, you're fucked."

CHAPTER 25

Mike drove the black SUV to the front of the Isgani mosque and parked beside the only other vehicle in the lot, a battered station wagon. A gentle slope covered with natural vegetation overlooked the front of the building and parking lot. On foot, he took a quick peek around the back and found a landscape of giant slabs of rock scattered among scrub and evergreen trees. There was only a single solid-looking fire door set in the rear wall. He nodded to himself. There would be sufficient cover for his team.

Returning to the front entrance, he held up his badge to the surveillance camera and rang the buzzer.

"Yes, officer, may I help you?" A male voice, slightly out of breath, responded after a moment.

"Agent Longstrum, FBI. May I have a moment to discuss an urgent matter?"

"Certainly." A loud buzzer sounded and the door lock clicked.

The lobby was austere, and the simple hallway led directly to a larger room where a man had just reached the podium that stood on a raised platform. Speaking into the microphone, his voice boomed across the space.

"Testing one, two, three. How does that sound, Agent Longstrum?"

"A bit loud, but clear."

The young man met him halfway across the room. "Yes, thank you. Our Grand Imam, who is giving a speech tomorrow night, is quite frail, with a quiet voice." He extended his hand. "I'm Abdul Korgani, the imam, the prayer leader of the mosque."

"Pleased to meet you. Tomorrow night is exactly why I'm here."

"Why, is there a problem?" Korgani placed his hands on his hips as his voice rose. "What, do you people think that our imam is here to preach violence?"

"Nothing of the sort. In fact, quite the contrary."

• • •

Abarque walked through the park with his head down. At the pond, he ignored the empty bench, choosing instead to keep moving as he emptied the contents of the popcorn bag along the shore. The birds rose in a frenzied flurry. He turned away.

At the college, he didn't bother gathering his cleaning supplies and instead proceeded directly to room 102. The last of the students leaving for the day were shouting and laughing in the corridor outside, but the classroom was empty and silent except for the creaking of the hardwood floor as he crossed to the computer. He didn't register his footsteps or the motion of his fingers typing.

The site loaded. The message was the same, a Tuesday night stag party.

His shoulders slumped. Grief seized him. Grief for a life not fully lived, not yet blessed with a wife and children. He choked back tears and expelled a long breath through his nose. Even if he did not die, if the FBI identified him as a terrorist, it would ruin all his hard work to bring his beloved sister to a better life in America.

Why did he feel compelled to sacrifice his life and destroy his sister's hopes and dreams? Truly, he believed in the teaching of the Quran: to enjoin that which is right, good and just, and to struggle against that which is wrong, evil and unjust. But was he truly a warrior? Or was he just fearful of this one man, Hamid? There was no point in asking for guidance from his imam. He already knew what the bearded old man would say. *Do what is in your heart and serve Allah however you can.*

As he switched off the computer, his tears broke through the dam and ran down his cheeks.

• • •

Fatima breezed through the security check at the end of the day. Other than the few moments it had taken to determine that Wizner had gone to work, she had concentrated only on doing her job, her real job, the thing that filled her with a sense of accomplishment and self-worth.

Today was just the beginning of the changes to come. Jenny never recovered from her late arrival and, for the first time in a while, Fatima had laid claim to first place on the leaderboard. The scowl on Jenny's all-American, made-up little face as she'd packed her bag had been more rewarding than the incentive bonus.

To celebrate, Fatima did some extra shopping on the way home. The grocery bag was heavy, the flimsy old door of their apartment loose and the lock sticky. As she struggled, the groceries slipped toward the ground. Trapping the bag against the door with her thigh, she almost fell through when it gave way. Samir appeared in a rush.

"Oh, it's only you."

"Yes, brother. Who else?"

Samir carried the bag to the kitchen counter without responding and quickly returned to his room.

Fatima shook her head. Thankfully, he would likely be in there for at least another hour. Lots of time to prepare his preferred meal of vegetables on rice and her special spicy hot sauce. Chopping the ingredients was tedious, but it was imperative to please her brother with good food if the evening was to be bearable. If she cut corners, he would accuse her of being too American and muddling up her priorities of home and family with a career and false freedoms. Then he would go off on some rant about Western civilization being a worthless relic and the need for a world caliphate.

The contents of the frying pan were simmering merrily when her brother entered the kitchen. He beamed.

"Oh, that smells good," he leaned over the stove and inhaled deeply, "my favorite. It is very special that you made this tonight. It will be good luck."

"If you say so. Go and wash. The meal is almost ready."

Over dinner, Samir seemed deep in thought. After swallowing his last forkful of rice, he looked up with furrowed brows.

"Have you learned anything else about this Wizner man?"

"No. Well, maybe. There were some recordings from the weekend. A lot of complaining. It made him sound like a hypochondriac."

"Why do you say this?"

"He told someone that he was scared that he had diabetes because he was peeing all the time and was going to see a doctor. He was very dramatic, insisting that he was going to lose a lung by coughing."

Samir nodded to himself and smiled. "That is very good information, Fatima. Very useful in fact. Thank you."

• • •

Mike arrived late for dinner. Mumbling only a brief greeting, he forwent the usual home-from-work hugs, kisses and ass groping, and instead headed to the bedroom to change. At dinner he was so preoccupied that he appeared to not even see Jenny, alternating his gaze at the blank wall behind her and his work phone.

She knew what he was like and that it would be a mistake to interrupt his thinking. Around his office, her darling husband had earned the nickname "Pitbull" for the tenacity with which he stayed on task. Today must have been intense; she let him be.

After clearing the table, Jenny sat opposite Mike. He was still mute, deep in his own world.

"How was your day?"

"Sorry, what was that?"

"I said, 'how was your day'?" Jenny checked the frustration in her voice.

"I'm a bit nervous."

"About what?" Jenny reached across the table to place her hand over his.

Mike flipped his hand over to grasp hers tightly. "You know that guy I've been watching? I got the go ahead for an operation. I'm lead."

"Oh." Jenny withdrew her hand and pressed her fingers against her forehead. "That's great" She scrunched her eyes closed as she gently shook her head. "What *kind* of operation?"

Mike shrugged. "Sorry, I've got to go back in tonight. I gotta work out a plan for tomorrow night and pick a squad from the list of available agents. It's far from a dream team, but it will have to do."

"Please, can't you tell me what you're doing?"

"A local group of white supremacists is planning an attack on the Isgani mosque tomorrow night. We plan on stopping them."

Jenny inhaled sharply. "Are you going to be safe?"

"Of course. The plan is solid. I've already reconned the mosque and have the cooperation of their leader."

"Are you sure? Those white supremacy guys pack a lot of firepower, and as much as they want to rid America of Muslims, you guys aren't exactly in their good books either."

"Have a little faith, honey. I know how to do my job."

"Oh, yes sir, Mr. FBI Agent, but you're also the future father of my children."

"OK, I'll wear Kevlar over my balls."

Jenny slapped Mike playfully on the arm and gave him a quick kiss before standing to wipe the table. "Aren't you going to ask me about my day?"

"Sure. How's your little conspiracy theory going?" He ducked just in time to avoid the wet dishrag she hurled at his head.

"It's your damn job that makes me paranoid!" Growling, she picked up the soapy sponge from the sink and held it like a Frisbee. "Conspiracy is every-where, even between dishwashers." She sent the sopping sponge twirling across the table, splattering Mike's shirt.

"Hey, my shirt!"

"It'll dry! Go save America!"

• • •

The night was young, but Billy felt juiced by his recent vigilante successes. He tapped his keyboard, rolling through the long list of suspicious sites. There was nothing new on the possible attack tomorrow night. But no news was still news. He rifled off an email to the FBI that there appeared to be no sign of a change in plans.

He loaded up Starcraft. Practice as he may, he still doubted he could earn a living competing in the e-tournaments. He'd started to consider changing his goal. A blog post he'd found said that not only consistent but also decent cash could be made as an online game host and commentator. Maybe tonight he would just watch the matchups and practice narrating.

Just as he was about to put on his headset, a notification ping alerted him to an update to his watch list. The 'Saturday' blog had a new post. In response to the notice of the stag tomorrow night, someone had replied, 'Bringing pizza'.

He frowned. Was there some subversive significance to 'pizza'? Ah, what did it matter? The FBI should be on this already. Besides, he didn't have time to speculate; the match between Stormmaster9 and JulieBlue2 had started five minutes ago.

He sent a screenshot on to the FBI and donned his headphones.

DAY SEVEN

Tuesday
July 3, 2018

CHAPTER 26

Abarque had not slept well. Every time he drifted off he'd awoken with a start. The loud cracks of thunder and snap of lightening outside did nothing to help settle him. All night long, every nightmare had concluded with his death. He was knocked off his feet by a hailstorm of bullets, each hole in his chest spewing blood like an erupting volcano. Then, he was lashed to a chair, a vague masked figure beating him repeatedly with iron fists until his ribs caved inward.

With the first light of morning, he got up and made tea. He could not waste a minute of this glorious day, his last day, even if it was raining like a monsoon.

In his closet hung his spare work uniform, a pair of jeans and two casual shirts. He half-heartedly packed the jeans and dark blue button-up into his duffel bag and slowly pulled on his uniform. His preference even on wintry days was bare feet and sandals, but today he donned socks and laced up his running shoes. He still didn't know if they were for the mission or his escape. Regardless, he was never returning here.

In his packsack, he placed his worn copy of the holy book and his passport. He wrote a note to his landlord explaining that he had been called back home on urgent business and would not be returning. He laughed wryly as he gave permission to the property management to sell everything in the almost bare apartment.

On his way out, he slipped the paper under the superintendent's door. For some odd reason it was comforting to keep the key.

There was enough change in his pocket to buy a jumbo bag of popcorn for the ducks and geese. He had a lot of hours to kill before work, and who knew when his feathered friends would dine so well again. First, however, he would take a long, cleansing walk in the rain.

• • •

Mike had arrived early at FBI headquarters. Behind the small podium in the briefing room, he rehearsed his spiel and fidgeted with the audiovisual controller until he was confident that he could run his PowerPoint presentation without a hitch. With nothing else to prepare, he paced the length of the room sipping his coffee, waiting for his team to take their seats.

A motley crew for sure, but at least they were punctual. By eight thirty everyone was present. Casting an eye over the five men and two women, all watching him intently, he couldn't help but think they were just waiting for him to fuck up. The expressions of the experienced field agents seemed to ask what this desk-jockey running his first operation knew about the real world. Added to the venomous mix were a couple of older guys who, passed up for promotion one too many times, probably had an axe to grind. Above all, none of them were shy and would eagerly tear him to shreds if they didn't like what they heard.

When the last agent was seated, Mike cleared his throat loudly.

"Good morning. Thank you for your prompt response on such short notice. You have been assembled because we've intercepted electronic communications appearing to indicate that the local white supremacist group the Lone Stars is planning an attack tonight. As I'm sure you are all aware, we have suspected this group of inciting hate crimes against Muslim targets for several years."

Stifling a yawn, Ken Jenkins, a seasoned veteran, raised his hand.

"What's your confidence level in this intercept."

"A similar threat was detected approximately three days ago. It was averted by publishing several communiqués making it known that we were aware and prepared to act."

"So what makes you think the recent communication isn't just a diversionary tactic?" asked Lisa Wernikie from the back row.

"We don't, but this group has not shown a high level of sophistication in the past. Also, their leader had been under surveillance since the first threat, and his behavior is consistent with the facts. Responding to a tip on Sunday that he had purchased bomb materials, we conducted a raid. There were no explosives in his possession, but residues were detected. He was taken into custody for wounding one of ours."

"So, it's over." Jenkins slapped his notebook closed and pocketed his pen.

"No, we still need to take this seriously." Mike took another sip of water. "The last communiqué was sent out after his arrest, and the timing of the possible threat coincides with an event at the Isgani mosque at 8:00 p.m. tonight. They are expecting a substantial crowd for a presentation by a visiting Grand Imam from New York City."

"What's the topic, free flying lessons?" Phil Dickerson was a sarcastic piece of work. He had just returned from another leave of absence in his ongoing battle with depression and made no bones about suffering from PTSD, triggered by his investigation work at ground zero in the days following 9/11. He had transferred to the other side of America just to get away from the constant reminders.

Mike took it as a good sign that no one in the room laughed. He was relieved to see several agents ready their pens, even Ken Jenkins. Agent 'Jerk'-ins never took notes.

But folding his arms across his chest, Dickerson wasn't finished. "What's the who, what and where of this electronic communication?"

"Agent Adams has been cultivating a contact who monitors websites on the dark net. He's previously observed spikes of activity on a certain blog correlating with mosque attacks."

Agent Wernikie raised her hand. "OK, but what makes this local?"

"Repeated reference to Standford. Look, guys, we have a chance here to prevent a massacre on our own turf and take down some really nasty dudes."

Agent Jenkins coughed and cleared his throat. "What you got in mind?"

"We'll beef up surveillance: two teams of two run on Ken Lowry, the second-in-command, and one agent on each of the other suspects. The remaining two agents and myself will set up at the mosque."

Lisa Wernikie perked up. "Are the potential targets aware?"

"Nominally." Mike took another sip of water. "It is imperative that things appear to be carrying on normally. Once we are certain an incident is about to occur, we will take all possible measures to ensure public safety while making the bust."

Jenkins was shaking his head. "That sounds a little airy-fairy. Cut the mumble jumble."

"Dan wants an open-and-shut case, so our mandate is to take these dudes down in the act without imperiling innocents."

Mike dimmed the lights before anyone else could speak and clicked the first slide of his PowerPoint. "This is Spitwell, the local leader of the Lone Stars."

Operational details always garnered everyone's attention. Starting on his prepared notes, he felt his heart beat steady, and the rivers of perspiration running down his flanks slowed to a trickle.

• • •

Entering the office, Fatima detoured from her usual path across the department. She stopped at Charlene's workstation, then Debbie's to say good morning. In her cubicle, she opened her umbrella and placed it on the floor to dry. As she adjusted her chair and arranged her pens and paper on her desktop, she softly hummed one of her favorite songs; "I Can See Clearly Now" had been stuck in her head since she woke up. Again, all Samir wanted from her today was to verify as soon as possible that Wizner had gone to work, nothing more. While she logged in, she kept her cell phone turned on and hidden in the folds of her skirt. Working swiftly, she scanned Wizner's activity log. Within minutes she was in the washroom sending the confirmation text. *Yes, there is bread in the fridge.*

Eager to post another productive day, she settled back in her chair and clicked on the first file requiring attention—then almost jumped off her seat when, behind her, someone cleared their throat.

"Congratulations, Fatima, your gift card for yesterday." Mrs. Perks was holding out a plain white envelope with a tiny Starbucks logo. "I'm glad you're feeling better, and I hope you have another productive day."

"Oh, thank you! I will try."

"I'm sure you will." Mrs. Perks winked. "Jenny called in sick today."

Fatima's mood soared past the clouds. Two days of being number one. Soon she would be running the department.

• • •

Jenny closed her eyes and let the hot water from the shower massage her neck. This morning Mike had been gone before dawn, mumbling as he dressed that he wasn't sure when he would be back. Eager to share her latest ideas about Fatima and Samir, she'd tried to catch him before he left, but his feet had hardly touched the floor as he flew out of the apartment, dripping peanut butter from the slice of toast between his lips.

Despite her irritation, it was impossible not to feel happy for him. Sitting at a computer all day was a jail sentence for Mike. It was only natural that the chance to run an operation would send a jolt of adrenaline coursing through his veins.

She also found his energy contagious. Today, she would be a secret agent as well, but one unencumbered by rules and protocols. If data sifting couldn't confirm her suspicions about the Khalifs, then it was time to go to the source.

Trying to keep the eagerness out of her voice, she had called in sick. When she casually asked Mrs. Perks if the rest of the department had caught the same bug, she was reassured by her boss's terse, "Thankfully not." Fatima was safely out of the way. It was a risk to assume that Samir would be driving BurBur Car all morning, but it was one she would have to take.

The morning traffic was slowed to a brake pumping grind by the heavy downpour. Finally, after detouring on side streets, she arrived downtown at the Khalifs' block just before ten. Their edifice was a sad example of the apartment-building boom of the sixties, the interior in desperate need of a facelift and the main glass doors stuck open. Every surface needed a good scrub.

She lingered in the lobby until an empty elevator car arrived. Her large purse was heavy from the small pry bar and assortment of screwdrivers she'd lifted from Mike's toolbox. From their painting supplies she had added a pair of latex gloves.

The upstairs hallway was empty and silent. In a few moments, she stood in front of unit 1210. Her hands shook as she slipped on the gloves, took a deep breath, and knocked.

No response. She exhaled.

Double-checking that she was unobserved, she inserted a heavy, flat-bladed screwdriver between the worn, ill-fitting door and the jam. With strength gained from hours of wrist curls at the gym, she torqued the handle and forced open a space, exposing the dead bolt. With her other hand she slid a smaller screwdriver along the bolt, probing for the end. Despite using all the pressure she could muster, it wouldn't budge.

The pry bar was her next tool of choice. With a little leverage, it was easy to bend the doorframe just a smidge. The very tip of the bolt was still catching.

She placed a small screwdriver on the bolt-end. Luck was on her side—the aging lock had an eighth of an inch or so of play. That was all she needed to slip the bolt past the receiving slot in the doorframe. She was in.

The living room was as bland as rice pablum. Sparsely furnished with mismatched wooden chairs, the small area was extremely tidy. The walls were bare, except for a simple framed seascape. She wasn't sure what she was looking for, but there were certainly no posters or books to suggest fanaticism.

The kitchen was immaculate. She sniffed. The pungent scent of unfamiliar spices permeated the space. Treading lightly down the hall she ignored the empty bathroom and peeked around the corner at the first bedroom. It was again neat and tidy, with a mirror and hairbrush on top of the dresser. Obviously Fatima's, and it offered no obvious clues.

The door at the end of the hall was closed. Putting her ear to it and hearing nothing, she slowly turned the handle and pushed. A waft of male musk greeted her, but nothing else. Across from the single, unmade bed, a powerful-looking computer rig dominated the small room. Two towers sat under the desk and a sea of cables connected a series of devices including twin screens. A bulky set of headphones lay to one side.

Was Samir a gamer? A tap on the space bar brought up a sign-in prompt demanding a password.

Jenny frowned—she had risked arrest for this? Not a single jihadist slogan painted on the walls or a scrap of bomb-manufacturing material on the desk. She turned away from the computer and scoured the rest of the room.

Under the bed were rows of sleek metal containers linked by cables. They looked like fancy battery packs, but she couldn't be sure. Odd.

She opened the closet. A few shirts and pairs of pants hung on metal hangers so mangled that they must have been reclaimed from a trash bin behind some dry cleaner. Overall, there was little of interest except a row of books on the shelf. She inhaled sharply as she scanned the titles—*Stability of Financial Systems in the Digital Universe, Developing and Protecting Your Online Marketplace*—bookended by editions of annual corporate reports and operational flowcharts from some of America's biggest companies in finance, tech and energy. She flipped through several; individuals' names had been underlined and crossed out.

She wasn't sure of the meaning, but something about the collection set off alarm bells in her mind. Mike needed to know about this. She snapped a few photos with her phone.

A loose-leaf binder sprouting multiple tissues as page markers stood at the end of the row. She reached up on tiptoes to grab it.

Undecipherable script covered the pages, endless paragraphs with no titles or pictures. There wasn't even a suspicious diagram. She laid it on the floor. It took both hands to steady her grip before the translation program finally worked. *Oh my God.* As fast as she could flip the pages, she clicked photos.

The binder was too large for the shallow closet shelf; it was a struggle to stand it upright again.

There's got to be something on the computer. Moving toward the desk, she jumped, nearly peeing her pants when a loud clatter erupted behind her. She froze, eyes squeezed tight, but there was nothing more, no angry shouts or cold press of steel at her neck. She turned back to the closet—the binder had fallen from the shelf, dislodging several of the tissue bookmarks. Replacing them quickly, she repositioned the binder and closed the closet door, this time making sure it clicked firmly.

That was enough. The insides of her plastic gloves were slick with sweat; her nerves couldn't take any more. At the apartment doorway she paused, reviewing her visit. No, she was sure that she had left nothing out of place.

Shit. The bend in the doorframe was obvious. With the pry bar and screwdrivers, she inserted the lock bolt back into its receptacle. Applying all her weight to the wide-blade screwdriver, leveraged over the pry bar, she bent the metal doorframe back into place as best she could. Standing back, she decided that the damage was not too noticeable from a distance. It would have to do.

CHAPTER 27

Wendy pushed back from her desk. Still warm from the run into work, she was sticking to her chair. It was time to stretch her legs and clear her mind with a trip to the coffee machine. Walking past the glass wall of the briefing room, she noticed Mike Longstrum behind the podium, a small group of agents seated before him. In the semi-lit room, a patch of light from the projector was reflecting off the thin gleam of sweat on his forehead.

She knew the feeling. The first team lead was tough for everyone. At least he wasn't yet bleeding from any razor sharp jabs administered by his audience. Just then he looked up, talking over the assembled heads, and momentarily caught her eye. She gave him a thumbs-up.

Not wishing to be a distraction, she put her head down and turned away, then almost collided with Tula Jones who was coming the other way. The two women offered a murmured "sorry" to each other. Wendy followed Tula's eyes toward the presentation room.

"Mike deserves this."

Tula nodded vigorously. "Yeah, and he looks great up there." She turned to Wendy with a lascivious smile. "And he always smells great too."

"Watch yourself, girl. He's a good man, and a married one. Jenny could, and would, crush you," Wendy snapped her fingers, "like that."

"I can dream, can't I? Besides, have you seen the rest of the guys in my department? They're all losers."

Wendy nodded. "I hear ya. All the men in my department are afraid of me." She grinned. "And so they should be. By the way, is Dan in?"

"Yeah sure, he's in his office."

"Good, I need to talk to him about helping Mike out. Maybe he could use a hand with his first operation." She grinned at Tula's jealous pout as she walked away.

• • •

Samir didn't use his own car for the trip to the Lakeridge Power Plant. At the front doors, he paid his cab driver cash with the promise of an extra tip if he returned in one hour. Why not be generous? The man had taken a direct route and not bothered him with the senseless small talk that so many cabbies mistakenly thought would earn a bigger tip. From the look of the man, he could use every dime.

Entering the foyer, Samir brushed several bits of lint off of his jacket, wiped the raindrops from his forehead and ran his fingers through his hair before presenting himself at the security desk.

"Good morning. I have an appointment at ten o'clock with James Wizner."

The guard, a hefty gray-haired man, verified the visit and slid a badge across the desk.

"Make sure this is visible at all times, even when you're going to the can. OK?" Without looking up he continued. "Now, please empty your pockets, place everything on the tray and put your briefcase here."

The man stood stiffly and directed Samir with a wave of his hand to pass through the metal detector while he slid the tray and the briefcase through a smaller scanner.

Extending his hand that held a cardboard tray with two coffees, Samir asked, "What about these?"

"Take them through the scanner with you, or if they aren't some fancy organic, tree-moss tea you can leave them here for me."

Samir smiled.

"Sorry, no luck today," he stepped through the arc of the scanner, "half-chai half-oolong and a soy milk macchiato sweetened with organic honey."

The man laughed. "That's enough to make a guy puke."

Samir collected his items from the tray. When he attempted to lift his briefcase off the counter the guard prevented him with a firm hand.

"Open it, please."

Samir complied without hesitation. The guard brushed his hand over the array of USB keys. "That's a lot."

"I do many different presentations."

Satisfied, the older man nodded. "OK, Dr. Khalif, put your signature here." He swung the visitors' book on his desk around and pointed. "Make sure that you sign out and return the badge when you leave."

He'd known there wouldn't be any problems, but Samir still sighed internally with relief. He had completed task one, entry to the facility. He smiled at the man again and thanked him.

"Swipe your card to open the door. Proceed down that hallway, veer left and wait at the reception area." The guard immediately turned his attention to the *Sports Illustrated* open on the desktop.

Halfway down the hallway, a sign mounted on the wall pointed to public information and viewing areas. Further along at a Y-intersection, the choices were Administration Offices to the left or Plant Operations to the right. Samir hesitated. At the end of the Operations corridor was a door with a large white sign and red lettering. He couldn't quite make out the words, but on the wall to the right of the door was what looked like a security scanner and keypad.

Consulting his cell phone and checking each door as he went, Samir wandered down the hallway, trying to look lost. When he was close enough to read the sign—Restricted Area Authorized Personnel Only—he squinted at the security device, searching for a name and model number on the faceplate. On the bottom right he could make out the letters S and T, but the surrounding writing was too small. He couldn't afford to get closer. He held up his phone and snapped a picture.

"Can I help you?"

He spun around. An attractive young woman stood behind him in a tight, short skirt and green sweater.

"Yes, I am looking for a Mr. . . . ," he brought his phone to his face and feigned reading something, "Wizner."

"Oh, good morning, you must be Dr. Khalif. Please come this way."

He followed willingly. Although he did not approve, he enjoyed the view for a moment before he averted his gaze. This woman should dress in a more conservative fashion, working in such a place, surrounded by men.

In the administration area she faced him, nodding at the coffee tray. "Is one of those for me?"

Flustered, Samir stammered. "No, no sorry I . . ."

"Relax, I was joking. But next time, remember Americano for me, iced in the summer, extra hot in the winter." She pointed at two plastic chairs against the wall with a long red fingernail. "Please take a seat. Mr. Wizner will be right with you."

The selection of magazines on the small end table consisted only of tattered old hunting and fishing journals. *Visitors must be rare.* The receptionist was right about the promptness of her boss, however. He had just cracked the spine of a Smithsonian-worthy copy of *Reader's Digest* when Wizner appeared.

The plant manager was rather casually dressed. Just above his belt, a sizeable belly pushed his checkered shirt open, to expose a patch of hairy white skin. The comb-over was not working, and the dark circles under his eyes looked permanent. Generally, he looked older than his Facebook photo. *It must be stressful to have such responsibilities at his age.*

"Good Morning, Dr. Khalif." Wizner extended his hand.

Clasping it with both of his, Samir replied warmly. "And to you. Thank you for taking time out of your busy schedule to listen to my presentation."

"No problem, come on in to my office."

• • •

Hamid paced the dirty linoleum floor of the small reception area at Louie's Truck Rental, waiting for the lone attendant to get off the phone. He'd chosen Louie's because the company was too cheap to paint a logo or name on its vans, but he was paying for it in the quality of service. He checked the cracked wall clock above the counter. The attendant had been talking for fifteen minutes.

To arouse the least amount of attention, he only wanted to rent one van and use it for the entire operation. Since Sunday, the guns had been cleaned, oiled and ready for action, but now he must ready the most important weapon. Some time and a few tools would ensure that it was operational, but his toolbox was too unwieldy to transport on his bicycle.

"How may I help you, sir?" The pimply teen behind the counter was far too perky-keen for this job. It was probably his first.

"I need a cargo van until Thursday."

"You're in luck, sir. There is a July fourth holiday special on for tomorrow if you take the vehicle after five today and return it by 7:00 a.m. Thursday. Pay just forty-nine dollars plus tax. Unlimited mileage is included. "

"*No*, I need it now. I cannot wait." The young man blinked, and Hamid chided himself. He couldn't make a scene.

"Um, what I can do, sir, is rent the van to you until five and then issue a separate contract for the special. That way you save thirty dollars."

"Yes, that is fine. Thank you for doing that."

"May I have your driver's license and credit card, please?" The printer was already spewing out forms.

Dropping his cousin's Georgia state license on the countertop, Hamid thumbed the bills in his wallet. "I don't have a credit card, but I have cash in full."

The attendant looked flustered. "We need to have your credit card information in case of damage."

"I will buy the no-deductible insurance and pay for everything, including gas in cash, right now. Please, may I have the truck?"

"Let me check with the manager." The lad stepped backward from the counter with his eyes still fixed on Hamid before turning toward the open door of a small side office.

Hamid watched the boy explain the situation to a fat, broad-faced, middle-aged man. The thin red hair pasted over the top of his gigantic head made him look like an orangutan.

While he waited, Hamid fiddled with the driver's license lying on the counter, scratching an itchy spot on his chin. He stared at the picture of his cousin. There was a vague familial resemblance, but they were far from identical. *It is good for once that, with our beards, we all look alike.*

The manager flashed a greedy smile and nodded. When the boy returned he was smiling smugly. "The manager said no problem, but he is asking for a deposit of five hundred dollars on top of the rental fee."

Hamid counted out the bills and slid them across the counter. Struck dumb, the boy fumbled to pick them up. The amount of cash was clearly testing his arithmetic skills to the limit. Hamid watched him check the number three times.

Hamid reached for the truck keys when they were finally offered. He wouldn't bother asking for the twenty-five cents in change.

• • •

"I brought you a Starbucks macchiato. I imagine your job is very tiring." Samir pushed the cardboard carrier across the desktop toward Wizner. "It might need to be nuked. Oh, sorry, microwaved."

"Impressive, you even brought my favorite. Thanks."

Withdrawing a small envelope from the breast pocket of his suit jacket, Samir smiled. "And two tickets for the Angels' game Saturday afternoon. Good seats, I think, ten rows up from first base. You better take your glove."

He extended his arm for Wizner to take the packet.

"Oh, wow, that's incredible. I'm a big fan. You sure know how to make an impression. Good thing they're not for tonight. I hear the weather is only going to get worse." Wizner kept the envelope in his hand, waving it about as he continued. "So tell me why you're here, then I'll go 'nuke' the coffee." He raised his fingers in air quotes and laughed, which developed into a deep rattling cough.

"Are you OK?"

"Yes, thanks, I'm just getting over the flu."

"Ah, I am sorry. Well, as you can see from my card, I have a PhD in computer science and robotics from MIT. When I graduated I realized there was a great need for enterprise security in this country. Three years ago, a colleague and myself began providing independent security assessments and solutions to protect against cyber attacks as well as the threat of EMP warfare."

"All very topical subjects these days. In fact, many of our current management priorities pertain to those very issues—in particular, the EMP threat. In other regards, I feel confident that, thanks to some recent software upgrades, we are well protected. In addition, we have installed a third-party internet security package, which we believe is more than adequate to secure our systems."

"Are all of your systems accessible online?"

"Yes, in this day and age remote access is a necessity. Everything is now password protected and it's mandatory that employees change their password each month."

"That is excellent to hear." Samir took a seat across from Wizner. "Are the actual plant operations accessible online as well?"

"Absolutely. I could run this plant from my living room," Wizner laughed, "while watching a ball game on my big screen when I don't have tickets. But," he dug in his pants pocket for a key, leaned over to unlock the top right drawer of his desk and held up a red dongle, "I need this for access to plant operations, and a password that is changed daily." He swung the dongle on its lanyard, hypnotically. "Hardwired security is required."

"Impressive." Samir rejoiced inwardly.

"Thank you, but we do still have a vulnerability when it comes to an EMP attack, so I would like to hear what you have to say about that." Wizner tossed the dongle back in his open desk drawer and dropped the packet with the baseball tickets on top of it. Standing, he grabbed a cup in each hand. "But first, the coffee. I'll be right back."

He left the room.

"Actually, mine is tea. It's the one with the tic on the lid," Samir called after him.

Wizner had left the office door open. Samir rose from his chair and looked down the hall. Clear. Popping open his briefcase, he sifted through the different colored and shaped USB keys and dongles. He felt a sudden pang of doubt. None of them were an exact match to the one in the desk drawer. Hopefully, Wizner would not notice his was gone. He reached across the desk, slid open the drawer and grabbed the red dongle.

He could hear voices in the hallway. Taking a moment to carefully reposition the envelope with the tickets, he settled back into his seat and tucked the dongle under some papers in his briefcase and closed it just as Wizner reentered the room.

Suppressing another cough, Wizner sat down and took a sip from his cup.

"Very good, thanks. OK, what you got?"

Samir made a show of clicking the locks on his briefcase and withdrew a folder but kept it on the desk close to him, tapping it with his finger as he spoke. "I assume you are aware of the threat posed by North Korea. It is very concerning that their recent ballistic missile testing over Japan had a perfect trajectory for an EMP attack. Now that Kim Jong-un's missiles can easily reach the US, it is necessary for all important infrastructure to be protected."

Wizner squirmed in his chair. "Of course, we are conducting an analysis of our vulnerability right now. Our planning and implementation committee has a meeting later this week, so your visit today is extremely timely."

Samir nodded and did his best to conceal his smugness. "I am very pleased."

He extracted a substantial document from the file folder, reached across the desk and handed it to Wizner. By design, it was over-the-top wordy, mind-bogglingly complex and exquisitely crafted to conceal the fact that most of it was bullshit. The executive summary and first few pages were convincing, but the document was hopefully daunting enough to make Wizner leave it on the corner of his desk for perusal some other day, week or month.

Samir began his presentation with a long introduction regarding the general effects of an electromagnetic pulse created by a high altitude nuclear blast. He had no doubt that a power plant manager knew most of this stuff, but he needed to waste time. It would take at least twenty minutes for the furosemide diuretic and digitalis heart medication he'd added to Wizner's coffee to take effect.

Fatima's opinion that Wizner was a hypochondriac had triggered Samir's memory. He had been seventeen when his adoptive mother's elderly mother came to live in the basement of their house. Never one to use drugs himself, he was always welcome at parties as a dealer. One night, searching for something to sell, he had snuck downstairs and raided 'Gramma's' medicine chest for a few of the morphine tablets the doctor prescribed for her knee pain. Why he also took the other pills, he didn't know—perhaps remnant instincts from his days scavenging in the trash heaps back home. He just hoped they still packed some power all these years later.

He rambled on while Wizner sipped away at his coffee. Finally, the man began to look pale and unwell. Putting up his hand, he rose shakily to his feet and grabbed the edge of the desk. "Excuse me, I really have to take a pee break. I'll be right back."

"You don't look very well, sir. Should I go and fetch someone?" Samir reached out to steady the plant manager and then, quickly coming around the desk, guided him back into his chair. "Let me loosen your collar. It will feel better, and you don't need these choking you."

Wizner made no protest as Samir slipped the two lanyards over his head. He groaned, looking paler by the second.

"Yeah, I feel like shit."

"Close your eyes. Please try to relax." When Wizner obeyed, Samir discreetly snapped a photo of both sides of the security badge.

He stepped back and pocketed his phone. "I will get you some help."

"No, no, it's OK." Wizner's eyes snapped open and he brought his chair upright. "I'll be OK. I'm just getting over a nasty flu bug. But I think I might have to take the rest of the day off. Let's schedule another meeting after I have read your report, yes? Thank you for coming in today."

"Certainly. I can show myself out."

"OK, thank you. Goodbye."

• • •

Too dizzy to stand, Wizner stayed in his chair until the tremendous urge to pee forced him up. Man, to feel this badly, his blood sugar must be astronomical. His mother's words echoed in his head. *Diabetic coma.* Staggering to the doorway, he panted through a sudden tightness in his chest, his vision fogged by a strange yellow hue. The last thing he remembered was reaching his office door.

CHAPTER 28

Jenny speed-walked down the hallway, away from the Khalifs' apartment. As she neared the elevator, there was a ding and the up button flashed. Jogging the last few steps to the stairwell door opposite, she hip-checked the bar-handle and pushed through. The heavy door had a slow close, so she pressed herself against the inside wall as the elevator opened. There was the thud of heavy footsteps on the threadbare carpet, and through the gap she caught a glimpse of a dark-skinned man entering number 1210.

This was too early. What BurBur driver wouldn't be taking advantage of late-arriving workers and morning shoppers? Was he sick? Or was something critical about to happen?

On the street she paused, squeezing her eyes shut while she concentrated. Damn the Khalifs—the always-jittery Fatima, her vastly underemployed brother—something just didn't sit right. The woman nearly fainted anytime you stepped near her cubicle, and her excuses for recording 'Wiz' were downright ridiculous. Now, besides books on cybersecurity and notes on nuclear physics, Samir had a curious interest in the names of business people. What was the missing link? What *business* did either of them have with—

Her eyes flew open. Business. Occupation!

Yesterday at work she'd barely had time to think, she was so busy trying to get ahead of Fatima. But risking a few minutes of 'overtime', she'd compiled a list of Alexandria customers in the Tillson area whose names started with Wiz and emailed it to herself.

The rain had temporarily abated, and she walked slowly, focused on her phone. At her car, she leaned against the passenger door, plugging each name into the search bar one by one. Some were practically non-existent on the net, but within forty-five minutes she was certain that she was on to something. Amongst the myriad of varying 'Wiz' occupations from banker and lawyers to shopkeeper, organic farmer and chronically unemployed, there was one newspaper article from last year about a James Wizner being promoted to manager—at the Lakeridge Nuclear Power Plant.

Hamid parked the van at the back of Safe Place storage, out of sight from the road. Methodically, he scrutinized all the sight lines to unit 56, before opening the rear compartment of the van and sliding out his weighty toolbox. Inside the unit, he uncovered the large luggage trunk and dragged it into the meager light.

Produced in Pakistan in the '80s, it was a knockoff of the shoulder-fired Soviet SA-7 surface-to-air missile used by the North in the Vietnamese War. The simple design was what made it so valuable. Even in the hands of untrained operators, the thirty-pound beasts had brought down many warplanes.

This particular weapon had remained hidden since 1990. Originally, the plan was to use it to take down a commercial airliner flying out of LaGuardia, but after the downing of a plane by another operative, increased airfield security had made it difficult to replicate such an attack.

The man in possession of the weapon had stored it and bided his time, but eventually he became disabled by illness. When Samir tasked Hamid with finding a heat-seeking missile, his contacts had located the prize buried under the floor of a basement in Brooklyn.

Not everyone who joined the cause remained true to it, and he nearly died during the collection. Some nasty bastards tipped off by the old man had made him pay dearly—with a lengthy physical 'interview' to validate his credentials and his cash.

In hindsight, it was good that so much time had passed — this beast would have been wasted on a single planeload of people. It had a far greater purpose now. Hamid closed his eyes and imagined the ensuing bedlam, the thought of the infidels killing each other over their unholy materialistic needs made him laugh grimly.

He spread out all the parts that he could remove and made sure they were clean and functioning. The SA-7 had not come with manuals, nor were there maintenance instructions online, but the electronics technician course he'd had to take for the security company served him well.

Finished, he cracked open the door of the storage locker and aimed at the hood of a passing truck on the highway. The thermal-seeking missile was in working order.

A surge of heavy rain drenched him as he loaded the two trunks into the back of the van and locked up the unit. He cranked up the heat in the vehicle, hoping to be warm by the end of the twenty-minute drive to the Capital Center building supply store.

In his jacket pocket, his cell phone buzzed. The message from Samir would mean nothing to anyone else. 'SecTec 8565'. *Good*. Ace Security didn't use that particular manufacturer, but their standard was an almost identical knockoff.

Caught in another sudden downpour, Jenny stomped her feet impatiently and ducked into the car. On the third ring, she received an out-of-office message and her call was automatically routed to the department secretary. She hung up without waiting to hear the annoying voice of 'Oh, my sweater must have shrunk in the laundry' Tula Jones. She could try Mike's cell, though he was unlikely to answer if he was out on a case.

She jumped when he picked up.

"Oh—hi, darling. It's me, Jenny."

"Yes, no one else calls me darling. Look, I answered because I want you to know everything is a go for tonight, so I won't be home until late. Don't worry."

"OK, be safe."

"Always."

"Wait. Don't hang up. I know who Wiz is!"

"OK, I'll bite. Who?"

"James Wizner. He's the manager of Lakeridge Nuclear."

"Interesting."

"It's more than interesting. It's critical!"

"Why?"

"Because Fatima's brother, Samir, has a lot of books about nuclear fission and stuff."

"How do you know this?"

"At break I asked her what sort of hobbies a PhD in physics has."

"Really, you asked her?"

"Indirectly."

"Right. Listen, I'm sorry, I really have to go. I've got a big day today. See you tomorrow?"

"Seriously? Don't you think it's highly suspicious that he's interested in nuclear physics, and his sister is spying on the manager of a nuclear plant?"

"Still need the why. I promise to check it out after tomorrow."

"There could be a mushroom cloud over Tillson by then."

"Honey, please don't call me for the rest of the day. I love you. Bye."

The line went dead. She shook her head in disbelief.

I know I'm on to something! Jenny had felt light and tingly since her escape from the building, but behind the wheel, heaviness descended. Her shoulders slumped. The thought of returning to her humdrum job held no appeal. Fixing the boring problems of petty customers seemed meaningless in comparison to stopping a terrorist attack.

Maybe she should stick around and see if Samir went anywhere. There was a café down the street with picnic-style tables sheltered from the rain by umbrellas. Why not indulge in a supersize latte? 'Sipping and surveilling' sounded like an excellent plan.

• • •

Abarque meandered to work, sheltering himself from the gusts of rain with a discarded newspaper he'd picked off the top of a trashcan. Despite the unusually nasty weather, he wandered the streets aimlessly, seeking comfort in the company of strangers rather than attending the mosque.

In the school basement, the supply room was undisturbed. He relocked the door and prepared the cleaning supplies he needed. Tuesday was desktop cleaning day, a spray of disinfectant wash followed by a quick going over with a polishing rag.

Wheeling his janitorial cart out of the utility room, he kicked the door closed behind him. The drudgery of his work routine had to be followed, no matter how little his heart was in it. No suspicions could be raised.

Behind him, someone cleared their throat. He froze. The district supervisor of custodial services was walking toward him down the hallway, toting a clipboard.

Mr. Thomas was an imposing man who carried close to three hundred pounds on his six-foot-plus frame. Hamid wondered if he'd been an American football player when he was younger. He favored his right knee, which could be from a field injury, although it seemed all Americans favored a knee or two, or sometimes a hip.

"Hello, Abarque, I just dropped in to see how it's going and if you need any supplies." Mr. Thomas extended a beefy hand. "You well?"

Abarque tried not to wince as he endured the vice-like grip. "Hello, sir. Yes, I am good, thank you very much. I believe we will need more paper towels before the end of the month."

"OK," said Thomas as he scribbled something on his clipboard. "If you don't mind, I'll just take a quick look in the storage. It's been a while."

Standing behind the man, Abarque's pulse quickened as the man inserted his master key into the lock.

"Good God, man, do you use any soap to clean the floors?" The big man chuckled. "This isn't Somalia, you know. You don't have to be so miserly with the stuff."

"Miserly? Oh . . . yes . . . I'm sorry. Old habits are hard to forget."

Thomas shut off the light. "I'm sure the school board is thrilled that you are saving them money, but if the floors are not clean, no one is going to be pleased."

"Yes, sir, I will use more soap."

• • •

Despite the impatience of the other drivers on the interstate, Farzaad drove exactly at the speed limit. There was no need to draw attention by getting a ticket.

Mouri was poor company, sleeping soundly in the passenger seat beside him. Yesterday morning, his younger brother had disappeared after being told about Hamid's message. His dinner went uneaten, and he had not come to the bakery in the morning. Farzaad had given up hope that he would ever see him again, but this afternoon when he pulled by the house with the rental car, his brother had emerged and solemnly took his seat. Pale with dark bags under his eyes, Mouri had not spoken a word since. He barely looked at him before folding his sweater into a makeshift pillow and falling asleep against the window. What had his little brother been up to for the past day and a half? Farzaad smiled. Likely what any young man would want to do before meeting his fate—defiling an infidel.

His brother may be no baker, but that's not to say that he didn't have talents. His Kabul street skills had been invaluable when procuring difficult-to-get items, particularly the explosives. Mouri's 'pizza' was hidden behind a side panel in the trunk of the car. He was glad his brother had made the right choice and returned.

The heavy rain was abating, and they were making good time. Hungry, Farzaad broke off a piece of this morning's bread from the loaf on the console between them. *Very good. Maybe next time a little more salt.*

He laughed out loud. What next time? His bread was as good as it ever would be.

• • •

Heidi slumped in the kitchen chair, watching the rain and counting the seconds between the flashes of lightening and corresponding bombs of thunder. She yawned, her jaw cracking. Becky's coughing had interrupted her sleep all throughout the night. Yesterday, she'd administered two additional physiotherapy sessions trying to relieve the congestion. Was it enough? It worried her that Becky chose to nap while the other children watched a movie.

She felt a sting of dread as Chuck emerged from the barn outside. Seemingly oblivious to the rain soaking him to the bone, he walked slowly, his head moving side to side, scanning the fields.

It hadn't been the most blissful day of matrimony. Still recovering from last week's double shifts, her darling husband had rolled back under the covers this morning when he saw the rain. He'd slept until after lunch and had awoken grumpy. The harder it rained, the more sullen he'd become. While she took care of Becky, he'd spent the afternoon banging things around in the barn under the pretext of repairing and maintaining the baling equipment.

Heidi swiveled in her chair toward the backdoor as it opened. "Find lots to do, honey?"

"Enough." Chuck slipped off his boots and strode directly to the front window. Pulling back the corner of the curtain, he peered down the driveway.

"What you looking at, the mailbox?" Receiving no reply, she stood to join him. "What's wrong? You seem jumpy."

Chuck blinked rapidly then pressed his fingertips into the corners of his eyes and massaged. "Nothing. I thought I saw Kevin Lowry's truck."

"Why would he be here?"

"No good reason." Chuck grunted something unintelligible and went into the spare room off the kitchen. When he reentered the kitchen, he was loading shells into his shotgun.

"What the hell, Chuck?"

"Lighten up. I'm just going for a stroll. I saw some coyote scat around edge of the pasture." He tucked the gun under his arm and stepped into his boots.

The back door slapped shut, which brought the two boys running into the kitchen.

"Mom, we're hungry! What's for supper?"

Heidi smiled wanly. Thank goodness for the Crock-Pot plugged in on the counter, filled with simmering beef stew. The appliance was a game saver.

Passing the kids some crackers to tide them over, she shuddered as the next horizontal sheet of rain raked across the kitchen window. The fields would be mud for weeks. *Oh well*. She reached over and turned the dial on the stove to 375°. Maybe she could muster the energy to bake a few cookies for dessert.

• • •

It had taken hours, but sifting through Wizner's mother's and sister's personal info, Samir had gleaned what he needed to reconstruct the daily password's encryption key.

Using that morning's email and the stolen security dongle, he logged in and brought up a virtual image of the Lakeridge plant's console. He scrutinized the miniaturized representation of every switch, dial and button. For many, he could decipher their function, and for the remainder he hoped that his binder of research notes would provide clues. Hopping up from his chair, he crossed to the closet.

The blue binder containing his physics notes on fission had fallen over and the tissue marking the section on temperature controls was missing. He looked down; it lay on the floor. The rest of his neatly arranged library appeared undisturbed.

He fumbled with the baseboard at the back and breathed out. The colt was still there.

Searching the rest of the room, he found no other signs of intrusion. He jogged down the hallway. The door and frame were so banged up it was difficult to tell if someone had tampered with it. Returning to his room, he tore it apart searching for listening devices or cameras. Then he ran complete diagnostics on his computer. Nothing.

This was very disconcerting. If it had happened months ago, he would be extremely worried—but thankfully, it would soon be too late to stop his plan, even if someone had caught on to it. He would question Fatima when she arrived home. In the meantime, he placed his gun within easy reach on his desk.

CHAPTER 29

Intermittent rain driven by wicked gusts of wind saturated the grass and bushes on the slopes surrounding the mosque. Locked and loaded, Mike's team was successfully in place, but the conditions made their observation positions uncomfortable and treacherously slippery.

It was less than two hours until the imam's speech. The reports from the teams conducting surveillance on the Lone Star members had been unremarkable to this point. They were maintaining their usual routines, heading home or dropping in at the bar for a brew after work.

The Grand Imam and the local mosque leader pulled up to the front door in a rusty old station wagon. Mike handed off his binoculars to Agent Jenkins

"I'll head in and give them the final brief."

Emerging from the bushes, Mike's unannounced presence startled the two preachers. They remained guarded until he held up his badge, and Abdul Korgani recognized him. Mike introduced himself to the Grand Imam. The elder was clearly still suspicious and extended his hand tentatively, demanding Mike's credentials. Holding the identification just past the tip of his nose, he eventually nodded his satisfaction and handed the card back.

"What can we do for you, Agent Mike Longstrum?" His voice was very soft and somewhat choked, but assured.

"Gentlemen, as I explained to Mr. Korgani earlier, we received information that your meeting tonight may be the subject of an attack. Now, we are certain."

"Oh, my goodness." The Grand Imam blanched and turned with questioning eyes toward the younger preacher. Korgani jumped in.

"Yes, sorry." Placing a reassuring hand on the imam's back, he spoke to Longstrum. "I was just going to bring our guest up to date."

The older man quickly regained his poise. His eyes were piercing as he alternated his stare between the two younger men. "We must cancel at once."

Mike held up his hand. "We disagree. If we're ever going to catch these people and prevent future attacks, we would prefer that you proceed as planned. We have a team in place, completely surrounding the facility. We'll be able to intercept the attackers before anyone is at risk."

"It sounds very dangerous to be in the middle of this . . . this conflict, no?" asked the Grand Imam.

"Your colleague will be wearing this." Mike held out a pager for display. "When it vibrates, everyone present needs to lie flat on the floor."

Korgani refused to accept the device. Mike softened his voice. "It is only as a precaution. We will not allow them to enter the premises. All of your congregation will be safe."

The younger prayer leader stepped back and shook his head. "No, I'm not convinced. I have changed my mind. It sounds too risky."

The Grand Imam hesitated, then reached out and put a placating hand on the younger man's arm. He addressed Mike. "We have confidence in you, officer. We place our faith in you. Please, we will take the device."

Once the men had walked away, Mike triggered his comm. Lisa Wernikie had called in twice during the conversation. "Yes, Lisa."

"Kevin Lowry drove into the country, and I had to lay back. Unfortunately, I think he made me anyway. He took off and I lost him."

"Shit. OK, I'll get Dickerson to help you. Let's hope that Lowry grabs something to eat at one of the usual spots."

• • •

Hamid nodded in satisfaction as he pulled the van into the loading zone behind Tech College. The security light over the rear door was off, an intelligent precaution. Abarque didn't own a phone, so Hamid was obliged to get out of the truck and knock. Before his knuckles struck the metal door, however, he heard the interior bolts being slid, and the form of his fellow Somali appeared in the doorway. Even in the gloomy darkness, Hamid could sense the thin man's nervousness.

"Praise Allah, brother," whispered Hamid.

"All is good," replied Abarque, his stance rigid, voice barely audible.

With a hand gesture from Hamid, the back door of the van opened and Farzaad and Mouri jumped down onto the asphalt.

"Please, follow me." Silently, Abarque led them through the darkened hallways to the storage room. He pointed a trembling finger to indicate which buckets to take.

Hamid grunted. "Where's the other stuff?"

Abarque pulled a box of glass jars from the back of another shelf. "Here is the potassium and aluminum material."

With the last container gone, Abarque locked the storeroom door and followed Hamid up the stairs to the parking lot. In the back of the vehicle, he could see stacks of barrels, batteries and timers. He wasn't stupid. They were making bombs. Panicked, he averted his eyes.

He knew that he must plead his case now or hold his tongue. When he turned from locking up the rear door of the school, Hamid stood waiting, holding open the van door, staring at him expectantly. Abarque swallowed hard.

Hamid took a step forward. "Brother, what is wrong?"

Abarque slipped on his packsack and inhaled deeply, steeling himself. "No, I am sorry, but I cannot do this right now." He stepped sideways, away from Hamid. "Please understand. I have provided you with what you wanted, but I wish not to be part of this anymore."

He started walking across the parking lot.

"You made a commitment." Hamid's voice was no longer friendly.

Still walking, Abarque half-turned to face the three men. "Please, I have family in Somalia to support and I must be here to be able to sponsor my sister."

Hamid's arm lifted.

Abarque ran, but covered only a few meters before a searing pain ripped into his lower back and his legs gave way, sending him tumbling to the pavement. When he opened his eyes, Hamid stood over him.

"Nothing and nobody can betray us. Our cause is too important."

Abarque closed his eyes as the hard coldness of the barrel pressed against his forehead.

CHAPTER 30

Jenny wasn't sure if she felt jittery from all the caffeine she'd consumed or from her anxiety. She'd lost count of her latte refills during the long, unrewarding wait for Samir to exit the apartment complex. Now back home, it was well into evening and there was still no word from Mike. *Did the takedown go wrong?* She paced the apartment.

The gummy blob of last night's reheated spaghetti remained in her bowl, barely touched. She couldn't tear her eyes from the TV screen, scanning the 24-hour news channels for any reports of an FBI agent being shot or an impeding nuclear meltdown—or both. There was some comfort in the fact that the local news items pertained solely to the deluge of rain.

She checked her phone again. Nothing. *Dammit.* The rolling thunder and sheets of lightening were putting her on edge. She had to talk to someone. Someone who could reassure her. Her best friend.

"Hi, Mom, it's me."

"Oh, hi, darling. How are you? Listen, don't you think that guy Bert is amazing, winning $35,000 on *Quizmasters* tonight? He could be the all-time champion!"

"I didn't watch. I'm worried about Mike."

"Why, what's up?"

"I can't really say, but something dangerous is going down tonight and he's the lead."

"Isn't being lead better that than being the first one through the door? Doesn't he get to stay back at the command center?"

"You don't know Mike. 'Lead by example' is his motto."

"Don't worry, honey. I think he can take care of himself. Besides, there is nothing you can do."

"I guess you're right. I feel so useless. I wish I had a gun."

"Oh, Jenny, don't talk nonsense. He'll be home soon. Go to bed. Read a nice book."

Jenny hung up.

"Fuck!" She slammed her palm into the couch pillow next to her. "I don't believe in fairy tales anymore, Mom."

• • •

Samir stormed into the kitchen. Fatima put down her book and rose to remove a casserole dish from the oven. *He must be starving.*

"Sit down!" Her chair screeched on the floor as she startled, and he gave her a stern look. "Did you touch anything in my closet today?"

"No, never! You know that I would never touch your things."

"Someone has disturbed my books."

Fatima watched Samir's knuckles blanch as he squeezed his hands into fists.

"Well, did you?" His voice was as threatening as the thunder rumbling outside.

Fatima flinched. Her brother was a scary man when he wanted to be. Desperately, she seized on a way to calm him. "This morning there was banging on the neighbor's wall. It sounded like construction, with a hammer or something. It made the walls shake."

Samir rubbed his hand over his mouth, then abruptly sat and picked up his fork. Fatima rushed to serve him. The lentil tomato stew looked as dry as Somali soil after being kept warm for hours, but her brother did not seem to care.

She put on a kettle for tea. "I did well at work. For two days in a row, I have been number one. I am sure that I will receive a raise in pay next month—it will help with our expenses."

"It will not matter," he said solemnly without looking at her.

"Pardon?"

A loud metallic clang sounded in the hallway. Samir flinched, dropped his fork, jumped to his feet and placed his hand on his waist.

"Brother, what is wrong? You are not yourself. It is just someone using the garbage chute."

Samir's shoulders relaxed, but when he turned back toward her, he was tugging on his shirt to conceal something tucked in his belt. When he noticed her staring, he merely shrugged, sat down, retrieved the fork and continued poking at his food.

He spoke into his bowl. "You will not go to work tomorrow."

Here we go again. "But I like my job. It is important to me and—"

Samir raised his hand for silence, speaking softly under his breath. "There will be no point. How much money do you have . . . in cash?"

"I don't know. I never carry much."

Samir emptied his pants pocket and a dropped a thick wad of bills onto the table. "Here, use this. You must go as far away from here as possible. Right now. Today, as quickly as possible."

Fatima inhaled sharply. When Samir stood, his shirt lifted, revealing a protruding gun handle.

He fixed her with an icy stare, quickly covered the weapon and checked his watch.

"I must go now and so must you. Leave right away." He touched her cheek delicately with the back of his index finger and smiled warmly. "My darling sister, just one more thing."

"Yes, brother?"

He pulled her to her feet, bringing her almost nose-to-nose. His smile evaporated. "Write down all your passwords for the computer systems at work." Extracting a pen and paper from his shirt pocket, he stood over her as she wrote.

When she finished, Samir briefly embraced her. "Go," he whispered in her ear and pushed her away.

Fatima stood unmoving as Samir snatched up the paper and, without another look, walked down the hallway and closed his bedroom door. She scraped his dinner back into the serving dish and tidied up the kitchen. Then there was nothing to do but go to her room and pack.

• • •

At his computer, Samir used Fatima's credentials to log into the Gazzel system. Then he uploaded and launched a program that would cripple their operations. Most of the coding was a simple undertaking, but he could not take credit for the real genius of this elusive electronic worm. It was amazing what you could barter for online these days. The new terrorists were hackers, preferring to wage war digitally either directly or by selling malware and asking for a dollar contribution to their cause.

The virus he had purchased was expensive but potent. Tomorrow the millions of Gazzel searches performed each hour around the world would return only a message about the virtues of Islam and the destruction of America, while in the background the malware overwrote vast swaths of memory, impairing the company's operations. It was only a temporary setback, but it would permanently ruin the company's reputation for security.

He wrapped his finger around the trigger of his gun and cradled it on his lap. Now, he would wait.

CHAPTER 31

Hamid fired another round, his silencer making the retort nothing but a sharp snap. Not bothering with the body, he picked up his shell casings, ran back to the van and threw himself behind the wheel.

He rammed the truck into drive. The clunk of the transmission coincided with a crash of thunder, and he ducked. Head down, he blindly wheeled the van in a tight half circle and sped toward the street. The bumper smacked down with a thud and ground loudly on the slope of the driveway. Hamid was halfway down the block before he expelled his breath.

He gripped the steering wheel tightly, *I must not fear*. Leaving Abarque's body in the parking lot had been a mistake. It introduced unnecessary sloppiness to an otherwise clean operation. Hopefully, the anonymity of America's constant inner city violence would make its discovery an unremarkable event. Or at the very least, their mission would be accomplished before the authorities figured out the connection.

Regrettable. We could have used the extra finger on a trigger. But if captured, the weakling might have talked. Although Abarque didn't know the rest of the plan, he could have identified Hamid. It had been right to eliminate the man.

Fortunately, they still had plenty of man and firepower to utilize.

• • •

The mosque was awash with an eerie glow from the incandescent spotlights, reflecting off the wisps of steam as cold rain struck the still warm ground. In the front doorway, departing worshipers stood bracing themselves to either run to their cars through the pelting rain or were pairing up to share an umbrella. A few of the more optimistic stood under the eves, glancing at the sky, waiting for the downpour to abate.

With every passing minute Mike's promotion dreams were drifting into the ether. Shivering, and wetter than a seal at Marine Land, it was time to admit defeat. At this rate, even allowing for post-presentation socialization, he predicted that by nine thirty the parking lot would be empty.

In his earpiece, Lisa Wernikie's voice sounded frustrated. "Lowry just arrived at work."

"Are you sure you didn't get made?"

"Not sure. Don't think so."

A lash of rain splattered across his FBI windbreaker. Mike closed his eyes and exhaled. "Fine. Thanks."

Suddenly he felt exhausted, the stress and restless sleep of the past few days were catching up to him. All he wanted to do was crawl into bed beside Jenny and pass out.

As he waited for the disaster to end, he contemplated all the possible ways he could shape the facts into something palatable for Smithers.

"OK, the last car is out of sight." Jenkins's sarcastic voice on the comm plunged him further into his gloom.

"Roger that."

He rolled his neck, trying to relieve the tightness banding his upper back. Triggering the mic, he mustered an upbeat tone.

"OK, stand down. Thanks, everyone. We'll tidy up the paperwork in the morning." Swallowing his disappointment, he continued evenly. "Our presence here tonight saved lives."

Behind the wheel of his SUV, he pounded his fist on the dashboard until his hand felt numb. The tires spun on the slick pavement as he throttled out of the parking lot. Someone was going to pay for this fuckup. He had to make sure it wasn't him.

• • •

With the kids tucked away for the night, Heidi and Chuck settled in with coffee to watch their favorite romantic comedy, Adam Sandler's *Fifty First Dates*, on DVD. Heidi was just about to use the pretense of being cold to snuggle in closer when her husband jumped sharply, his forearm clipping her on the ear.

"Ouch." Heidi pulled away. "You sure know how to wreck a romantic moment."

Chuck said nothing, staring at his vibrating phone as it jittered across the coffee table.

"You gonna answer that or let it shake the coffee cream into butter?"

Chuck grunted and flicked off the TV. Grabbing the phone he rose and moved toward the kitchen.

"Hi, what's up?"

The conversation only lasted a minute, but when Chuck returned, he was wearing his jacket.

"Was that Spitwell calling you to work?"

"No, Kevin Lowry." In response to her quizzical look he continued. "Spitwell's been arrested. I gotta go now. Two guys from the afternoon shift went home sick."

"I thought you said you were taking a break."

"He said that if I didn't come in, I could look for another job."

• • •

Fatima sat on the edge of her bed, her hands clenched in the blanket beside her. She'd known this day would come, but she hadn't expected to be cast to the wind like a kite with a cut string. She realized now—they had never been in this together. Maybe his cause was just, but Samir had used her.

She always knew he was serious about taking action, but what in the world was her brother about to do? She'd figured he would take down the financial system for a day or two, or knockout part of the electric grid. Maybe she'd been naive.

Despite her fear, resentment roiled in her. Would it ever be safe to return to this apartment, to this city? If not, Gazzel would miss her for a week or two and then hire someone else. But this had been her job, one that she had grown to like. She would be giving up a once-in-a-lifetime opportunity to put her foot in the door of a growing company. Once again, Samir was an obstacle on her path to becoming independent, free.

A surge of anger swelled inside her. Was Samir truly following the teachings of the Quran? His rage was no longer an abstraction. How much damage would he do? She stood to look out over the city, shaking her head. Downtown, the billboards and store signs flashed invitations of choices and hope—trivial, perhaps, but innocent. The average American meant no harm, so why hurt them?

The district police station was only three blocks away.

She shuddered. No, she couldn't turn in her own brother. Scrambling in her closet, she crammed her few toiletries and best clothes and shoes into the same pink Samsonite her foster mother had given her for the trip to Tillson. Her eyes smarted. Besides innocence, her mother's warm, perfumed embrace was what she craved, but it was not to be. If she could protect anyone, it would be Marj. She took one last look around her room. It seemed so empty now.

At Samir's door she paused, then continued past. He would detest her weakness if she tried to say goodbye. Locking the door and walking to the elevator, she cast an eye back toward the apartment.

"I forgive you."

CHAPTER 32

The windshield wipers of the police cruiser barely kept up to the deluge flooding the dimly lit parking lot of the Value Food supermarket. Police officer Manny Rodriquez tilted his thermos until the end hit the vehicle's ceiling. A drop of sugar-laced coffee dripped onto his uniform, spreading out into a sticky brown splotch. It made no difference that he was alone or that it was dark outside, he fastidiously cleansed the area with a moistened paper serviette. Content, he reached into his lunch bucket for the second half of his chicken pesto sandwich.

The dash radio crackled into life.

"Suspected murder victim behind the Rackford City Tech College on Third Street." Loretta Minceur's voice was angelic, no matter the static or topic of the call.

Still chewing, Manny held the microphone for a moment while he swallowed. "This is Bravo 10. I'm two minutes away."

"Roger that. Secure the scene and wait for the detectives."

"10-4."

He had never met Loretta, but someday soon he would march into the dispatch room and find out if the personality matched the voice. Cramming the last bite of sandwich into his mouth, he switched on the rooftop flashers. There was no need for sirens; why rush for a corpse?

• • •

In the detective office on the ground floor of the fifth precinct station, the dispatcher's voice blared through the overhead speaker. Arnie Samulson looked over the other members of the night shift squad before lifting the phone from the cradle. Receiving an approving nod from his partner, Enzo Merphin, he responded.

"Dispatch, this is team S and M. We'll take this one." Samulson tossed a stack of paperwork back into his in-box. "Thank goodness. Enough of this paper crap. Let's go, partner."

Merphin was already heading for the side exit. Outside, he clamped lights to the roof of their unmarked car. "You drive."

Samulson turned the wipers on full and swung a wide turn across the parking lot. "Raining enough for you, Enzo?"

"My tomatoes are going to get root rot."

"You need better drainage, bust up the clay." Samulson flicked on the lights and sped for the downtown campus of Rackford College.

Reports of a body were commonplace in the downtown core, the victims usually members of the drug trade. If the dealer kingpins considered murder the cost of doing business, then Samulson couldn't get too emotional about it. He just wished they would clean up their own mess.

At the scene, a triangle of three squad cars formed a perimeter around a motionless form lying in the middle of the parking lot. The wet asphalt glittered like fairy dust in the headlights.

Samulson parked close by and greeted the patrol officer who stepped up to the window. The man looked like a storm-drenched sailor, his face glistening.

"Hi, Manny, brutal night. You first on the scene?"

"Yes."

Samulson smiled. Personally, he appreciated the man's curt professionalism. Manny Rodriquez was a fifteen-year veteran who loved being on the streets and turned down every promotion offered to him. Notoriously difficult to get along with, he rode without a partner, but everybody regarded him as a true pro.

"So what we got?"

Rodriquez did not disappoint. "Male victim. Deceased. Two small-caliber gunshot wounds. No witnesses so far, called in anonymously. I notified the coroner already."

Outside, Samulson slipped on gloves and knelt down beside the corpse. The man was certainly dead. The rain had washed away most of the blood, making the bullet hole in his forehead easily visible. The location between the eyes suggested a gang-style execution; it was code that the last thing an enemy should experience was going eyeball to eyeball with his killer. From the expansive puddle of blood under the man's lower back, he must have been shot from behind first, likely when he tried to escape.

The scene was otherwise unremarkable. There were no shell casings and the parking lot was dark, devoid of vehicles and people. The nearby high-rises overlooking the school could be a source of possible witnesses. He wanted more information; something here didn't quite jibe with a drug-trade assassination.

Standing, he brushed wet asphalt debris off his knee. "Manny, tell dispatch that we need forensics."

"Done," said Rodriquez. "Ten minutes ago."

Hamid checked again that they were not being followed. Satisfied with the empty road behind them, he tilted the rearview mirror to watch Farzaad the baker and Mouri the failed engineer make their final preparations in the back of the van.

"You are ready?"

"Just a few minutes more." Farzaad's answer was muffled.

"Good, we are almost there. The next piece of road is rough. There will be some bigger bumps."

Hamid slowed the van and turned onto the narrow, rutted access road into the valley. The scrubby vegetation of this remote terrain reminded him of the landscape at home, but he felt no nostalgia. He had traveled enough of the world to realize one could find similarities between different places and people everywhere. It was a waste of time to be sentimental about such trivial things.

Personally, he believed it was unrealistic to think Islam should be the only religion of the world, but he did not welcome the arrogance of the modern-day crusaders either. He smiled to himself and caressed the AR-15 assault rifle propped between the front seats beside him. The Americans were good for one thing, at least.

Ahead in the misty rain, a double line of massive electrical transmission towers loomed into the night sky. The dashboard display showed that they were ten minutes early. Everything would be on schedule.

Hamid parked close to the base of the closest tower, shut off the engine and stepped out. Drawing up his hoodie for warmth, he pushed through the long wet grass to the back of the van. By the time he opened the rear doors, his pant legs were wet and heavy.

Mouri jumped down. He wore an enormous backpack and, without saying a word, jogged away toward the nearest tower. Farzaad slid two large plastic drums across the bed of the van and then lowered himself down to help Hamid lift them to the ground.

"These are not very big for ANFO bombs. Are you sure they'll be enough?"

"In Afghanistan, after they stopped making ammonium nitrate in Pakistan we switched to calcium ammonium nitrate. It is half the nitrogen, so we started adding potassium chlorate and aluminum powder. It will be a good bang."

Hamid nodded, but he was still glad for the additional explosive device Mouri was placing.

Dragging the first barrel to the base of the closer tower, they strapped it tightly against one of the giant steel legs. Mouri, climbing as effortlessly as a mountain goat, was already a third of the way up the system of climbing pegs.

When the second container was in place, Hamid sent a text to Samir. Together they double-checked the remote detonation system before returning to the van to wait for Mouri.

Detective Samulson yawned. The corpse was a Black man, but this one's gaunt facial features were strikingly different than their usual victims. The forensic team leader handed him the victim's wallet and passport, which had apparently both been on the body. Abarque Abouani was a twenty-eight-year-old male Somali with landed immigrant status.

"Hey, Enzo, something's not sitting right with me about this one. We better run this guy by the FBI to see if he's on their surveillance list."

A few minutes later Merphin returned from the cruiser, shielding his notebook from the rain as he scribbled. "Arnie, you're on the ball tonight. He's on their terrorist threat list but was considered low risk."

"OK, let's go check out his apartment." Samulson noted the address on the health insurance card—school board issue—then dumped the wallet into the plastic bag held out by the forensic officer.

"Do me a favor will you? Let me borrow the guy's keys for an hour."

• • •

Chuck entered the parking lot and scanned the vehicles. In the far corner of the lot, he could see Lowry's metallic red pickup truck next to a lamp standard. A shot of nervous adrenaline made his foot heavy and the tires spun. At the lamppost, he came to an abrupt stop.

Lowry's truck was empty. Chuck stepped out, squinting to scan the surrounding shadows and dark spaces between vehicles. At the rear bumper of his truck he froze. *Behind. The crunch of a footstep.* He turned—too late.

The snap of the chokehold made him gasp; his hands instinctively flew to his neck. His Adam's apple felt like a shell in a nutcracker. Unable to get a grip on the arm at his throat, he rammed his elbows back into his attacker's flanks. When their grip slackened slightly, he tried to twist away but struck his head on the open truck door, sending a shower of stars across his vision.

Dazed, he knew that he was easy prey. He tried to raise his arms but his sore shoulder screamed like it was being torn from his body. The pain somehow increased as both arms were forced behind his back. Using everything he could muster, he threw himself backward into the side of his truck, eliciting a satisfying groan from his attacker.

Before he could take advantage, however, a blow to his belly doubled him over. Someone grabbed the hair at the front of his head, nearly ripping it from his scalp, and whipsawed his neck skyward. Lowry's face loomed, so close that Chuck could feel his hot beer breath.

"Spitwell tells me you ratted him out."

"I don't—know what you're talkin' about." Chuck's urgent gulps for air sliced his words.

Another punch took his breath away completely. Vomit surged into his throat.

"Who else would know about the ammonia?"

A knee in his lower back sent him to his hands and knees. The puking was sudden and profuse. Another wicked kick to his kidney sent him sprawling on his side.

There was the crunch of gravel near his face. "If you don't want a skid load of struts to accidentally crush the snitch-shit out of you, then you better keep your fucking mouth shut."

Strong hands grasped Chuck under his arms and pulled him to his feet. He staggered, nearly falling until he managed to find the truck door. "I have no—"

"Oh, yes you do. Now, get your act together for night shift." Lowry stepped forward and slipped something into his shirt pocket."

"That's a discipline card. One more and you lose your seniority and benefits package." Lowry affected an exaggerated, hacking cough. "Poor wee little Becky."

CHAPTER 33

Jenny woke to the sound of the front door opening. Slipping on her housecoat, she met her husband in the front hall as he stripped off his rain-sodden jacket.

"You're shivering. You must be frozen."

"Yeah, it was a little damp." With a grunt, Mike pulled his shirt over his head and tossed it toward the laundry closet.

"How about a hot shower, then let's get you to bed, honey. You must be bushed."

"I didn't expect you to be up." Pressing his cold bare chest against her, he drew his arms tightly around her.

"I was worried. How did it go?"

"I don't really want to talk about it."

"Sure." She stood on her toes and looped her arms around his neck to give him a kiss. *This would not be the moment to discuss the success of my own work today.*

She pulled him closer and kissed the side of his neck. "You smell so good and taste even better."

• • •

Wizner opened his eyes. Everything was yellow and hazy. His heart pounded, but so slowly it felt like an unendurable eternity between beats.

He tried to sit up. Lightheaded, he grasped at the bedrail for balance. His mouth felt like the inside of a grungy wool sock. Bedrail? Where was he?

His left forearm felt constrained, pinched tight and immovable. He blinked at it. An intravenous line stretched up from his hand to a hanging bag dripping clear fluid. There was an annoying beeping sound coming from somewhere above him. He turned his head to look. A thin green line traced across a screen, occasionally rising into a peak. The number 34 flashed beside the large letters 'HR', and some smaller red flashing ones that spelled 'Alert'.

He felt a firm pressure on his shoulder and the murmur of a woman's voice, but both seemed miles away.

"Take it easy, Mr. Wizner. You've had a rough day, but don't worry. You'll feel better soon. Now, just lie back."

"What happened? Where am I?"

"You're in the cardiac holding room in the emergency department of East Memorial Hospital. You took an overdose of digoxin."

"I did not," he protested indignantly. "That's insane."

This was why he hated hospitals. They were fearsome places, stripping away a person's control when they were most vulnerable.

"Will I live?"

"Indeed you will . . . if you want to." The nurse gave a motherly smile and squeezed his hand gently.

Wizner shook his hand free. "What's my blood sugar, my electrolytes?"

"Completely normal, as were all the tests for a heart attack or stroke."

"When can I go home?"

"As soon as your heart rate stays over fifty beats a minute and the psychiatric team has a little chat with you." The nurse fluffed his pillow. "Is there anyone we can call to pick you up, dear? Someone has to keep an eye on you overnight."

"I'll just rest a little longer, then I'll take a cab home."

The woman patted his hand. "We'll see what the doctor says about that."

He closed his eyes so that the nurse would shut up and leave him alone. Digoxin? There must be a mistake. Sorting that out would have to wait, however, because all he wanted to do right now was sleep.

• • •

Detective Samulson opened Abarque's apartment door with one of smaller keys on the crowded ring. He surmised the remainder of them must be for the school.

The apartment was bare except for a futon, prayer mat, and some papers in a neat stack under a rock paperweight. There was no computer, TV or other electronics—not even a charger to indicate a stolen cell phone. There was no landline either.

The papers under the rock revealed very little except pay slips from the school board. The most recent was from the First County bank for a foreign money transfer to an account in Somalia. Besides the health insurance card and several hundred dollars, the only other item in the victim's wallet had been a bank card. The lack of statements would indicate that no credit cards were missing.

Overall, there was nothing suspicious except the money transfer.

Emerging from the bathroom, Merphin stood in the middle of the kitchen shaking his head. "There's barely enough stuff in the rest of the place to go on a camping trip."

Samulson waved the bank receipts. "All I got is a wire transfer to Somalia. Do you think the FBI would find that interesting?"

"Personally, I don't think it's worth bothering them . . . yet."

"OK, let's check out the school, his employer and what mosque he went to." On his way out, Samulson tossed the key ring to his partner, freeing his hands to pull out his phone.

Merphin locked the door behind them, musing aloud. "If there are no cards missing and his wallet was still in his back pocket filled with cash, then it wasn't a robbery. There are no known Somali gangs in town, but it was clearly a targeted attack. So who would want to kill this guy?"

CHAPTER 34

Hamid scanned the horizon for intruders as they waited for Mouri to descend the transmission tower, tapping a frantic beat on the steering wheel with his fingers. He checked again that the machine gun lying across his lap was loaded and ready.

The back door of the van slammed shut. In the rearview mirror, Mouri gave a thumbs-up. Hamid tapped his phone to alert Samir, then slammed the gearshift into drive. The tires spun on the rain-slick dirt and gravel before the van lurched forward, and he dropped his phone onto his lap. To maneuver up the rough hillside back to the road required two firm hands on the wheel.

Two hundred yards down the road, Hamid pulled into a small clearing with a partial view of the towers. The range of the detonation device was limited—he couldn't go too far. He pulled the burner phone from his pocket.

"Praise Allah."

His companions echoed his words, and he dialled the number.

The tower nearest to them convulsed, then toppled inward toward its twin as impressive explosions ruptured its high voltage lines. It landed on the remaining lines, stretching and snapping them amid bright flashes of light. Yellow and white sparks soared upward.

The fireworks were awe-inspiring, but they dared not linger. This was just the beginning.

• • •

Samir dropped his phone and swiftly entered Wizner's ID into the power grid interface. Two clicks, and the transmission network map appeared. All lines were green.

His palms were moist; the index finger he held poised over the keyboard trembled with anticipation. An alert box at the top of the screen flashed red.

He hammered down the F6 key, launching the misinformation program he'd inserted into the repair dispatch code. Sent again from Wizner's account, the virus-containing email had been opened without question by the night-ops department. Samir had simply renamed the attached document 'version 2' based on a previous exchange of correspondence and asked them to update the file. The faithful employee had dutifully complied.

The lights in Samir's room flickered and went out. With a reassuring click, the back-up power packs under his bed activated, seamlessly maintaining electricity to his computer. On the screen, the grid system alert box continued to flash its warning. The company would dispatch a work crew to investigate, but Samir's modifications would place the location of the fault over sixty miles away on another line.

If everything worked to plan, just as the repair crews arrived they would be informed that the site of the fault had been incorrectly identified. Anticipating the movements of the crews, the software would continue to change the location accordingly, creating a bewildering cat-and-mouse game to find the outage.

With the night-ops' attention diverted, Samir switched his focus to the reactor's control software. Design modifications introduced after Three Mile Island had made American nuclear reactors nearly impossible to push into meltdown. But when the reactor reached a certain temperature, it would trigger an emergency cooling mechanism to prevent overheating. It was this fail-safe measure he was counting on.

Samir anticipated that there would be other safeguards that he would need to circumvent. In fact, he wasn't entirely sure that what he sought was even possible. All he could do was acknowledge that there would be obstacles, trust his months of research and pray.

First, he had to manually override the plant's cooling system. Accessing the control console required being in 'live mode', and for that he would need the daily password. An additional prompt asked for the security dongle. He inserted Wizner's into the USB port.

Under the cooling system controls he clicked on the red override button. Immediately, a warning appeared on the screen asking if he was sure. His yes response triggered yet another pop-up. *Damn.*

He ran his hands through his hair. Maybe . . . yes, he could trick the system. His fingers flew over the keyboard. He inserted a software patch into the feedback program controlling the cooling. Then, copying the last hour of normal running stats—including core temperature—he fed them into to the input module. He smiled. Now the system operator's control panel indicators would display the false numbers in a continuous loop—while unleashed, the reactor marched closer to meltdown.

Hopefully, the deception would keep the plant employees oblivious to the overheating core. Eventually, however, he would need to completely disable the system. This time, Allah must grant him the wisdom to find a way.

He checked under the bed. The power packs still blinked green.

CHAPTER 35

Without streetlights or traffic signals, the drive back to the Tech College had taken Samulson and Merphin longer than expected. When they arrived, the forensic team was just lifting Abouani's body into the back of the coroner's van for transport to the morgue. Mr. Carson, the campus director, stood at the back door of the building, huddled under an umbrella.

Inside, the school official said very little, obviously displeased to be roused from sleep for such a trivial matter as a dead janitor. Initially reluctant to divulge personal information, he confirmed, after a gentle reminder of the seriousness of the matter, that Abarque Abouani was on the college payroll.

"But with the power off I can't pull up his human resource file on the computer." Carson hurriedly rebuttoned his raincoat.

Merphin patted the file cabinets he was resting his arm on. "You mean to say there's nothing in here? Most organizations require the employee's 'wet ink' signature on a physical copy of their assessments."

Carson grimaced and said nothing. Unlocking the top drawer, he flipped through the contents and handed Merphin a folder without making eye contact. Merphin scrutinized it under the dim light of the emergency fixture.

"In the quarterly review there's a note about an oversupply of floor soap," he chuckled, "and a suggestion to use more of it. But there's no mention of suspicious behavior, missing items, etc. In the annual evaluation . . . ," he ran a finger under the words as he read, "although Abouani's work history is exemplary, he will not be considered for promotion until his English language skills improve."

Detective Samulson jotted a quick note as he spoke. "Did Mr. Abouani have any signing authority for supplies?"

"Yes, but with a strict dollar limit," Mr. Carson said brusquely. "Any ordering or purchases over one hundred dollars would require review by his supervisor."

"May we see where he worked and any supplies that he may have ordered?" Samulson struggled to keep his tone polite.

"His station and janitorial storage room are in the basement. I assure you that it contains nothing more than toilet paper and cleaning supplies. Mr. Thomas, our maintenance supervisor, inspects once a month and he is very strict. He would have noticed anything out of the ordinary."

"I'm sure, but we need to cover all the bases."

Standing at the supply room door, the school official appeared flustered, frantically searching his pockets. Samulson smiled and held out his hand, dangling Abarque's keys.

Slipping on his reading glasses, Carson studied the choices.

"Front and back door . . . master key to the classrooms . . . leaving either of these two for the storage . . ."

Merphin cleared his throat. "Sir, could you please try them?"

"Certainly, certainly." Visibly relieved that the first key worked, Carson pushed open the door and stood back.

Samulson reflexively tapped the light switch before Merphin switched on his phone flashlight. The weak beam revealed shelves overflowing with supplies. Above each section a handwritten note on a strip of masking tape described the products and their uses.

Noticing the detectives' attention, Carson explained from the doorway. "Mr. Thomas told me that he put those up when Abarque first started work. Coming from the third world, the poor man didn't have experience with many of these things."

"I see that Abarque took Mr. Thomas's directive seriously." Merphin pointed at the empty shelf below the label 'Floor Washing Soap'.

"I suppose he could have been stealing it and selling it." Offered Carson as he drew the door closed, striking Merphin's heel as the detective exited.

Merphin grunted and let Carson pass. "So what you thinking, partner?"

Samulson tapped his notebook with his pen. "There was no soap at his apartment." He called ahead to the school official, already several paces ahead on his way to the exit. "Sir, perhaps the victim's boss Mr. Thomas could send us the product ID so we can follow up on the missing soap."

"You think he met his demise over a bad soap deal?" Detective Merphin grinned. "Dirty deed without a clean getaway, ha."

Detective Samulson tried but failed to keep a straight face. Scurrying ahead like a startled rat on a drainpipe, Mr. Carson did not laugh. When they stepped outside, he was already closing his car door.

Merphin snorted. "There's a man eager to return to his warm bed."

Samulson shook his head. "Whatever happened to civic duty?"

• • •

The city was dark, sirens wailing in the distance as Hamid pulled up beside the large garbage bin in the deserted parking lot of the self-serve car wash.

"Throw everything in there," he instructed Farzaad and Mouri.

They also needed to wash down the inside of the van, but with no power they would be lucky to get more than a few drops out of the pressure washer.

"Mouri, buy some of those cleaning cloths from the machine over there. We will need to wipe the van."

The young man jogged over to the dispenser but quickly returned. "It is not a mechanical machine like for condoms. It does not work without power."

Farzaad gave his brother a piercing look.

"How would you know about such things?"

Hamid intervened. "Of course, I should know better."

Mouri extracted a cloth handkerchief from his front pants pocket. "We can use this." He pointed to a puddle of soapy water on the floor of the wash bay.

"Yes, yes good."

Farzaad and Hamid finished tossing away the soap containers while Mouri scrubbed. With the van empty and clean except for the two luggage cases, Hamid bowed his head to the brothers.

"Until tomorrow."

With a nod, they disappeared into the obscurity of the night.

Hamid drove several blocks with the headlights off. Parked at the end of a quiet cul-de-sac, his work van awaited him. Bright yellow, with 'Ace Security' emblazoned on all sides in bold red letters and an assortment of extension ladders strapped to the roof, it would have been too conspicuous for tonight's work. But tomorrow it would be perfect. What business wouldn't be panicking about their security system during a prolonged power outage?

He backed the rental truck up to the rear doors of the company van. As quietly and quickly as he could, he transferred the two suitcases.

With the weapons hidden under a drop cloth, he closed and locked the doors. Stepping back, he regarded the logo and slogan painted across them. 'Ace Security—The ace up your sleeve against crime.' He laughed.

"Tomorrow, it will be the joker."

Back at the truck rental, Hamid searched for the darkest-of-the-dark parking spots among the other vehicles. The least conspicuous place to abandon it was in plain sight among its compatriots. Giving everything a last once-over, he finally wiped off the steering wheel and door handles inside and out with Mouri's handkerchief.

Thanks to having prepaid with cash, he merely had to drop the keys in the night return slot, but he didn't want the rental company to know it was back. Tossing them on the mat, he pressed the door closed with his back. Losing the deposit for damages and gas was inconsequential; there would be no one alive to pay them.

Glad to be finished, he yawned. It was time to get some sleep—he needed to be well rested for phase two tomorrow.

CHAPTER 36

Standing in the long queue for bus tickets, Fatima fidgeted with her purse strap and cast a wary eye over the other late night patrons. Her breathing was slowly calming to a normal rhythm, but she continued to shiver. She wasn't sure if it was due to fear or cold. During her trip to the station, all the streetlights had gone out. Walking at this time of night was bad enough, but in the pitch black it had been terrifying. In her haste she had also left the apartment without an umbrella, and her wet clothes clung to her skin like used dishtowels.

With no electricity, the self-serve kiosks were inoperable, and the two ticket agents were forced to write out everything by hand. If you didn't have cash, you were out of luck. With the electronic board that usually listed destinations dark and dead, Fatima had no idea what ticket she wanted.

Spreading her cash out on the counter, she felt like a runaway teen. She asked the agent the farthest she could go on the earliest bus.

"This time of night? Las Vegas," he replied, smirking at her headscarf.

"Yes please, that is fine." While the man counted her bills she smiled inwardly. *Won't this be different? What better place to break free from my brother than Sin City?*

Squeezing into a small gap on the wooden bench —begrudgingly liberated by the bum-shuffling of two men four times her weight— the rage she felt toward Samir resurfaced. Soon, any woman wearing a hijab in public would be an easy target for revenge. After what he did tonight, would she ever be safe in America?

• • •

It had been a hard-fought battle to reassure the hospital psychiatric team that Wizner was not suicidal. Despite feeling like he had spent thirty-six hours being pummeled by rubber hammers in those test labs for sports gear, he'd used all his powers of persuasion to convince the young doctor that he was well enough to take a cab home. Now, steadying himself against the hallway wall of his condo, he wished he hadn't.

As he lay on his bed, the room swirled. *Maybe I should call an ambulance.* No, he could tough this out. For reassurance he reached into his pants pocket, but his phone wasn't there. It would still be at the office.

Work. Power outage. During the cab ride home, he'd been only vaguely aware of the enveloping darkness. Right now, he really didn't give a shit. All he wanted to do was sleep. The crew could manage without him. If they really needed, they could use the emergency radiophone.

After a moment, he sighed and rolled to the edge of the mattress. Reaching down, he dragged the cumbersome handset and its behemoth battery pack out from under the bed. *No one could ever say I'm a bad manager.*

He collapsed back onto the bed. It was so much softer and more comfortable than the hospital gurney. He would just close his eyes for a minute and then get up and email in to report his recovery.

Disoriented by an odd buzzing sound and total darkness, it took Wizner a minute to gather his bearings. *Where am I?* Right, hospital, taxi, condo. The racket was coming from the damn radiophone. *Shit.*

He swung his legs over the side of the bed, groped for his glasses on the bedside table and stood. The room reeled; he dropped to his knees.

With his forehead firmly planted on the carpet in a vain attempt to stop the spinning, he dragged the phone receiver to his ear. There was a voice speaking on the other end, but Wizner's tongue was held hostage by the glue of dehydration. Pulling himself upright, he sat on the edge of the bed, took a long sip from the days-old glass of water on the table and tried again.

"Wizner here."

"Hi, boss, it's Brian. You need to get in here pronto. The shit is hitting the fan big time. There is a massive disruption on grid-lines one and three."

"Why are you calling me? Just wait for the report from the scene and reroute around the problem."

There was a pause and he could hear the night-ops taking a deep breath. "The tower damage sensors are sending the work crews all over hell's half acre and they're coming up empty. Our system is totally black and for some reason we can't reroute replacement power."

"Shit. OK, OK, that sounds messed up, but I'm afraid I'm quite sick. You'll have to give me some time. I'll be there as soon as possible. In the meantime, do what you can."

Staggering toward the open window he pushed aside the blinds and inhaled the rain-freshened air. Without the glare of streetlights, the inky black storm clouds seemed more ominous. He watched the rain pounding across the pavement in sheets; *by morning I'll need a boat to get to work.* A cold spatter struck his face. He shut the window. Weaving his way back to the bed, he dove under the covers.

The dry, rattling rat-a-tat-tat from Becky's bedroom jarred Heidi from a sound sleep. She clicked the lamp switch, but the room remained dark. *Crap.* Her daughter's mist tent must have gone off with the power.

The good Boy Scout that he was, Chuck had bought a big-ass gas generator for times like this. Of course, now he wasn't here to start the damn thing up.

Dashing across the hall, Heidi yanked up the plastic wall of the tent. She could just make out Becky, her wide eyes reflecting the little light coming from the window. She was panting, clearly panicked.

"Mommy, I can't breathe."

"It's OK, honey, the electricity isn't working. I'm going out to start the generator and everything will be fine. Hang in there. I'll be right back."

God dammit, this thing is heavy. The generator caught on another lump of grass as she struggled to drag it over the lawn. To facilitate moving it from the barn to the house, Chuck had put the machine on a dolly, but her dear husband obviously hadn't done a test run. The wheels were too small to handle the rough ground and wouldn't budge. Putting her shoulder against the generator was painful; the hard edges dug in as she struggled up the rain-slick grade to the side of the house. She pushed until she couldn't take another step.

Unraveling the entire length of thick cable, she walked gingerly through the flowerbed, hoping she was close enough. When the cord pulled taut, she drew her hand across the siding, searching in vain for the electrical panel. She chastised their lack of foresight. This was not a straightforward task on a dark, moonless night. A simple magnetic flashlight attached to the generator's metal casing would be a godsend right now.

Eventually she located the connection behind the thorny protection of the rosebush. The cord just reached. Thank goodness the generator motor wasn't a hand-pull and the engine chugged instantly into operation with the push of the button. What a wonderful sound!

Becky's breathing would soon ease and they would be able to run the necessities. Until the fuel ran out. *At least we were smart enough to stash away several cans of gas in the garage.*

• • •

Billy was pissed. His hope that the power would be restored by morning had remained unrealized; the South Koreans would be racking up victories and his ranking would undoubtedly fall out of the top ten.

What was going on? Blackouts usually only lasted a few hours. The technological age didn't accept long outages—without electricity, the world would come to the same apocalyptic end as a nuclear holocaust. For Billy, life without his computer was an unfathomable void.

He stared at the blank screens. It was disconcerting to think something major could be happening and he wouldn't have a clue. Maybe there was enough charge on his phone to get some news.

The screen illuminated, but the network icon had a 'No Service' line through it. The budget southern Oregon-based provider must be without power.

• • •

Samir sat transfixed at his computer screen, tapping a staccato beat on the floor with his feet. This was a better feeling than any worldly pleasure he had ever allowed himself, better than the bus trip to the science museum when Linda Bellingshire had flashed him. The virus was working flawlessly. Every request made to reroute the electricity to feed the local grid he immediately denied. So far, the repair crews had been dispatched to three different locations in the past six hours, none of which were remotely near the damaged towers. The diversion was allowing him time to complete his bigger plan. After the night of heavy rain, Hamid and the others would wreak havoc, adding more ingredients to their toxic brew of destruction.

Standing to stretch, Samir walked to his bedroom window and admired the drenched, sleeping city. The darkness amused him.

On bedside tables all over the city, phones were not charging, in the morning alarms would not be ringing and when all the poor bastards jumped out of bed late for the day, they wouldn't even be able to make a cup of coffee. If they dared to go to work, their computers would be dead. Panicked, trying to buy emergency supplies, their useless credit cards would drive them to hysteria.

If he and Hamid achieved nothing else, by tomorrow night the citizens of Tillson would have experienced a taste of anarchy. With security system batteries drained, business owners would sleep in their unprotected shops with loaded guns at the ready. Soon houses and stores would begin to stink as frozen meals thawed and rotted in fridges.

Finally, his long-dreamed-of social experiment was coming to fruition. Why not recreate the conditions Somalia suffered and see how the Westerners dealt with it? Take away the necessities of life—electricity, water, gas and food—from thousands of gun-toting citizens and see how long their precious 'civilized' society lasted. The world had declared Somalia a failed state. Now it would be America's turn.

And with a little Chernobyl thrown into the mix, who knows what could happen? The fake status data scrolled by in a minimized box at the top left of his screen. With a flurry of keystrokes, he took a peek at the real numbers, another triumph. His little 'fix' to the temperature feedback loop was also working like a charm. The reactor was heating up.

DAY EIGHT

Wednesday
July 4, 2018

CHAPTER 37

It was still dark outside, but Hamid could not pretend to sleep any longer. He had been restless all night listening to the heavy rain—so perfect for the next part of the plan. Now that the deluge had stopped, he drew back the drapes to reveal a breathtaking palette of purple, pink and royal blue. Pools of water reflected the first light in every little depression of the gardens and lawns across the street.

Turning away from the window, he heaved the heavy gym bag off the floor of his closet and over to the bed. In the bag were all the things he might need if he survived the day—a change of clothes, his passport, cash, assorted protein bars and several bottles of water. He tucked his revolver in amongst the three pairs of underwear and selected a clean work uniform from the closet. His name was embroidered on the pocket and his title underneath, then the company logo, Ace Security.

In the mirror, he stared at his reflection until he faded away, replaced by a warrior. Then he steadied his straightedge razor and shaved thoroughly, including the little hairs on his ears. He must be clean if he was to enter heaven today.

It was almost time to pick up the others, but first he had to empty the van of all unnecessary items to make way for the heavy cargo they would load. His landlady's unlocked garden shed at the side of the garage would suffice, and he would borrow her collection of shovels while he was at it.

With the duffle bag of ordnance under his arm and his gym bag in hand, he gave his room one last inspection. He felt no remorse leaving it. His time here was done.

• • •

The shit storm is starting early today. Behind the reception counter at the front of Station 5, police officer Rob Clark picked up the hollering phone. Maybe it just seemed early. The emergency backup power provided only minimal lighting.

"Fifth precinct, Officer Clark. How may I help you?"

"Hi, listen, I don't usually complain, 'cause, like, you know, people are always dumping their shit in my bin, but this time I think you can track down the asshole who filled it with their fucking empty cans."

Clark shook his head. *Didn't this guy have bigger concerns in the midst of a major power outage?* As an experienced officer, however, he was well practiced at concealing his surprise at what the public thought was important.

"Why is that, sir?"

"One of the cans had a packing label stuck on the bottom. It's addressed to the Maintenance Department of Rackford Tech College. You'd think they would have their own trash bin."

"What is your concern? Did the cans contain toxic material?"

"No, the label says soap."

"Soap?" Officer Clark rolled his eyes and placed his hand over the mouthpiece to hide his grumble of exasperation. Across the office, shift-sergeant Mulholland cast an inquisitive look over the top of his coffee cup. Officer Clark shrugged, raising his eyebrows silently. "OK, let me take your details. We'll check it out, sir, but with the power outage and the July fourth holiday it may be awhile. With the lights out we've got a lot of officers directing traffic."

"Tell me about it. I run a carwash. I'm going broke, man."

• • •

As forecast, the weather had shifted and dawn sunlight now streamed into Samir's window. He rubbed his eyes and smiled. The rain had stopped and the treetops bordering the small park across the street were bending under the force of a strong wind from the north.

Samir massaged the base of his neck. He must have fallen asleep briefly but was relieved to discover everything remained on track: the reading lamp on his desk was still without power, the grid status light on his computer was blinking red and the reactor core temperature was climbing, albeit more slowly than he wished.

Perusing Wizner's emails, he saw that repair operations had been suspended until the glitch in the dispatch system was resolved. That was good news and bad. The distraction of the grid problems had been quite useful. Without them, would the plant operators notice his real objective? Another crucial email sat in Wizner's box just below the first, like a cherry ready to be picked from the tree. He opened it and committed the daily security code to memory.

At midsummer, the winter road maintenance depot on Elm Street sat quiet and unused. Behind the chain-link fence, the tall piles of sand waiting to be spread on icy winter roads sprouted a scraggly crop of weeds.

The key lock on the gate was not a problem; the depot's security contract with Ace allowed Hamid entry 24/7. With the van safely parked out of sight behind the building, the three men emerged and made their way quickly through the yard. In the nearest shed sat stacked fifty thousand empty burlap bags—the city's emergency supply in case of flooding. Hamid grabbed an armful and dropped them at Farzaad and Mouri's feet.

"Start shoveling, my friends."

• • •

In the underground parking below his apartment, Wizner sat behind the wheel of his electric car, thankful that it had started. It was normal for the battery to be fully charged as he rarely used the thing, preferring to car-pool to work, but today was the Fourth of July. All his usual chauffeurs were having a blissful sleep-in.

The roads were slick from the overnight rain. Still feeling slightly off-kilter, he drove slowly, fearful of sliding into a telephone pole. He was perturbed. The latest news at shift turnover was unchanged: the grid was off line and there was no outside power available for the city.

On holidays, Lakeridge ran with only a skeleton staff, so the parking lot was mostly bare and the building appeared deserted. When he swiped through the lobby doors the security guard, seemly caught unawares, jumped up from his chair and waved him through, not bothering with the usual formalities.

"Working the Fourth of July, Mr. Wizner. There really must be a big problem."

"That would be an understatement, Henry."

With the plant on emergency power, he didn't bother going to the administrative area. The control room had priority for electricity; his office and computer would be dark. Waving his badge in front of the reader, he punched in the day's code and entered the operations area. The man at the console remained engrossed in his work, studying several readouts and tapping on his keyboard as Wizner approached.

"What you got, Derek?"

The day-shift operator, in his late thirties with long, perennially dirty-looking hair, looked up.

"Hey, glad to see you, boss. Man . . . you look like shit."

"Yeah, I've been better."

"Like Brian told you on the phone, I'm beginning to think the entire system has gone wacky. The reported location of the fault keeps jumping around every few hours. Unless we can figure out the software problem, we'll need to put eyes in the sky and locate the issue by chopper."

"That is a very costly option. What else you got?"

"Every request to reroute power to resupply the city is being rejected."

"By who?"

"By us."

CHAPTER 38

The suburbs of Tillson were still awakening when Hamid pulled into the well-to-do enclave known as Highland Heights. Blessed with an amazing view over the city, it was the preferred neighborhood of many wealthy retired couples. The Ace Security van would not seem out of place; many of the luxury homes displayed the company sticker in their windows.

Taking a left at the Y in the road, the vehicle climbed Linsen Drive. At the first curve where the roadway began a steeper ascent, Hamid pulled close to the curb and parked. From the back of the van, Farzaad and Mouri dragged out two stolen traffic signs—'Road Closed' and 'Men at Work'—and placed them in the street.

With coordinated teamwork, the three men began rapidly placing sandbags, three high, along the contour of land leading toward the storm sewer grate. Once finished, they got back in the van and moved up the street to the next drain, and the next.

• • •

Back at work after only a few hours of sleep, Detective Samulson sipped the acrid black coffee from his oversized mug. He shut one eye to rub away the crust of sleep from its corner then blinked rapidly, trying to summon some moisture to relieve his dry, scratchy eyes. When he was tired, his left eye wandered; he struggled to focus on anything farther than his desk. The office looked nothing like it usually did. Operating under emergency power, a barely adequate yellowish light cast odd shadows and left corners—dark as a war-time bomb shelter.

With his vision finally clear, he logged into his computer. He was fortunate that it was one of the few designated to remain on. Judging from the length of the department-wide action report spilling across his screen, it had been an eventful night. A power outage was a green light for the city to get up to all sorts of shenanigans. As expected, the reports of gas theft by siphoning were numerous, but that wasn't his concern unless someone was murdered in the process. He read on. It was his firm belief that staying aware of all events in general was good practice. One could never know when an item might relate to one of his open cases.

His personalized report was filling rapidly as well. Sherlock was an incredible tool, a powerful AI engine that had been developed in conjunction with the computer giant IBM. Any information or inquiry he entered about a case was put against the database and vetted by relevance to all other cases, using advanced algorithms generated in consultation with the nation's most talented detectives. The entire department could add data, from the superintendent down to a beat cop.

A list of hits with their assigned relevance score filled the screen. Each entry could be expanded with a right click to reveal the reason the information may apply to one of his cases. Scrolling down the list, Samulson's eyebrows rose. Sherlock had flagged a relevant addition to last night's murder of the Somali male. He clicked the entry open.

At approximately six o'clock this morning, a phone call received by a desk sergeant, Robert Clark, at the fifth precinct had reported over a hundred empty soap cans dumped at a Triple Clean car wash. The owner wanted action because he was "sick of paying the haulage on other people's trash." Samulson grunted. Didn't this guy know there were bins with lockable lids?

He checked his text messages. The brand of cleaner matched the one called in late last night by the college's janitorial supervisor, Mr. Thomas. *Excellent.* Finding out who'd bought the stolen soap from Abouani could bring about the quick arrest of his murderer.

The complainant stated that one can still had a shipping label attached, but Officer Clark had not bothered to record the details. In the action column, there was no notation that an officer had been dispatched. Samulson jotted down the address. Perhaps it was time to give the cruiser a scrub.

There was a click behind him, loud in the empty room, as Merphin entered juggling a coffee, donut and newspaper in one hand. A dark growth of whiskers exaggerated the deep lines of fatigue in his partner's features. He looked like he hadn't slept at all.

Samulson rose and grabbed his hat before his partner could sit down. "Hey, Enzo, you ready for a dumpster dive?"

"No thanks, I already had breakfast."

"Yeah, yeah, let's go. I have a lead on last night's case." Samulson rubbed a hand over his own clean-shaven cheek. "What's with the face fuzz? You going for the metro male look?"

"Electric razor."

• • •

While the boys ate an early breakfast, Heidi nipped outside to check the generator. The tank was less than half-full. Becky's frequent aerosol treatments would require lots of juice today; it would be best to take care of the job while she had a free moment. She jogged over to the barn to fetch the gas.

While she was there, she might as well fill the feed dispenser for the animals. Hoisting the heavy pail of grain mix, she groaned. *If weight-bearing exercise prevents osteoporosis, I have no worries.* As the cows drifted in to investigate, she gave the newest calf a pat on the head. They were pretty cute, despite all the work.

Heidi paused as the hum of the generator outside sputtered and stopped. *Is it out already?*

Lugging the ten-gallon gas container made for a slow slog back to the house. At last rounding the corner onto the driveway, she looked up to judge the rest of the distance.

"Shit."

The fuel can dropped with a thud. The generator was gone, and a black pickup was racing away down the driveway.

• • •

Rounding the final bend of the road, Chuck let his shoulders relax. He was glad to finally be home after a tedious and unprofitable ten hours. The shift foreman had held the crew at the plant all night waiting for the power to return, only to dismiss them just before seven with the union-prescribed minimum four hours of pay. Worse yet, he couldn't lie down for naps like the other guys due to the bruises from Lowry's 'warning'. He'd spent the night pacing the workroom floor. On his first trip to the urinal his stream had been bright red with blood, but after several bottles of water it was just a slightly pink.

He was only a hundred yards from the house when a black pickup truck came barreling down the road. Chuck swerved. Fish tailing erratically, the other vehicle sped past, raising a blinding spray of mud. At the entrance to the driveway, the intruder's tires had carved deep ruts into the gravel.

Dropping his foot on the gas, Chuck sped toward the house. As he rounded the last bend a flash of blue filled his vision, and he yanked the wheel just in time to avoid colliding with Heidi's little Ford Focus. With the brakes locked in a skid, his truck lurched into the small ditch beside the lane and came to a stop.

Sucking back waves of nausea at the knifelike pain in his side, he rushed to the car.

Heidi was pounding the steering wheel in rage. Lowering the window, she started to speak and dissolved into tears.

"Some asshole just stole our generator."

Teetering for balance on the clasped hands of his partner, Detective Samulson reached into the dumpster and managed to grab the lip of a soap container. Before he dropped back to the ground, he saw that there were over a hundred more at least, identical and nearly covering the other garbage beneath.

He pulled off the lid of the one he'd grabbed and inhaled. A pungent aroma greeted his nostrils, not the perfumed scent of soap but something more industrial. There was a familiarity about it that triggered a memory; a happy recollection of sitting on a wicker chair, sipping lemonade in the sunshine on his grandmother's enormous wraparound veranda while she doted on the lush garden sweeping its border. He remembered her wagging finger as she frequently reminded him, "You must use one with lots of nitrogen, Arnie, to make the garden green."

Plant fertilizer.

"Enzo, these smell like plant fertilizer. I think we have something other than black market soap deals to worry about."

"What, the attack of the giant killer tomato?"

"Nitrogen."

"You think somebody is making a bomb?"

"Could be. Definitely makes the connection to our perps and Mr. Abouani much more interesting."

Nodding his agreement, Merphin pointed toward the office of the car wash. "Too bad this video camera is pointed the other way, but hopefully somebody saw who took him out at the college. Any more witness calls last night?"

"Apparently one lady claims that she saw the body from a distance as she cut through the parking lot on her way home from work," Samulson snapped his notebook shut, "but she didn't check it out 'cause it was raining too hard.'"

Merphin snorted his contempt. "Then I guess it's time to go door to door at those apartment buildings."

"And call the FBI."

Samulson snapped his notebook shut and tapped on his cell phone. "After that we can check out the hardware store. It's open at seven thirty."

CHAPTER 39

Mike Longstrum woke to thin hints of daylight squeezing between the slats of the bedroom blind. It must be late. Sleeping in was not like him.

He rolled over and groaned. The face of his phone was black. In his exhaustion last night, he must have failed to plug it in. He snapped in the spare battery. Shit.

Judging from sounds emanating from the kitchen, Jenny was already up. A moment later, she appeared in the bedroom doorway with a laden tray.

"Hi, I let you sleep."

"Why aren't you at work?"

"Because there's no power."

"But honey, you should have woke me up. I still have to go in."

"Not so fast. I made you breakfast. After last night's amazing performance, you need some nourishment. But I'm afraid without a stove all I can serve is cool-not-cold milk and Cheerios."

"Sounds great."

She slid the tray onto his lap and sat down on the bed.

"I got the impression it didn't go well last night. Want to talk about it?"

He grunted. "Could have been worse, I guess. On the plus side there was no massacre, but on the other hand, I'm not sure there was ever going to be one. I think someone is playing us."

"Who?"

"Some Internet freak who's been feeding us a pack of bullshit, that's who."

"What are you going to do?"

"Find him and slap him around." Mike caught Jenny's startled look. "Kidding."

He slid the breakfast tray off his lap and started searching for his underwear on the floor. "Best damn breakfast I've ever eaten in a power outage."

"Cereal and milk won't get you through the day."

"I know, but I gotta go. I'm late as it is."

"Give me a second to make you some sandwiches. The sliced ham in the fridge will just go bad."

She was already heading to the kitchen. "It'll only take two minutes. There aren't going to be any restaurants open today, and the vending machines won't work."

"You're right, thanks. Everything will be on emergency power at work and I have to file my report about last night, ASAP. I'm more than a little worried about how Dan's going to react."

Mike followed her down the hallway, hopping, one leg in his pants.

"Well, after you're done you really need to check out Samir and the connection to Wizner."

Mike gave her a quizzical look. "I was pretty uptight yesterday. Remind me."

Jenny began puttering with the dishes noisily.

"Oh, nothing really. You know, just another one of my paranoid theories." She slammed the cutlery drawer shut with a hard hip check. "Your sandwich will be ready in a minute, *darling*."

"Ouch. You know I respect your ideas. I've been busy. Haven't I told you before to apply to the Bureau? You'd be a great agent."

"Cut the crap." Jenny turned with a half-smile holding out a lunch sack. "Here you go. And drink lots of fluids. You better hurry up before Samir blows us all up."

Mike accepted the offering but didn't leave.

"No, no, I'm listening. Tell me again."

• • •

"I still think we should file a police report for the generator." Heidi poured two cups of coffee and sat down at the breakfast nook table.

"Yeah, sure. When the power's back on and I can find the paperwork with the serial number."

She swirled the cold cereal around in her bowl and watched as Chuck inspected the bruises on his side, her appetite non-existent. "You still haven't told me what happened to you."

Chuck's laugh was cut short and he clasped his side. "I tripped on a power-skid. It could have been worse."

Heidi shook her head.

"Lucky."

Pushing away her breakfast, she couldn't hide the tremor in her voice. "Speaking of worse, Becky is having a rough time."

"You don't have to tell me, I can hear it from here." Chuck put down his fork and pinched the bridge of his nose. "But we can't afford another hospital admission right now. The last one used up her ten-day allocation for the quarter."

"Damn that insurance. She can't survive much more damage to her lungs."

"But we can't afford the intravenous antibiotic treatments on our own." Chuck slid his hand over the table toward Heidi's. "If we had electricity we could step up her treatments here, but—"

Heidi slammed her hand on the kitchen table, their plates jumping with a clatter. "What about Sam Rayleigh on county road 91? He must be completely off the grid with all those solar panels on the roof of his barn."

Chuck nodded slowly, then with more certainty as he pushed away his lukewarm leftover hamburger casserole, also barely touched. "Good idea, I'll pack up her aerosol equipment."

Heidi hurriedly grabbed several days' worth of medications from the crowded refrigerator shelf reserved for Becky's supplies and dumped them into a plastic shopping bag.

Chuck returned to the kitchen with the electric pump, tubing and nebulizer in a plastic box under one arm and his shotgun tucked under the other.

"What the hell are you doing with that?"

"Being prepared. It seems pretty damn nuts out there."

● ● ●

James Wizner stared at the operator's console. It had been three years since he'd had to work the controls, ever since his promotion to management and then plant manager. Luckily nothing had changed—except for how the system was behaving.

The readouts still showed that the reactor was fine, but the grid was fucked. Frustrated, he drew in a breath, then exhaled slowly. How could the plant be denying their own rerouting requests? Was it a software glitch or could there be outside interference?

"OK, Derek, reboot your terminal and reload the grid diagnostics software from backup. And take the entire system offline while you do it."

Impatient, he clicked his fingernails on the counter rapidly as Derek began flicking switches. "Anything I can do?"

Derek turned to him with a wry smile. "Yeah, boss, you could stop the racket."

"Ah, sorry. I think I'll go get something to drink."

Standing brought on a wave of dizziness. He kept one hand on the wall all the way to his office.

After fumbling for a moment in the dark fridge, he took a long draft from a half-empty water bottle. It was barely cold enough to be refreshing but better than nothing. He tossed the empty bottle in the recycling bin by his desk and turned to leave, then went back. While he was here, he might as well grab his system access dongle.

The lanyard was not in its usual place in his upper right desk drawer. He shook his head. Had he taken it home? Yesterday was such a blur, but that made no sense. His cell phone was there and so was the envelope with the baseball tickets that PhD guy had left.

Weird. He shrugged. Whatever. A second dongle was only necessary if they had to go manual, and hopefully that wouldn't happen.

Back in the control room, Derek was just bringing the grid software back online.

"How's the reboot going?"

"OK, I think. The tower sensors say the problem is about forty miles out of town in the Samata Hills. It will take over an hour to get the guys there. So, I say keep the team where they are for a while and make sure the system doesn't change its fucking mind again. If not, then maybe we're good to go."

"Dispatch the crew anyway."

"What? The closest one is on the other side of the county."

"Just do it. What do we have to lose? In the meantime, try making another rerouting request."

Derek typed rapidly for several seconds and then waited, hunched over the keyboard, his attention fixed upon the screen.

"OK, so far so good —*dammit*." He pounded his fist on the counter. "Denied."

"Shit." Wizner slumped in his chair. He was already tired, and the most challenging day of his career had just begun. "OK, let's go old school. Call HQ. We need to talk to real people, not a computer."

• • •

"OK, hear me out." Jenny placed the cutting board and knife in the sink and turned back to Mike. She took a deep breath: the words tumbled out of her.

"I checked out Fatima and Samir's place." She couldn't help but giggle. "I broke in with a couple screwdrivers."

"You did *what*?"

Mike threw the lunch bag across the counter. Jaw clenched, nostrils flared—he looked angrier than she had ever seen him. "How did you know they weren't home?"

Jenny backed away a couple steps. "I made sure Fatima was at work and I assumed he was too."

"Assumptions are what get you killed! If the man's truly a terrorist, he'd be armed." Mike clenched and unclenched his fists. "And you could've been arrested for B and E."

"I just took a look." Jenny took another step back and bumped into the stove. She felt a thick lump developing in her throat. "I didn't steal anything."

"This is insane! Are you trying to end my career?"

"No! If you would just listen to me. It was weird. He's got battery packs attached to his computer." She picked up her phone from the counter. "I took pictures of one of his notebooks and used meTranslate . . . ."

"Oh my God." Mike turned and faced the wall, running his fingers through his hair several times, panting, almost struggling for air.

"Are you alright?"

"I can't hear this." His voice was quiet. "Not now, not ever."

Jenny reached out to comfort him but Mike pulled away from her with a jerk. "You're compromising everything I've worked for."

"But this is important. The notes were about nuclear reactors."

Without looking at her he slipped on his jacket.

"I was only trying to help."

She stood motionless in the center of the kitchen, waiting for the apartment door to re-open, until the faint clunk of the stairwell door told her he was gone.

• • •

As Detectives Samulson and Merphin entered the hardware store where Mr. Thomas had stated the victim bought his cleaning supplies, the man behind the counter held up his hands.

"There is no cash here."

Merphin held up his badge. "Relax, police. Are you the owner?"

"Yes, but I'm closing since there are no credit or bank cards working. But man, am I ever glad to see you guys. Two assholes just stole my last generator. Before that, it was all my candles and matches. I've given up hope that the power is coming back so I'm locking up. Not that a few deadbolts will stop anyone; with the battery on full-time, the alarm system is dying. I expect the store will be empty by tomorrow."

"Sorry to hear that, but actually we just want to ask you a few questions."

"Do you recognize this man?"

Samulson held up the photocopy enlargement of Abouani's passport photo.

"Sure, he's the evening janitor at the tech college down the street. Comes in all the time to pick up little things. Seems like a nice guy. Very quiet, but maybe that's just because his English isn't that good."

"What does he buy?"

"Window cleaner, small tools, fertilizer for the plants and shrubs around the building. Sometimes small packages of nails and screws."

"How often does he buy the fertilizer?"

"At least a container a week ever since he started over a year ago. He says his expense account has a weekly limit."

"Do you mind if I open a container of the fertilizer, just for a quick smell?"

The storeowner gave Samulson an odd look. "Whatever turns your crank, Detective."

Merphin snorted.

"Yeah, Samulson, sniff away. Do you want some glue to go with that?"

"Har har. You're a laugh a minute. Let's head over and do a door-to-door at the building behind the college. They should be out of bed by now."

"Yeah, and with nowhere to go this fine Fourth of July."

CHAPTER 40

It was only a short trip up the hill from Highland Heights to the sewage treatment plant. On his reconnaissance trips over the preceding months, Hamid had verified that it was not a secure facility. There were no CCT cameras or security guards, nothing but a rusty old chain-link fence with three strands of barbwire stretched along the top.

The only movement was a steamy mist rising from the series of concrete settling tanks. Atop a thick concrete pad at the far end of the complex, a grouping of large green metal valves regulated the inflow of raw sewage from most of the city. But the storm sewers that drained from the older section of the downtown core were also connected to the main sewage pipes. To prevent the holding tanks from being overwhelmed during heavy rain, these valves automatically restricted the flow of sewage entering the plant when necessary, creating a backlog waiting to be processed.

At the near end of the settling tanks, behind a retaining wall built into the side of the hill, several similar valves regulated the outflow of treated water into Hansen Creek as it passed by on its way down the slope.

Eight months ago, Samir had provided Hamid with a link to online blueprints of the system and a set of instructions. The idea was another example of Samir's brilliance—an application of basic physics to wreak havoc on the city's infrastructure. But annoyingly, Samir had never given the go-ahead, stating that by itself the attack was only an inconvenience, not crippling. "Wait for the bigger plan," he'd said. Hamid was pleased they were done waiting.

They would achieve the first prong of their attack by blowing away the side of the plant. The blast would release millions of gallons of partly treated effluent into the Hansen, which meandered its way through the city before joining Masta Creek in Regency Park. Here, the creek water was used to fill a series of picturesque lagoons. The sudden surge would instantly breach their banks, destroying the downtown green space before flowing into the streets and eventually the Hansen River.

It was more complicated to create the second wave. Farther along the hillside, the storm sewers of the old subdivision of Highland Heights also fed rainwater directly into the system. The street grates there drained into the last section of the old main pipe from the downtown core, just before it entered the treatment plant. As an additional precaution, after last night's heavy downpour, the intake valve to the plant would also be completely closed to prevent the mix of sewage and storm water from exceeding the capacity of the holding tanks.

Samir had noticed that the feeder system of the old downtown system consisted of smaller diameter pipes. By applying sufficient water pressure on this side, a water hammer effect could be achieved. A large enough mass of water flowing downhill from the large pipe into the small ones could create enough propulsive force to drive the water back up the pipes and out the storm sewer grates, further flooding the city with sewage.

Luckily, the water source they needed was just above them, and its flow would be directed into the storm sewers by the strategically placed sandbags. With the plant's intake valve closed, the pent-up mixture of rainwater and sewage would surge back into the city like a toxic tidal wave.

About fifty yards below the sewage plant, Hamid pulled into the access point for the public hiking route that wound along the bank of the creek. There Farzaad, dressed in green camouflage and a matching packsack, slipped out of the back of the van and ran up the slope into the cover of the brush.

Hamid watched Farzaad climb on his belly, a folding shovel across his forearms. After a few minutes, he reached the retaining wall below the outflow control valves. A small cascade of dirt slid down the hill as he dug in close to the concrete base, before reaching for the packsack and starting to pull out bars of Tovex. Stolen from a highway construction site, only a small amount of the blasting material had been needed to blow the electricity tower last night. This would require everything they had left and, unfortunately, maybe more.

Once the detonation device was wrapped around the package, Farzaad slid back down the hill to the waiting van. When the time was right, what a shitstorm it was going to be.

• • •

Mike arrived at his workstation to an ominous scene, Smithers sitting in his chair and Wendy poised on the edge of his desk. Smithers spoke first.

"Agent Longstrum. Good morning."

"Not really." Mike opened his desk drawer and snapped a recharged battery into his phone aggressively.

"Yeah, that was a bit of a fuckup last night."

"We thwarted the attack."

"Perhaps, but according to Wendy there was no traffic on the site to indicate a mission abort. Perhaps they spotted the surveillance or your team at the mosque."

"Impossible, we were—"

Smithers shrugged impatiently. "Mike, frankly, I think you've been had."

"The bomb is still out there."

Smithers nodded. "Granted. So we'll keep up the surveillance on the Lone Stars, but with that and the holiday, we're a little understaffed so I'm pulling you," he waved the file folder he was holding, "to work on this."

Before Mike could respond Smithers began reading. "Two city detectives investigating the murder of a Somali man uncovered something of possible interest. The victim worked for approximately the past year as a janitor at the downtown campus of Rackford Tech College."

Wendy took a turn. "Nothing at the college seemed unusual except that the space reserved for soap in the janitorial storage room was empty. According to an onsite inspection by the victim's immediate supervisor the day of the murder, the shelf had been overflowing with containers during his visit. The school official suggested to the detectives that perhaps the man was selling the school's cleaning supplies on the black market."

Mike opened his mouth to express his bafflement, but Dan held up a hand and flipped forward a page in the docket. "This led to an investigation of the dumping of approximately one hundred large soap containers in a garbage bin behind the Triple Clean car wash near Thirty-second and Maple. Several of these containers bore packing slips with the school address. Because the detectives suspected fertilizer residue inside, they called us."

"Their opinion is based on one of the detective's sense of smell, but the store clerk of the nearby hardware store did confirm that the man bought fertilizer weekly using the campus account," Wendy interjected.

"I'm no expert," said Smithers, "but it sounds like this guy was stockpiling enough nitrogen to cause a serious blast. Guys, we're stretched. So I need you two to check this one out. Wendy, you're lead."

"Sir, I'd appreciate the opportunity to—"

Smithers shook his head. "With power in short supply, neither of you can do your usual computer voodoo witchcraft thing. She's senior, so it's her case. Now get out there and do some real work."

• • •

For the second part of the plan they drove past the Highland Heights subdivision, farther uphill to the city's principal water tower. Again, they parked in an area designated for hikers. A hundred feet in the air, the enormous metal bulb resembled a giant, shiny gumball on a stick.

A clean source of drinking water warranted more stringent security than the city's waste. With the limited time available, they needed a creative way to circumvent the multiple protective measures of barbwire fencing, motion detectors and surveillance cameras.

The three men struggled to slide the three-foot-long drone out of the van.

"It's a little joke between us. For years, I try to teach Mouri to bake, yet the only thing he can make is pizza dough—but he sure can cook up some spicy C-4."

Hamid attached the drone's wings and taped the payload to its underbelly. "Where did you learn to make plastic explosives?"

"Easy, the recipe is online. The hard part was finding the ingredients."

Farzaad tousled Mouri's hair. "But he mixed up one good batch and this is the perfect place to serve his homemade pizza."

Hamid handed Mouri the controller. "You sure it works?"

Farzaad laughed. "No doubts. The test blew the lid of my best cast-iron casserole through the ceiling."

Mouri verified the code on the remote detonator wired to the C-4 and stepped back.

With a soft hum, the black whirlybird lifted into the sky and soared on a perfect trajectory toward the platform at the base of the water tank. Farzaad shook his head in awe.

"How did you learn to do that?"

Mouri grinned. "Video games."

Hamid slapped Farzaad on the back and pointed down the slope toward Linden Street. "See, the water will funnel through there and create enough force to backwash all the shit and piss we release by blowing away the plant."

The instant the drone set down on the platform with a faint metallic click, they ran back to the van. Soon, just like the third world countries the citizens of Tillson pitied, their own streets would be overflowing with human waste and disease.

• • •

Mike and Wendy caught up with Samulson and Merphin outside the apartment buildings that overlooked the parking lot of the tech college. Neither of the city detectives looked happy, but they acknowledged the display of FBI badges with a perfunctory nod.

"What you got, boys?" asked Wendy.

Samulson spoke first, holding open his notepad but not bothering to consult it. "Like we said on the phone. A Somali male, Abarque Abouani, was shot in the parking lot behind the tech college last night somewhere between 7:00 and 9:00 p.m. We called you because over the preceding year the deceased had bought a considerable quantity of nitrogen-based fertilizer and appears to have stockpiled it in soap containers inside the college."

Merphin took over. "Overnight, someone dumped 105 empty canisters matching the brand of soap used by the college in a dumpster over on the east side. We haven't checked them all but the ones we did were contaminated with fertilizer residue."

"Is this confirmed by the lab?" asked Mike.

"Not yet." Merphin cleared his throat and continued. "We just spoke to a witness who was taking a smoke break on her balcony last evening about 8:00 p.m. She observed a light colored, possibly white van parked behind the college being loaded with similar containers. It was too dark to make out plates or markings on the vehicle. When her cigarette was done she went inside to watch the TV and did not see an altercation or hear a gunshot."

"So she says." Samulson closed his notebook. "That's all we have. Although they're a dime a dozen, we put out an alert for a white van and we were going to check recent rentals."

Wendy nodded. "Thank you detectives. Do you have the passport or a copy so we can run him through our system?"

"Yeah sure, but we already checked through our liaison officer. He's on your terrorist watch list." Samulson smirked as he handed over the paper.

Wendy expressed no reaction in her crisp reply.

"OK, we'll start cross-checking with the rest of the watch list." In exchange for the photocopy of Abarque's passport, she handed over a business card. "Keep us in the loop and we'll do the same."

As they walked back to the unmarked SUV, Mike shrugged. "Well, that isn't much to go on."

"It sure isn't, but that's why we get paid the big bucks."

"We need to run this guy through the system."

"And get some coffee," Wendy added as they drove past a dark, shuttered Starbucks. "I hope the generator holds out."

• • •

Samir watched as the grid icon changed to off-line then returned to active status. To his annoyance, the system was now showing the correct location of the downed power lines. The reboot must have cleared his nasty little program out of its memory.

It could only mean that the operators were onto the misdirection. How long before they figured out the other deception, the fictitious core temperature readouts? A quick study of the real data showed that although it was steadily rising, the core was still a good way away from needing emergency cooling.

He was running out of time. The status indicator on the power supply under the bed was down to the final two bars. He needed the plant off-line.

Well, if they could reboot with backup software, then so could he. Taking remote control of the cursor, he scrolled through the shutdown options and selected 'restore to previous'.

CHAPTER 41

To keep himself occupied while Derek rebooted the grid interface, Wizner refreshed his memory of the console controls and indicators. Still thirsty, he drained a second large bottle of water and surmised that his intake of fluids must be helping because in the past hour his mind was clearing. And amazingly, he didn't need to pee.

Trying to release the spasm in his upper back, Wizner leaned back and stretched his arms over his head. When he returned his attention to the control board, a slight pause in one of the readouts caught his attention. The reactor reading had showed that it was too hot, but only for a millisecond before the numbers returned to a normal level. He was perplexed. The core temperature never fluctuated more than a few tenths of a degree over the short term.

He looked up as Derek spoke. "OK, the grid status program is up and running and so far, so good."

"Are we are still showing the same fault location?"

"Yup." Derek took a sloppy bite of his sandwich, dropping something half-chewed and green on the console.

"You're not supposed to be eating in here."

"Come on, boss. Not only did I draw a holiday shift, but a shitty one at that."

"All right, sorry, it's just that my stomach is a little off. Well, at least one thing worked and we can locate the issue in the grid."

Derek, his mouth crammed full, gave a thumbs-up and turned back to his screen. Then he nearly choked. "Shit no, wait a minute, the damn screen just froze. Now it's blank. OK, there she goes, but man the keyboard is lagging big time. I think the system just rebooted by itself."

"That's insane. Something fishy is going on." Wizner reached over the system op's shoulder, went into the system preferences menu and selected network settings. The rainbow beach ball of death appeared, spinning mockingly on the screen. "Take the module off-line."

"OK, done."

"We might be hacked. Stay off-line. I'm calling security at headquarters."

"But then we'll never find the breach in the grid, unless . . ."

"Yup. It's time to send up the chopper."

• • •

Heidi and Chuck sat in tense silence as the pickup truck sped along the winding gravel road. All three children were buckled in across the back bench seat. Tim, perennially antsy, was pinching his younger brother's leg.

"Ow! Stop that!"

"Behave, you two," Heidi snapped.

"Do you think Mr. Jones will have enough power so we can watch TV? I don't want to miss *Power Puppies*."

Peter's whining voice grated across her nerves like sandpaper across a wound.

"I don't know and it's not important right now."

"Yeah, that's not why we're going to see him, moron," huffed Tim.

"I know. It's 'cause of her." Peter jerked his thumb at Becky.

"That's enough of that," barked Chuck.

Chuck turned into Sam Rayleigh's driveway. The heavy metal gate was chained shut and secured with a huge padlock. The lawn was a rutted muddy mess that served as a parking lot for several trucks and ATVs. The ornamental scrubs along the front of the house were well on their way to being trees. An American flag hung from a pole attached to the veranda that was listing and rotting.

Heidi let out a deep sigh. "I wonder if he's home."

"You guys stay here. I'll go see." Chuck turned off the ignition.

Heidi placed a hand on his. "Chuck, people are rattled, take the gun with you."

"That's just asking for trouble." Chuck jumped down from the truck and climbed over the gate. He walked toward the house with his hands visible, held well away from his side. The driveway was long, but he had a good sight line to the front door. He tried to stay relaxed. It's fine. *We're neighbors, aren't we?*

Twenty yards from the house, he pulled up short as Bert Jones stepped out of the bushes onto the flagstone walkway. His eyes were slits squeezed between an untamed gray beard and a bleached out Angel's baseball cap. He wore only rubber boots and overalls. The deep red-freckled tan on his arms stopped abruptly at the elbows. Butted firmly against his shoulder was an old but well-maintained rifle.

"Stay where you are."

Behind him, the front door swung slightly ajar and the barrel of a second rifle emerged through the gap.

"Whoa, take it easy there. It's just me, Chuck Schelmer from over on the fourth line. We've met a few times at the county picnics."

"I don't give a fuck who you are. We don't got nothing for you."

"We aren't asking for much, just a few minutes of electricity."

"Tough. You shoulda been prepared. If you were smart, you'd know something like this was coming."

"What do you mean? Like what?"

"The Russians, shit for brains. Not with nukes. No need, all they have to do to fuck us over now is shut off the power and screw with the Internet. They want anarchy. Once we destroy ourselves, they'll just march right in and take over."

"I'm not sure what you're talking about. Look, we have a sick daughter who needs a simple medical treatment. All we want is enough electricity to run a small machine for twenty minutes, two times a day."

He took a step forward.

"I said stay put or I'll shoot. Now turn around and leave us alone."

Chuck took another step. "Look, I'm not here to—"

The shot struck the stone walkway near his foot, spraying shards of stone. A searing pain dropped Chuck to one knee.

"What the hell! Are you *crazy*?"

"Maybe. Now get goin' or I'll aim higher next time."

Chuck stumbled to his feet and backed away down the driveway.

• • •

Enzo Merphin replaced the receiver on the phone with a flourish. "Bingo."

"What you got?" Samulson leaned back in his chair, yawning.

"You know that sketchy truck rental place on the east side?"

"Yeah, Louie's. I'm surprised he doesn't own his own tow truck the number of times you see those vehicles broken down."

"And charge the customer for the tow. Anyway, our good friend Manny Rodriquez checked it out and they rented out a white van with no markings for cash on Tuesday."

Samulson sat upright. "Sounds promising."

"I've got the plate number," Merphin waved a piece of paper, "and a name. Some guy from Georgia."

"Did they copy any photo ID?"

"Come on, it's Louie's. But the renter was Bashiir Hassan from Georgia."

"Right. Let's broadcast an APB."

"Roger Wilco," replied Merphin, the receiver already pressed to his ear, "but remember he could have swapped the plates."

Samulson waved his hand dismissively. "Just do it. I'll call FBI."

Merphin already had the phone to his lips. "Hello. Loretta? I need a city-wide all points on a white van, plate number Bravo Charlie 749."

"Everything is good?" Hamid watched in the rearview mirror as Farzaad and Mouri checked and rechecked their weapons.

Farzaad kissed the stock of his automatic rifle and gave a thumbs-up. Mouri didn't look up but nodded curtly.

A deep pothole brought Hamid's attention back to the road as the van jolted and labored up the steep grade to the Naskas reservoir.

"We are blessed. Everything has gone to plan so far this morning." He grinned at the pair in the rearview mirror. "Now it's time to create even more havoc."

The huge man-made lake supplied all the water for the city, but for such an important facility, it was almost as poorly guarded as the sewage treatment plant. The main control room for the massive sluice gates was often left unattended while the two-man crew worked elsewhere.

When the city had hired Ace Security to install an intrusion alarm at the main building, Hamid had recognized the opportunity. Tasked with the installation and performance of regular maintenance checks, the staff was accustomed to seeing the Ace van parked at the gate. It was also useful that the master code to bypass the security system was one he chose.

The Easton dam soared above them. Like doors to a giant's castle, the six metal sluice gates were arrayed across the thick span of reinforced concrete. Obtaining sufficient explosives to blow the dam was an impossible fantasy. Instead, it would be a simple matter to fully open all the gates from the control room.

Like with much older infrastructure, there were no online manuals. With no opportunity to learn the workings of the controls beforehand, Mouri, with his engineering background, was the natural choice for the task. When the reservoir crew finally discovered the pending disaster, the young martyr's AR-15 would greet them.

Seeing the look on Mouri's face in the rearview mirror, Hamid tried to reassure the young man. "You are doing Allah's work."

Farzaad enveloped his younger brother in a vice-like hug, then drew back and kissed him on the forehead. Tears streamed down his face.

Without a word Mouri undid the safety on the AR-15, opened the back door of the van, slipped out and scampered up the grassy embankment. He did not look back.

Hamid slid the shifter into low gear and orientated the van downhill. There was no time to waste; it would not take long for the electric gates to open. Only if the emergency generator ran out of diesel would Mouri have to manually turn the large wheels of the mechanical backup.

He could already see more water beginning to flow under three of the sluice gates, a bubbling, churning cauldron that rushed to join the Hanson River as it flowed directly toward the center of town. Without the dam regulating the surge of water from the rainfall, the vast tracts of recent development on the plains surrounding the city would soon be submerged. It would be a flood the likes of which Tillson had not seen for a hundred years.

At the bottom of the hill, Hamid looked upward and smiled. All six gates were already one third up and, Allah willing, Mouri would ensure they stayed open.

CHAPTER 42

Wendy replaced the receiver on the phone console. "That was Samulson. They have a cash rental of a van to a male Somali."

Mike slid his finger down the computer screen. "Who knew there were so many Somali in the area?" He took big gulp of coffee, crushed the paper cup and threw it in the waste bin. "God, that was bad."

Wendy finished her own and slid the cup over the edge of the desk into the garbage. "Making coffee with lukewarm water sucks."

"Roger that." Mike stood, balled his fists into his lower back and arched into them. "But it makes no sense that the Lone Stars and Abouani are related unless they needed more nitrogen and he was their backup."

"Or do we have two bombs?"

"No way! That's too surreal."

Wendy pushed back from the keyboard. "Well, it is the Fourth of July."

"Where do you want to start?"

"What about this Hamid Hassan character. Same last name as the guy who rented the van." Wendy's cell phone buzzed. "Adams here. Oh, you again?"

Mike watched her face turn from neutral to concerned as she hung up.

"What?"

"Local PD located a suspicious van parked in front of the Federal Tax Office on General Standford Boulevard."

"White?"

"Didn't say, but there's an active shooter."

"Let's go!"

• • •

Hamid looked briefly at Farzaad, sitting in the passenger seat, staring blankly out the windshield. The man's eyes were still glistening with tears. He poked him on the thigh. "It is time."

Farzaad nodded and smiled thinly. "My brother is braver than I thought."

"Yes, he answered the call. Praise Allah."

As they crossed the bridge that led to the ring road, Hamid could see the waters of the Hanlon creek surging, only inches from the bank. He handed Farzaad his phone. "Blow the sewage plant." He pointed at the clock on the van console. "Wait five minutes and blow the water tower."

• • •

In the parking lot Mike wheeled the Lincoln SUV in a tight U-turn, weaving strips of black on the asphalt before speeding down the ramp onto the street with thump. Entering the older section of downtown on Main Street, they turned onto General Sandford and were met by a sea of cruisers, their flashing lights illuminating the storefronts like Christmas.

With the police occupied and the power out, a few citizens were taking advantage. Down a side street, Mike spotted two men playing tug-of-war with a flat panel TV in front of a smashed storefront. There will be more of that, thought Mike, if the power stays off. Dozens of people had gathered to enjoy the spectacle. They kept to the sidewalks because the streets were an inch deep in water. The storm sewers appeared to be overwhelmed by the heavy overnight rain.

Sitting on the hood of his car, Samulson waved them over with his ever-present notebook in hand. "Patrol noticed the vehicle." He jerked his thumb over his shoulder at a light gray van farther up the street. "Wrong plates but ran them anyways."

Merphin took over. "Stolen last night. It's registered to a numbered company that we're tracking down." He nodded at Samulson to continue.

"With all the buzz about a bomb, the first officer on the scene called for backup. As he approached on foot somebody took a shot. Fortunately, his flack jacket took the hit but he's pinned down." Samulson pointed at a doorway twenty feet behind the van. "He couldn't determine where the shot came from, except across the street."

"Classic cop-popping—set up a trap to draw in first responders then," Merphin shook his head grimly in disgust and shot an imaginary finger-pistol, "pick them off, one by one."

"We've established a safety perimeter and are waiting for the Tac and bomb squads." Samulson snapped his notebook closed.

Mike loosened his tie. "Keep everybody back. I'm checking it out."

"No, you're not!" Wendy grabbed Mike by the arm. "Wait for the Tac team."

"If it's a bomb and if it's the Lone Stars, we need to start rounding them up ASAP. From what Spitwell implied, this could be just the start of the fireworks they've got planned for today."

"Understood," Wendy pursed her lips, "but they could trigger the bomb remotely."

"Not yet. They want a crowd so they can have a shootout and—"

Wendy started nodding. "Blow the thing at the right moment. Otherwise, it would have detonated it by now."

Merphin furrowed his brow into deep lines. "If that's the case, there may be multiple shooters."

"Hope not." Mike scanned the buildings across the street from the van, then turned to Merphin. "Any alarms triggered on that block?"

"Nothing on the radio."

"So, without breaking in, where would a shooter have access?" Mike drew a line from a partially constructed building to the van. "There. If I keep to that side of the street and stay under cover, I can get across from the van."

Merphin shook his head. "Yeah, but you got to get back across the street, four lanes."

"No prob. Varsity ball, forty under five seconds. But I'll need a distraction." Mike wiped away the damp film on his forehead with the palm of his hand.

Wendy glanced around. "When he's in position, get that officer with the rifle to start taking shots."

"What, at random?" Samulson threw his hands in the air, sending his notebook skittering across the hood of the car. It landed with a splash in the murky water. "Ah, shit."

As his partner sloshed around the hood of the car to retrieve his book, Merphin continued. "I'm not sure if that is a safe idea."

"I don't give fuck if they hit nothing but bricks." Wendy shook her head. "Drawing return fire will give us a target soon enough." She turned away from the detectives. "Officer, give me that rifle."

Behind the line of cruisers, Mike splashed across the street, his shoes weighing heavier with each stride. The entrances of the high-rise condo and adjacent boutiques were all protected with blue, gold-trimmed awnings. Staying close to the building facades, he approached as quietly as he could manage through the water.

Across from the van, he ducked into a doorway and raised his arm. Using the concrete step as a starting block, he took up a runner's crouch, then let the arm drop. The crack of Wendy's rifle and the splintering of brick and mortar overhead reverberated down the street.

With every fiber of muscle he possessed, he pushed off. A shot rang out. Ahead, to the left, a spray of water flew up. He veered right, then planted his foot and cut back hard to his left. Another crack of fire and an eruption of water on his right. Lunging toward the old Mercury wagon parked just ahead of the van, he grabbed the grill and swung himself around the front bumper. Protected behind the wheel well he waited, heart pounding in his chest like a pile driver.

After a few deep breaths, he shuffled to the rear bumper, braced himself, then darted to the van. At the side window he popped up. The bad angle and grimy glass made it difficult to see. With hands cupped around his eyes, he peered behind the front seats. Four large barrels sat in a row—the stenciled print, 'Mission Hill Farm Co-Op', was clear. *The arrogant fucks hadn't even bothered to paint over it.*

Just as he crouched again, the window above his head exploded, showering him with shards of glass. He slid along the van to the rear bumper and signaled for another round of covering fire, then dashed across the street.

Breathless, he arrived back at Wendy and the two detectives. "It's a bomb for sure and it's got to be the Lone Stars. Let's go get our warrants and round them up."

Wendy handed back the rifle and nodded at the detectives. "We'll take it from here."

Merphin laughed. "You can have it."

"I'll let Smithers know." As Mike raised his phone to his ear, it rang. "Longstrum here."

"It's Dan."

"Perfect timing. We just found Spitwell's bomb, we need warrants and—"

"Great. Let Wendy handle it. We just received a call from the head of security at American Atomic Power. It seems the power outage is not due to the weather. They are concerned that their computer system at the Lakeridge plant has been hacked. Because it involves a possible cyber attack on infrastructure of national importance, it falls to us and specifically to you."

Mike wanted to groan. Was he just some pinball to be smacked from one case to another? At least this one had been his baby. Now, he had to listen to some inept fool try to explain away the fact that their system software lacked a proper firewall.

"It's an active situation here."

Voice softening slightly, Smithers added, "Mike, you're our best Internet security guy. You have to admit that if this is true, it's a very disturbing development, considering the power outage."

"Sure, Dan. I'll come back to the office now."

"Great. I'll come help out Wendy."

"Who's the contact person at Lakeridge?"

"James Wizner, plant manager."

"On it."

Mike slipped his phone back into his jacket pocket. He looked at Wendy and opened his mouth, then stopped.

"Holy fuck."

CHAPTER 43

Leaning against the mobile command center down the block from the tax office, Merphin swiped a finger across his phone screen and chuckled. "You gotta love Manny."

Dodging around various personnel scurrying about, he strode over to his partner and tapped him on the shoulder. "Got a sec?"

"Why, what's up?" Samulson reluctantly interrupted his conversation with the Chief Superintendent of Police.

"Rodriquez found the missing van. Clean as a whistle."

• • •

The headquarters of OTC, the Oregon Telephone Company, was a massive building, containing not only all the switching hardware for the regional telephone system and the Internet fiber optics, but also a vast complex of powerful, newly installed computer servers to support the company's nascent cloud-computing business.

For Samir and Hamid, the location had become a very important target about eight months earlier, when the local news reported OTC's procurement of a large federal contract. Numerous press articles explained how the company's technology would store the massive amounts of data required to underpin online government services such as immigration applications and customs. It would be more challenging to take the government's online processing down completely, but by destroying the flow of information to the system they could stymie the movement of people and billions of dollars of commerce passing through the borders of the USA.

Parking near the loading docks, Hamid watched in the rearview mirror as Farzaad leapt out of the van, shouldered a packsack and slipped the safety off his own AR-15. Abarque's rifle still hung on the cargo hook.

"I am sorry you must do this alone. May Allah be with you."

Once the rear doors were closed, Hamid gunned the engine. He needed to get over the bridge at Tenth Avenue before it was underwater. There was only an hour until he had to be in position.

• • •

Wendy pulled up to the Bureau without a word.

Mike stepped out. As he closed the door, he remembered a quick "Thanks," but she pulled away quickly without responding.

He couldn't blame her; he'd been lousy company. But his head was reeling.

At the vehicle pool office, he signed out a black, unmarked SUV. Sitting behind the wheel, he stopped to think, running over all Jenny had told him.

The battery packs under the bed meant that Samir had expected a power outage. *Why?* Had he caused it? Was that the extent of the sabotage, or was there a second bomb threat?

Jenny had thought Fatima was monitoring Wizner at home. Why would she do that? Were they blackmailing him? Was he in on it? If Samir was hacking the nuclear plant from home, then . . .

This was no time to go to his desk. Lakeridge was a more urgent assignment than he'd thought, but a little side trip was in order. He picked up his phone. It was also time to apologize.

"Honey, what's the address of Fatima and Samir's apartment?"

"620 Sixth Avenue, apartment 1210."

"Thanks. Put your phone on power saving mode. It could be awhile before we have any electricity."

"You're not going to Samir's alone, are you?"

"I need to check a few things out before I call in the troops. I can't afford another screwup like last night." He softened his tone. "Honey."

"Yeah?"

"Sorry for not listening. You did great work. I love you."

"You should listen to me more often."

"Don't ruin the moment."

• • •

In Officer Stan Olensky's opinion, detectives Samulson and Merphin walked around with their heads up their asses most of the time—but this morning's AP bulletin had to take the damn cake. Stop every white or light-colored van—to check plates? What was Enzo thinking? It would mean pulling over every delivery and rental van in the city.

Luckily, on a Fourth of July holiday during a blackout, traffic was light. So far, all the vehicles he'd stopped were clean. Several of the drivers, exceedingly annoyed at the extra inconvenience, subjected him to some choice profanity.

Truly, this had not been his favorite day on the job. All tedious stuff, and worse, he had been too far away to respond to the excitement of the day, the bomb threat at the federal building.

When the unmarked, white van whipped by the end of the street where he'd parked to have lunch, he figured it was just a cruel joke meant to send him into early retirement. Shaking his head, he pulled out and flicked on the lights and sirens.

Shit. He floored it.

• • •

A flood of nervous adrenaline surged through Hamid's blood at the sight of the red, white and blue flashing lights in the rearview mirror. If the contents of the van were examined, he would be arrested on the spot. He must not be stopped.

Accelerating, he reached over to the gun on the passenger seat and released the safety. The vehicle pitched onto two wheels as he took a high-speed turn, the crate with the SAM missile slamming against the wall of the truck. He winced. It better still work.

• • •

Olensky was about to call in the pursuit when the dispatcher's voice crackled through the radio.

"Cancel APB on van, plate Bravo Charlie 749. Repeat cancel APB."

He tapped his mic. "What's up Loretta?"

"It's been located."

"Where?"

"In the back corner of the rental company's parking lot."

• • •

Hamid loosened his grip on the steering wheel. In his rearview mirror the police car carried on past the intersection, lights still flashing.

The forced detour was taking him out of his way, but he could recover quickly. In his career, Hamid had installed alarm systems over most of the city. Turning right onto Walker Mountain Road would force him to travel a few extra miles, but from there he could turn on Old Vernon Road, go down the ridge and be in position.

The path to glory beckoned.

CHAPTER 44

Farzaad wasted no time watching the van leave. The quicker he entered the building, the less chance he would be detected and stopped.

Breaching the solid-looking door beside the loading zone would be too time consuming, and the view through the small window into the hallway beyond held no promise of access to the computer center. Stooping low below the neatly trimmed hedges, he ran along the side of the building toward the main entrance.

• • •

Behind the security counter of the OTC lobby, John Poer flicked through the pages of *Hired*, a magazine dedicated to the real-life tales of mercenaries. The soldiering life still held appeal to him even after two tours in the Middle East, but his fiancée wanted him to stay home and be a family man.

The closest thing to the military he could find in Tillson was the security business. Hampered by his lack of a high school diploma, he was forced to start at the bottom. But with time and night school business courses, he hoped to move up the rungs and into management. He missed the adrenaline rush of the front lines, but he would do anything for his Annie and the twins.

With the day shift all checked in, he was enjoying the relative peace that settled over the lobby after crew change. It was quieter still today because of the reduced Fourth of July staff. For the rest of the afternoon, he could enjoy reading his magazine and sipping cups of the horrible vending machine coffee. And monitoring the closed circuit TV feeds, of course.

Arrayed in front of him, the black and white images on the sixteen screens constantly cycled through their predetermined pattern, occasionally revealing the two other guards patrolling the halls at the far ends of the building.

Holiday calm prevailed on the retail operations side, but in the administration block, there were a few ambitious white-collar types putting in hours, fearful that the mandatory mid-week break would wreak havoc with their schedules.

The electrical outage was creating a real buzz in the technical department. The emergency power provided by the huge diesel generators on the roof kept the place operational, but resources had to be rationed. From what he understood after chatting with the techies, power to the cloud-computing center was the priority. Shutting off a few customer support computers or slowing the Internet down was a minor price to pay for maintaining the US government's access to their data.

Something caught his eye on screen seven. Peering closer, the sides of Poer's cardboard coffee cup buckled in his hand. The camera for the rear entrance showed a man with a large bundle over his shoulder and something in his hand that looked like—

He thumbed the microphone on his radio. "Alpha two and three, this is control. We have a potential threat at the rear service door."

On the monitor, the figure disappeared, apparently stymied by the secure door. He would probably head to the front entrance next.

Poer placed his hand on the holster cover of his revolver and quietly thumbed it open. Nearby, a few people were taking their break, gossiping outside the corporate accounting office. He didn't want to alarm them by pulling his weapon.

Military training had taught him the tactical advantage of not being found in the obvious place. Duck-walking behind the security counter, he took cover behind a pillar and waited. His heart was pounding. This could be just another empty manifestation of his hyperreactivity to any perceived threat, but that's exactly what had saved his ass more than once in Afganny.

Or . . . it could be his moment of glory.

• • •

The lobby was a big open space, sparsely decorated with two rows of concrete planters, each containing a small tree. Office windows circled the three-story space and a row of vending machines and tables lined one side wall of the lower level.

Oddly, the security station was empty. *The holiday, perhaps? Regardless. Praise Allah.*

Farzaad whispered, "Allahu Akbar," and burst through the revolving door into the lobby, rifle held at chest height. Screams erupted from his right. Two young women pointed at him before running away down the hallway behind them. It didn't matter.

Sprinting to the security checkpoint, he leapt over the metal fence on the far side of the desk. Crouched behind the concrete planter behind it, he paused to catch his breath. The corridor to the operations area was just ahead.

Poer raised his gun and tracked his target, but eased off the trigger when the man dipped out of sight behind a planter. Better to bide his time. Taking care to stay out of sight, he crawled back to his station and set off the silent alarm.

Then he stood, assuming a solid, shoulder-wide stance. He didn't have to wait long, as a blur of green khaki bolted toward the technical operations area. Poer let loose a round, but the edge of the planter took the hit.

"Fuck." He wished he had his Marine M17, not this crappy little pistol.

Poer gave chase as the man disappeared around the bend of the hallway. Before he made the corner, there came the loud rat-a-tat of machine gun fire. No screams; the man must be blasting through into the computer center.

Pressed flat against the wall, Poer slid sideways until he could see the metal door, now standing ajar and bullet-riddled. One step, two, three, and then his back slammed against the far wall next to the doorframe. He sidestepped into the opening, leading with his barrel. The target was running down the center aisle of the switching arrays. Poer leveled his gun and pulled off two quick rounds.

• • •

Farzaad was thrown to the ground by the impact. Despite the searing pain in his leg, he remained calm. There was no reason for panic.

Forcing his body to comply, he twisted and fired several shots back toward the man in the doorway. In the ensuing pause, he slipped the bulky packsack off his shoulder, pulling the bag in front of his chest.

• • •

Having pitched himself to the side after he fired, Poer was only grazed by one of the target's bullets. Ignoring the sting in his shoulder, he crept on all fours to the edge of the nearest immense power supply unit.

A quick peek around the corner showed the wounded intruder sitting half-prone, his weapon pointed down the aisle. *Good.* The man's aim had not adjusted to Poer's new position; the barrel was pointed high and to the left. His mistake would be deadly.

Placing his foot against the solid metal base of the power unit, he pushed off and fired. The moment he hit the ground, he rolled twice. His first two shots had been defensive, intending only to suppress return fire. Landing firmly on his stomach, his aim steadied.

Two kill shots went wide. He kept squeezing the trigger.

CHAPTER 45

Perplexed, James Wizner stared at the screens on the console. The issue with the grid was an enormous problem, but what concerned him now was the security of the plant itself. That was truly his responsibility.

There, again! A millisecond pause in the core temperature readout. And the first sequence of numbers after the pause were exactly the same as those an hour ago, right down to the last decimal place. Possible, but highly improbable.

Without his security USB device, his access to diagnostic mode was denied.

"Hey, Derek, get me into the operations system. I need to check something."

Scrolling over the data from the past twelve hours, he immediately detected a pattern. The same numbers were appearing in a loop, with the only exception being the first readout at the top of the hour.

"Holy mother of god! The reactor is compromised."

"What—How could that happen without us knowing?"

"I don't know, Derek, but the core is approaching critical."

"How can you tell?"

"The numbers in the core temperature readout are constantly repeating; it's been put on a loop. But the first entry at the top of the hour is different. Whoever hacked us was very clever, except for one tiny glitch. The rest of the data is fake except for these entries, and they're rising."

"We have to go into manual override as soon as possible."

"Yeah, but we need a second . . ."

Frantic, Wizner ran back to his office and ransacked his desk and packsack. Nothing.

"I can't find my security USB. We need another sys-op. Get Grant here, stat."

"He's in Leaville taking his family to Wonderworld today."

"Who else has a dongle?"

"The emergency backup from the rota sheet for today . . ." Derek pulled a clipboard off the wall and scanned it, "would be Matt Molson, but he lives out in Maryton."

"Find him." Wizner massaged his temples. "Cut us off from the internet, completely now."

A few minutes later, Derek picked up his cell phone and whistled a long, low note. "I just got a text. Matt won't be here for at least another thirty minutes."

Face now buried in his hands, Wizner's voice was barely audible. "Start the emergency protocol. We need to evacuate."

• • •

Peace flowed through Farzaad. His breathing slowed and the pain in his leg faded into the distance. It would not be much longer before he was in paradise and this place a flaming torch.

And thanks to Mouri's handiwork at the dam, when the fire crews arrived and opened the valves on the fire hydrants, they would produce nothing more than a few useless drips. His body felt light, floating. He lifted his gaze skyward, trying to imagine that the banks of fluorescent lights were the sun, shining brightly in a clear blue sky.

The fifth and sixth bullets penetrated the canvas packsack on Farzaad's chest, striking the metal gasoline container inside. Its explosion set off a chain reaction of bullets ricocheting around the room and detonated the twenty-two fragmentation hand grenades that had been strapped to his belt.

Riddled by shards of metal, Farzaad and his enemy died instantly. Within minutes, their bodies were consumed by the blaze.

• • •

Samir struck the desktop with his fist. Someone had taken the plant controls off-line again.

He dropped to his knees to look under the bed. The caution light on the front of the reserve battery system was blinking yellow. His computer would die soon.

He had one more task to accomplish with the remaining power.

• • •

Mike felt the rear tires slip sideways as he sped around the corner on to Sixth Avenue, the road seeming unusually slick. He fought to regain control and cranked his neck to check building numbers. There, 620. Sliding to a stop, he jammed the truck into park and grabbed his phone.

"Dan, it's Mike."

"Yeah. Sort of busy."

"You guys better go bust down Hamid Hassan's door."

"Why?"

"He's a local Somali, high on the threat list. Before I go to Lakeridge I've decided to check on another Somali, Samir Khalif. There might be a connection between these guys and the nuclear plant."

"Shit. Keep me posted. Gotta go. The Tac team is about to take out the shooter."

Mike reflexively checked his shoulder holster, then stepped down from the truck. Moving toward the apartment building, he startled at a loud noise behind him. As he whipped around with his gun drawn, the storm sewer grate a few feet down the curb gurgled again, then burped like it had guzzled too much beer and pizza. The waft of foul air smelled like it too.

He reholstered his gun and entered the apartment foyer. The door was locked. He ran a finger down the call buttons and jabbed the one labelled Superintendent three times. Nothing. *No power.* Mike rapped his knuckles on the glass until a door just past the elevators opened and a man in his sixties dressed in blue jeans and a pajama top ambled across the lobby.

With his badge pressed against the glass of the door, Mike urged him to hurry. The man nodded and pressed on the latch. Mike shouldered past.

"Hey, what's the hurry? You gotta take the stairs."

"I know. Where the fuck are they?"

"One here and another at the back, down that hall."

• • •

Samir inserted Wizner's passwords and security information into an encrypted email and addressed it to the hacker (possibly multiple) that he had found on the deep net. He did not know their nationality or motivation but assumed that they had something to do with the Soviets or North Korea. It didn't matter. In trade for access to American Atomic corporate computers, which were linked to the national grid, they'd guaranteed to unleash a tsunami of ransom-wear, denial of service attacks and other malware designed to bring American infrastructure and commerce to its knees.

Their only previous communication had been months ago to arrange the price of access to the American power grid. In exchange for the information Samir provided, Bitcoin would be paid into an ISIS controlled, cryptocurrency, virtual vault. This would be another, although anonymous, part of his legacy. Combined with other donations from benefactors around the world, the ongoing war against America would be funded for years to come.

Enough of that. Right now, he needed to take back the nuclear plant.

He pressed send and shut down his system. Pulling on his suit and tie, he strung the lanyard with Wizner's security dongle around his neck and tossed his gun into his otherwise empty briefcase.

Samir locked the apartment door and strode down the hall toward the rear stairwell. Knowing the parking garage door wouldn't be working, he had parked outside, in a visitor's space. While he unlocked the car, he drew in the fresh scent of rain-cleansed air and smiled.

• • •

Breathless after climbing the twelve flights of stairs, Mike stood with his hands on his knees in front of Fatima and Samir's apartment. This damn desk job was putting him out of shape. Taking a last gulp of air, he straightened, withdrew his gun and held up his badge.

There was no response to his knocking. After counting to thirty and delivering a second round of loud raps, he twisted the handle and pressed his weight into the door. It held firm. Bending his knees, he exploded like it was an opposing lineman on fourth down and one to go. The door creaked and gave way abruptly, sending him stumbling to the floor.

"FBI." He rolled to a crouch, swinging his aim side to side. Nothing.

He went straight to the bedroom at the end of the hall. It was deserted, but an extension cord trailed from under the bed to the elaborate computer rig on the desk. He hit the on button, but the desktop didn't stir. The power packs must be out of juice.

In the closet, men's clothes hung on the rod and near the floor was a displaced piece of trim. On his hands and knees, Mike probed the cavity behind, but it was empty except for drywall dust.

Standing, he took a last look around the room. A discarded baggie lay on the floor near the bed. He picked it up and wiped his finger across its interior. Gun oil.

Mike bolted down the hallway.

He descended the stairs two at a time, arriving in the lobby in minutes. There, he hesitated. He should call Jenny and let her know he was OK.

His cell had no signal. *Weird.* He pulled out his service phone. It was for exactly this type of situation the FBI maintained its own secure server. Wracking his brain for a moment to remember Jenny's number, he tapped out a text. 'I'm OK. Love U.' Anything more would have to wait. He needed to call Dan.

Holding the phone to his ear, he pushed back out through the stiff doors one-handed. A moment later, he was stumbling back inside, hand slapped over his nose. The air was putrid.

He aborted the call and peered through the glass. A brown, sludgy liquid was gushing up and out of the storm sewers with such force that the iron grates were dancing like popping corn on a skillet. Spreading along the street and over the curbs like a giant carpet, the smell reminded him of the rancid muck he used to hose off the killing floor of the abattoir where he worked as a teen.

Tiptoeing to the truck limited the coating of raw sewage to just his shoes, but when he closed the driver's door, he retched. Swallowing hard he forced himself to breathe shallowly, then redialed.

"Dan, it's Mike. I'm heading to Lakeridge now. I'm pretty sure it's the target."

"Why?"

"Another Somali who's been studying nuclear reactors knew in advance there was going to be a blackout. And he's armed."

"There's no way the amount of nitrogen Abouani gathered would put a dent in that place."

"Yeah, I haven't figured exactly what's up yet."

"OK. We're just wrapping up here. Check it out, but don't do anything until we get there."

• • •

Olensky sat in his idling cruiser, one of several that formed the barricade blocking West Thirty-Fourth. In the distance he could see orange flames erupting through the roof of the OTC computer center. Thick black smoke curled out of a partially collapsed corner of the structure, with the occasional pop sending a shower of sparks rocketing skyward.

"Attention all available units east of Twentieth." Lorretta's usual calm, silky voice was tight and shrill with panic. "Proceed to Old Vernon Road and Finch. Implement evacuation of Zone One and Two around Lakeridge Nuclear. This is not a drill. I repeat—this is not a drill."

Zone One and Two, he thought. That means big problems, bigger than sitting here. He tossed his sandwich aside and put the cruiser in gear. The radio was a cacophony of overlapping voices as other squad cars began to respond.

CHAPTER 46

Driving in the city always made Heidi nervous. Chuck usually took Becky to the hospital downtown; most of her travel was only on the back county roads. Today, the further distraction of pulling over for emergency vehicles as they sped by, sirens blaring, was tying her stomach in knots.

Approaching the First Street Bridge, Heidi gripped the steering wheel ferociously as she maneuvered to avoid numerous abandoned cars, stalled by the rising water in the street. Beside her, Chuck was pale as a ghost, trying his best to put pressure on the gushing wound above his knee. The two boys sat silently in the back, staring wide-eyed at the destructive force of the water surging around them. Between them Becky had her eyes closed, exhaling through pursed blue lips.

The First Street Bridge was the fastest way Heidi knew to get to the hospital, but the water was at the front bumper and the truck was struggling to maintain momentum. As she shoved the gas pedal to the floor, there was a loud crash on the passenger side and the cab rocked sideways. A horrible scraping sound had the boys yelling and covering their ears.

The vehicle refused to budge another inch.

Shifting into park she undid her seat belt and half stood, her hands on the dash, trying to see the front of the truck. An upside down wooden picnic table, snatched away from someone's backyard by the floodwaters, had wrapped itself into the passenger side bumper and wheel well. The torrent of murky brown sludge swept around the truck with alarming force as other projectiles began to crash into the door panels. The boys began crying, their wails rising in a crescendo each time something new struck the truck.

Silent so far, Heidi had assumed Chuck was passed out. When he spoke, she jumped. "Stay here with the boys and I'll carry Becky the rest of the way."

"No damn way. You're in no shape to do that."

She lowered the window and sucked in a disgusting nose-full of foul-smelling air. Chuck could contract a serious infection wading through the polluted water. If he failed, she might lose them both.

"I'll take Becky."

"The current—"

"I can handle it." Without waiting for a response, she climbed onto the central console and faced into the back seat. "Boys, stay with your father. You're safe here. Do not get out of the truck."

Reaching out to Becky, she spoke in a softer tone. "Darling, undo your seat belt and put your arms around my neck. We're going to get out of the truck through my door. You must hold on as tight as you can."

Becky nodded and allowed herself to be pulled into the front seat. Heidi opened the truck door with one hand, bracing her daughter's back with the other. Brown foam bubbled over the floor. The roar of the water was deafening.

There was a cedar hedge along the side of the road leading toward the bridge. All they had to do was to cross the ten-foot gap from the front end of the truck to the first trunk without being swept away. Easy.

With Becky's panicked grip almost choking her, Heidi put a foot down, searching for the pavement. The force of the water funneling under the truck shocked her. "Becky, I have to let go of you so I can grab the truck. Hold on tight, with your legs too."

At the front tire, Heidi halted, swaying with the current. The open stretch of churning brown water looked insurmountable. Whirlpools and eddies spun debris like the teacup ride at the county fair, and the torrent of water disappearing into a sink hole down the bank made an horrendous sucking sound.

Planting her feet wide for balance, she let go of the wheel well.

Five endless minutes later, she clutched the trunk of the first tree, her legs trembling. Becky's breathing next to her ear was labored. Moving haltingly, she was stopped again at the end of the hedge. There was another gap, nearly twenty feet, between the cedars and the bridge railing. There, the ground seemed to rise toward the bridge, the water shallower but flowing even faster.

Halfway to the railing, something hard and sharp struck Heidi in the calf. *Fuck, that hurt.* Gritting her teeth, she forced herself forward, barely able to control her steps. At the concrete abutment, she doubled over.

"Becky, I am going to set you down on the railing for a moment so I can take a rest. OK?"

Lips quivering, the little girl nodded.

"Are you all right, Mommy?"

"Yes, honey, and we don't have far to go. Hang in there."

"You too."

A hard lump rose in her throat, and Heidi turned away, blinking hard. A few moments later, wiping her tears with the back of her hand, she drew her leg out of the water to assess her wound.

She didn't understand. A broken piece of two by four, about ten inches long, lay flat against her calf. Was it caught in her pants? She reached down to pry it off.

Pain lanced up her leg as the two sets of nails embedded in her flesh slid out a fraction of an inch. She gagged.

If she fainted from shock here, she would be swept away. Gritting her teeth, she pushed the piece of wood back against her leg.

"OK, Becky, grab hold again. We're going to go over the bridge to the hospital and find Dr. Bronson."

Two-thirds of the way across the span, Heidi was shaking. The current repeatedly battered her with unidentified objects, slamming her against the railing and nearly off her feet. But there were only thirty more feet to the other side. Like an oasis in the desert, a short distance past the bridge the street sloped upward to dry land. They would make it.

Out of the corner of her eye, she caught sight of the large item hurtling toward her only seconds before it hit. The metal garbage container struck her in the ribs, crushing her against the railing. Excruciating pain erupted in her chest. She couldn't breathe.

Desperate to remain upright, she let go of Becky's legs so she could grab the metal struts with both hands. She could feel her daughter's grip around her neck weakening.

"*Hold on, Becky!*"

Her scream was lost in the roar of the water.

CHAPTER 47

At the locked doors of Lakeridge, Samir waited patiently under the watchful eyes of two mounted video cameras. The arthritic guard hobbling across the deserted plant lobby was the same man as yesterday. Samir watched as he slowly inserted a key into the lock on the inner wall, but only the outer set of doors opened. When Samir stepped forward, they closed, detaining him in the vestibule.

Holding up a hand, the elderly man made his way slowly back to the security station, assumed his position behind the counter and pressed a button on the desktop. With a loud click, the locks on the interior doors sprung open.

Samir crossed the lobby smiling. "Good morning."

"Sorry about all that. Off hours security procedure."

"No problem, I understand."

The guard pulled the visitors' book toward him. Over top of his reading glasses he scrutinized Samir's face with a scowl.

"I wasn't expecting anyone."

Then a brief flicker of recognition crossed his features and he flipped back a page, finger running over the list of names from the preceding day.

"Ah, Dr. Khalif. What brings you here this fine Fourth of July? There aren't too many folks around."

"I understand you have an emergency issue."

"No kidding! No power on the Fourth of July sure's goin' to put a damper on the party."

"Darkness will be good for the fireworks."

"I guess." The guard placed a pen on the visitor's book and turned it to face Samir. "So why are you here?"

"Mr. Wizner has called me in to help out."

"Humph, really?" The man squinted at him. "You forgot something."

"What's that?" Samir could feel a bead of sweat forming on the edge of his hairline.

The man smiled. "I don't see my coffee."

"Oh, yes. Sorry. Everything is closed today."

"I know. Just joking." The guard checked a scratch pad by the phone. "He didn't tell me anything about you coming, so I'll have to call him. I'm sure this will only take a second. Meanwhile, pop open your briefcase."

As the man reached for the phone, Samir clicked open his briefcase, removed the revolver and put a bullet through the guard's forehead.

He'd never pulled a trigger before. The power of the recoil surprised him, but he felt nothing as the man snapped backwards, bounced off his high-backed chair then pitched forward onto the desktop. Tucking the gun in his belt, he reached over the counter, grabbed the guard's badge and pressed the release button for the door into the plant.

Over the past few days, with his full access to the company's website, Samir had perused the orientation module for new employees and studied the schematics of the plant. He'd confirmed that the operations center was behind the Restricted Access door he'd seen yesterday.

He inserted and withdrew the guard's badge into the security scanner with a stuttering motion. A warning appeared on the screen: 'Card unreadable. Try again'.

Damn. But all was not lost. He held down the star and number sign keys for ten seconds, activating the failsafe mechanism unique to SecTec 8000 series hardware. In case of an emergency, it allowed technicians to perform a manual override.

A login box appeared on the scanner screen. *Thank you, Hamid.*

Opening his phone, he entered the employee ID and badge number from the photo he had taken of Wizner's security pass. With the addition of today's passcode, the door mechanism released. Praise Allah there was no iris or thumb scan required.

Samir pushed the door open. Across the room, two men sat in front of an enormous control board, engrossed in their work. One was Wizner. His companion spoke without looking up from his screen.

"It's about time you got here, Matt."

CHAPTER 48

From Samir's apartment, the quickest way to the nuclear plant was through the downtown core. Mike figured the traffic would be light with everyone home from work, so he avoided the highway ring road and cut up the hill to Jones Avenue and over to Main Street. There, he was forced to a standstill; a foot-high wall of water surged down the street.

The clearance of the SUV was adequate, but the water level was rising dangerously fast. Just ahead, brown froth was breeching the concrete retaining wall lining the riverbank, and the bridge road surface was completely submersed. He couldn't chance it. Stymied, he racked his brain for alternative routes when his eyes caught on a terrifying sight.

Hunched over and barely visible above the floodwaters, a woman with a child wrapped around her neck was leaning backwards over the railing of the bridge. The child's legs were dangling over the side, buffeted by the turbulent flow.

Mike put the black Suburban in gear. As he got closer, the woman raised her head, her face contorted in pain. Fighting to stand, she looked exhausted. It was only a matter of seconds before the pair would be swept away.

As he edged closer, there was a teeth-rattling crash against his door and a loud grating sound emanated from somewhere underneath him. Cranking the steering wheel, he attempted to gain higher ground by mounting the sidewalk. With one tire over the lip, the truck lurched and the tires began to spin. He turned off the ignition.

The driver's side of the truck was now tilted down, deep into the water. It was impossible to open his door against the current, so he slid across and out the passenger door. Dropping into the water, the strength of the flow threatened to sweep him away. Planting his feet wide, he plunged deeper.

As he neared the railing, a surge in the current caught him off guard. The water slammed him against the concrete side of the bridge. *Dammit, what are all those hours in the gym for if I can't do this?* Bracing himself against the bridge, he slowly righted himself. Railing grasped in one hand, he thrust forward with his thighs, slicing through the water toward the woman and child.

He wasn't sure if the little girl was still alive. Her eyes were closed; the only color in her face was the deep purplish blue of her lips. With an unfocused, wild look, the woman thrust the limp body at him.

"Take my daughter to Central Memorial. They know her, she has cystic fibrosis. Dr. Bronson—"

He shouldered the girl and wrapped his arm around the woman's waist. "You're coming too."

Hoisting her over his other shoulder, he made his way back to the Suburban. The little girl was limp and silent, but the mother groaned with each step. As gingerly as possible, he lay her across the back seat and placed the little girl on her chest. Stepping back, he gasped in revulsion when he saw the scrap of wood nailed to the side of the woman's leg.

He slid back to the driver's side, awkwardly jousting with the shift lever. Pausing to catch his breath, a new worry struck him. With the water level over the wheel wells, would the motor be too wet to start?

Thankfully, the engine roared without hesitation, but when he put it in gear the van only lurched, tires spinning. Reverse made no difference, nor did four-wheel drive. With the window rolled down, he lifted off the seat to look. The waxy leaves of an enormous potted umbrella plant bobbed in the current, its planter wedged tightly between the running board and the front tire.

It wasn't that far to the hospital. He hoisted the woman back over his shoulder. After an initial moan of complaint, her form went limp. Delicately bringing the young girl to his chest, Mike set out into the flood.

• • •

Samir pushed the two bodies off their chairs onto the floor. He had fired three shots before either had even looked up.

The cell phone, on the blood-smattered console where the greasy-haired young man had been sitting, vibrated. He checked the screen. It was a text notification from about forty minutes ago from someone named Matt: "Be awhile. Stuck in traffic." There were no messages since, and the indicator at the top of the screen showed no service.

The console screen showed the system page with the manual overrides entered and a prompt underneath: Insert USB key. Samir pulled up a clean chair and sat down.

On the virtual system, his computer screen had been too small to display the entirety of the plant's controls; the symbols had been grouped, forcing him to page up and down to see them all. In real life, the array of dials and gauges spread out before him was daunting.

Not surprisingly, there wasn't much easily accessible information on how to operate a nuclear reactor. Despite all his research, he didn't understand everything. That was OK. He only had to know how to bypass the system's safety checks.

He removed Wizner's lanyard from around his neck and slid the red dongle into place. Swiftly deactivating his previous software overrides, he opened the system monitor. Now streaming real data, the readout displayed the actual core temperature. Since his last look just over an hour earlier, the number had been steadily climbing, now a tantalizing 1,600 degrees.

Within seconds, the system detected the overheating. Ignoring the flashing red light at the top of the panel, Samir checked the system status. On the small LED screen directly at eye level, a prompt flashed: "Initiate shut down?"

Selecting 'no', a siren began to sound. He hit the alarm override and entered Wizner's password.

Samir wondered if Wizner had discovered the problem and warned anyone. Would the authorities be organizing an evacuation? From the lack of service on the phone, he concluded that Farzaad's attack on the OTC had been successful.

He laughed out loud. How could the police warn people? Drive down the streets with bullhorns? The citizens of Tillson would be sitting ducks.

CHAPTER 49

The emergency department of the Central Memorial Hospital was bedlam. Prepared with emergency power from rooftop generators, all departments were still functioning except the elective surgical suites. With a body on each shoulder, Mike stood at the triage desk and waited for the nurse to look up. Finally, the man spoke but his eyes remained fixed on his screen.

"Go ahead."

"Got a woman with a leg wound and a very sick child with cystic fibrosis."

"Have a seat. What are their ages?"

"I have no idea. I found them in the flood waters."

"Do they have insurance?"

Mike shifted the woman higher on his shoulder and reached inside his jacket pocket for his badge. "Agent Mike Longstrum, FBI."

"So?"

"Look, I don't have time for your bullshit. I have an emergency to respond to. I'm leaving these two with you. Send the tab to the agency."

Stepping into the triage station, he placed the mother on a gurney and then slid the little girl across the desk into the arms of the nurse.

"They're your responsibility now."

Back outside, Mike sprinted down the hill toward the river. The torrent of murky water was subsiding, and the planter wedged in the wheel well was more visible. Most importantly, the truck's back hatch lid was now above water level and easy to open. From the side storage compartment, he snapped open the plastic catches holding the tire wrench.

Standing over the planter, his first whack hit the running board. The second bounced off the tire, striking the chrome edge of the wheel well and sending a jolt of pain through his wrist. Against the resistance of the water, there was no way to get enough power in his swing to crack the son of a bitch.

Damn the paperwork. He drew his firearm.

The shot shattered the thick ceramic container instantly, a swill of muddy water, shards and tattered leaves washed under the truck and out of sight.

With the bridge impassable, he would have to take the longer route to Lakeridge. Anxious to recover lost time, he flicked on the lights. The rear end of the truck shimmied sideways across the slick pavement as he pulled a slow U-turn, then tore up the hill.

• • •

The sudden quiet of the winding country road was soothing after the stress of the last few hours. Letting himself relax fractionally, Hamid contemplated the fate of his fellow compatriots.

Without a partner, there was little doubt that Farzaad had died at the OTC. He knew the improvised bomb had exploded; there was no service on his regular phone anymore. Mouri would have defended the control station at the dam until his last breath. At the nuclear plant, Samir would soon pay the price for his actions, if he hadn't already. Most likely they all met their fate face-to-face with the enemy. In comparison, his task was cold and impersonal. Praise Allah, he might even live to fight another day.

He brought the van to a skittering stop on the steep gravel road and pulled through an open gate into the recently cut hayfield beyond. The last time he'd been here he had walked only a short distance in from the road, and the tall grass and alfalfa had hidden the roughness of the ground. Now, the van lurched violently, the thumping on the undercarriage so jarring he was worried he might break an axle. He would have to leave the van out in the open and walk the rest of the way.

He parked and opened the back doors. At the edge of the hillside, the footing was slippery, and the SA-7 launcher wasn't exactly light. Not looking at his feet, he tripped over a large rock and smashed down to the ground. Holding his ribs, he regained his footing and soldiered on, gritting his teeth and grunting in discomfort with every step. When he inhaled, a knifelike pain stabbed him in the side. Had he punctured a lung? This was not the time to be weak. He must honor the sacrifice of the others by completing his task.

In the cover of the aspen grove at the edge of the field, he leaned the missile launcher against a tree trunk and rested. When his breathing had recovered, he hoisted it again and slid on downhill, through the thick undergrowth until he could see the nuclear plant, about two and a half miles away. Sprawled out on the flats below, surrounded by an asphalt apron, it appeared like a cluttered serving tray with two gigantic, gray concrete stacks as the centerpiece, belching steam like tall teacups. In front of them sat the biscuit box—the long, windowless, three-storey containment building.

He brought the weapon to his shoulder and sighted through the eyepiece. The target was clear and well within the launcher's three-mile limit. At over five hundred yards per second, the missile would arrive in seconds. He only had to wait for the signal.

CHAPTER 50

On cursory inspection, Mike noticed nothing out of the ordinary as he approached the main entrance to Lakeridge. When he received no response on the intercom, he pressed his face to the glass door and cupped his hands beside his head to cut the glare.

On one side of the atrium-like structure was an array of chairs, on the other was a set of educational display panels. Farther back, a lone guard sat slumped at the security checkpoint, his head resting on the desk, partially obscured by an open briefcase.

Mike pivoted, searching for something, anything that could help. Pushed to one side of the concrete pad was a metal poster stand displaying visitor information. He seized the heavy base, raised it like a baseball bat and swung for the fences. His third blow brought a cymbal crash of shattering glass.

Gun drawn, he ran across the deserted lobby. The guard was dead, his weapon still in its holster. His head rested on a *Sports Illustrated*, surrounded by a congealing pool of dark blood. Under his outstretched hand, the logbook was open, but the visitor's column for the day was blank except for crimson splatters.

Mike holstered his gun. A blackout, a bomb and a zealot well read in nuclear reactors could only add up to one thing.

He grabbed a visitor's badge from the wooden basket on the desktop and jumped over the counter. Holding the plastic card to the reader, he was met with silence. The heavy security door remained locked. Running back, he pulled the dead man up in his chair and frantically searched for his badge. Nothing visible around his neck. He fumbled in the shirt pockets. A shopping list. He shoved the man harder against the chair. There it was—clipped to his belt, underneath a corpulent stomach.

Through the door, the corridor split into three. Ignoring the directions to administration, he turned down the long hallway to his right. It was a dead end at the visitor's center. He retraced his steps and took the next. At the end of the passage was a door labeled 'Authorized Personnel Only', a security scanner mounted on the wall beside it.

He pulled out his Bureau phone and spoke as loudly as he dared.

"Dispatch, I need backup at Lakeridge Nuclear. One civilian casualty at the entrance. Entering to investigate."

The door handle didn't budge, and the keyboard on the scanner gave him nothing. Was there another way in?

As he spun around, the sudden, deafening ring of a klaxon forced him to cover his ears. Mercifully, it stopped after only few seconds.

With the condition of the streets, who knew how long it would take for the troops to arrive. He was the only officer on the scene, confronted by an immediate threat. He had to act. Now. Alone.

He pounded on the door with his open hand.

"FBI, open up."

Nothing.

Taking a step back, Mike aimed three shots around the lock and a fourth directly into its center. Sufficiently compromised, the door yielded to his hard kick.

With his shoulder against the door, he pushed forward, maintaining a two-fisted grip on his revolver. Barely halfway through the opening, there was the sharp retort of a gun and the door slammed back against him. The metal edge blunted the blast, but the bullet ricocheted off the doorframe behind him, and a split-second later found its home in Mike's side. Stunned, he staggered backwards then dropped to his knees. He could feel wet heat flowing between his fingers as he clutched his aching abdomen.

With his free hand he pulled out his phone and called Smithers directly.

"Dan. I'm at Lakeridge. You better send the Tac squad."

"What's going on?"

"I've got at least one shooter inside the control room of the plant and I'm pinned down." A deep, shooting pain in his stomach took his breath. His head was feeling odd. "Other than that I know fuck all. The main doors . . ."

Splotches of black were appearing in his vision.

"Mike, are you all right? Talk to me."

He barely heard the clatter as the phone fell. Lifting his hand away from his abdomen, he watched with detached interest as bright red blobs dripped off his fingertips onto the floor.

"Mike?"

CHAPTER 51

Samir kept a wary eye on the partially open door as he skirted around the perimeter of the room. Hearing no movement, he kicked the door closed and swiftly wedged it shut with a folding chair.

It had been too easy, taking out the intruder with a single shot. Other threats would arrive soon. He was confident the rest of the plan could be accomplished quickly though, even if it meant holding them off at gunpoint. He would wait just a little longer.

But not much longer. The core temperature was approaching 850 degrees Celsius. Originally, Samir had hoped to turn Tillson into another Chernobyl, but his research had quickly dampened that dream. Unlike in the movies, even if the core melted down, it was unlikely to explode and breach the thick walls of the containment building.

In the American reactors, before that was even remotely possible, the system would douse the core with water to cool it—creating a massive amount of high-pressure radioactive vapor. Removing this dangerous buildup of pressure necessitated that the vapor be vented gradually, in measured amounts to the outside. Charcoal scrubbers would reduce but not eliminate the radiation released, the hope being that the low levels left would dissipate before the gas reached populated areas.

A console light blinked. The core was being shut down—there must be another automatic fail-safe built into the system, overriding manual control.

The situation was closing in on him. It was time. A few keystrokes, and the command was sent. Certainly, if there were an award for the worst nuclear reactor operator, he would win hands down.

Within seconds of the emergency water's release, the pulsing bleat of another horn blared through the loud speakers. The red phone attached to the console began to ring; to the right a screen flashed rapidly.

Another blinking red light appeared, warning that the opening of the emergency discharge vents was imminent.

Now it didn't matter whether he lived or died. Nothing could stop the venting, and with today's favorable wind, the ion cloud would blow right over the city.

But greater impact was possible. If he could disable the carbon scrubbers, the dose of radiation delivered would be devastating, even lethal. He just needed to live a little longer.

• • •

Mike shook his head groggily. Everything hurt. Why was he on the floor?

A shout reached him, echoing like he was underwater. Somebody in a white hazmat suit carrying the helmet in their hand was running down the corridor toward him. When the man got closer, he stopped abruptly and raised his hands. *Oh yeah, I'm holding a gun.*

"FBI." Mike held up his badge, his voice weak.

The man's brow glistened with sweat.

"What the hell is going on? I need to get in there and talk to ops. They're not answering their phone. The system is hot and there could be a breach."

"Who are you?"

"Ralph Nestor, maintenance. I got to go in there."

"Well, Ralph, I wouldn't advise that. There's a shooter inside."

"Oh my God." Suddenly, the man seemed to notice Mike's prone state and the dark liquid pool beside him. "Are you OK, man?"

"Not really. When you say breach, what does that mean?"

The man knelt beside him. "First, let me get some pressure on that wound. I'm going to help you get your jacket off."

Mike groaned. Twisting his torso to free his arms made it feel like a lance was running him through.

Nestor folded the lightweight coat into a square and placed it over the wound, then moved Mike's hand on top.

"Breach means the core is overheating and the safety controls are not being activated. We've got to get in there before there's a massive release of radioactive vapor to the outside."

Mike grimaced. "Is there another way in?"

"Not really. Well, except for the emergency exit on the other side of the room," Nestor took a swipe at the beads of sweat dripping into his eyes, "but there's no way to open it from the outside."

"OK, good to know. I've called in a tactical team. We better wait until they arrive."

"Sir, with all due respect, we don't have the time."

• • •

Dan Smithers took shotgun in the lead vehicle with Wendy Adams. Close behind them followed the procession of Tac team armored trucks. Even using lights and sirens to circumvent the stampede of traffic, their progress had been painfully slow. On several occasions, the only way forward was onto the sidewalk, through green spaces or across empty mall parking lots.

Up ahead a patrol officer held up his hand, forcing them to a stop in front of a roadblock of local police cars. From his other hand dangled a service revolver.

Dan shifted forward in his seat until the seat belt locked. "What the fuck?"

Wendy lowered the driver's window, presenting her badge. "FBI. What's the problem, officer?"

"Lakeridge Nuclear Plant has issued an evacuation order. Naturally, there's been mass panic, but some assholes seem think it's a good time to do some looting." He lifted his weapon. "I've had to use this once already."

"Smithers, station head, FBI." Dan leaned over, holding his badge up. "Understood, officer, but we need to get through. There is a terrorist situation at the plant."

"Be my guest and all the power to you. In a few minutes, I'm getting the fuck out of Dodge. I don't want to be near that thing if it blows. I got a wife and three kids, and we are driving as far away as possible."

"Good luck with that." Wendy clunked the truck back into gear. "The freeways are totally blocked."

CHAPTER 52

Another alarm sounded as the pressure in the containment building triggered the opening of the release vents. Everything was unfolding as predicted, but Samir was increasingly nervous. There had been nothing but eerie silence in the hallway outside. It couldn't be much longer before a flash grenade exploded and troops came crashing through.

He scanned the controls and monitors, but the charcoal filters were apparently autonomous. That was OK. Tough problems required powerful solutions.

• • •

In the full embrace of adrenaline and endorphins, Mike's spirits soared at the sight of the Tac squad charging up the hall toward him. He held up his badge and gun in supplication.

Kneeling beside Mike, the squad leader reached for his wrist.

"Longstrum, it's Peters. You OK?"

"Been better."

Peters triggered her helmet microphone. "Agent is wounded but alert, pulse rapid. Location southeast corridor outside control room."

She looked up at Nestor, who stood with his hands in the air and helmet held between his knees. "Who's he?"

"Maintenance. He says there's gonna be a massive release of reactive gas into the atmosphere. We don't have much time."

Peters blinked. "What's the situation inside?"

"At least one shooter. The only other access point to the room is the emergency exit on the far side. You'll have to blow it."

"Good work, Longstrum. We can take it from here. Do you think you can walk?" Peters slid an arm under Mike and lifted.

Mike groaned deeply, expelling breath through clenched teeth. "Not very fast."

"OK, stay put. The medic will be here soon." She pressed her mic. "On the way back to rally point. Plan for contact in five minutes. Send a medic with the team to the east door of the control room."

Turning back to her team at the end of the hallway, she began shouting orders. "Outside! We need explosives for the door, flash grenades and a look at the floor plan so we don't fucking shoot each other."

• • •

"Praise Allah."

The control panel showed the emergency vents were fully open. Would the pressure be enough to blow the filters right out of the vents?

Samir didn't have the luxury of time to find out. Prepared for the local cell service to be out, he switched to his satellite-enabled phone and selected the only name in his contact list.

• • •

"What are all those alarms and sirens?" Mike had to shout to be heard over the racket.

"Emergency venting."

Nestor started pulling on his helmet.

"Don't we all need one of those suits?"

"You're relatively safe inside the building, but I have to follow protocol. I need to get visual confirmation that the vents are open, then monitor the exterior radioactivity levels."

"Don't you need someone here to run the controls?"

"Be my guest."

• • •

The satellite phone in Hamid's hand vibrated with a single text: 'Now'.

Activating the heat seeking capability of the launcher, he sighted toward the nearest release door on the containment building. Its signature glowed brightly on the screen. He flipped the engage switch.

The thrust of the missile release jammed hard against his shoulder.

The smoky trail arched gratifyingly across the sky toward the target. Not bothering to watch the effect, he began loading the next missile. This was a skill he wished he'd had the opportunity to practice more. His movements were clumsy, hampered by the burning stiffness in his side.

The third round slipped out of his hand, rolling away across the ground. When he reached down for it, the pain in his ribs erupted.

There was no time to fuss. He took another from the bag beside him.

Pushing one heavy steel bookcase of manuals in front of the emergency exit, Samir moved another so it sat between him and the compromised door. Catching his breath, he sat down heavily in the control ops chair and closed his eyes.

Most of his compatriots would all have fallen by now. Fatima was far away—ready to build the new future. He was ready for his fate.

Blowing up the control board would take only a minimal amount of explosives, but the effect would be immense. There would be no way to shut down the reactor. Once it died, it would require years, if ever, for them to clean it up.

Tucking his gun under his belt, he lay down and wiggled his way under the control panel. The sweet spot was the conduit in which all the cables passed through the wall into the console. Hopefully, there would be sufficient explosive charge to challenge the integrity of the reinforced cement containment barrier as well.

He withdrew the C-4 plastic from his suit pocket along with a wad of sticky tack. Just as he pressed the explosive into the putty, the floor beneath him shuddered.

Good man, Hamid.

CHAPTER 53

The FBI cavalcade rapidly arrayed itself in front of the Lakeridge Plant. Wendy watched the tactical squad set up their command post with practiced precision, before a tight formation of heavily armored agents moved swiftly to the shattered front door.

Smithers stood beside her, behind the door of their SUV as they listened to the relay from the Tac squad's radio.

Wendy slammed her palm on the side panel of the truck. "Shit! Mike's down." She stepped out around the door. "They're calling for a medic."

Smithers grabbed her by the wrist. "Where you going?"

"To talk to Tac."

"Stay cool. Wait until Peters is out and can brief us."

A thundering explosion shook the building, accompanied by a flash of light. Wendy tried to find the source as a wave of dust and debris rolled toward them, but her eyes seared with pain. As the percussion shock arrived, she threw herself into the vehicle, taking refuge below the level of the dashboard.

She lifted her head. Outside, Smithers was in a ball on the ground, holding his eyes and moaning.

"Dan, are you OK?"

Smithers rolled on his side to face her, blinking rapidly. "Yeah, but I can't see shit."

"Stay down. I got this."

The source of the sound seemed to be a row of metal doors on the side of the long rectangular building, each emitting long, narrow white jets of steam—except for the closest one. Where it had been, a smoldering, gaping hole gushed a massive white plume.

Wendy slid out of the van and began to move toward the front entrance, when a man in a hazmat suit rushed out, arms waving frantically. As he neared the emergency vehicles, he reached up and pressed the mic on his helmet.

"Radioactive leak, clear the area!" He turned and pointed at the plumes of steam. "Someone's blowing holes in the containment building. Get out of here!"

Wendy scanned the area. The parking lot was empty except for their convoy, and she couldn't see any devices near the building. The explosion must have been internal. Radiation or not, they had to get inside as soon as possible. She turned toward her team.

The agents were all huddled in their vehicles, looking alarmed. Wendy wanted to scream. There was no time to call the bomb and hazardous material team. Behind her, two members of the tactical squad emerged from the building and sprinted to their command post. Captain Julie Peters grabbed the arm of the medic running toward the plant and held him back, yelling.

"Gear up! We got a shooter inside."

As Wendy reached the first armored vehicle, there came another high-pitched whistle, then the ground shook. She turned. A second vent was gone, amidst more clouds of billowing steam.

Wendy frowned. That whistle had sounded like—

She raised her eyes to the sky, away from the plant. A thin line of smoke trailed away into the blue. It was quickly dissipating in the strong wind, but she crudely marked its origin on the wooded hillside behind the plant.

The situation was incomprehensible, but there was no time to waste. Tactical would have to deal with the situation inside.

Wendy dashed back to the truck. Dan was up on his knees, but his complexion was a ghastly gray and he clutched the armrest of the door for balance. She couldn't leave him lying in a cloud of radiation. Gripping him under the arm, she half-dragged, half-pushed him into his seat.

"Come on, Dan, we're no good here. We gotta take out a missile launcher."

CHAPTER 54

Swimming back into awareness, Mike felt a surge of panic. Nestor was gone. How long had he been drifting? The medic and tactical teams should have reappeared by now.

Inside the control room, he could hear a metallic scraping, then a dull thud. Then a larger thud and a teeth-rattling vibration shook the entire building.

"What the fuck?"

His shout echoed down the hallway, but there was no response.

He couldn't just sit here as the place came down around him. Pulling off his tie, he wrapped and knotted it as securely as he could over the folded jacket pressed to his stomach. With his back against the wall, he got his legs under himself and slowly began to stand. He was almost upright when his foot skidded sideways, the jarring motion sending searing pain through to his back. Glancing down, he saw that he'd slid in the thick slick of his own blood.

Gripping his revolver in one hand, the other fisted to his wound, he stepped toward the partially open door to the control room. The waves of nausea provoked by each footstep forced him into a rigid, half bent posture. Ignoring another stab of agony, he lifted his leg and eased it through the gap.

A few inches in, the door hit something and stopped. He slipped his hand through the gap and slid a metal chair softly to the ground. The room was stark, lined with shelves of binders and a few credenzas. A high metal cabinet stood sideways, blocking his path. Twisting his body as gently as he could, he held his breath and gingerly shuffled inside. Hopefully, the staccato clangs blasting from the ceiling speakers were loud enough to conceal the sounds of his clumsy movements.

At the corner of the filing cabinet, he took a moment to recover before peering carefully around the corner. There was no movement. Two bodies lay awkwardly crumpled on the floor next to a large board of meters and dials. The lights blinking on every panel were brighter than a Macy's Christmas tree.

The legs of a third man extended out from under the edge of the control console. He was wearing suit pants and dress shoes, so probably not a worker. Was he a plant manager? The location and pose seemed logical for another victim, but was he alive or dead?

• • •

Under the console, the twisting metal and wires above Samir nudged his memories—tree branches, dreams of robots and rocket ships, so long ago. His ears were nearly bursting from the alarm bell, but he paid it no mind. Calmly attaching the C-4 to the conduit cover as it emerged from the wall, he inserted the detonation wire into the soft material.

There was no adrenaline left in him to make his hands tremble. Almost ready.

His revenge would be toxic, and avenging his father's murder, oh so sweet.

• • •

Edging around the corner of the file cabinet, Mike's clumsy attempt at a tactical crouch was met with overwhelming pain. Gasping, he retreated.

There was a three-ring binder on the credenza behind him. Readying his revolver, he grabbed the book, then turned and threw it around the corner, aiming for the console. But the legs were gone.

The shot was deafening. Its force slammed him backwards against the metal desk behind him, and his left leg buckled.

As he fell, he made eye contact with the man underneath the console, now raised on one elbow. His face blazed with icy hatred, the gun in his hands leveled at Mike's chest.

Mike fired three shots before he hit the ground. All found their target.

His vision fading in and out, Mike blinked down at his leg. Blood was spurting out of his thigh. Every movement felt like he was swimming in molasses as he undid his tie from his abdomen and wrapped it tightly above the wound. Then, energy spent, he toppled.

CHAPTER 55

There was no direct road up the hill from the plant, so Wendy drove across the highway and into the ditch on the far side. Ramming the floor-mounted shifter into low four-wheel drive, she forced the SUV up the bank.

At the crest of the hill, a barbwire fence marked the boundary of a mowed pasture. She shifted into high four-wheel and jammed down the accelerator. As it crashed through, the Suburban dragged several fence posts from their holes. There was a metallic screech as the barbwire slid away underneath the vehicle.

Across the field, the only remaining obstacle to the gravel road leading up the hillside was a wooden gate.

So far, Dan hadn't said a word. She took a quick peek. He still had his hands over his face.

"You OK?"

Dan dropped his hands and turned toward her. His left eye was unfocused and blood red.

"I must have taken a frag hit in the left one, cuz I can't see anything out of it. The right one is fuzzy."

"Shit. Keep 'em both shut."

The gate of weather-damaged two-by-fours exploded into a spray of splinters on impact. Beyond, Wendy eased the truck over the rutted tractor access onto the roadway and began the steep climb, tires spewing streams of stones.

She estimated they had another two hundred yards of elevation to cover before they would be near the shooter. Unfortunately, the road was tortuous, switchbacking repeatedly across the face of the hill. Dan groaned and grabbed the strap above the door as they struck pothole after pothole in the washboard roadway.

Coming around the next tight bend, Wendy braked hard. Farther up the hill, a bright yellow van sat oddly askew in the middle of a recently cut hayfield.

The SUV dipped deeply as she whipped it across the narrow bridge of dirt crossing the ditch into the field. From a small grove of trees at eleven o'clock came a loud bang. A white trail erupted out of the treetops, lancing across the sky toward Lakeridge.

"We got 'im, Dan! Hold on."

Revolver aimed across the dash, Wendy pulled alongside the other vehicle, then circled around the back. The rear doors, splashed with a red Ace Security decal, stood wide open. It was abandoned.

The powerful vehicle heaved side-to-side, bucking over the rough terrain like a rodeo bull as Wendy pushed it across the field toward the grove. Halfway across, however, a low, untidy wall of stones halted her progress.

"Dan, stay put. But have your gun ready. If the next person you hear doesn't identify, shoot."

Hopping out of the truck, she hurdled the wall, slipping on the pebbly downside of the slope when she landed. A small landslide of dirt and rocks came with her as she skidded a slalom course through a bramble of bushes and into the tree line.

A short distance below her, a man kneeling among the trees turned his head toward the noise.

Still sliding, she aimed her revolver, arm bouncing too much to fire.

"Hands up! FBI."

The man pivoted, whipping the rocket launcher around to point at her.

Wendy fired two rounds as she threw herself across the hillside toward a mossy boulder. When she peered around the rock, she saw the man was unhurt. Weaving around trees and rocks, he was picking his way toward her, a smaller gun visible in his hand.

She needed a better vantage point. Scrambling for footing in the loose shale she worked her way along the face of the slope, ducking behind rocks and trees.

A bullet whizzed over her head and she dropped, rolling downhill. She came to rest against a massive log just as another shot rang out. Wood exploded above her head, showering her with splinters.

Shoving herself up, she slid over the log, slamming down hard on the other side.

Damn. She was pinned. Raising her head as much as she dared, she scrutinized her surroundings. Downhill to her left, the far end of the log disappeared into thick brush.

One ear on the crashing sounds of her pursuer, Wendy dug a deep groove in the gravelly dirt with her heel. Selecting a good-sized rock, she tossed it toward the other end of the log. At the same time, she shoved out with her left foot, sending a small avalanche cascading into the bushes.

Using her makeshift foothold, she pushed in the opposite direction as hard as she could, rolling once before taking a quick look over the log. About ten yards away, the man was rising from a crouch. He fired twice, aiming for the movement in the bushes.

Wendy got off three rounds, but the last two were unnecessary. Rising to her feet, she picked her way up the slope, maintaining her aim at the prone form. His eyes were open to the sky. The lower half of his face was lighter, freshly shaven and flecked with red shaving nicks—his expression was peaceful.

She holstered her gun and made her way back up the hill to the missile launcher. It looked like a relic, but the damn thing obviously still worked. The fabric bag beside it was empty, but a gigantic, lethal looking round lay on the ground ten feet away at the base of a tree.

In the distance, she could see five ragged holes in the side of the nuclear plant. A torrent of steam rushed from every one.

Scrabbling the rest of the way up the hill, she sprinted to the SUV.

"Dan, don't shoot! It's me, Wendy. Everything is under control. The perp is dead."

"What about Lakeridge?"

"I don't know, but I'm taking you to a hospital in the opposite direction."

CHAPTER 56

In the hallway outside the control room, Julie Peters pressed against the wall beside the doorway. There was a large pool of blood on the floor, but no Mike Longstrum.

She was impressed at his resolve, but a fellow agent inside made her task more complicated. She triggered her microphone.

"No covering fire. There's one of ours in there."

Eight clicks sounded in her headset. Message received.

She swallowed hard. "Alpha team, you ready?"

Click. She raised her fist. "Bravo team, it's showtime."

Immediately behind her, the first two of the four agents crouched. All had weapons raised.

"On my mark." She unclipped a flash grenade from her waistband. "1-2-3—*now*."

A loud whoomp and surge of dusty air enveloped Peters as she burst through the doorway. From the far side of the room came a dull thud and then a crash as Alpha blew the fire door open, toppling a file cabinet.

Both teams fanned out, taking cover where they could. Peters rushed forward to the file cabinet that blocked her view of the main workstation. She brought Bravo team forward with a hand gesture, then launched herself through the gap, two fingers tight on the trigger.

"Two dead on the floor." She dropped to one knee. There was a leg under the console. "Target under console."

"Alpha 3. Got it."

The prone form jerked with the impact of the high velocity round, but remained inert.

"Target down." Swinging her sights around the room, Peters moved forward. "All clear."

Turning, she inhaled sharply. Longstrum's body lay slumped against a desk, his face a ghastly gray-white.

"Medic! Agent down!" She knelt and placed two fingers on his carotid. "Alpha one, help me."

Together, they slid Mike gently to the floor onto his back. Another agent raised his legs.

Peters ran back to the hallway. "Is the system operator here yet?"

"Affirmative."

Around the corner, a figure in a hazmat suit appeared, escorted by two plainclothes agents. Peters waved the plant operator forward. He slipped off his helmet as he strode briskly into the control room behind her, but at the sight of the carnage he froze, face blanching.

"Oh my God, is that Derek? Jim?"

Peters slipped an arm around the trembling man's shoulders and gently pushed him forward. "I'm sorry, but we don't have time. Can you get this under control?"

He expelled a stuttering breath. Pulling a clean chair to the console, she guided him into it.

"OK. I'll do what I can, but with the vents disabled a hell of a lot of radioactivity is still going to be released."

"Meaning?"

"Everybody in a fifty-mile radius has to be evacuated immediately, and even further in areas downwind. All the crops and livestock will be contaminated, as well as wildlife."

"For how long?"

"Depends. Could be fifty, a hundred, depends—maybe a couple hundred years."

CHAPTER 57

Mike woke to the sound of soft beeping. His body felt heavy, like he was being pressed into the mud at the bottom of an ocean, fathoms of water above—yet his mind was floating just past Mars. Blissfully, he was no longer in pain, though something was squeezing his hand quite tightly. Slowly, he opened his eyes. Blond hair filled his vision. The skin on his lips felt like it was ripping when he tried to smile.

"Hi, beautiful. Where am I?" His voice was husky.

"In Oz. Actually, it's Denver. The Sister Grace Hospital."

"Colorado. How the hell . . .?"

"Tillson and most of the outlying districts have been closed down. You were airlifted out."

"So . . . are the lights on in here, or am I glowing in the dark?"

"Being the smart man that you are, you decided to get shot in the safest place — inside the plant."

"I don't actually feel so bad. How long have I been out?"

"Almost a week. You have some catching up to do."

"Jesus." He made a vain attempt at clearing the gumminess in his mouth with his parched tongue. "Wait, are you OK? What about the radiation?"

"I was initially far enough away and got out on the medevac flight with you."

"Thank God."

"But a lot of the first responders to Lakeridge are gonna have to be tested for leukemia and thyroid cancer for the rest of their lives. It's pretty bad. The land south and east of Tillson is going to be our version of Chernobyl for a long time. Tillson is a ghost town and may stay that way. Lakeridge is shut down indefinitely. Without cheap power, whole industries have walked away. The evacuated are all reluctant to return, if and when they get the OK. That includes me. We need to start over."

Mike squeezed her hand and nodded. "So what happened?"

"Some guy was blowing holes in the containment wall with a rocket launcher, until Wendy stopped him."

"Alone?"

"Yup, she's the big hero. She's getting a citation and a trip to the White House. Probably a book deal too."

"And Dan?"

"Unfortunately, he was hit by debris from one of the explosions. He'll never see out of his left eye again, but otherwise he's fine. He's actually happy. With a full disability pension, he can spend more time with his kids. Odds are that Wendy will get his job."

"Great."

"Come on, don't look so glum. You're a hero too."

"For what, getting shot in line of duty?"

Jenny tutted and ran her fingers through his hair, combing it off his forehead. "Everyone knows what you did at Lakeridge was incredibly brave. Rumor has it that things could have been a lot worse. You are a hero."

Mike turned his head away. "But not enough of one. I should have listened to you earlier. Without the stuff you figured out . . . who knows, I might not have gone to the plant at all. So really, Jenny, *you* are the hero."

She winked. "Well, you got that right at least." She drew him toward her with a finger under his chin. "And you got that Spitwell thing right too. Samir wasn't the only terrorist in town."

Mike smiled and pecked her on the lips. "I assume it was Samir that I shot, but what happened to Fatima?"

"Yup, and I told Wendy and Dan what I knew, and now she's on the most wanted list."

"Well done. You'll be in the FBI before you know it."

"Thank you. Oh, also, not only are you a hero, but you're famous too. It has nothing to do with shooting bad guys though."

"What?"

"Well, apparently Agent Mike Longstrum carried an injured mother and her dying child over his head five miles through neck-deep floodwater to the emergency room of the hospital."

Mike laughed. "Urban myth alert." He squeezed Jenny's hand. "Is the little girl OK?"

Jenny squeezed back. "I checked for you. She'll be fine." She grinned. "But despite that Herculean effort and taking down a terrorist, you are in serious trouble with the Bureau."

Jenny withdrew her phone from her purse and read from the screen. "Someone in the ER department posted a blog report that got picked up by the wire services. The gist of it is that the triage nurse took offence to your little tantrum, and for the rest of his shift he put the charges for every patient without health insurance on the Bureau's tab."

"Oh, God."

"On *Good Morning America* they named you 'The Robin Hood of the FBI'."

"Ring my nurse. I think I need heavy sedation."

"Oh, honey, it gets even better."

Giggling, she scrolled through her phone. "Here, 'FBI Fights Terrorism'." She leaned and angled the screen so Mike could get a clear view of the grainy image.

"My big tough guy."

"I don't—"

"This clip went viral." She pressed play. The dark, shaky image of a man in water over his knees stood beside a black SUV, holding a gun. "You wanna tell me why you were shooting your vehicle?"

"It was a planter in the—I shot a planter . . ." The retort of the shot could clearly be heard above the roar of the floodwater. "Oh, my God. I guess I need another job."

"First, you better get some rest. Once you recover, you have an opening spot on *Saturday Night Live* and a raft of daytime TV interviews to do." She giggled and ruffled his hair.

"Sure." When the looped clip started to replay, Mike turned away again, pushing his face deep into the pillow. "Turn it off, OK?"

Jenny dropped her phone into her purse and pressed her check against his. "I love you."

"Love you too." Mike looked up, his eyes moist. His attempt to rise on his elbow and kiss her was met with a shot of pain in his side. He gasped, screwed up his face and moaned softly.

Jenny gently helped him to recline on the bed. "Take it easy, cowboy. Let me do the kissing."

• • •

Fatima shifted in her seat on the 809 train, resisting the urge to stretch. After a grueling bus and train trip, the next stop was finally Grand Central Terminal.

Readying her bags, she tucked the newspaper she'd been reading into the seat pouch in front of her. Most of the articles concerned the effort to seal the nuclear plant's containment building, the consequences of the leak and horrific pictures of the flood and sewage damage. Carried on the wind, the radioactivity would render a large swath of the state uninhabitable for a long time. Many first responders were critically ill with radiation illness. Untold people had died in the flash flooding, and of course, disaster had spurred deadly violence.

The photo essay that documented the difficult search and rescue effort still underway was particularly disturbing. The first image was of a pickup truck covered in muck and severely battered by debris, while the next captured a crew in hazmat suits using the jaws-of-life to pry open its passenger door. The final shot made tears well in Fatima's eyes. Tended to by heavily protected rescuers, the terror in the eyes of two rescued boys was painfully visible, as they stared at their father lying lifeless on a gurney beyond.

It was difficult to believe that Samir had been able to keep the magnitude of his plan from her. Besides his need for secrecy, she had to believe it was a precaution to protect her. But she had been complicit, no matter her ignorance. Even if the authorities believed Samir coerced her to cooperate, she would bear the burden of hundreds of deaths for the rest of her life.

Stepping down from the train, her footsteps echoed on the terrazzo floor of the station. With US borders closed, the crowd was thin. People were somber. In the washroom, Fatima studied her reflection for a long moment, then removed her hijab and stuffed it in the trash container.

Outside on the street, the rush of people threatened to pull her away. A gust of warm air whispered by, and she realized that the wind had never ruffled her hair before. She would enjoy it while she could. The nearest police station could not be far.

The End

ACKNOWLEDGEMENTS

I want to thank my early readers Brenda, Kieran, Tony, Sandy and Blair for their invaluable input. A special thanks to Aislinn Cottell of Granville Island Publishing for her patience and guidance as she pushed me to do better.

John D. May was born in London, Ontario. He has balanced multiple passions over his life, including his work as a biologist, his career as a physician, his volunteer service at medical outreach clinics in Guatemala, singer-song writing and storytelling. He has written several songs for well-known Canadian artists and released two CDs available on iTunes and Spotify under the name Johnny May. His time is divided between his rural farm property near Toronto and the south of France.

Johnny May Words and Music
http://johnnymay.ca/